Kate Fennigate

BOOTH TARKINGTON

Kate Fennigate

DOUBLEDAY, DORAN & CO., INC.

Garden City   1943   New York

PRINTED AT THE *Country Life Press,* GARDEN CITY, N. Y., U. S. A.

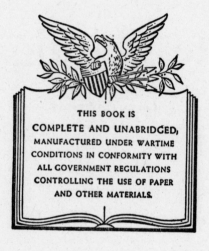

THIS BOOK IS
COMPLETE AND UNABRIDGED,
MANUFACTURED UNDER WARTIME
CONDITIONS IN CONFORMITY WITH
ALL GOVERNMENT REGULATIONS
CONTROLLING THE USE OF PAPER
AND OTHER MATERIALS.

bw
.T1745k

To
Linda Tarkington

Kate Fennigate

A STRANGER IN THAT STILL ENLARGING CITY MIGHT SEE
Kate Fennigate at any of its selective social gatherings without particularly noticing her; or, even if he were properly sensitive to the
looks of people, he'd probably fail to recognize her as the most
remarkable person present. "Remarkable" has always been Mr. Henry
L. Roe's word for her character and mind, and, as nowadays he is not
seldom called the city's Henry Ford, any adjective of his is worth
examining. More, old Mr. Roe has known Kate Fennigate long. Once,
for a year or so, he employed her, and he knew something, too, of her
childhood when she'd already begun to be remarkable.

This portrait of her must take account of that childhood, for she
was then her essential self as much as ever she became. Of course in
every portrait of a woman all other women must find at least a bit
of themselves, and in the childhood of the subject of the picture there
must have been something of all other children; but even in childhood
Kate Fennigate had a local celebrity as an exceptional little girl, not
to say a peculiar one. Among her known ancestors, migratory English
of the Seventeenth Century and their descendants, westward-adven-
turing New Englanders, nothing accounts for her any better than
Benjamin Franklin's commonplace similar outfit accounts for him.
Genius, and especially female genius, seems to leap out of nowhere.

This is not to say that as a child Kate Fennigate was recognized
by the people of her town as a genius. She was never called one even
by those who loved her, and probably Henry L. Roe is the only person
who has ever suspected the truth.

It was when she was about twelve that rumors concerning her singularity began to drift through the groups of citizens longest established as the worldly foremost. Then, before the very portals of the Carlyle Club, that sanctuary for the town's most seclusive gentlemen, she gave a performance rich in entertainment for everybody except her father.

He had lunched at the club that day; but, instead of returning to his law office, had remained to engage in a game of bridge that lasted through all the bright May afternoon. The clubhouse, a fine old mansion half way downtown and half way uptown, faced National Avenue, the wide thoroughfare leading into the disappearing "best residence section"; and all that afternoon a wide plate-glass window of the second floor framed the profile of Mr. Fennigate as he sat examining his cards or playing one of them or dealing all of them, smoking cigars and sometimes lifting a glass to his lips. He was a portly man, dignified, with an impressive big Roman head; though, as the afternoon progressed, upward glancing passers-by may have thought he looked flushed and somewhat too ripe.

This opinion was repeatedly expressed within the clubhouse after five o'clock when members on their homeward way began to arrive for stimulants to help them undergo their dinners; commentators visited the card-room to observe the long-lasting game, then returned to the large and leathery apartment adjacent, exclaiming. It was agreed that bridge less scientific or more inebriated had never been seen in the Carlyle Club.

"Go look, if you don't believe it!" William Wriothesly Jones, the youngest member not a year out of Harvard, urged newcomers. "Mal's bootlegger delivered a case for him at the club's basement door just before lunchtime. The party's on Mal, and those four have been playing twenty-five cents a point, all i.o.u., for five hours and nobody knows anything except that Mal Fennigate owes all of 'em, he doesn't know how much. Neither do they and none of 'em ever will. I went on the water-wagon last week, but fell off just looking at 'em. When you watch a game like that you either got to drink or go crazy. Look yonder. That's a good un!" His reference was to a colored man in the club's quiet livery who passed into the card-room carrying a calling-card upon a silver tray. "Somebody downstairs calling on one of those souses; I hope it's a clergyman!"

In the card-room Mr. Fennigate was repelling the proffered tray. "Don't push things at me, Sigmund. Use your eyes. Can't you see we're occupied? Don't intrude. Take it away. I don't want any callers, Sigsmund."

"Yes, suh." Siegfried, the colored man, still offered the tray. "It's a lady, Mr. Fennigate."

"A lady?" All four of the card players looked offended; Malcolm Fennigate set down upon the table not only his cards but the fizzing glass from which he was about to drink. "Since when are ladies condoned in this club, Sigmuss?"

"She ain't, suh," Siegfried replied. "She waitin' outside. She ring front door bell, say, 'Please be so kind hand Mr. Malcolm Fennigate my card, tell him I'm waitin' he please come take a drive wiv me.'"

"Take a drive with her? A drive? Did this lady say a——"

"Yes, suh, Mr. Fennigate. Drive whut she say, suh."

"Who is she?"

"It say on the card, Mr. Fennigate."

One of Mr. Fennigate's opponents, youngish but baldish Mr. George Cooke, had an idea. "Maybe it's your fairy godmother, Malcolm," he said. "She's probably come to change you into a bridge player. Go down and tell her to go away; we like you better the way you are."

Frowning, Malcolm Fennigate took the card and examined it carefully. The name upon it was not engraved but neatly written with a pen and purple ink: "Miss Kate Fennigate". He stared at it long.

"Doesn't it say who she is or anything?" Mr. Cooke inquired, after a time.

"It seems—I mean it appears—I mean it would appear to seem to be my daughter. Where'd you say she is, Sigmund?"

"She settin' right down there, suh, waitin'. You can see her out the window."

All four of the card players looked down from the window. The short front lawn was separated from the cement sidewalk by a low but imposing fence of carved limestone, and beyond the sidewalk was another strip of clipped grass edged by the curbstone. There

stood an elderly speckled horse, all bones and drooping patience; and
to him was attached a vehicle even then, 1920, almost extinct, a
fringed surrey. In the front seat the driver, a colored man as shabby
and elderly as his horse, sat looking browbeaten. From the upstairs
window he was fully visible; but of the occupant of the middle of
the rear seat the top of the surrey permitted to be seen only a pair
of small patent-leather pumps and two insignificant ankles. Not observing these, George Cooke made a suggestion.

"I don't see any daughter, Mal; it must be the horse that wants you
to take a drive. It's been years and years since I've seen any horse
calling at the Carlyle Club. If you want to quit the game as big a
loser as you are, Mal, why don't you go on downstairs and take a
drive with this horse the way it wants you to?"

"I won't do it!" Fennigate put the calling-card on the window-sill
beside him. "I won't go! I can see her feet; but I decline to go. Sieg-
fred, go down there, tell her I'm very, very busy so I can't come, kindly
go home to her mother and then come back and tell me she's gone
and bring another round with you."

"Yes, suh." Siegfried departed but was stopped as he passed through
the next room where several members were staring interestedly down
from the front windows.

"What goes on, Siegfried?" young Jones inquired hopefully. "Has
somebody come here in that terrible surrey to call on one of the
gentlemen in the bridge game?"

"Yes, suh; callin' on Mr. Fennigate. Card say Miss Kate Fennigate.
She ve'y li'l young lady. Mr. Fennigate say she his daughter. She tell
me say he please come take a drive wiv her; he say she got to go
home to her mamma. Scuse me, suh."

Siegfried descended to the lower floor, returned five minutes later
with the liquid "round" Malcolm Fennigate had ordered, delivered it,
descended again, and, within a quarter of an hour, was back, bearing
a tray upon which was a calling-card. He entered the card-room and
presented it to Mr. Fennigate. George Cooke looked annoyed.

"What's this? More horses calling on him, Siegfried?"

"No, suh. They ain't gone away. Same li'l young lady ring door bell some more, hand me card again, say air so nice wouldn't Mr. Fennigate injoy come down take a drive wiv her."

Malcolm Fennigate placed the card with its fellow upon the window-sill; then rubbed his forehead with the knuckles of his right hand, striving to concentrate. "I'll have to think of something," he said. "Something that'll make her go away."

"You'd better," his friend, Cooke, advised him. "Due to our changing partners, you now owe each and every one of us as many as probably seventy dollars more or less; I mean more. I've been thinking I know that horse, myself, because who's driving it is old Thomas, our ash and trash man. I mean our trash and ash man, whichever way you care to put it. I think he's your ash and trash man, or trash ash man, too, Mal, because that's certainly Thomas and his horse. He comes in an ash and trash wagon usually, though, so I don't know the surrey; I'm not acquainted with it."

"It's mine," Mr. Fennigate said. "It's my surrey. It's been standing in my stable all silent for ten years. She's hired Thomas to hitch it to his horse because I've got the car and she's come to break up our game in the surrey. It's all her own idea, too, I penetrate, because her mother doesn't have 'em. I don't like it. I tell you I don't like it."

George Cooke pointed downward from the window. "Look, he's changed hips; I mean the trash horse. First he rests one hind leg on the rim of his hoof and that makes the other hip higher. Then he changes. I can see her feet now, too. She's a good daughter, your little Kate, Mal; but I wouldn't like to have her. The way I look at this matter, she knew you'd come to the club for lunch and I bet she called up your office and found you hadn't gone back there and thinks maybe probably it's pretty certain by this time you'd better not drive your car home. All this talk about pure outdoor air and taking a drive, I speculate it's just camouflage and she'd take you straight home, no pleasure-carriage driving at all."

Fennigate turned sternly to Siegfried and used a word that delighted young Jones, who had spyingly followed the messenger. This word, a bibulous compression of "bullied" and "persecuted", was therefore to be often repeated to its creator, later. "I decline to be bullycuted, Sigsmund! Tell her I've already gone home by myself."

Siegfried looked embarrassed. "She can see you settin' here, Mr. Fennigate, suh."

"She can? Well, then, tell her I'm lying down and left word not to be disturbed."

Siegfried became more embarrassed. "Iffen I do, she go' think I ain't tell the trufe. She can see you jes' the same, no diffunce which I tell her, suh."

Young Jones offered a suggestion. "Mal, why don't you just send word you won't be bullycuted?"

"That's jargon," Malcolm Fennigate returned. "I don't know what you're talking about. Sigmuss, go tell Miss Fennigate I'm occupied having discussions on matters and'll be dining here, so you're requested that she needn't wait because her mother might get worried about her. Do so immediately, Boy; do you hear me?"

"Yes, suh." Siegfried went forth with his vacant tray, and, about seven minutes later, returned with another card upon it. Malcolm Fennigate, badgered, cried out dolorously.

"She must have written herself a whole pack of these cards! She's too young; it's a waste. What's she say this time, Sigsmund?"

"She say gittin' to be such a nice cool evening she like you to take nice drive wiv her, see the sunset in nice fresh air."

"I decline! Merely state to her that I decline. Go back and tell her I permanently decline. Can you pronounce that word, Sigmund?"

"Yes, suh," Siegfried replied, without trying to prove it, went again and in time returned again with yet another card.

Kate Fennigate's father uttered sacred names, and from just outside the doorway came, in low tones, the barber-shop chordings of a quartet organized by William Jones:

> *"Father, dear father, come home with me now,*
> *The clock in the steeple strikes one . . ."*

Malcolm Fennigate rose to his feet. "This is beyond all reason and bearings! I'll go down and send her away, myself. Don't deal till I come back; just give me half a minute——"

He walked carefully from the room, haughtily passed through the quartet and descended the stairway, assisting himself at times by a hand that slid upon the massive walnut rail. He emerged from the front door accompanied by Siegfried, who carried a black derby hat, a pair of chamois gloves and a silver-headed Malacca walking-stick. At the top of the stone stoop Malcolm Fennigate paused and said crossly: "Boy, what are you doing with those? Aren't those my hat and things?"

"Yes, suh, Mr. Fennigate. She say when you come out you mos' likely go' think you goin' back but I better bring 'em for you 'cause you might forget 'em."

"Return them back into the club cloakroom at once!"

Siegfried paused, uncertain; then, as the annoyed member descended the stoop, followed deferentially, bringing the hat, gloves and stick with him. Malcolm Fennigate, concentrating his faculties, walked out to the surrey and looked at his daughter as fixedly as he could, which wasn't over-fixedly.

She was a fair-haired, brown-eyed little girl with an exquisite profile. Small for her twelve years, she was quiet, demure and non-committal. Appropriately for a call at the Carlyle Club she wore a dainty white dress with a lace-edged collar; upon the wavy fair hair was a white straw sailor hat; round her inconsiderable waist was a glisteny black patent-leather belt; white stockings descended to the patent-leather pumps that had been observed from above. Her delicately shaped childish hands, resting in her lap, clasped a green silk card-case.

"Thank you, Father," she said. "I mean for coming out to take this drive with me." She spoke to Siegfried. "Please give Mr. Fennigate his hat and gloves and cane now." Siegfried, obedient, offered them somewhat pressingly. Mr. Fennigate pushed them away. "Wait," his daughter said, and stepped from the surrey. "Give them to me, please." She took the hat, gloves and stick from Siegfried, stood on tiptoe, placed the hat upon her father's head and the gloves and stick within the flaccid grasp of his left hand—actions pleasedly observed from the now rather crowded upper windows of the club. From the green silk card-case she produced, after some rummaging, a nickel and gave it to Siegfried. "That's for you," she said graciously. "You've

been very kind; but you can go now. Father, don't you think we'd
better get in so we can begin to take our drive? So many people seem
to be looking at us out of those windows I think maybe we're com-
mencing to seem conspicuous."

The air of outdoors, somewhat encumbered by the growing city's
smoke, had not refreshed the reluctant father; but it had produced
a disturbance in his mind, confusing him. He was under the impression that he ought to go back into the clubhouse. There was something he wanted to do there; but for the moment he couldn't
remember just what it was. "Con—conspicuous?" he said. "Where?
I see no reason. Go home to your mother, child. I left my car in the
garage behind the club. When I decide it's time for me to come
home for perhaps dinner I'll go and get into it and——"

"No, no," the little girl interrupted. "I got Thomas to go to all the
trouble of hitching his horse to our surrey and he even had to oil
the axles. Thomas'd feel hurt if you didn't come with us. Wouldn't
you, Thomas?"

"Ma'am?"

"Of course Thomas would, Father!" she said. "Besides that, he's
cost me seventy-five cents. Won't you please get in, Father?"

Malcolm Fennigate glanced vaguely back over his shoulder at the
club and at the windows saw smiling faces that mystified him. "What
is all this?" he said wistfully, and, with the slight assistance of his
daughter, climbed into the rear seat of the surrey. She lightly took
her place beside him, and the anomalous vehicle began to move slowly
up the street. The speckled old horse refused to call upon himself for
better than a walk, though when Thomas mechanically said, "Get up,
you!" and languidly applied the stump of a former carriage whip, the
animal hunched his hindquarters slightly upward as a promise that
presently, after he'd thought it over, he might break into a trot. He
didn't, and the upper façade of the Carlyle Club continued to be
animated until the fringed surrey was out of sight.

Within it there was silence for a time; then Malcolm Fennigate
expressed a new puzzlement. "Where—where did you get seventy-five
cents?"

"I have plenty of money," the daughter said calmly. "Thomas

charged it to me because I've thirty-six dollars in the savings bank so he knows I'll pay him."

"Is your mother aware?" Malcolm Fennigate spoke with care. "Has your mother taken cognizance——" He made gestures with his yellow gloves toward Thomas and the horse and the top of the surrey. "Cognizance of all this? I mean does your mother know about—about all this?"

"No, I don't believe she does, Father. She was taking her nap in her room, I think."

"Perhaps—perhaps it's just as well."

"Yes, Father."

They drove slowly up the street, upon which automobile sales buildings had begun to intrude, here and there, displacing houses and green yards. It was still a "residence street", however, lined with big shade trees and at intervals agreeably whitened by bridalwreath in bloom. Sunset was emblazoning the fresh Maytime greeneries of the short cross street into which the surrey finally turned at a corner three-quarters of a mile north of the Carlyle Club; the sad old horse walked half a block farther, then stopped before a "frame" house painted green, but not recently, and, like most of its fellows on this brief thoroughfare, East Cherry Street, displaying the turreted architecture once fondly called "Queen Anne". Small Kate Fennigate jumped out and offered a helping hand.

"I'm afraid our drive's all over. Here we are at home. Don't you think you'd better come in, Father?"

He seemed to be thinking with his eyes closed, but murmured, "What, what?"

"We're home and it's dinnertime. Let's go in."

He said, "Home?" opened his eyes, looked about him inquiringly; then, moving with caution, descended to stand beside his daughter. "Home? So it appears; so it appears."

"That's all, Thomas," the little girl said. "You'll be paid. You can drive around the alley way and leave the surrey in the stable and get your own wagon out. Be sure and feed your horse all he wants, Thomas."

"Yes'm." Thomas drove away, and across the street a handsome

woman rose from a wicker chair on a verandah to obtain a better
view over the clumps of tall lilac bushes that gave her small front
yard some air of privacy. Risen, she looked hard at the father and
daughter standing in the warm sunset glow before their house; then
the handsome woman's gaze went from them to the snail's progress
of the departing surrey and she laughed aloud—loud enough to be
heard across the street.

This laughter perplexed Malcolm Fennigate. "What is that noise,
Kate? Is somebody laughing?"

"It's only our neighbor, Mrs. Capper, Father. She's always laughing.
Let's go in."

"One moment." He looked across the street, saw the handsome
Mrs. Capper upon her verandah, smiled indulgently; then slowly
put on his yellow gloves, placed his cane jauntily under his arm,
removed his black derby hat and made Mrs. Capper a gallant, somewhat effusive bow; upon which she laughed the more loudly. "She's
a darling," he murmured.

"No, she's not," little Kate said. "Father, I think Mother's expecting
us to dinner. We'd better go in, hadn't we?"

"Why, certainly," he said briskly, replaced his hat and suffered her
to lead him within the house.

II

INDOORS, AS IN MOST OF SUCH HOUSES, THERE WAS A
smallish, flowery-papered hallway, with the "front stairs" ascending
one side of it, the dining-room door at the inner end of it, and, opposite the stairway, two pairs of double doors, one pair giving admission
to the small parlor or "reception room", the other to the larger living-
room. Malcolm Fennigate, whose face now expressed gratification—

he was reviewing his bow to Mrs. Capper—placed his hat and stick upon a narrow table and, still wearing his gloves, walked into the living-room, followed thoughtfully by his daughter.

"Good evening, darling!" he said heartily. "Darling, good evening!"

Mrs. Fennigate, seated in an upholstered rocking-chair beside an open window, didn't look away from the book she was reading, a borrowed old copy of "Three Weeks" by Mrs. Glyn. Forty-five and short, she'd encouraged a former comeliness to be everywhere bulbously overlaid; the chair creaked faintly as it rocked and upon the window-sill beside her was an open box of chocolate candy. This was the climax hour of her day's pleasure: in the afternoon a long, long nap to unsettle her lunch, then the rocking-chair, a novel either a little illicit or about weaponed adventures, and the box of chocolates open beside her. Thus she read, rocked and ate from the end of her nap straight through till dinnertime; it was routine.

"You home?" she said in response to her husband's caressive overture; her eyes were still upon her book. "Better call the child in if she's somewhere out in the yard; Editha has already rung the bell twice for dinner. I suppose you had to go over and sit with that gangling Lucia Capper on her porch about an hour again before you could coax yourself to come in your own house."

"No, he didn't, Mother," young Kate said quickly. "He and I came in together. Editha is ringing the bell again."

"I have ears, haven't I, child?" Mrs. Fennigate, feebly querulous, put down her book, placed the cover on the box of chocolates, and rose. "What are you so all dressed up for?" she asked her daughter, and, without caring to hear the reply, spoke complainingly to her husband. "You're all flushed again. You've got that funny look around your eyes. Can't you ever learn when you've had enough? No, it seems like not; I give up. Come on to dinner." In the dining-room she showed more interest. "What you giving us to eat, Editha?" she asked of the gaunt colored woman who'd cooked the meal and now stood waiting to serve it. "Something good?"

"Liver, boil' potatoes, carrots, boil' rice, rice-and-raisin pudding."

Mrs. Fennigate sighed. "Oh, dear! That's the same as we had night before last, Editha."

"Yes'm. I can't do everything."

Malcolm Fennigate, having seated himself opposite his wife, felt a pressure upon his right shoe and opened his eyes, which he'd again been obliged to close. The pressure came from the foot of his daughter who had edged her chair nearer his than usual. He looked at her inquiringly and she whispered the word, "Gloves!" from the side of her mouth.

"What?"

Mrs. Fennigate was busy with a dish offered by Editha. "Hadn't you better take off your gloves?" Kate whispered. "We're having dinner, Father."

"Yes. Yes, to be sure." Under cover of the table top he removed his yellow gloves and limply dropped them on the floor.

The quick-eyed little girl let her napkin fall from her lap so that it covered them; then she picked up the napkin and the gloves within it. "Miss Carroll's going to have the school give a play, Mother," she said. "Laila Capper's going to act the principal part. She's the best actress."

"She ought to be," Mrs. Fennigate returned discontentedly, "with that mother! Never knew her to stop acting. It gets the men, though, doesn't it, Malcolm?"

"Men?" he repeated. "I beg your pardon. What about men?"

"It's a splendid play," the daughter intervened hurriedly. "It's all Scandinavian about folk lore, and Laila and I are going to do a dance in it and sing a duet, too. I'd like to tell you the story of it. In the first act——" She interrupted herself to whisper to her father, "Eat something!" Then she went on with the story of the school play, to which neither of her parents paid any attention. At intervals she pressed her father's foot with her own, whispered earnestly, "Eat! Eat some more!" and continued the story of the play. Mrs. Fennigate ate thoroughly, and the meal might have been thought dismal for an intelligent person of twelve; but the small Kate was interested, anything but bored, because she was doing the kind of thing she liked to do: she was managing, so to speak, both of her parents.

When coffee came she contrived that her father should drink four of the small cups of it without his being aware, himself, that he had more than one (he didn't care for coffee) and without attracting the attention of Mrs. Fennigate, who ate diligently of rice-and-raisin pudding after the daughter's recommendation to cover it thickly with powdered sugar. The coffee revived in Malcolm Fennigate the capacity for at least sluggish motion, and, when his wife returned to the rocking-chair, "Three Weeks", and the chocolates, he walked out to the verandah accompanied closely by his daughter and almost not needing her delicate steering.

They sat, he in a wicker chair and she upon the verandah steps, while warmed May dusk grew deeper, and, after a vagrant mild spell of hiccups, he lighted an expensive-smelling cigar. A few moments later he snored once or twice, and his daughter rose watchfully, tiptoed to him, took the cigar from between his unconscious fingers, descended the verandah steps with it, and rubbed out the spark on the brick path that led to the sidewalk. Then she tiptoed back to him and softly slid the almost unused cigar into his waistcoat upper pocket. This done, she sat down again, a patiently inscrutable little figure.

Upon other verandahs and in the small yards along the short street children of her own age were playing squeally, and several times there came unanswered calls for her out of the darkness: "Oh, Kate! Oh, Kate Fennigate! Come on out! Why'n't you come on over, Kate?" Directly across the street adult voices were making merry upon Mrs. Capper's verandah after dinner. Several men seemed to be telling jokes there, and the laughter of their handsome hostess was almost incessant. Malcolm Fennigate had slept more than half an hour before it awakened him.

"Well, well!" he said, fumbled in his pocket, found the cigar, lighted it, rose and took two steps forward before his daughter's quiet voice stopped him.

"Are you going to bed now, Father?"

"Bed," he echoed. "Bed? Is that you, Kate? No, I just thought I'd stroll across the street a few minutes before dinner and——"

"Before dinner?" She laughed rallyingly. "Father, wake up! You must still be asleep. You've had a nice splendid long nap since dinner; but I guess you haven't noticed. You ought to begin to get a good night's sleep now, oughtn't you, because aren't you going to make that grand speech to-morrow?"

"Speech? To-morrow? Where?"

"Why, in court," she said. "Don't you remember telling Mother and me about it yesterday evening—how maybe if you win this case against Mr. Roe he'll probably want to have you for the lawyer on *his* side after this? I'm sure he would, too, because he's such a nice man. I'm getting to know him awfully well lately, Father."

"You're what? Getting to know whom?"

"Mr. Roe, Father. He likes to walk home from downtown and sometimes he passes the school about when I'm getting out from my music lesson, so I walk this far on his way with him. We talk and talk and I've been telling him about your being such a good lawyer without having him notice I was telling him. You have to be in court by nine o'clock to-morrow morning, don't you, Father?"

"To-morrow morning? No—not till Friday."

"To-night's Thursday," Kate said, as if absently.

"Thursday? Yes, of course, of course. Anybody knows that!" He advanced a few steps farther. "Well, I suppose your mother's gone to bed, so I believe I'll just drop over across the street for a few minutes and——"

"Yes, of course, Father, if you think you'd better." Kate rose and stood before him, in his way. "Mrs. Capper's such a jolly woman, isn't she? I suppose she thought she had a terrible joke on us, the way she was laughing at us when we got home this afternoon, Father."

"Laughing at whom?"

"At you and me, Father. You remember when we got out of the surrey after we had our drive from the Carlyle Club—well, we were just standing there a minute or two but she looked across and just laughed and laughed at us!"

"She did? Yes, of course, of course. Let's see; I was thinking of something else at—at the time—and I hardly noticed. Of course I didn't go over there and speak to her or—or—— Let me see. One forgets these things. No, I didn't go over there—or did I?"

"No, Father, you didn't. You just took off your hat and bowed to her and she laughed some more, maybe harder. It wasn't very polite because of course there wasn't anything to laugh at. She's got lots of men over there to-night, laughing all evening."

"She has?"

"Why, Father! Don't you hear 'em?"

"Yes, I do." He frowned, stood in silence for some moments; then extended an uncertain hand to pat his daughter's head, which he missed. "Goodnight, my dear," he said, recovering his balance. "I've been losing too much sleep lately on account of work. If you'll excuse me I think I'll go up to bed."

"Yes, Father dear."

He turned, went into the house, and could be heard slowly making his way up the stairs. Alone, little Kate Fennigate sat down once more on the top verandah step, and into the darkness she smiled contentedly.

What accounts of her afternoon's exploit were already being given here and there in the town's "best residence section" that evening she didn't suspect; the mind of childhood leaves wide vacuums in the computation of consequences, and, competent as she was even so early in life, she didn't foresee how talkative Malcolm Fennigate's next appearance at the Carlyle Club would be. Neither did she realize that she'd convinced the club's active members of something useful, and this was that henceforth her father'd come home at once if she merely telephoned to ask if he wouldn't like to have her come and bring Thomas's horse for a drive in the fresh air. She herself, though, didn't yet comprehend that telephoning would be sufficient. The horse was nice, so was Thomas, and she could easily again spare seventy-five cents; she was prepared, gladly, to do the same thing any time her father stayed away from his office all afternoon, not on business.

She loved him tenderly, more than he understood, and he'd have been startled if he'd ever realized how much she knew about him. She knew, for instance, that he was disappointed in himself, in life generally and in Mrs. Fennigate. He'd been openly disappointed in Arthur, Kate's much older brother, who'd been dropped from college, gone wild, ruined his health and now lived in New Mexico on cheques that had to be sent to him; but those other disappointments had never been mentioned, and young Kate understood that it wouldn't do to let her father see that she knew about them. Her thoughts of his disappointment in himself were acutely sympathetic; she comprehended that he'd expected to become a great lawyer and she was sure that he could have been regarded as one—if it hadn't been for the hidden disappointments that made him go to call on Mrs. Capper so much and worry people about his driving his car.

In the mild May evening dark she sat with her elbows on her knees and her cheeks between her hands, puzzling over plans to make her father a great lawyer. Other children of East Cherry Street played more and more boisterously as bedtime approached, and Laila Capper, tall for thirteen, passed along the sidewalk, meandering closely with a boy—out of school Laila Capper was always with a boy and always walked too close—but the small figure on the Fennigates' verandah steps remained alone, silent. Kate didn't see how she could do anything about the disappointment with her mother; but she thought that maybe if she could go to court some day and watch her father's conduct of a lawsuit and hear him make a speech about it she could see what was wrong with his way of doing it and sort of confidentially tell him how to do it better.

III

She thought that if her father's practice of the law could get brilliant enough to dazzle Mr. Henry L. Roe a little, Mr. Roe might put all the law work of the Roe Metal Products Company into his hands. If that happened, her father wouldn't be disappointed in himself any longer, because lots of people talked about the Roe Metal Products Company nowadays and how it was growing to be the most important Works in the city or anywhere around. Mr. Roe was one of the nicest old gentlemen in the world, not aristocratic like the Fennigates, of course, because he'd come to the city instead of being born there and so he didn't belong to the Carlyle Club or have family, though Kate had heard her mother's friends saying he had lots of trouble with his son, Henry L. Junior, who was bad. Mr. Roe was good and had repeatedly asked her all about Sunday School; he and his wife hadn't missed Prayer Meeting any Thursday night in eleven years and five months, he'd told her.

Sitting long on the steps that spring evening in her thirteenth year, Kate Fennigate hoped that Mr. Roe wouldn't hear about her father's not believing in Prohibition and that maybe the grand speech in court next morning would work the desired wonder. It worked no wonder at all. Malcolm Fennigate, not feeling well when he rose, overdid the usual remedy, hair of the dog, and at the trial was by no means at his best. Mr. Roe, perceiving why, and irritated by several irrelevant and unwarranted attacks on the validity of some of the Roe Metal Products Company's patents, couldn't see how such a red-faced, dissipated, spiteful man could have so lovely a little daughter. Malcolm Fennigate lost the case, was more disappointed in himself than ever, and, the next time Kate walked part of the way home with Mr. Roe, the old man changed the subject back to Sunday School as soon as she began to mention that her father hardly ever read anything except his law books.

She wasn't one to abandon an ambition easily. With elaborate tact she persistently did her unavailing best to get Mr. Roe excited about her father's ability, and, the better to prepare these daughterly hints, she talked to her father a great deal about the practice of law. He responded absently, though he laughed one day when he'd explained to her that everything depended upon a lawyer's proper preparation of his case and she asked if it wasn't even more important for a lawyer to know how to coax the judge and everybody else in court to like him ever so much and be on his side.

"You might be right, at that," Fennigate said, and laughed again.

"Yes, Father. So if I was a lawyer I guess I'd be thinking up all the best ways to make them like me and think I was right. The trouble is people pretty often can't see what makes other people not like them and think they're wrong. For instance, you take Laila Capper: she thinks the girls ought to like her and admire her because at parties she gets all the boys, so she thinks she ought to be just as prominent among the girls too; but they simply despise her for it and she'll never, never see why. You understand what I mean, Father?"

"Yes, I think I'm able to follow you that far, Kate."

She wasn't sure of this. "Well, then, Father, look at your own sister, Aunt Daisy. She always, always thinks she's right, so pretty nearly nobody thinks she ever is. That's what makes it so hard for Cousin Ames to like her, especially because he's her son-in-law and's so poor he and Cousin Mary haf to live at Aunt Daisy's house. If Aunt Daisy didn't think she has to act as if she's so terribly right about everything all the time, Cousin Ames and everybody else would like her and maybe get to thinking maybe she *is* right about certain things now and then. I mean if I was a lawyer, why, when I went in the court-room and talked to the witnesses and made speeches and all those things I'd be ever so agreeable, as if everybody had a right to their own opinions but if they'd think again maybe they'd see mine was the best one. Mightn't that be one of the best ways to be a good lawyer, Father?"

"Really I don't know but it might. In fact, I've always rather inclined to think so, myself." He laughed again, and then was thoughtful, rather sadly.

After that she more than ever wished to watch her father's conduct of a case in court, to see if he knew how to be a good lawyer as well as he seemed to believe he did. School interfered, however, and he hadn't many clients; it wasn't until her spring vacation when she was fourteen that she had her chance to see him in full legal action.

The case was a hard one—a cross, shabby man on crutches, with his sad wife and four restless children sitting all the time just outside the railing behind him, wanted a hundred thousand dollars from an old lady who owned a building. He thought he ought to have all that money because he'd fallen down a coal-hole in the building's sidewalk, and Kate's father was against him and for the old lady. Everybody else seemed to be down on her, angrily so, even after several men and two strange-looking women swore that the man on crutches had been drinking among them too much when he fell into the coalhole. The trial lasted four days, and Kate didn't miss a session, though her father failed to observe her presence. Neither did her mother know she was there, for Mrs. Fennigate seldom inquired either where Kate had been or where she was going.

The young girl sat, always intent, far back among the spectators. She came, really, as a constructive critic, expecting to make useful indirect suggestions later; but hour after hour of the trial passed without her father's doing a single thing she thought ill-advised. He was precisely what she would have had him be, easy, never unfriendly, offhand and yet alert as if amusedly so. Fine points of law at times came up for discussion, and here he was masterly but in the kindest, most tolerant way, especially when he had to straighten out the judge's mind for him. Kate felt more and more pride in him; she'd never dreamed how many important mystifying things he knew or how delightfully he could be both powerful and ingratiating at the same time.

In the large high courtroom with its prevailingly plebeian crowd, both room and crowd somewhat begrimed with the downtown smoke, he looked fashionable, too, which pleased her; but his fine big senatorial head was the center of interest, not his attire. Kate had always loved him but now she began to find him fascinating, and when he made his argument, on the fourth afternoon, she reached the point of worship. His speech was quiet, more like talk than oratory. He seemed only to be explaining things, at times humorously but always with the greatest care that the clear truth of them should be fully understood. The lawyer on the other side sneered, denounced and often shouted overbearingly; but Malcolm Fennigate was genial unanswerably. When he finished his speech, smiling and cordial, and sat down, his daughter, trembling, heard two men behind her speak of him.

"Didn't I tell you? The verdict's a cinch and there isn't a lawyer in the state that can touch Fennigate when he's on the water-wagon. Of course he'll fall right off again; but if he'd stay that way he'd have 'em *all* beat."

"Yes, guess he would. Wine, women and song's too much for many a big man, though. To-day shows what Fennigate can do when he lets 'em alone. You're right about the verdict, of course. They thought they were going to have a walk-over; but Fennigate's knocked 'em dead. Yes, sir, when he wants to be, he's absolutely a wiz!"

Kate began her walk home from the courthouse to East Cherry Street, her small chest bursting with a pride that nevertheless contained an ache. Her admiration for her father was overwhelming. Surely, surely he was a great lawyer, so why, why didn't everybody else know this as well as she did? "Wine, women and song" one of those men behind her had said. Women? Song? Sometimes, though rarely, she'd heard her father humming a tune, but never singing out loud, and he didn't seem to pay any attention to any women especially, not even her mother—except Mrs. Capper. He liked to go over there, just across the street, and stay pretty late sometimes, which usually made things uncomfortable at home for a few minutes after he got back; but calling so much on Mrs. Capper certainly didn't interfere with his law business the way that other trouble did. No, what did most of it must be the wine, and maybe, when he realized how much letting it alone had done for him in this case he'd just won, he'd quit taking any wine altogether. Then everybody, especially people like Mr. Roe, would just *haf* to understand that he was a great lawyer and bring him more cases and she wouldn't always have that pang in her heart even when she was proudest of him.

Her keen ambition was still for him to be Mr. Roe's principal attorney. She'd heard it said that this would be a "gold mine" for any lawyer in the country because the Roe Metal Products Corporation (not Company any more) now grew so great, and on that account had so many lawsuits, it made everybody rich who had anything to do with it. Kate yearned to tell Mr. Roe, as if absent mindedly, about her father's triumph of that afternoon; but she didn't know when she'd have the chance. She still had her piano lessons at the school at the same hour; but he didn't walk by there on his way home now. He'd built a house far, far out on the new extension of National Avenue, so he had to use a car and she saw him seldom. Nevertheless he did at times happen to come driving by as she walked home from the

piano lesson, and he'd picked her up and taken her with him the
few blocks to the corner of East Cherry Street; so, though their chats
were brief, the friendship lived.

The trouble was it might be a month or two before he'd happen
by again at the right time, and even then maybe Mr. Roe'd be worrying too much over his son, Henry L. Junior, to listen properly. Kate
had heard her mother's friends saying that Henry L. Junior was the
talk of the town, was treating his wife and their twin babies just terribly, had driven his mother into the grave and his father almost
crazy. Kate was fond of old Mr. Roe and wished she could do something with Henry L. Junior for him; she was pretty sure she could
if she had a chance.

Walking up National Avenue on her way home, exalted by her
dear father's triumph and fairly confident that some day she'd be able
to help old good Mr. Roe with his dissolute son, she went more slowly
as she passed before a wide-fronted brick house near the corner where
she was to turn into East Cherry Street. This biggish house, well back
from the street and standing among tall old trees in better than an
acre of green lawn, was her Aunt Daisy's now; but Kate Fennigate
was conscious of it as being in a special family way a part of herself,
for her grandfather had built it and her father had been born in it and
grown up there. It was part of the reason why he'd looked fashionable
in the courtroom, part of the sense of "class distinction" that was in
the fourteen-year-old girl's thoughts when they touched upon the
Fennigate family.

Since her infancy she'd had the continuous impression that the
Fennigates, and a limited number of other families originally of this
neighborhood, belonged together in a confederation, as it were, somewhat above the rest of the population. Just how "above" wasn't clear
because of course one was supposed to be friendly to everybody, and
some people, like the Cappers, for instance, almost belonged to the
confederation—and yet almost belonging to it was in certain ways a
good deal worse than being completely outside of it like Mr. Henry
L. Roe. Young Kate, passing, looked at the broad old brick Fennigate
house not with proprietorship, since now it was Aunt Daisy's, but
with much the same expression she wore when at times she looked

at the medal she'd won at school for leading her class in scholarship, deportment and character. It's true that like other able executives she had her moments of complacency.

Her Cousin Mary, a wan young mother leading a four-year-old child by the hand, walked round the nearby corner where Cherry Street crossed National Avenue, and the child, a little girl, broke away from her mother and rushed upon Kate, shouting lovingly. Cousin Mary was wearing a flannel hat, a green silk jersey, a white linen skirt and rubber-soled white shoes. "Oh, hello!" she cried. "I've been over to your house looking for you; but your mother didn't know where you'd gone. I wanted to see if I could get you to look after Celia for a couple of hours. Ames wants me to go out with him to the Augrens' to play tennis and we can't take Celia because their dogs are always running about the place and don't like children. There's nobody here but the cook and Mother, and the cook can never do anything at all with Celia, and Celia says she won't stay with Mother."

"I mon't," Celia said, sat upon the pavement and squirmingly embraced Kate's ankles. "I mon't stay wif Granmuzza. I mon't!"

Kate pulled her up. "Yes, Celia's wicked; but I'll stay and play with her, Cousin Mary."

Little Celia was delighted. "I'm wicket!" she shouted and pounded at Kate's stomach. "I'm wicket! I'm wicket! I'm wicket!"

"You are. Very!" the child's mother agreed, and the three turned into the bricked path that led toward the low stone steps before the front door of the house. "We'll be ever so obliged, Kate, if you'll just play around the yard with her an hour or so till we get back. That'll be before dinnertime."

Cousin Mary put two fingers in her mouth and produced an accomplished whistle; it brought forth from the front door a tall slim young man in white flannels that had seen better days. He was black-haired, dark-eyed and had what's often called a "good" face, with well-shaped manly features and an expression that seemed to be an habitual odd combination of both worriment and gayety. At sight of him Kate Fennigate stood still, and, not heeding little Celia, who had begun to pound her again, looked at him examiningly. He waved one of the two tennis rackets he carried.

"Hello, hello, hello!" he called, in a cheerful deep voice, and came forward. "This is fine of you, Cousin Kate. We were afraid Celia'd get bitten if we took her along. She's always after us to get you for her to bully. Think you can stand her?"

"Yes," Kate said gravely, continuing to look at him. "Don't you think you're getting too thin, Cousin Ames?"

He laughed. "Look at yourself! You're just a sliver, and besides, it's time you were beginning to grow some if you don't expect to be a midget. Here's Celia only four years old and you don't look any-where near twice her weight. Fat up!" He touched Kate's cheek lightly with a forefinger and turned to his wife. "Come on, Mary; we'd better trot if we're going to catch a Jefferson Boulevard street-car. Good-bye, ladies! Let's run, Mary."

Young Kate, serious, watched them out of sight, her gaze more upon the young husband than upon the pale wife he seemed rapidly to tow along; then little Celia, shouting importunately, had her way and the two began to play at being wild animals among the trees and budding shrubberies in the yard.

Celia was a romping rowdy, one of those inexhaustible children incessantly in extremities of motion except when they sleep, and Kate, though strong for her small size, was glad when at last Aunt Daisy opened a side door of the house and called them in. Aunt Daisy was cold-faced and always wore stiff, dark clothes; she looked at people as if she knew something about them they'd rather she didn't. Ordi-narily Kate wasn't pleased to see her; but after an hour and a half of playing with the child, Celia, any intervention was welcome.

"Bring her in," Aunt Daisy called. "I never heard such a racket! It's time for her bread-and-milk. Bring her in."

"Yes, Aunt Daisy," Kate said. "I think if you're going to take her now, I'll be going home. Good afternoon, Aunt Daisy. Good-bye, Celia."

Celia squawked to split the ear. "I mon't! You shan't go home! You shan't! I mon't come in! Go 'way, Granmuzza!" She charged into Kate's back, leaping upon her, pounding her with two round fists, screeching. "You haf to stay! I mon't! I mon't! I mon't!"

Aunt Daisy looked cross but beaten. "Stop screaming! If your

Cousin Kate stays you'll come in and have your bread-and-milk, won't you, Celia?"

"Yes."

Beaming sweetly, Celia took Kate's hand; the two entered the house and followed Aunt Daisy into the dining-room where Aunt Daisy lifted Celia into a high-chair, fastened a small tray across her, thus imprisoning her, set bread-and-milk and a spoon upon the tray and said, "There!" as if she said, "There, darn you!" Kate moved toward the door.

"Well, I believe now I'll just run on home because——"

"No!" Celia shouted, and hammered the tray with the spoon uproariously. "I mon't! You shan't!" She seized the bowl of bread-and-milk dangerously with both hands. "No! No! No!"

"Sit down, Kate," Aunt Daisy said, and was obeyed. "Nobody knows why children take these fancies. Sit down. Eat your bread-and-milk, Celia; eat it."

Celia laughed unbecomingly into a spoonful of bread-and-milk and looked at Kate as if to say, "I'm clever, what?" Then slowly she consumed the bread-and-milk, and, sighing, closed her eyes. Almost instantly she was asleep in her chair. Kate rose to go.

"Sit down," Aunt Daisy said, and again was obeyed. "You can talk as loud as you please and it wouldn't wake her; but if you take any steps toward the door she'll be squalling again. I know her. For heaven's sake don't wake her up! She's killing her mother, and goodness knows she's too much for me. It doesn't make any difference when you get home, anyhow. Your mother never had dinner on time in her life and why should she? Your father wouldn't be there to eat it—not till everything was cold. That old food-spoiler of yours, Editha, complains to my cook that you've been trying to run the house a good deal lately, giving her orders what to have for meals and all that. Have you?"

"Well—I've been trying to help a little, Aunt Daisy."

"I'll bet you have!" Aunt Daisy laughed vocally, without altering the severe contours of her face. "Everybody says you're the bossiest little girl in this neighborhood and even your father's afraid of you. I wish you'd try your hand on my esteemed son-in-law. Somebody'll have to if Mary and Celia are to be kept out of the poorhouse."

"Cousin Ames is lovely," Kate said, and her eyes were deeply meditative. "I just noticed to-day he's too thin but looks like the pictures of Daniel Webster, except Cousin Ames's hair's shorter and of course he's lots younger. Everybody says for a young man he has the finest brains in town and's going to be a prominent citizen."

"'Prominent citizen'!" Aunt Daisy echoed hootingly. "'Daniel Webster'! I wish a few of 'em had to put up with what I do from him." Her expression and her voice both became more unpleasant as she began to elaborate a theme already familiar to the niece. "Look what he's done to my daughter. Married her without a cent before either of 'em graduated from the state university, and went off and joined the war; then came back without a cent and got his diploma and's been in Law School ever since, living here on his wife's family——"

"I don't think so." Young Kate's interruption was firm. "Cousin Mary told me he's always paid you board, Aunt Daisy. She told me he works himself to death being a stenographer night-times after his Law School work."

"Night-times!" Aunt Daisy grew more bitter, as she usually did. "Yes. Night-times when he doesn't drag Mary around to silly whooping parties where he can sing and play the piano and show off to their crowd of young ninnies. I ought to have sent her to Miss Carroll's and never let her go to the state university. I didn't see then that the reason she wanted to was because Ames Lanning was going there. They were practically engaged already when they were freshmen, seventeen years old. I didn't dream such a thing! None of the Lannings ever made any money; his father was a Unitarian preacher, and I guess that's enough to know! Now Ames is going to be out of Law School in June and what's he going to do?"

"He's going to be a lawyer—like my father, Aunt Daisy."

"Just about!" Aunt Daisy uttered another strictly vocal laugh. "That's a fine prospect for my Mary, isn't it? He's going to be a lawyer like your father. Just about!"

Kate's brown eyes, enlarged, regarded her gravely. "Have you ever heard my father plead a case in court?"

"Good heavens, no! Has he had one? I didn't suppose he could spare the time away from the Carlyle Club and his charming Mrs. Capper. Your mother certainly is a strange woman; but I suppose she's kept herself stuffed with food so long that by now she probably doesn't care about much else. Most of her family were like that—fat but not jolly, just sleepy. She lost her looks within two years after she married, and if she ever had anything else I'd like to hear of it. You'll have to look out you don't take after her when you grow up."

"I'm almost grown up," Kate said mildly. "I'm fourteen. I'm not very fat yet, Aunt Daisy."

"No." It was easy to see why Aunt Daisy wasn't popular. "You're the runt. You're the first one—everybody big and lumpy on your mother's side, everybody tall on the Fennigates'. Well, what's going to happen to us now I don't know. Half the people in this town now-adays don't even know who the Fennigates are! Look at all this new crowd that've been coming in, more every year, getting rich out at that vulgar common old Roe's Metal Products factory. People I never heard of driving big cars past my door and building showy houses out north. The town's being ruined!"

"It isn't Mr. Roe's fault, Aunt Daisy. He isn't common and vulgar; he's good and very nice."

"Excuse me!" The aunt became satirical. "I forgot I was speaking to an authority on all matters. Perhaps you'll permit me to say that at least the Fennigate family's being ruined. Look at this very house. What's going to happen to it? There's a new automobile salesroom going up in the next block, and those beastly Augrens sold their house across the street last year and moved miles out, and now the old Augren house is going to be torn down and a disgusting flats building put up right against the sidewalk. Where'll real estate values go? As if I wasn't poor enough already!"

"Are you, Aunt Daisy?" Everybody in the family maintained that Aunt Daisy was rich and terribly afraid somebody'd find out that she was. "Wouldn't it be a lovely present you could make to Cousin Mary, though, if you'd have a nursery governess for Celia?"

"Nursery governess!" Aunt Daisy plainly struggled to control herself. "When half the time I don't know how or when I can pay my cook! One servant in a house as big as this, and me working my fingers to the bone trying to keep the place decent in the smoke that's thicker every year!"

"Why don't you sell it, Aunt Daisy? Then you'd have plenty of money. I've been thinking about that."

"Have you? Then you'd better think again. My parents left me this house, and it's a sacred trust. Your father and your Uncle James took their share in money. James's went for a stained glass window and an alcove in that useless college when he was drowned, and your father spent his long ago. Every cent of it! He let your brother, Arthur, get about half of it away from him, and how he keeps Arthur in New Mexico and you in Miss Carroll's School God only knows but——"

"I don't want him to, Aunt Daisy," the niece interrupted. "I've asked and asked to go to high school instead; but he won't let me."

"Poverty-pride," Aunt Daisy explained. "Keeps you at Miss Carroll's because he's poverty-proud. Same reason he pays his dues at the Carlyle Club and owes for an acre-size sealskin coat he let your mother get from Heisberg. Nursery governesses! Don't talk to me! If you're in one of your planning fits, young lady, you'd better let it work on somebody else, not me. Maybe you could stir Mary up to do something with that husband of hers except drag around to play tennis with him. She ought to make him quit Law School and get a real job to-morrow! Mary hasn't had a single day of health since this selfish child here was born."

"I don't think Cousin Ames looks so very well, either, Aunt Daisy. He's too thin and——"

"No such a thing. He's an ox. He and Celia could wear out a regiment. He——" Aunt Daisy interrupted herself as an old-fashioned bell jingled in a passageway behind the dining-room. "That's the front door. They're back. I wouldn't trust him with a key; there's no telling what hour he wouldn't be keeping her out. Go let them in, Kate; I'll watch this pest. She's waking up. Hurry or she'll be squalling after you!"

Kate ran from the room; then walked through the wide, ugly hall, with glimpses of heavy Hayes and Wheeler furniture seen through the open double doorways of the cumbered, large, dark rooms on each side of it. She opened the front door and had a hearty quick greeting from Cousin Ames Lanning.

"Hello, angel midget! Still here; good for you! Afraid we're late. You're a sport, sticking to Celia this long. Thanks a thousand!"

"She's been asleep in the dining-room," Kate said, and, as Mary slipped by her and hurried through the hall, spoke in an undertone. "Aunt Daisy's sitting with Celia, Cousin Ames. You ought to change your clothes after tennis, oughtn't you? You always play so hard. Aunt Daisy and Cousin Mary'll put Celia to bed now. Hadn't you better hurry upstairs and get your other clothes on before they come by here?"

He looked at her out of the side of his eye, smiling ruefully. "Maybe I'd better."

"I would," she said, stepped into the vestibule and closed the door softly behind her.

She went home, walking the short distance slowly, engaged with thoughts of her father and Cousin Ames Lanning. It seemed to her that Cousin Ames was much too thin but had a beautiful face. That way he had of looking gay and troubled at the same time made one like him and be terribly sorry for him, too. The gayety must be the way he'd like to feel all the time if he could, and the trouble must be Aunt Daisy and being so poor.

He had a great future, though. Everybody who knew him said so, because he'd worked his way through college and yet had been at the head of his class. He'd gone to war, and now was said to be the top-most of all the students in the Law School. Her father was really a great lawyer, no matter what people thought, and Cousin Ames was going to be one. Then they ought to be together. That was an idea! As soon as Cousin Ames finished Law School he ought to join in her father's office—Fennigate and Lanning. Solemnly happy, far inside her, she began to plan how to bring this about.

IV

AT HOME, WHEN KATE ARRIVED, EDITHA HAD THE DINNER on the table waiting dismally. Mr. Fennigate was not in the Carlyle Club nor had he been there, the telephone in that refuge replied to the daughter's inquiries; and afterwhile, when Mrs. Fennigate roused herself from a peevish lethargy, she and Kate sat down to the less than lukewarm meal.

"You needn't save anything for him, Editha," the mother said through cake in her mouth, as they finished. "Whenever he's this late it means he won't be able."

Kate, looking anxious, protested. "But to-night I'm sure he will, Mother. It's different to-night. You see he's won this lawsuit so splendidly, didn't I just tell you, and all week while it's been going on he hasn't taken anything except food—and water of course."

"Yes; but it's over." Mrs. Fennigate walked heavily back to her rocking-chair in the living-room. "The lawsuit's over. If he sticks to food and water after one's over, it'll be the first time. You needn't ex-pect it."

"But I do, I do," Kate said faintly. "I do expect it."

That expectation failed, as hours passed. Mrs. Fennigate had gone to bed; but her daughter still waited when Malcolm Fennigate ar-rived at eleven in a taxicab. The driver helped Kate to get him into the house, and departed; at the foot of the stairway Malcolm Fenni-gate summoned all the powers of his will and was able to stand un-assisted except by his right arm round the repulsively varnished wooden pineapple atop the scratched newel-post. "You're—you're mistaken to sit up so late," he said to his daughter. "You're too young and I have no time for collversation."

This was the end of his effort. His arm slid from the newel-post; he buckled into a reclining posture upon the lower steps of the stairway, closed his eyes and slept as promptly as had little Celia in the afternoon. Kate looked from him to her slight wrists and hands, comprehended that these were inadequate to the task of conveying him upstairs to bed, and seated herself upon a bleak hall chair to watch over him. That is, she watched over him; but after the first moment or two didn't look at him, because his mouth was open and his face wasn't like itself. Throughout her childhood she'd never cried much and she didn't cry much now; but before long, though her face was not contorted, two lines of tears were sliding slowly down her cheeks. She was giving up her new great idea; she understood that Cousin Ames had trouble enough with Aunt Daisy and it wouldn't be fair to plan that there should some day be a legal firm of Fennigate and Lanning.

Upstairs her mother was sleeping peacefully—or anyhow she was sleeping—and Kate wondered if this other slumberer, lumpish at the foot of the stairway, wouldn't have been able not to get like that if her mother had been more interesting. Of course her mother couldn't help not being an especially interesting woman and so, probably, her father couldn't help being the way he was now—and liking Mrs. Capper better. Maybe, though, from the time her father and mother got married he hadn't cared much to stay home in the evenings and so her mother maybe gave up trying to be an interesting woman. The way married people acted toward each other seemed to have a great deal to do with the kind of people they got to be; but, on the other hand, maybe the kind of people they already were when they got married caused them to act toward each other the way they did.

"Either way it isn't much their own fault." So ran the young girl's thoughts. "If somebody else made me be the way I am I'm not very responsible for it, and if I already *was* that way anyhow, then my ancestors must be responsible for it, and Who's responsible for *them?*" There didn't seem to be much use in blaming anybody for anything; but since maybe people *were* a great deal what other people made them be, then the only thing for you to do was to make them be the best you could.

More than an hour passed before Malcolm Fennigate woke. At first he didn't open his eyes but seemed trying to adjust one of the stairway steps under his head as a pillow. "What's the matter with it?" he asked. "It's all wrong. What's the matter with it?"

"Nothing, Father." Kate didn't rise. "It's all right. Hadn't you better sleep some more?"

"Sleep?" He pushed himself up to a sitting posture and began to get his eyelids apart. "I'd better be moving along toward home, I think. I've got a wife and child, you know. Let's all go home."

"You're home, Father. It's all right." Kate rose and extended a hand to him. "Would you like to go to bed, Father?"

"Bed? Oh, yes; bed, of course. Yes, if you'll excuse me, I believe I will." He ignored her hand, and, using the newel-post, pulled himself up. "Yes. I've been working too late o' nights this week and losing all my sleep. Excuse me, please." He tried to ascend the stairs with no aid except from the railing; but he made a perilous failure of it and Kate jumped to help him.

"Put your other arm round my shoulders, Father."

"It isn't practical," he said. "Pardon me, but it's entirely un-impractical."

"I know, but just try it anyway."

"Oh, if you say so, if you say so," he assented, and leaned upon her; but, though she sagged, she strugglingly got him upstairs and to the door of his own room, where he bade her a formal goodnight, floundered in and closed the door. She heard him fall upon the bed, and went to her own, where she wept again, grieving for the firm of Fennigate and Lanning that would never be.

She'd had a bad drop after the exalted hours in the courtroom; her pride in her father had turned all to ache now. One thing that her Aunt Daisy had said cut sharply into her, too—the reference to her father's spending the money to keep her at Miss Carroll's School. Kate knew that it wasn't what Aunt Daisy had called it, "poverty-pride", that made him go to this expense; it was his affection for his daughter. He really did love her dearly, Kate always knew. The public schools were excellent; but Miss Carroll's was a rare and noble institute of learning. Nowhere in the land was there a better school and nowhere else was there a Miss Carroll. As Kate had told her aunt, she had begged her father repeatedly to transfer her to a city school, and, though she begged in earnest, she adored him the more for not consenting. The tears upon her pillow that night after she'd seen him glorious in court and then helpless on the stairway made a wider splotch of dampness because of his goodness to herself.

Except for two rainy days of melancholy study indoors, that was the end of her Easter vacation. She was glad to be on the way to school again Monday morning, though a little sorry that Laila Capper skipped across the street to walk with her. The two were day pupils at Miss Carroll's, and, counting merely by the time they spent together, Laila Capper was Kate's most intimate friend; but the intimacy was all on Laila's part. Kate never, so to speak, felt intimate toward Laila.

A year the older of the two, Laila was already taller than Kate Fennigate would ever be. One of those stirringly black-eyed young beauties that males of all ages become curious about a block away, Laila at fifteen was fully conscious of her increasing shapeliness in feature and figure, and was adventurously aware of the prestige she thus gained among the boys. Mystifyingly, she seemed to know boys all over the town—some of them pretty odd and some pretty old, too —for she was always interested in new ones; and, though Kate wondered where and how certain of them had been introduced to Laila, it wasn't imaginable that any of Miss Carroll's girls had ever let herself be picked up on the street.

"How's your old man?" Laila asked, as they began to walk toward National Avenue together, and her voice, in spite of the years at Miss Carroll's, was as wrong as the inquiry, Kate thought. Laila's mother and father had the same kind of voices, too, placed close behind their noses, indistinct on consonants and terrible on short A's. Probably it was one of the causes why the Cappers couldn't ever quite belong to the confederation, though of course Aunt Daisy could tell you lots of other reasons for calling them "common". "I mean after the other night when he got that big bun on," Laila added. "Mom was at a front window and saw the taxi drive up with him and we all went out on the porch to rubber. You and the taxi man sure had a giddy time of it! Looked like that Laocöon thing we had in the art course last month. Mom said it was the worst she ever saw him because he 'most always knows anyhow how to navigate. Where'd he get it?"

"He wasn't well," Kate said. "He'd been working too hard and he——"

"Come off the perch!" Laila laughed and pushed her. "Always trying to put it over; you're the funniest little canary I know! I bet in your heart you haven't got any more respect for your parents than I have for mine."

"Indeed I have!" Kate was a little superior, and perhaps meant to be, she was only fourteen. "I both respect and honor mine."

"Go fly up the creek!" Laila pushed her again. "Me, I don't pull any bunk about the dear old home life. I was onto Mom and Pop by the time I was eleven years old. Yes, and they know it, too, because I laugh at 'em. Sometimes Mom can't help laughing, too, because she knows I know about her. I told Pop to his face the reason he got blackballed at the Carlyle Club when Mom had your father try and get him in, it was because the club thought Pop was too close to being a professional gambler. Yes, and that's just about what——"

"Laila! He isn't any such thing and you oughtn't to say it. He's a broker."

"Yep. So the sign on his office says, Miss Fennigate; but Pop plays other things besides the market, you bet! My whole life, sometimes he'll have a roll big enough to buy Mom a mink and the rest of the time we're standing off the butcher for weenies. When they get a grouch on at each other both of 'em have plenty to bring up, so it runs pretty even between 'em. Your father hands me a bigger laugh than either of 'em, though."

"No, he doesn't," Kate said. "I don't know what you're talking about."

"You do, too! Prig! Trying to act like that old pious Æneas, so crazy about his father he carried him around on his back? Gosh, that stuff runs into one of my ears and out the other. I'd make Mom let me quit school altogether except everybody thinks it's snooty to be at Miss Carroll's. You know as well as I do your old man's been after Mom since Noah was a babe. I bet it's never really got him anywhere with her, though. She certainly knows how to string 'em along! Guess he thinks he's high man with her; but he isn't. This year it's the new one, that old slick-face with the half grey moustache, Mr. A. Villrid Barnes. Tried laying on of hands with me, too. There's a laugh! He's a promoter and's got that big white Marmon you notice in front the house half the time lately. Pop kind of hates him; but he don't mind your father. Sort of likes him. Listen. Aren't you kind of related or something to that Martha Gilpin's family?"

"Yes. They're my cousins. Why?"

"Listen," Laila said again. "Those Gilpins make me tired. Excuse me if they're your cousins, but I've been sitting next to that squinty little Martha Gilpin two years in French and she acts like I'm some kind of arsenic. What's she got to be so up-stage about, just she's a Gilpin and belongs to the Country Club and her folks are going to blow her off to a big May Day party out there? I guess I heard all you other girls my age talking about it just before spring vacation commenced, didn't I? Nice for me, wasn't it? Me the only one in the class not going to be invited! You're supposed to be my best friend, aren't you? Well, what about it?"

"I think I can," Kate said. "If you want to go very much, Laila, I think I can get you an invitation."

"Atta girl!" Laila patted her friend's small shoulder. "I'm not going on being left out of everything in this old town, I can tell you! Just wait a while; I'll show 'em. Just wait till I once set eyes on the right man!"

" 'Man', Laila? You don't mean somebody you'd want to marry?"

"Why don't I?" Laila's girlish laugh was high-pitched, nevertheless a buccaneer's. "Oh, I'll not be in any hurry. I'm going to have lots and lots of fun first, and afterwards too if I want to, because that's really the only way clever women get their share out of this life; but the man I pick's got to be the right kind of hubby, not like your pop or mine, or I'd give him the hoof in a jiffy."

"Laila, you're absurd! You're not even sixteen yet and——"

"Yep, not sixteen; but little Brighteyes knows her oats, young Missy! The hubby I pick's going to be right, I tell you. I'm going to be a bird in a gilded cage; but the cage isn't going to have any top on it. Some day your priggy Martha Gilpins and these other stuck-ups that try their best to leave me out are going to haf to use smoked glass to see my tail feathers!"

Kate looked up at her puzzledly. "Why do you care what they'll see, Laila?"

"Never mind! Just follow me and you'll wear diamonds." Laila became more serious. "Listen. Will you come over after school and push me through this horrible new geometry stuff she's going to poke us into to-day? I can't keep my mind on it in class, it bores me so, and I know I'm not going to understand a word she says. What say, kiddo?"

Kate said yes, though she wished she weren't always acquiescent with Laila, and she knew very well how Laila "worked" her. A lithe marvel in the dancing class and a flashing, whooping belle at parties where boys were, Laila in school was dumbest of the dumb and couldn't have remained if her small neighbor across the street hadn't coached her.

Kate, wondering why, did most of the "home school work" for both of them and continued to do it, although other franknesses of Laila's even less enjoyable than those of that morning's walk to school were often upon the older girl's lips. What thinking Laila did was mostly aloud, mainly about boys, and, though she had her secrets, her talk sometimes gave glimpses of doings that Kate preferred should remain but glimpses. She did not lack curiosity; but she desired not to know the secretest parts of Laila's secrets and Kate was, herself, by far the more secretive of the two. Laila couldn't have guessed Kate's opinion of her and had no thought at all of Kate except as somebody to talk to and to use for dreary lessons and other advantages.

The companionship of the two girls, like many another, was only geographical, caused by the location of their houses. Kate found Laila a somewhat interesting person, often unpleasantly so, but for the most part an oppression upon her.

Laila was beautiful, really beautiful everybody admitted; and, by the time she was seventeen, she had a knowing, rather mocking look when her eyes met those of men, as they always did when they had that chance. Kate's mother naturally didn't like this look of Laila's and had her own definition of it.

"She's getting so fast looking," Mrs. Fennigate said to Kate. "Of course she would, with such a mother; but I wish you wouldn't feel you have to be with her so much. You ought to stop being nice to her."

"I couldn't very easily, Mother. She's——"

"Oh, I know," Mrs. Fennigate grumbled. "Always running over here, and you've never known how to be rude. Well-bred girls are careless nowadays; they let the common ones in and'll get contaminated. We hear horrible rumors lately about something called petting parties—of course only among the most ordinary young people; but that's the kind Laila'd know, outside of you and Miss Carroll's School. I'm sure she's the sort of girl that gets talked about, and with good reason, too! Of course she couldn't lead you into anything really improper; but if you keep on being seen with her so much——"

"Seen with her? I don't think I am, Mother. Nobody ever looks at me when I'm with her."

"No, I suppose not—on the street. Those loud 'come hither' girls with the long curves get all the common staring; but I do hope nice people won't begin to think you're much of a friend of hers. Besides her looking fast and the Cappers being very, very ordinary, it isn't becoming to you to be with her. She already looks too grown-up and you still look like a child. I don't mean you're not pretty enough. Your hair's not so flaxen as it used to be, but it's nice and wavy, and your eyes are a nice bright brown color and you have that good profile and you've grown some and filled out a little, so you're really a very good-looking young girl; but always being seen with a show piece a foot taller than you——"

"Oh, not a whole foot, Mother. I've been growing a lot. I'm fully five feet and almost an inch and three-quarters already, and Laila isn't more than——"

"Well, I'm only warning you," Mrs. Fennigate said, sighing with her weight of flesh. "These wretched ailments that have been gaining on me don't give me much chance to watch over you, so all I can do is say 'Be careful and don't let nice people get a wrong idea of you.' I'm sure your father's got himself talked about, going over there as much as he always has, and I certainly don't want anything like that to happen to you. I do wish that family had never moved into this neighborhood or that we'd never had to live here in this inconvenient cheaply built house, ourselves. Another thing, child, do try to get along with this new cook better than you did with the last one. Really, I wish you hadn't interfered with old Editha, trying to get her to make all those things she couldn't learn how. How many have we had since her? About seven, isn't it? With my asthma the way it is and all this arthritis setting in, and the doctor hammer-hammer-hammering at me to diet, I'm simply not up to doing the house-keeping any more. What did you tell her to give us for dinner? Something good, I hope. You've been making our meals too skimpy. Whatever there is to-night, I hope for once there'll be enough of it."

Kate reassured her upon this point—falsely, for she was trying hard to reduce her mother's weight. Later in the day the daughter thought seriously about the maternal warning not to be seen a great deal with Laila Capper and found something ironical in it. She was as little with Laila as she could contrive to be without open unfriendliness, and herein she recognized an inconsistency in herself, one amounting to a weakness of character. She liked to advise people deftly, also to control them by suggestion and maneuver. She was so eagerly of this type that Aunt Daisy, repetitiously prompted about a nursery governess, often asked her niece why she didn't run for Mayor?

On the other hand, with all her managings, Kate was unable to be severe. Something within her compelled her to be almost supinely accommodating; she could neither be discourteous nor bear to disappoint anybody. Thus Laila put herself upon the small neighbor across the street, and, when the moment came, gave her a lasting hurt.

V

It's NOT ALWAYS A DISADVANTAGE FOR A GIRL TO GROW UP
in what's known as "an unhappy home". True, a whining nature may
therein fall into habitual self-pity; but a good mind acquires more
knowledge of the world, more experience of our human inwardness,
than if sheltered within sunnier walls. A hard-drinking father pushed
to pay his bills, a mother become an invalid through physical self-
indulgence, and a dull ugly house never once the scene of heartfree
merriment, moved young Kate Fennigate to no self-pampering. Seventeen, she had no envy of happier girls or of richer ones; she was a
planner of improvements—mostly for other people. Usually the plans
didn't work very well; but some of them did and she was too shrewd
to plan the impossible. She did most of Laila Capper's school work,
for instance; but didn't waste energy trying to elevate Laila's character.

Laila was still an oppression upon her, nevertheless so rewarding
to the eye that Kate liked to look at her. For other observers the two
girls, seen together, were a charming contrast—though of course a
noticeable time elapsed before the glance of a passerby rested (if it
did that at all) upon Laila's demure, small companion. At eighteen
Laila was blossoming indeed; her vitality made her conspicuous.
She seemed radiantly always in motion, even when she sat. Her arms
swept in wide gestures, her knees crossed and uncrossed, her expressive feet were seldom still, animation continually re-shaped the handsome face, her large coal-black eyes did really seem to dance; and her
restless, insistent voice never stopped. Beside her, Kate Fennigate
seemed almost voiceless: one was doing all the doing, the other all
the thinking.

The one that did the thinking was the star of Miss Carroll's School, an outshining lustre in the climax of the two girls' final year, though at the senior dance, two months before Commencement, a stranger would have mistaken the class's dunce for its prize girl, Laila's look that night was so triumphant. She was all over the place, had to push boys away from her; her happy laughter outdid the violins, and her dancing held upon her even the unwilling eyes of other girls' mothers.

Mrs. Fennigate's eyes were not included; she was at home with asthma, arthritis and indigestion, and her husband, preferring even this to a school dance, had begged to remain to look after her. Aunt Daisy had said that "the family" must be represented, however; and Cousin Mary, fond of Kate, had easily persuaded Cousin Ames not to spend the evening alone in the house with Aunt Daisy, so he was there, too. They sat on the sidelines, and Cousin Mary was pleased to see that boys liked Kate and her dancing.

"You're quite popular, dear," the young Mrs. Lanning said, once when the schoolgirl cousin came to sit with them between dances. "You must be pretty proud to have so much attention and know that you're going to graduate at the top of the class and get all the best prizes, too! Ames and I are quite set up, being allowed to be your chaperones. I think Ames'd like to dance with you, if you don't mind his age."

"His age?" Kate laughed, and her color heightened as she looked at the thin long young man. "Will you, Cousin Ames? Will you dance with me?"

"Maybe it'll give me a reputation for learning," he said. "I've been noticing the deference Miss Carroll shows you—yes, and the other teachers, too, when you've been talking with them. I don't think the family have understood what a celebrity we have among us. Seems to show we don't recognize celebrities until we see them in their own field."

Kate gave him a serious glance. "I don't mind your laughing at me, both of you." She saw a boy coming toward her, rose quickly and put forth a hand. "The music's beginning, so if you really can stand it, Cousin Ames——"

"Stand it? Not I! You'll have to do that."

They began to dance, and, looking up from not quite the height of his shoulder, she saw that he was smiling indulgently. "Once you told me to 'fat up', Cousin Ames," she said. "I have—some—haven't I?"

"Yes, enough for it to be quite becoming."

"But you haven't," she said. "I don't think you eat enough and you ought to drink lots of milk. Aren't you working too hard, too?"

"I think not harder than a clerk in a law office has to if he's to hold his job."

"Don't they give you any cases yet, Cousin Ames?"

"Me?" He laughed. "They let me work up a few details sometimes."

"But don't they know where you stood in the Law School and what everybody said about you? It's pretty stupid of them!"

He laughed again. "Oh, Mary and Celia and I'll get along some-how!"

"Why, of course!" she said, and then for a while devoted herself solely to dancing.

Cousin Ames danced well, she was pleased to discover, and, in spite of the difference in height, they moved sweetly together. She became aware that his arm was about her, that his hand clasped hers, and never before had she noticed such a thing; partners' arms and hands in dancing were technicalities. For the first time in her life they didn't seem to be only that and she felt a startled, strange joyousness because they didn't. Ever since she'd first seen this cousin-by-marriage, just before his and Cousin Mary's wedding, she'd thought a great deal about him, and lately almost as much as she'd thought about her father; but suddenly now, as she danced with Ames Lanning, she thought about him much, much more poignantly than ever before. As suddenly, she thought about herself, too. If this thought about herself could have been put into words uttered by her voice, it would have been the astonished outcry: "Why, I'm happy!"

She'd never in her life asked herself the question "Am I happy?" or "Am I unhappy?" Now, all at once, she knew she was happy—because she was dancing with Ames Lanning. For the moment her thought of him left out "Cousin"; he was just Ames Lanning. Something unknown but dear and lovely was happening and nothing else had value. Her breath quickened, and, not knowing that she spoke, she said, "Oh!"

"Murder!" he exclaimed. "Did I step on you?"

"No, no, no! You dance better than anybody I've ever known. Do step on me!"

"What? Why?"

"I'll keep the slipper."

"No wonder you're popular!" Ames laughed aloud and expressed his jocular approval in the flying twirl he gave her. "Never mind; I'm game. A cousin's the best possible old stick for you to practise that sort of thing on."

Kate laughed, too, a little breathlessly, glad that he took it that way. She'd spoken too quickly and without quite knowing what she said; but it was true. She would have kept the slipper, though of course it was better for him to think that she'd been joking. Why better? Why would she keep a slipper if he'd stepped on it? Why had she asked him to step on hers? What was the matter with her? Whatever it was, it was more dazing and delightful than anything that had ever happened before to anybody. She didn't look up at his face. Her downcast eyes saw only the black cloth of his coat as they danced on.

He was speaking again, and his pleasant deep voice seemed enrichingly changed, as if she'd never heard it before. "I mustn't monopolize you. I'm afraid I've noticed several hoverers trying to work through to cut in."

"You want to stop?"

"No, no; but I'm taking too much of your gala time, and besides I'm afraid I ought to be getting Mary back home. She isn't strong, you know, and the exertion of talking to people tires her pretty easily."

"Oh, yes, of course; I'm very thoughtless." She stopped dancing instantly and they began to move across the crowded floor toward Mary.

A girl's loud laugh intruded closely upon their ears, and Laila Capper, dancing with a short boy, bumped into Ames lightly but with almost plain intention. For a moment her face, laughing and beautiful, was within an inch of his. "Good gracious!" she exclaimed. "Do pardon us!" and she swept away, still laughing.

"Who is that?" Ames asked, looking after her. "I've seen her before —often noticed her. Rather dashingly magnificent, isn't she? Not one of your classmates, is she? Seems rather too grown-up, I'd say. You know her?"

"Her name's Laila Capper."

Kate wished that he hadn't asked her about Laila, who of course had tried to make him notice her; but his curiosity was only momentary. Cousin Mary rose as they approached her, and she put her hand rather tiredly upon her husband's arm. To Kate, Cousin Mary oddly looked a little changed since the beginning of that dance. There seemed to be something different about her; somehow she wasn't quite the same Cousin Mary, and her putting her hand upon her husband's arm in that familiar possessive way didn't appear to be right. Everything was being pretty peculiar; but if Cousin Mary was in some strange manner changed she didn't seem to know it, herself.

"Ames and I'll be trotting along home now, dear," she said. "Of course we wanted to put in an appearance to show that the family appreciates the honor you are to it; but I'm a frail reed these days and besides Celia might be waking up—she has dreams that scare her and makes the most frightful row—so goodnight, dear. Run and have a good time with the boys. Goodnight."

Ames tapped Kate's cheek with a friendly forefinger. "Yes. You dance like a fairy ballerina, young cousin. Have a big time with the boys I've been cheating. Goodnight."

"Goodnight. Oh, thank you—thank you for coming, both of you! Thank you for dancing with me. Goodnight."

Kate watched them through the door and then turned to a boy who was waiting to dance with her; but everything was anti-climax after that. The big room, crowded, lost significance; amber light turned grey—and yet there was something new about everything. Once, while the orchestra rested, Laila ran to her.

"Listen, kiddo, who was the sample of the older set? I mean that Hamlet-looking tall bird you were dancing with and bumped into me. Isn't his name Ames Lanning or something?"

"He's my cousin," Kate said. "He isn't very Hamlet-looking, Laila; he keeps his hair short and he's cheerful. Yes, his name's Lanning."

Laila laughed and pushed her. "Why the frosty tone? Come off the roost! Think the Fennigate family's so sacred I can't even ask about its cousins? If you aren't the darnedest little priggy snob sometimes! Olive oil!"

Kate felt an inside shock and injury. Something infinitely sensitive seemed to have been intruded upon and insulted, though she didn't know how—except that Laila had shown a characteristic, prospector-like interest in Ames Lanning and shouldn't have thought she had a right even so much as to speak his very name. The matter was entirely different, a little later, when Miss Carroll mentioned him. Miss Carroll was the highest possible type of woman, and a precious angel, too; the finest, most secret things in the world were safe when her quiet voice mentioned them.

"I was delighted to meet your cousin, Mr. Lanning, Kate. Of course I know your Cousin Mary; but I'd never met him. It's a pleasure to see a young man who looks to be all the good things one hears said of him. I'm sorry your father and mother were unable to be here, dear; but since they couldn't I'm glad you invited Mr. and Mrs. Ames Lanning."

At home, Kate repeated this to herself, word for word, especially "It's a pleasure to see a young man who looks to be all the good things one hears said of him." She loved Miss Carroll worshipfully, and it seemed as right and dignified to think of Miss Carroll and Ames Lanning together as it was stupid and unpleasant to think of him and Laila Capper in the same breath, as it were. Kate tried to put Laila's freshness out of her mind entirely, so that she wouldn't think of Laila and Ames in the same moment. She didn't like to think of Ames and Cousin Mary in exactly the same moment, either; and this seemed to be because of that peculiar change in Cousin Mary at the end of the dance with Ames. What was that change?

Kate Fennigate was only seventeen, a young girl alone in her room thinking back over a school dance just ended; but she was able to see within herself somewhat. All at once she knew that it wasn't Cousin Mary who had changed. Color rose high and burningly to Kate's forehead as she discovered her own secret. Color rose even higher when she remembered saying, "I'll keep the slipper." She'd

said it not knowing what she said, and by the mercy of heaven he
hadn't understood that she meant it and so hadn't despised her for
a crazy little fool.

"But this must have been going on in me all the time," she thought,
discovering with amazement something more. She wasn't sorry, she
was glad, and had no envy of Cousin Mary but now an added tenderness toward Mary and little Celia both, since both belonged to him.

It was late, late before she fell asleep, thinking how more than ever
she adored Miss Carroll because she'd spoken so appreciatively of him.

VI

WHEN THE SHAFT OF MORNING SUNSHINE FELL ACROSS
her bed, Kate woke in her meager little room feeling all new and
strange and rich. A celestial necromancy seemed to have been done
upon her, transfiguring her life into a brilliancy she hadn't dreamed
could exist. How queer that she'd been seventeen long blind years
in the world not even suspecting what dazzling treasure it held!

After breakfast there shone a happy thought. She had six dollars
and there was no school to-day, Saturday; when she got the house
straightened up, she'd go downtown and spend the money for a
doll for Celia—not to please Ames with herself but because Celia was
his and loved new dolls. The errand was delayed, however. Mrs.
Fennigate's asthma became acute for some hours and it was not until
the middle of the afternoon that her daughter could leave her. Kate
almost ran the whole mile to the downtown shop that kept the jolliest
dolls.

She found the right one, for five dollars and a half, and, with it in
a blue-wrapped white box under her arm, she had walked two blocks
upon her homeward way when the mischance befell her. She'd left

the thickest Saturday afternoon shopping throng behind her; the sidewalks were less crowded here, and then, not ten yards before her, she saw Laila Capper skip adventurously out of the doorway of a restaurant known even to schoolgirls as the town's most influential speak-easy. Laila wasn't alone, and one of the two men with her was also known even to schoolgirls, though strictly not better than by sight.

He was a small, pale, button-nosed young man, had insane grey eyes set near to each other in a silly face, and he was too noticeably dressed in green and fawn, with an orange feather in the ribbon of a blue velours hat. The other man, older, bigger, a little shabby, fat-faced and laughing approvingly, was plainly some sort of follower or sycophant. Kate had never seen him before; but the younger of these two startling friends of Laila's she recognized as Henry L. Roe, Junior, nowadays entitled to be defined as notorious. Kate had long ago given up her childhood's hope that she could some day help poor old Mr. Roe with his worse and worse son; tales of him dealt with more than escapade, and to see him as apparently a familiar friend of Laila's —he had her by the arm and was certainly familiar—ran close upon the appalling. There were blanks in Kate's knowledge of Laila; but recklessness so deep as this hadn't been even vaguely imagined.

Kate hesitated, slowed her pace. The three were crossing the side-walk to an open yellow touring-car that stood at the curb, one of its brass lamps gone and the mudguard heavily dented. People were staring at the flushed and laughing Laila and her pair of visibly sporting-life companions. Among those interested was a grey-haired lady of fine appearance who'd just stepped out of a stationer's small shop directly across the street. She didn't pause; but, as she walked away, her gaze, through nose-glasses, examined the opposite side of the street. The lady was Miss Carroll; Laila saw her instantly but pretended that she didn't and acted upon a brazen inspiration.

Kate tried to pass unnoticed behind the three as they reached the yellow car. Laila'd seen her too, and, just at the moment when Miss Carroll's glance began to turn that way, stretched forth a long arm, caught Kate above the elbow and drew her impetuously into the group. "Hi, old girl!" Laila cried gayly. "You're just what we're looking for to make the party even. Say how-do to Harry Roe and Mr. Emil Horsch; then hop in the car and they'll take us out to——"

"No, no, no!" Kate said; but was pushed hard into the open tonneau door of the automobile, and in this movement the fat-faced man, Horsch, assisted Laila.

"Get in, kid, get in!" he urged in a whiskied old voice. "These two been playin' me for a gooseberry all afternoon and I certainly need cheering up. I don't mind your being only about thirteen; I want company."

Across the street Miss Carroll had ceased to gaze in that direction, and, moving away, turned the next corner; but both Kate and Laila knew very well what she must be thinking she had seen—a party of four, two of them Carroll School girls, climbing into Harry Roe's raffish car in front of a known speak-easy where they'd apparently been entertained by the notorious youth and his friend. That was the picture Laila'd made.

"Let me go!" Kate hotly resisted the pressures upon her. "What have you done, Laila Capper? You saw her! You did it on purpose! What have you done to me?"

Laila was laughing wildly. "Just trying to give you a good time, Snooks. These boys are the most fun I've had since Heck was a pup. Stop being a wet smack and get all the way in. Get in!"

"No! No!" Kate contrived to release herself from both Laila and the lamenting Mr. Horsch. She sprang from the car's running-board, turned her back, strode away furiously, followed by three mocking cries:

"You'll be sorry, kiddo!" "You don't know what you're missing, baby!" "Sure you won't change your mind, little lady?"

Kate was angrier than she'd ever been in her life; but, after she'd delivered the doll, and Cousin Mary and the child, Celia, had made a grateful fuss over her, she became more philosophic. Miss Carroll knew her too well, she was sure, to believe in the mere appearance of things that were really impossible. At eleven that night, alone downstairs working upon the address she was to make on Commencement Day, she heard a tap upon a front window, went to the door, admitted Laila and was able to be calm with her.

Laila looked tired. "Listen," she said. "Lend me a couple of safety-pins, will you? That fellow's an Indian. I'm sorry for Horsch; he has a job trying to keep him out of jail. Never again for me, birdie; never again! I don't mind a little gossip; but I don't intend to have my name batted about all the speak-easies and roadhouses around this town and I'm not setting out to be the second Mrs. Harry L. Roe, Junior, either. Horsch says his old man knows he's crazy and won't leave him a cent, and I expect to be Somebody in this town some day, thank you, when I decide to! Listen, you don't think she'll do anything about us, do you?—I mean on account of what she saw."

"I don't know."

"Go on, of course you do! She isn't going to get rough with our Valedictorian this late in the day."

"Yes, that's what you counted on—but I don't know."

"Pooh!" Laila said. "You're her Exhibit A, and she's got to let me off if she does you. She won't do a thing. Listen, has Mom telephoned over or anything to ask if you knew where I was?"

"No."

"Well, that's a relief," Laila said. "We had supper at a chicken-dinner speak out on Route Eighteen, and who should we run into but Mom's and Pop's and my dear old family friend, A. Villrid Barnes! I let on not to see the naughty old rascal and he did the same for me because I wish you could have lamped what he had with him! Oh, boy! But of course even A. Villrid Barnes'd set up to be shocked at anybody's running around with Harry Roe, so I was afraid he might've telephoned Mom. She's a pretty liberal old girl, herself; but Harry Roe—no, not quite! I guess old Barnesy didn't, though, or she'd have been telephoning all around to locate me. Looks as if Barnesy wants to make it fifty-fifty—he'll not tell about me if I won't about him. Quit looking so up-stage, kiddo. I've had enough along this peculiar line, thanks, and won't get myself in such a jam again, you bet! Just forget it, will you?"

"I'll try to."

Kate was never to forget it. On Monday morning when she arrived at the school she was told that Miss Carroll wished to see her. Miss

48 KATE FENNIGATE

Carroll was looking out of a window in the Principal's Room when Kate came in, and she didn't turn immediately.

"Close the door, please," she said, and stood silent for some moments while Kate waited.

"Yes, Miss Carroll?"

"I——" Miss Carroll hesitated; then turned but didn't look directly at Kate. "I've never assumed to stand in loco parentis for the day pupils of this school. Their mothers and fathers are of course responsible for their conduct—and companions—outside of the school. You understand that I take this ground, don't you?"

"Yes, Miss Carroll."

"Very well," Miss Carroll said. "I've called you in to explain two things that are difficult to make quite clear. The first of the two is that I don't act upon hasty judgments. For instance, if I saw any of our day pupils downtown apparently doing something unpleasantly astonishing, or being with—with extremely unsuitable companions— I shouldn't leap to the conclusion that such a thing was habitual. I'd not deny that it could be interpreted as impulsive or even almost accidental—something that probably hadn't happened before and wouldn't happen again. That's the first of these two things. You understand it?"

"Ye-es, Miss Carroll."

"Very well, then. The second is this: it seems to be understood that your relationship with Laila Capper is of the girl-team variety; you and she are what is called 'best friends'. It's always surprised me a little, though of course I realize that propinquity makes girls who live across the street from each other likely to be intimate. Since you *are* that intimate with her, though, and therefore naturally interested in what concerns her, I've called you in to explain why I prefer not to acquiesce in her enrollment as a graduate of this school. It's very exceptional to drop a girl from the school within a few weeks of what would otherwise be her graduation; but in this case it has been decided to take that step. We have informed her parents."

"Laila's——" Kate drew a quick breath. "Laila's being—being expelled?"

"Dropped," Miss Carroll explained. "She's being dropped because her school work, always below the mark, has fallen so low this final term that all of her instructors agree that it would be useless for her to take the coming last examinations for a school diploma. As you're the president of her class besides being her closest friend, I'm giving you the facts and you may repeat them to the other members of the class."

"I—— Miss Carroll——"

"Yes?"

"I——" Kate stopped again.

Miss Carroll's tone throughout was neither cold nor unfriendly; but there was a difference in it, an unusual formality. She spoke as does one who impersonally performs a duty, and never before had she so dealt with this most favored pupil, Kate Fennigate. More and more, through the years of Kate's schooling, the loved teacher had been almost girl-to-girl when they were alone together, often and often gayly confidential; and this difference was ominous. Miss Carroll didn't change easily and if she did she stayed changed. Kate stood dumb, looking up at an adored face, eyes that had lost affection and didn't fully meet her own.

In this queer clash it was not the teacher who knew the student's mind but the other way round: "She thinks she can't get at the truth. She believes that in spite of what she's always known of me, there are maybe other things about me that she doesn't know, and, as I'm supposed to be so thick with Laila, I'm after all just possibly the sort of girl that might have been on a wild party with her. What Miss Carroll saw on the street was exactly that, and she thinks if I *am* that sort of girl I'd never tell her the truth about it; I'd claim it was a sort of accident and that I'd joined up with them to sort of protect Laila and hoping maybe to get her away. Miss Carroll's had a long experience with many kinds of girls and's sometimes been shocked by finding how little she's known some of them she'd been sure she knew all about. Her mind is all doubt of me. She thinks maybe I did really join them hoping to get Laila away; but, since that's what she thinks I'd claim anyhow, she wouldn't truly know which would be the truth, so she'd prefer I didn't try to explain what she saw. What she didn't see was Laila's jerking me into the party. She just saw me with them, getting into Harry Roe's car, and of course it looked as if I'd been in that speak-easy with them."

"Yes?" Miss Carroll said. "What is it?"

Kate went on thinking what Miss Carroll was thinking: "She thinks that whichever way it was she has to give me the benefit of the doubt. She can't help the doubt and I can't say anything that would really change it. Telling her the truth, that Laila grabbed me, would just be ruining Laila worse with her, a treachery to my 'best friend', and even if Miss Carroll believed me she'd see the treachery and feel that a treacherous person is always to be doubted. So she's got the doubt and will always have it the rest of her life. It isn't her fault; she can't help it. She would if she could because it hurts her; but she can't. She'll never be the same with me again."

"Well?" Miss Carroll said.

"Nothing. I haven't anything to say, Miss Carroll."

Miss Carroll turned again to the window. "That's all, then."

"Yes, Miss Carroll."

VII

LAILA WAS WAITING AT THE NATIONAL AVENUE CORNER of East Cherry Street when Kate came from school that afternoon.

"It's all over the whole dear old Carroll institute of learning by this time, of course," Laila said, as they turned into the home street together. "Buzz-buzz-buzz all day, what? 'Oh my, girls! Have you heard the big news? Laila Capper's flunked out!' A hell of a lot I care! What's the dif? Guess you thought I'd be hanging out the crepe, didn't you?"

"No, I didn't."

"Why should I?" Laila asked. "I'm not fired; I'm merely dropped for low term marks. Well, at that you don't suppose anybody'll think

I got 'em because I'm dumb, do you? This whole town knows I never paid any attention to her silly old curriculum. People have been asking me for years when I ever took time to pay even the slightest notice to my lessons. All this'll be it'll be a joke with the whole crowd, and Mom isn't making any fuss over it. She says she's been expecting it for years, because she never saw me so much as open a schoolbook. Pop doesn't count. He doesn't come home over two or three times a month nowadays, anyhow. Old Carroll fixed it up pretty for you, though, didn't she?"

"No, not very."

"Get out! She did. She's a sly old cat, slicker than I thought she was and she's put a fast one over on me. I thought she'd haf to let us both alone and just forget what she saw Saturday. Not she! But if she fired me for *that* she had to include you in it, too, and that would never do! Fire Kate Fennigate, what? Demoralize every girl in school! No, no, no scandal, see; just ease out Laila Capper for poor scholarship. Fine! Leaves dear little Kate Fennigate sitting pretty and everything perfectly jake. What'd she say to you?"

"Miss Carroll?" The two girls had paused, facing each other, before Kate's house. Kate was serious and pale, while Laila smiled down upon her satirically. "How do you know she said anything to me, Laila?"

"Cut out the Sunday-school teacher with me, Kate Fennigate! Can it, will you? Don't you ever get just plain human and natural for as much as a minute at a time?"

"I'm sorry." Kate looked at her steadily. "What you mean may not be possible. For me the way I am seems natural, Laila."

"All right; stay that way!" Laila's smile was more cutting. "Of course Miss Carroll called you in for a heart-to-heart. Trying to put it over on me that she didn't? Poot! What I'm curious about is what you told her."

"I didn't tell her anything."

"Baloney!" Laila laughed aloud disgustedly. "Don't come that on me, little sweetikins! I know what you told her just as well as if I'd been there, myself. You said, 'Oh, Miss Carroll, how could you think such a thing of me! That big bad old Laila Capper practically threw me into Harry Roe's car, and if you don't believe me I'll show you the bruise marks on my arm!' And then Miss Carroll said, 'Oh, my darling pet, how could I *ever* have mistrusted *you!* But it's all right, don't fear, because I never did like that Capper person anyhow and I only let her stay in my sacred school this long because she's *your* friend, baby-doll, and now we'll just quietly and pleasantly throw her out for being a bum at scholarship. Won't that be nice, little starlight?' So you said, 'Yes indeed, Miss Carroll!' and then you two had a nice long good big sweet cry in each other's arms and——"

Kate interrupted with an authoritative sharpness that surprised both of them. "Don't be such a damned fool, Laila!"

With that, in a maze of astonishment, the smaller of these two young girls turned upon her heel and went into the house, leaving the taller staring after her open-mouthed but furious.

Indoors, Kate began busily to attend upon her ailing mother, who was mountainously in bed, wheezing for air, and, as the work continued, somewhat easing the querulous patient, amazement wasn't abated but grew. Kate realized that she had a quarrel on her hands— and that she had sworn. Years earlier girls had begun to use swear words with some fluency and she'd once mentioned this inquiringly to her father who, in the matter of profanity, was abstemious. He'd explained to her that violent language was the resort of a meager mind unstocked in vocabulary and thus unable otherwise to seek to be impressive; swearing was only a sign of weakness.

To the daughter this had seemed true and she had always the habit of seriously thinking over things that appeared to be true, then of trying to guide herself accordingly; but now she'd just called Laila Capper a damned fool. "Damned" was a commonplace with many girls, of course, and modernly not regarded as actually profane; but she'd never said it before. Was her character changing or was she just growing up? Was the quarrel, too, a part of her growing up—like falling in love? Did people's characters become worse, possibly weaker and coarser and more selfish—as they grew up?

Changes appeared to be happening within her and outside of her, too, for people were changing toward her. Two people had changed toward her to-day, Miss Carroll and Laila Capper. Neither of them would ever again be the same with her. The change in Miss Carroll was one to break the heart; the change in Laila Capper could be despised. Nevertheless it was astonishing: Laila was certain that Kate had betrayed her and Laila would always more or less hate her for it, be in reality a sort of enemy—and yet Laila'd "done the whole thing", had instinctively and instantly exposed her friend to possible utter ruin in order to benefit herself, and now sincerely believed herself betrayed by that friend!

The real truth of this and of everything seemed all mixed up and contradictory, and so did people. Her father was the finest lawyer in town and clients knew it but wouldn't come to him because he drank; whereas if enough of them came to him he wouldn't drink—at least not so much probably. Her mother was a good, kind woman who'd never done any harm in her life, except to herself by over-eating poor food, and yet now in this sickness nobody came near her to help or even inquired about her, except absentmindedly if they happened to think of it. Aunt Daisy, her own sister-in-law, spoke spitefully of her without any reason whatever; Aunt Daisy spoke spitefully of everybody, for that matter—and why? There wasn't any sense to it. Old Mr. Roe lived a good life, gave thousands of people work—and it must just about kill him to have Harry Roe for his only son. Cousin Mary lived the life of a gentle angel but never had any health. She had Ames, though—and with this thought Kate's breath quickened again as it had during the dance when both she and Ames Lanning seemed to change so strangely and brilliantly.

Nothing conformed to the shapings of life one expected. Laila'd often taunted Kate with being Sunday-school-teachery, which indeed she was. She'd been a churchgoing child and now herself taught a class of little girls on Sundays at St. John's. At Miss Carroll's the English courses were elaborate and so were those in French. She'd read all the required books and plays, hundreds of others not required, and at home she'd skirmished among modern novels; she was not unaware of Freud and the "new psychology". All of this seemed to imply that life and the behavior of people, though plastic, must conform to certain patterns—and they weren't doing it at all. Things weren't as represented.

Who and what was she herself? She'd never been worried about this before; but now, all at once, she seemed to have lost herself, or, rather, never to have had a known self to lose. One thing she did know about herself, though, was that she'd always felt superior to Laila Capper. Of course Laila had long since perceived this, maybe subconsciously, and wasn't that why her resentment had broken out at last so crazily over a thing she'd herself brought about and that had nothing to do with Kate's superiority? It must be that people often had quarrels about things other than what they thought they were quarreling about, things that didn't even get mentioned.

Kate Fennigate, seventeen, found the world shapeless and herself wandering in it, an inconsistent shadow. She was glad that Ames hadn't yet come home from the office when she'd brought the doll to Celia. She dreaded seeing him again because she was afraid that the next time she saw him she'd find that what had happened to her while she danced with him had vanished and that she really wasn't in love with anybody at all.

She was right about the changes in Miss Carroll and Laila Capper; both alterations were permanent and even the despised one could make her wince. On an evening of the second week after the quarrel Laila sat whooping with four or five boys on her verandah and saw Kate come out of the front door across the street and seat herself upon the steps. Laila shouted at her guests, "Talk to yourselves a while, roughnecks!" jumped up, ran across the street and stood before Kate in the dusk. "I just thought I'd ask about your mother," she said in a friendly voice. "Mom says she's afraid she's pretty sick again. Is she?"

"She's better just now, Laila. The doctor was here a while ago and gave her something. She's gone to sleep. Thank you for asking."

"Not at all, not at all," Laila said. "Of course Mom and I'd be glad if there's anything we could do."

"No, I think not. Thank your mother for offering, though, Laila, and you too."

"Oh, that's nothing, kiddo." Laila paused. "I suppose everything's going big at the school, getting ready for Commencement. I expect

it'll be a big disappointment for your mother if she won't be well
enough to see you graduate."

"Yes, I'm afraid so."

"It wouldn't be a disappointment to Mom about *me!*" Laila
laughed. "She'd have been bored to tears sitting among all the high-
brow parents and 'friends of the school'. Not very congenial to Mom's
high, wide and handsome sporting nature, what?" Laila's tone became
confidential. "All the same, Mom's got a good heart; she thinks it's
a shame the way your father keeps coming over to our house when
your mother's so sick. Don't blame her, Kate; I just wanted to tell
you. She's been trying to make him go home this last half hour."

Kate spoke impulsively. "Oh, is he——"

"Yes, didn't you know? Yes, all the time the doctor's car was out
in front here. They're sitting inside with highballs; but the windows
are open and I could hear her telling him over and over he oughtn't
to be there, he ought to be home. Of course she laughed; but she
meant it. So don't blame her, Kate. That gang's getting rough on our
porch, so I can't linger. Toodle-oo, baby!"

She whisked back to the boys across the street, pleased with the
flinch she'd seen upon the face of Malcolm Fennigate's daughter.

He came home an hour later, crossing the street somewhat stum-
blingly to where Kate still sat upon the steps; and a hot wave of pity
drenched her heart as she realized that even by moonlight anybody
could see how much balder his big head was becoming. He ascended
to a wicker chair upon the verandah and talked to her of many things,
blandly and with rich wisdom, until a gasping murmur from overhead warned them that Mrs. Fennigate's opiate had worn out its
effect and she needed help.

On the hot afternoon of Kate's Commencement, the suffering
mother made a heroic effort, got into her best and tightest afternoon
attire, and, attended solemnly by her husband, sat in the front row
between him and the child Celia, the greater part of whose chair
she necessarily occupied. Loyally present, next beyond Celia, were
Cousin Mary and Aunt Daisy; and Kate, uttering her Valedictory
in a spirited brave young voice, was more conscious of the family
group than of the words she spoke. The words were all projected

from her correctly, and the Valedictory was to be widely hailed as
the most maturely eloquent ever heard in the school; but to Kate it
seemed that she was making vocal sounds of little meaning.

On the flowered platform, never looking directly down upon her
relatives, she was aware of Celia's squirmings as the little girl repeatedly strove to push some of Mrs. Fennigate back where it
rightfully belonged. Kate saw, too, how Cousin Mary struggled
whisperingly to share a part of her own chair with Celia; but Celia
wouldn't accept it, being determined to possess what was legally
hers. The young speaker's mind was preoccupied with these two,
Cousin Mary and Celia, for they seemed part of that absentee of
whom she'd thought with every word she'd written of her Valedictory. It was to him she'd written it; but she was glad he wasn't
there—not because she still feared that when she saw him again she'd
lose what she felt about him. She'd seen him often since first she'd
had that fear, and she'd lost nothing, alas! Why "alas", since she was
glad? She didn't know.

There was a deep loss, however, felt woundedly all the while she
spoke. Since the morning when Miss Carroll had explained the
expunging of Laila Capper, the teacher's manner toward the student
had been "perfect", and Kate knew that the perfection, which was
as crystalline as pure ice, would be lifelong between them. This was
the change that hurt and would go on hurting Kate Fennigate to her
dying day. It was sharp in her as she went back to her seat in the class
and saw Miss Carroll applauding with the rest, but formally.

One of her hearers, an elderly man in the distant rearmost row of
chairs, did better by her, though his manual enthusiasm went unnoticed and the young speaker herself didn't see him, couldn't have
imagined his taking the trouble to be present. During her address
he'd nodded affirmatively as she made her "points" and he concluded
these noddings with a double one in approval of his own judgment.
"Yes, sir, I'm right," Mr. Henry L. Roe said to himself. 'Always
thought she was the smartest girl I ever knew, and she is." Then, not
needing the distribution of diplomas and prizes to confirm him
further, he went out quietly to the hot June afternoon and drove
away.

Malcolm Fennigate had already heard the valedictory address—it had been rehearsed before him—but as it had come now from the lips of his daughter, a slight fair-haired white figure gallantly facing all these people and challenging the hidden forces of all the years lying in wait before her, his heavy-lidded eyes began to blink unaccustomedly. They blinked again, a little later, in the "old Fennigate house", when Kate's health was drunk by the small party of kinsfolk who'd been present at her Commencement. Aunt Daisy had insisted upon this tribute to the new graduate as a festal conclusion of the great day.

"It's only iced tea," she explained when the six gathered round the pearl-inlaid ebony table in her cherished drawing-room, and she added, not lowering her voice, "Of course we ought to drink the Valedictorian's health in something better and I have a little—a very little—of my pre-Prohibition wine left in the cellar; but I thought it'd be advisable to make it just iced tea—on account of Malcolm, you know."

This wasn't what set Malcolm's eyes to blinking again. His emotion was incited by the performance of the child Celia. Aunt Daisy filled six cut-glass goblets from a clinking silver pitcher. "Now, Celia, say your little speech," she said.

Celia faced Kate obediently, and in a high and hurried monotone spoke the words Cousin Mary had taught her: "Dear Cousin Kate, you have finished your school days in triumph and we all hope and believe that the rest of your life may be as rich in reward as your career at Miss Carroll's fine institution has been. May you live happily ever afterward because you are wise and good and we all appreciate and love you. With this wish we drink your health."

"Going to sob into your iced tea, Malcolm?" Aunt Daisy inquired. "For heaven's sakes I should think you'd be pretty glad not to have Miss Carroll's bill hanging over you every term after this. Sit down, everybody, and Mary'll pass the jelly cake."

They sat and Celia seized upon Kate, pulling her to one of the heavy sofas, but was silent there, devoting herself to iced tea and the two wedges of cake she'd irretrievably grasped while being forbidden to do so. Cousin Mary put the glass cake-stand back upon

the table, sat beside her uncle Malcolm and began to talk to him; but
Aunt Daisy's voice, addressing Malcolm's wife, who panted in the
largest chair, dominated the high-ceilinged room.

"Of course with a nice convenient small house like yours and
Malcolm's, housekeeping problems amount to nothing; but how I'm
to keep on managing here I don't know! Ames thinks I ought to give
it up. Just like him, telling me what to do when he can't even afford
to join any of these new country clubs that are springing up, not
even the cheapest of 'em, and let Mary have a little fresh air. I'd no
more give up this house than I'd fly; it's the one sacred trust of my
life. Look at all these wonderful beautiful things that have been
handed down to me. That very chair you're sitting in Grandfather
bought in Cincinnati in Eighteen fifty-six from the most expensive
firm there. They were the best furniture makers west of the Delaware
River. Look at those teakwood sofas. Mother bought the brocades for
'em in New York, and that oil view of the *Salute* in Venice my great-
uncle Laurie gave my mother under Chester A. Arthur. Good artists
who've seen it say it's by Bonington and it's priceless. Every stick of
that gilt furniture in the reception-room is mahogany under the gilt;
Mother had the gilt put on when that style came in. Well, all these
precious things have to be kept up, don't they? I can't let 'em just
crack up and go to pieces, can I?"

"I don't know, Daisy," Mrs. Fennigate gasped. "I suppose not."

"You 'suppose'? Good heavens, what a way to put it! You've certainly been in the family long enough to know that if it wasn't my
duty to keep this place up I'd be only too glad to sell it and move out
of all the grime and soot and smoke we're getting down here. Look
at my white lace window curtains! How many times a year do you
expect I have to take 'em down and wash 'em and then sit up night
after night repairing 'em where all the washing wears 'em out? I'd
like you to guess just how much of my time has to be given to the
lace curtains in just this one room, if you please!"

"I couldn't, Daisy; I couldn't guess."

"No, of course you couldn't, nor how I have to drive and drive to
keep my inside shutters clean enough to show what they're made of.
They're black walnut, and only fourteen houses in this whole town

ever had inside shutters of black walnut. Living the way you and Malcolm do, you couldn't dream what a care such a house as this can be!"

"No, I'm sure I couldn't, Daisy."

"Of course you couldn't—and look how the whole neighborhood's simply set on ruining it! That apartment house straight across the street from me, a boarding-house next door, and I hear they're going to tear down the Lockwoods' on the corner below and put in a gasoline selling station. Here I am working my fingers to the bone and everybody telling me I ought to move, and all these things get done to me! Wouldn't I be only too glad to go live in a quiet small place out of the dirt if I were willing to see my father's and mother's and grandfather's treasures and beautiful house defaced? Never! What's more, Mary's got to keep it up after I'm gone; I'd never, never consent to anything else. I swear——" Aunt Daisy interrupted herself. "Oh, dear! Here he comes. I suppose he'll think he has to join the party. I'll never get used to his thinking he's really one of the family."

She referred to Ames, who came in breezily. "Hello, hello, hello, everybody!" he said in his gay and manly voice, went to Kate and took her hand. "A thousand congratulations, young woman! I'd have been to see you in your glory, but I had to argue a case in court—at last!"

Kate had jumped up. "What was it? You've won it, haven't you?"

"I'm afraid not. Our firm let me defend a restaurant keeper in a suit brought by a man who'd found a dried mouse in one of the restaurant's raisin pies. I did my ferocious best to bully him into admitting that such an accident might have happened to one of his own mother's pies; but the judge's sympathies seemed to be against me. No, I'm afraid I didn't shine and that the heads of my firm won't entrust so much responsibility to me again."

"Oh, I'm—I'm sorry, Cousin Ames." Kate looked stricken.

"Splendid!" Aunt Daisy's laughter was prompt. "Old Amy Huling, Ames's great-aunt, was here the other afternoon telling me everybody says he's going to be a great man some day. She's in her second childhood. Lo, the mountain was in labor and brought forth a mouse! They put a case in his hands at last—it's about a mouse in raisin pie.

Raisin pie! He gets a case about a mouse's mummy—and loses it. Congratulations, Ames! Oughtn't we to drink the mouse's health, too?"

"Mother, Mother!" Cousin Mary said softly; for, though Ames only laughed, his color had risen. Kate was redder than he; she felt that Aunt Daisy ought to be killed. How could anybody live in the same house with Ames Lanning and forever be so viperish? Aunt Daisy'd better do a little sewing for him instead of vilifying him; his shirt collar showed a frayed edge against a faded old blue necktie. It wasn't right that he should be so poor—and so neglected.

Cousin Mary had given him cake and iced tea, and he turned to talk local politics with Malcolm Fennigate. Kate, standing where he left her, saw something upon the floor at her feet; it was a button from his coat, one that had dropped evidently when he shook hands with her. She picked it up and showed it to him. "Cousin Ames, you've lost a button from your coat. Would you let me sew it on for you? Cousin Mary'll lend me a needle and thread. Won't you——"

"No, indeed, dear. It's a useless one from the cuff of my sleeve or, rather, from where the cuff of men's coat sleeves used to be. Clothing makers still insist upon furnishing us with those vestiges of the extinct, nobody knows why. There were formerly two on each of my sleeves; but the other three have been gone for quite a while, I've noticed, and now I look more consistent with none. Throw it away, Kate."

"Yes, if you say so, Cousin Ames."

Mrs. Fennigate just then gave up trying to fan herself and listen to her sister-in-law. "Kate," she said strugglingly, "I'm afraid I've done a good deal for one day. You and your father'd better try to get me home now."

They came to help her, got her home and let her rest in her rocking-chair for a time before attempting the stairway. Breathing was less difficult for her in the chair than in bed, anyhow, she said, and patted Kate's hand. "You're so kind to me, my dear daughter, so kind!" This was an unusual speech; but the Valedictory, and the sight of Kate standing forth alone upon the platform, and the significance of the day, had stirred something within the mother. There were things she wanted to say if she could. "It's hard on you to have to spend so much time looking after me, Kate, and it's been hard on you a long time—taking all the care of the house, too. I wish Malcolm could afford to send you to college. I think he ought to try."

Malcolm agreed painedly. "Yes; you're right. I ought—if I could. I——"

"No, no!" Kate protested earnestly. "College isn't needed for anybody that's been through Miss Carroll's School, you know. It's useful for girls from other schools but not from Miss Carroll's; it'd only be duplication of a great deal that she's given us and'd be a waste. Besides, I absolutely wouldn't leave you, Mother, until you're well again."

"Well again?" Mrs. Fennigate's voice was vague, as if she spoke of something too strange and remote to be comprehended. "I wish Malcolm could send you for a trip abroad, then, if you don't think college is needful. A trip abroad would be——"

Kate stopped her. "No, it wouldn't, Mother. I love—I love my own city and I don't want to go away from it. I don't ever want to go anywhere else at all. It's—it's just beautiful here!"

"You think so?" Mrs. Fennigate persisted in her idea. "You haven't seen much else. If it were only a few months abroad it'd be worth while. Even I had that much, myself, when I got out of school. Malcolm, you ought to be able to manage it somehow, now that Arthur isn't costing us anything and you don't have to send him cheques as you used to. It's certainly a providence, his getting a father-in-law that put him into the ranching business or whatever it is. I wish he'd come home, though, just once anyhow. I'd like to see him anyhow once again and what his wife looks like outside of a kodak. Don't you think maybe you could scrape up enough for Kate to have just two or three months abroad, Malcolm?"

"I—I—— We'll see, dear. I can't say just at this minute. We'll see."

"She ought to have it," Mrs. Fennigate said. "Kate, I'm afraid I'll have to admit I never knew how much you stood out from other girls until to-day. I knew you were very bright, of course, and more intellectual and smarter; but I really didn't ever before see how much. You don't get it from me, of course; it's from Malcolm. I wish I'd saved enough from housekeeping to send you to Europe. We ought to've done more for her, Malcolm. We were proud of you to-day, Kate."

"Yes," her husband said, hesitating. "I—I'd like to say so, too, Kate."

"We ought to've done more for her all along." The mother dwelt upon this sadly. "You must try to do more from now on, Malcolm. You really must. Look at the Gilpin girls—everything just thrown in their laps. Daisy ought to give Kate a coming-out party. We couldn't very well do it, ourselves, not in this house; but Daisy could and she ought to. She talks about her sacred duty to that big house; but what does she ever do with it that's any good to anybody? She ought to give Kate——"

"Mother, I don't want a coming-out party. I don't need to——"

"She ought to, though," Mrs. Fennigate persisted. "She knows it, herself, too, and that's why she had the iced tea and jelly cake for us to-day. She knows it ought to've been a coming-out party, instead; but of course she'll never do it. I certainly know that much. I don't know much; but I know that much." She began to pant more laboriously. "Well—maybe you'd better try to get me upstairs if you can, the two of you. Maybe we can make it." She smiled lopsidedly as they contrived to lift her to her feet, and she added with a rueful humor, "And maybe we can't!"

Twilight made Kate's room vague before she was able to be there alone, for a time, until she'd need to return to her mother. She sat by the open window, and the evening was so still that although automobile horns honked on National Avenue, half a block away, she could hear the light rustling of leaves as birds moved among the branches of the maple tree that had grown so tall in the narrow yard as to darken her window. Her right hand rested in her lap and upon its open small palm was the button from Ames's coat sleeve. She bent her fair head above this button, looking at it woefully. Cousin Mary didn't seem strong enough to take as much care of him as he needed; Celia used all the time and strength that Cousin Mary had, probably, so she couldn't look after his clothes—much less protect him from the eternal goadings of Aunt Daisy. Aunt Daisy was rotten to him—rotten!

"Oh, *damn* Aunt Daisy!" Kate Fennigate said aloud, and all that was religious in her rose to confront her with her sinfulness.

Laila Capper had often called her a prig; but the truth must be that she was really a sanctimonious hypocrite. Prigs and Sunday-school teachers weren't given to cursing people and falling in love with married men! Yes, here she was, passionately in love with one, a member of her own family, intending to keep a button from his coat forever, and profanely hating another member of her own family, his mother-in-law.

"That's the kind of girl I am," she thought. "I'm not even likable. He doesn't dislike me, or like me, and'll never think about me enough to do either. My father and my mother love me; but that's only biology. I thought Miss Carroll loved me; but she didn't. She didn't even know me. The girl I've been most with, growing up, my 'best friend', hates me. Nobody that really knew me would like me. Are all human beings the same way, so that if we all knew one another really thoroughly we couldn't like anybody at all?"

So, through the twilight of her Commencement Day, she who'd been voted the "Most Respected Girl" by her class sat bending over a clandestinely caressed button, finding life unmanageable and herself not even respectable.

VIII

"EVEN DAISY ADMITS YOU'VE BEEN BETTER FOR ME THAN the best trained nurse could have been," Mrs. Fennigate said, finding the strength for this final appreciation, upon a rainy March morning. "Maybe I ought to've let your father get one; but they charge so terribly high nowadays and I thought maybe he'd save the money and put it into that trip abroad for you. My heart's set on it, Kate, and he promised to if—if he could. He'd mean to keep his promise—he always means to keep them—but you'll have to hold him pretty closely in hand, Kate. I never could, but you can; you're the kind that does. He'd spend it all on a honeymoon if you'd let him."

"What?" Kate stopped shaking down the mercury in the clinical thermometer. "Mother darling! What are you——"

"Oh, yes," Mrs. Fennigate said. "Of course he'll want to marry Mrs. Capper, now she's a grass-widow. Daisy told me weeks ago the divorce has been granted. The husband was going to be in some sort of trouble with the authorities and thought it wise just to disappear quite a while ago. Of course poor Malcolm'll want to marry her."

"Mother! Stop talking like this!"

"He will," the mother insisted. "He'll want to; but it mustn't happen, Kate dear. He'd try to be fair to you; but you'd be utterly sacrificed—with as selfish a step-sister as that. She's your most intimate friend, I know; but I've never been able to understand why or even to like her. You must believe I've tried to, on your account, dear. Of course your father thinks he'd be happy with a jolly good-looking common woman like that; but he wouldn't. He'd be upset about other men, because she'd never let 'em alone. She'd take presents from 'em. She always has and even poor Malcolm gave her a seventy-five-dollar jade pin he still thinks I never knew about. You'll have to somehow manage to stop it, Kate."

"Mother, please don't talk so! It's grotesque! You're getting better and——"

"Let me—say my say." Mrs. Fennigate struggled to breathe. "You—you always try to tell me I'm better; but it can't go on like this—much longer. I've been very selfish with you—letting you spend all these months on me, ruining your whole first year as a young lady, when you ought to've been just going to parties and getting new clothes. At least, though, I've had this much of an excuse—that I thought maybe he'd save the money a nurse'd cost and you'd get your trip abroad. Don't interrupt me to claim you don't need it or want it. Maybe you think you don't—and that all you want is to get to work as so many other girls do nowadays. Well, you could do that after you come home from Europe, couldn't you, if you still feel you'd like to? I see now I've always been very self-centered with you——"

"Mother, you haven't. *I'm* the most self-centered little——"

"Please stop interrupting me, Kate; I can only talk a—a little. I see now I've been a very self-centered mother and I'd like to feel that at last I'm going to get something done for you—just one thing, any-how. He's promised me he'll somehow give you this trip abroad and I want you to promise me now that you'll let him. It'll be almost the only thing I ever did for you except bringing you into this mean old world and I want to know that you're going to take it. Let me—let me —hear you say you promise."

"Mother, I tell you I don't——"

"No—no. Say you promise, Kate!"

Kate looked at the pitiably anxious fat white face pushed forward by the supporting pillows. "I promise."

"I can—rest now," Mrs. Fennigate said. "I like to hear the rain splattering on the window-panes."

Her rest was almost complete; she was conscious only once again. This was a week later. Arthur and his wife had just arrived; Ames Lanning had met them at the station and brought them to the house, where Aunt Daisy and Cousin Mary were in the act of taking them into the living-room for hushed information. Upstairs Malcolm Fennigate and his daughter sat beside the bed, leaning toward it intently, when Mrs. Fennigate's eyes half opened and she looked intelligently at Kate, then at her husband, then at Kate again.

"What a stupid woman I've always been!" she said faintly, and a few minutes later Malcolm went downstairs to tell the son brokenly that he'd come too late.

Malcolm's grief was astonishing and racked his daughter. Stagger-ing under what she herself felt—the pathos attending the departure of a harmless and seemingly meaningless life can be unbearable—she had to carry him through what was undeniably a genuine agony. At the funeral he leaned upon her even physically, and when they returned from the cemetery shut himself in his room and would see neither her nor his son. Arthur, for that matter, was a stranger to both his sister and his father; and Arthur's wife, Aunt Daisy said with unfailing instant dislike, was just what she'd have expected—a Southwestern chatterbox in the wrong clothes.

The chatterbox made Arthur call good-bye to his father through the closed door, a few hours after the funeral, and took him away to return to the Southwest as quickly as possible; she'd had enough of Aunt Daisy. Cousin Mary, Aunt Daisy, Ames, and the Gilpin cousins of the Fennigates all told Kate comfortingly that she must get some rest now, she'd better go to bed. They went home, leaving her in the startlingly empty house in which there was only the muffled sound of her father's slow incessant footsteps as he paced his room.

The amazing depth of his sorrow was given a lamentable interpretation by the mind of Laila Capper. Kate hadn't seen her since more than a month before Mrs. Fennigate's death; but Laila came with some formality, at the outset, to pay a call of condolence a week after the funeral. The inevitable things were said, and for a while Laila was sympathetic both in voice and thought; then she asked, "Are you going to go on wearing black for a whole year?"

"I don't know, Laila."

"Well, if you do it'll take you clear up into being nineteen and a half before you're in colors and start going around much again. Seems too bad; but of course your mother was an awfully nice woman and I don't blame you. I never remember her being anything but kind to me ever since I was a little girl. I guess it hurts most of all when we lose that sort of a mother, always sort of easy with you and never objecting to anything much."

"Yes, Laila."

"But of course," Laila added, "you've got your religion to fall back on. Funny. All that Sunday-school and Bible stuff's looked just the bunk to me ever since I was about ten. Way I look at it, when you're dead you're dead so you better grab what you can while you're not." She uttered a thoughtful chuckle. "Singular, but Mom's kind of half way religious; she kind of believes in souls living on and all that. Believes it because she was brought up to, I guess—before she began to have too much fun! She wanted me to tell you how sorry she is about your mother, Kate."

"Yes, Laila. Please thank her for me."

"I will." Laila looked at Kate quickly and oddly; then looked away. "Everybody says your father's been feeling it dreadfully, dreadfully."

"Yes—he does."

"Too bad." Laila seemed to check an impulse. "That black's becoming to you. Your hair's been getting a little darker, not so blondie as it was, and of course you've always got that cute profile; but you'll have to have the skirt taken up some before long, Kate—they're getting shorter and shorter. I'm having my spring skirts just to the middle of the knee-cap. I'm pretty tall for that; but I guess neither of us need worry. You and I've both certainly got something to show." She laughed. "I guess the Follies might as well go out of business. Have you noticed where the men look first as they come toward you on the street?"

"No. I haven't been out much lately, you know, Laila."

"No, of course not. I forgot," Laila said. "I'm sorry. Maybe you wouldn't notice much where the men look, anyhow. I'll tell you something, Kate. I've often wondered if you're as shy and cold a little thing as you seem to be."

"Do I? I didn't know."

"Is it real? Or do you only put it on?" Laila laughed again, but leaned forward interestedly. "I bet you don't know which it is, yourself. We're a funny pair to've teamed together all this time. I've been thinking about you; I don't really know you at all. But look at me, now; I'm just what I am: I like the boys and they can tell I do. I never saw a nice fellow in my life I didn't want to jump in his lap and then fight him if he'd try to keep me there. Oh, murder!" Laila was astonished by her own outburst of frankness. "I do say the damnedest things. They just slide out. Shocked to death, aren't you?"

"No, not any, Laila."

"Meaning you always thought so, Priss? Well, what of it? Yes, I like 'em; but I'm not pulling any more dumb plays like that Harry Roe business. They say his father's tired of spending fortunes hushing things up Harry's done and's trying to get him put in an asylum. Gosh, I came awful near getting my fingers scorched that time, hon! I suppose you and your father are going to go on living here just the same as always, aren't you, Kate?"

"No. We've been planning to sell this house, Laila."

"You have? Going to move?"

"We're going abroad," Kate said. "I really don't want to go."

"You don't? Me neither; but I'd take the first end of the trip any day. I mean as far as New York. That's the burg for me! Never got there but once—that time Pop took me on one of his splurges. I was too young to take in more than half of it; but oh, boy! If you don't want to go abroad, Kate, why on earth——"

"My mother'd set her heart on it," Kate explained. "My father and I both feel it's keeping a promise we made to her."

"You say your father feels that way, too? He's going with you, Kate?"

"Yes; I've persuaded him to."

"So?" Again Laila looked quickly and oddly at Kate, then away. "I don't suppose you had much trouble persuading him. No, I rather wondered if he'd care to go on living here any more—since all that's happened. Things have been occurring over at our house, too, you know, Kate."

"Have they?"

"You didn't even know?" Laila's smile was wise and commiserative. "You didn't realize that he was pretty upset about our new prospects across the street?"

"I don't know what you mean, Laila."

"We're going to have a wedding." Laila's eyes were lively with amusement now. "Oh, a very quiet one, of course—Mom and Mr. A. Villrid Barnes, who's absolutely no good I'll inform you confidentially, though that's a point where Mom and I loudly disagree. Yes, oh, yes, and Mom thinks it'll be just great! She did hate to tell your father about it, though, because she really is good-hearted, I'll say that for her. She kept putting off telling him till she just had to. That was just before—well, just before——"

Kate stood up. "I can't talk to you any longer just now, Laila. I have some things that need attending to."

"Oh, excuse me!" Laila rose, too, and went to the door. "Of course you've got lots on your hands and I oughtn't to've stayed so long. See you often again, of course, before you're off on your trip, and I'm sure you know that if there's anything either Mom or I can do to help——"

"No, there's nothing."

" 'Bye-bye, then."

Laila was gone, and Kate too well knew what she'd meant. Dead Mrs. Fennigate couldn't even enjoy the spiritual monument of a widower's grief, since his sorrow was for himself in losing Mrs. Capper —yet Kate believed that this was not all of the truth nor as much as half of it. Self-reproach was hounding him, and whiskey didn't check it. She could see no help for him except that ancient remedy, "change of scene", and keeping the promise made to her mother brought a painful satisfaction as if, in a measure, husband and daughter assured Mrs. Fennigate that they were trying to make up to her for her bleak and neglected life. Thus, and as an atonement for the sin of reluctance to leave the place that held Ames Lanning, Kate planned to be away at least a year.

" 'Whom the gods would destroy'!" Aunt Daisy suggested, making a midsummer call in the depleted house. Workmen were carrying furniture out to be removed to a warehouse. "I always said Malcolm's crazy; but I didn't know you were, too, Kate. I must say he looks it— a great big portly man all withered up in just these last few months. I suppose alcohol does burn the tissues away at last. I'd rather think it's alcohol than watching his dreadful Capper woman performing her new connubialities across the street! How much money have you got out of the sale of the house? I suppose the purchaser assumes the mortgage; but nobody's thought proper to inform me."

"We'll have almost six thousand dollars, Aunt Daisy."

"Well, of course you and Malcolm'll have to live at *pensions* if you expect to make it last a year and a half, which I understand is your present plan. A fine investment! You'll come home flat broke without even a house to go into and your father's law practice gone where the woodbine twineth! Clients don't wait around a year and a half for a lawyer to come back and attend to their affairs—or perhaps you hadn't thought of that."

"Yes," Kate said. "Father and I have considered it carefully."

" 'Carefully!' " Aunt Daisy exclaimed. "Good God!" Then she laughed. "Oh, I see! His law practice is so close to utter disappearance already that it really doesn't matter. That's what you mean by considering it carefully! Well, when he comes back what's he to go into—

at his age? Fat chance! I suppose you and he have considered that carefully, too?"

"I've learned shorthand and I'm a good typist," Kate said. "I've been to see Mr. Roe. He's always been a friend of mine and he appears to think I'll be capable. He says when we come back he'll be glad to take me on. He's very liberal with his employees, and Father and I can take a small apartment somewhere."

"And Malcolm can go on reading the papers and playing bridge and storing his bootlegger's supplies at the Carlyle Club? On a typist's salary?"

Kate was able to laugh. "Those are bridges to cross when we come to them. A year and a half's a long time."

"You think so? You'll know better when you're my age, Kate Fennigate. I'm sixty-three, and a year and a half goes like the snap of your fingers or people dying or the way this town keeps growing. What's the use my telling you, though? Old people can't tell young people anything. That's why young people don't know anything. Look at my son-in-law! Just like your father, except Ames doesn't drink. Some people used to say your father was going to be a great lawyer; I guess it's about time they quit saying that of Ames—he hasn't had a single thing to do except clerical work ever since they gave him that dried mouse case he lost. Couldn't even beat a dead mouse! That's a record, isn't it?"

Kate was deeply relieved when Aunt Daisy let her go back to the packing, and her heart was almost light on the day of departure. East Cherry Street, the ugly house where she'd grown up, her long "friendship" with Laila Capper—these were attachments that were really her Old Men of the Sea, and her shoulders were being freed from them. There was another attachment, though, one that went with her as she lay in her berth on the eastbound train. Ames had told Cousin Mary to say good-bye and *bon voyage* for him; he hadn't come with the others to see her and her father off at the station, though even Laila Capper did that much.

"I'll try to be gone a long, long time," Kate thought. "While I'm away maybe I'll meet somebody—somebody else. Maybe when I come back I won't feel this way. Oh, I hope not!"

IX

"SHE WRITES GOOD LETTERS TO YOU, MARY," AUNT DAISY said, and of course neither she nor her daughter suspected that the letters were "good" because of a hope that Ames Lanning would read them or hear them read. As it happened, he'd been listening to this one, though absently. "Her descriptions make you see the places and the people," Aunt Daisy continued. "I liked it better when they were in England and Paris and then Italy last year. Malcolm and she've been in that Munich *pension* over six months now and I bet she's practically running the place herself by this time. She would! Never could touch a thing on this earth without trying to manage it. She's certainly been able to make the money hold out. That old Roe may be right about her having a capacity for being a business woman. I hope she keeps as tight hold on Malcolm as she does on the dollars. He's got away from her a few nights, though, I'll bet!"

"Poor Kate," Cousin Mary murmured. "I hope not."

"She'd never tell us if he did," Aunt Daisy said. "Never knew anybody tighter-mouthed. Always did seem to believe her words were jewels and she couldn't spare any."

Ames looked up. "Why, no. Think what long letters she writes."

"Why, yes!" Aunt Daisy retorted. "She writes by the hour about music and German politics and French factory strikes and that tiresome League of Nations; but all she ever says about herself and whether she's got that Swiss professor wanting to marry her is zero nothing. I bet she worries about Malcolm and won't tell us. I didn't like that withered look he had before they went away—kind of dried-up and puffy, too. Malcolm's getting old, besides, and German brandy's bad for anybody. He never did like beer. They must be getting near the end of their string. American money goes a long way in Europe these days; but even on the cheap two travelers can't live there forever on less than six thousand dollars. She's strung it out long past the year and a half she calculated on; it's almost two years. I hope they don't expect to land on *my* hands when they ge*t* back."

"Mother! Kate told you Mr. Roe's going to have a place for her."

"Suppose he does," Aunt Daisy said. "They'll have to go somewhere till they can get settled down, won't they? I merely said I hope they don't expect to come here to my house. Malcolm may be my own brother; but I couldn't put up with his coming in at all hours of the night in heaven knows what condition and I certainly wouldn't be able to have him stay here if he turns out to be really sick—not with all I have on my hands looking after this house. In her latest letters she's mentioned three times he's been to a doctor. She never says why or what he's got, just says the doctor's helped him and he seems 'pretty well'. I'll bet she brings Malcolm Fennigate home an invalid and even if they don't expect to stay in my house she'll be thinking I ought to go and spend whole afternoons with him while she's busy with Henry L. Roe's office work."

"Mother, what nonsense! She hasn't written you anything that even hints Uncle Malcolm's going to come home an invalid."

"No, that isn't her way; but you just wait and see. When I turn out to be right, kindly remember that I saw it all beforehand. Malcolm Fennigate wasn't a well man when he left here. He's going to be an invalid when she brings him back, and, in spite of all she knows I've got on my hands and your never having a day of health, yourself, Mary, she'll expect to use us to keep him entertained. You'll see! She's got it all planned out in her mind, I tell you. I can read her like a book and you remember what I'm saying!"

. . . Mary did remember, but was too weakly peaceful to say so. Like almost all other habitual prophets, Aunt Daisy couldn't bear to eat her own words but when any predicted event didn't come to pass, or happened otherwise than as prophesied, simply altered her memory of the prediction and applauded herself for a new evidence of lifelong foresight.

"I knew exactly what was going to happen," she said, the day after she had the cablegram from Geneva. She addressed Mary and the elderly cousin, Mrs. Herbert Gilpin. "I told Mary and Ames that this was going to happen four months ago in this very room. I sat in this very chair and told Ames and Mary that if Kate kept Malcolm Fennigate over there any longer he'd never live to get home. We could tell from her letters she was dragging him around from one doctor to another all over Europe, and I came very near writing her, myself, that if she didn't show sense enough to cut that out and bring him home where he belonged, she'd come back here a full orphan. Nobody ever listens to me, though, until it's too late. Mary, you remember what I told you and Ames when they were in Munich. Didn't I say if she didn't come home I'd never see my brother alive again?"

"Did you, Mother?"

"Did I? What on earth do you mean, asking me did I? Even Ames'll be able to remember that much. I'll ask him to your face and if he says he doesn't——"

"No, no," Mary interrupted hurriedly. "I remember you were worried about Uncle Malcolm's health and——"

"Worried about it!" Aunt Daisy exclaimed. "I absolutely knew that if she kept on dragging him around among foreign doctors nobody knows anything about he wouldn't have the faintest chance of getting home alive. That's precisely what I told Mary and Ames over four months ago, Roberta Gilpin, and you can tell all the family connection I said so."

"It's strange," Mrs. Gilpin said. "Kate's had so much experience of sickness I should think she'd have brought him back before it happened. Of course she always has liked to have her own way and——"

"Uncle Malcolm didn't want to come," Mary interposed. "She told us so in the last letter we've had from her. He wanted to stay over there as long as they could possibly afford it."

"Pooh!" Aunt Daisy said. "She had Malcolm where he'd say he wanted anything she decided on. Roberta, kindly tell me what you think of her not bringing him home to his own family lot? Did you ever hear anything so crazy? Burying Malcolm Fennigate 'way over there in the Alps! Never occurred to her that he's my brother and she might consult my wishes!"

"It might have been too expensive," Mrs. Gilpin suggested. "Maybe she didn't have money enough left. Of course she's got to get home, herself, somehow and—— What on earth?" She referred to a squealing and squawking interruption from outdoors, where young Celia had become active in altercation near one of the open windows.

"It's that child," Aunt Daisy explained desperately. "She has fights with boys from that horrible apartment across the street. She gets them to fight one another and then joins in like a wildcat. Oh, me! I can't hear myself think! Mary, I'm afraid you'll simply have to——"

"Yes, yes; I'll try to stop them." Mary rose, sighing. "I'll see if I can't coax her into the house."

"'Coax' her in!" Celia's grandmother said, alone with the guest. "Did you hear that, Roberta? 'Coax' her! Nobody has the slightest authority over that child. Mary hasn't the strength physically or mentally to cope with her, and as for Ames—he's about as much help in that way as he is in others! I could have stood an ordinary tomboy about the house; but Celia is—— Well, I can only say it's one of the mysteries of Providence that as peace-loving a woman as I am should have a hellion for a grandchild!"

"Hellion, Daisy?" Mrs. Gilpin's elderly voice quavered in protest. "Of course we all know you've always liked to use startling words sometimes but——"

"Me? Never! 'Hellion's' an understatement, Roberta. Nobody in this whole family's ever been able to do a single thing with that child, except Kate Fennigate. Here she is almost eleven years old, and Dr. Powls insisting that Mary must never make the slightest over-exertion, and Celia having to be dragged out of God knows how many fights a week with these rowdy boys that have come to live in the neighborhood! Think of it—Mary, who ought to be receiving the greatest care and attention herself! She really ought to be in the hands of a trained nurse, Roberta, because her life's just nothing but sacrifice, sacrifice to that husband of hers and this child!"

"Yes," Mrs. Gilpin assented. "On the other hand, a great many people as frail as Mary seem to live about as long as anybody else and she's had that fading-away look for quite a number of years now.

If you're worrying about her, though, why don't you get a trained nurse for her, Daisy?"

"Why? That's rather a strange question, Roberta! Who'd be paying a nurse's wages? Ames Lanning?"

"He couldn't?" Mrs. Gilpin inquired, and added, "I've always heard he's considered the most promising young man in the city."

"Yes indeed!" Aunt Daisy uttered a snapping laughter. " 'Always' is right! He's been considered promising so long now it certainly does seem like always. He keeps his wife and child in sustenance and clothes—just barely! I bet there isn't a trained nurse in the city doesn't make more than he does."

"Dear me!" Mrs. Gilpin spoke timidly. "Daisy, I've been wondering—I suppose Kate'll certainly be coming home now. I understand her plans were that she and her father would take an apartment somewhere; but now that he's gone, where do you suppose she intends to live? Of course these modern girls are dreadfully independent; but I wonder if you've thought——"

"Yes, I have." Aunt Daisy glanced out of the window; then lowered her voice and became confidential. "I've thought about it a great deal because I have exactly the same feeling that you have, Roberta. In spite of all these absurd new modern freedoms there are a great many old citizens of this city, people brought up the right way, who'd be horrified to see a girl member of the Fennigate family living all alone as if she were a man. What's more, I'm opposed to her going into business, trying to be a typist or secretary or something out at that ordinary old Roe's factory. I'll never consent to it."

"Well, but Daisy——"

"There's no 'but' to it," Aunt Daisy said. "She simply can't be allowed to do it and I want your help to influence her. I want every relative we have to get to work on her the minute she's back here. I've cabled her to come straight to my house when she——"

"You have? I see. I think that's the very wisest thing that could be done, Daisy, and very thoughtful of you. You have so much room in this big house she could live here much more happily for herself than anywhere else and——"

"Certainly she could." Aunt Daisy's expression became that of a woman frankly just at all costs. "It's the right thing to do for her, my own niece; but I don't claim that I'm not considering others besides, including myself. She's very practical and would be a great help."

"Yes, she would so." Mrs. Gilpin looked thoughtful. "She took care of her mother so long, and now with all the added experience she's had with poor Malcolm I don't suppose there could be a professional nurse anywhere that'd be any better. Then, as you say, her influence with Celia and being able to control the child——"

"I'm going to put her in the next room to Celia, Roberta—a very nice room. Celia still has those nightmares—no wonder, the way she tears round every minute she's awake! Of course, as I say, Kate's my dead brother's only daughter and he'd have a right to reproach me from his grave if I didn't offer her a home now she has nobody else; but I don't deny she'll help to take a load off my shoulders. I've had nothing but burdens all my life and I don't expect to be in this world much longer. Of course she'll try to manage the whole house and me too; but I won't mind letting her think she's doing it. The sooner she comes the better."

Kate didn't think so and had no intention of accepting Aunt Daisy's cabled invitation. More than two months elapsed before a slight and comely figure in black emerged from the railroad station downtown and walked up National Avenue in the smog that gloomed a December morning. The city was at its ugliest. For seven months of the year foliages that screened its architectural inequalities and even somewhat softened its hell-colored signboards had been frosted away, Nature thus leaving multitudinous works of man brazenly exposed, abhorrent to any sensitive eye. Kate Fennigate's eye, lately come from regions of anciently seasoned harmonies, was a sensitive one and the scene about her as she walked northward from the city's business heart didn't please her. She saw alterations, too, not for the better æsthetically, and she had all the discomfiting sensations of a long absentee who returns to find everything uncomfortably both familiar and unfamiliar.

Then why had she come back? Because there'd be a place for her in the Roe Metal Products Corporation? No, she could have made a living elsewhere; the Swiss professor's sister had wanted her as a colleague to teach English and American history in Lausanne. Kate had come back because this was home and she could never get over knowing that. She had no dwelling-place; but this was home, and the noise and smoke, increased since she'd left, were the well-known adjuncts of well-remembered home. She had the feeling usual in such circumstances that the day upon which she and her father had set forth upon their adventure was long, long ago and yet but yesterday.

The faces about her, downtown, were also familiar-unfamiliar, more American than the faces she'd seen during the day or so she'd stayed in New York. These Midland people were the creatures she best understood and would always best understand of all that walked the earth; but she felt it would take her some time to be one of them again. Her absence had blurred them to her, as it also blurred her old self to her present self. She remembered that on the train, as she'd left here so long ago and so little ago, she'd hoped she'd get over being in love with Ames Lanning. That certainly seemed to be accomplished.

She'd almost forgotten his features, though she was still sure that there was something about his face very kind, able-looking and agreeable; but it was long, long since she'd known herself to be in love with him. She'd thought of him, yes, warmly and affectionately and probably almost every day. She'd thought of him especially when she wrote her letters to Mary, and it was true she'd aimed those letters at him, hoping they'd interest him; but the pictures she had of him in her memory had receded. He'd grown so dim that perhaps—perhaps now when she'd see him again she'd be almost amused to remember the girl-self that had been so unquestioningly in love with him.

She passed the group of coupled brick buildings that had been the Carroll School, and she had a twinge of unexpected sharpness. Across the façade of the middle house there was a long black and gilt signboard, already dingy: "Railroad Men's Building and Loan Insurance Corp." Mary had written her that Miss Carroll had moved the school to a wooded region far out, "where everybody that can afford it's gone to live now"; but the cause of the twinge wasn't only the sight of the buildings in what seemed their grotesque masquerade. There was one

of the "old Carroll girls", a star pupil in her day, who wouldn't be
visiting the school in its new quarters. Miss Carroll would be better
pleased not to be reminded of distressing old questions.

Beyond the shell of the school there were other changes, other
houses with signboards upon them, a row or two of new business
buildings, "used car" salesrooms, and then, half a block before her,
the broad front of Aunt Daisy's treasure, the Fennigate house—and
beyond that, most familiar-unfamiliar of all, the corner she'd turned
many thousands of times, the corner of National Avenue and East
Cherry Street. She didn't wish to turn that corner and had no need
to; just now she was only going as far as Aunt Daisy's.

From the rear of the big old yard there came the sounds of pre-
adolescent voices shrill in abuse, and Kate stopped for a moment.
Over the tall grey old wooden back fence, three hundred feet from
the pavement, boys were scrambling, shrieking taunts as they made
the escalade. A shabby girl of about eleven, grown too fast for her
clothes, ran at them, hair flying, voice and all limbs at their utmost,
as she swung a long-handled dripping mop murderously. Celia!

Kate went into the yard, to the front door, and rang the bell. Aunt
Daisy came from the interior with a dust-cloth in her hand and an
anti-dust towel round her head. She stared; then she shouted, "Kate
Fennigate! Kate Fennigate, how dare you?"

"May I come in a few minutes, Aunt Daisy?"

"What on earth do you mean not letting us know when you were
coming? Where's your baggage?"

"I'll tell you." They exchanged a tribal cheek-salute, Kate stepped
forward, they went together into the living-room. "It was lovely of
you to invite me to stay here, Aunt Daisy; but I can't possibly. I left
my baggage at the station until I can find what I need. There used to
be any number of rather pleasant boarding-houses that I knew of,
and, after seeing you and Mary and Celia a few minutes, I'm going
on to look them over. They may have changed or disappeared since
I went away, so maybe you or Mary could tell me which one you
think——"

"You can't do it!" Aunt Daisy, who'd sat down, jumped up and
became voluble. "It's abominable your not letting anybody know

when you were arriving! You can't go living around town in board-ing-houses; you'll have to show some regard for your family's wishes. The Gilpins, every one of 'em, have been talking and talking about it, and so has everybody else, insisting there's only one place for you to be and that's right here in your own family's house. When your own dead father's only living sister asks you to stay in it I think you'll have to show a little consideration! You go straight to the telephone and have your baggage——"

"It's most kind of you, Aunt Daisy; but I'll have to get myself set-tled down as permanently as possible at once. As soon as I've found a room I'm going to see Mr. Roe, if he's in town and——"

"You'll do no such a thing, Kate Fennigate! You'll telephone for your baggage this minute; it'll be here by the time we've had lunch and then we——"

"No, no, I really can't. I——"

Aunt Daisy stamped her foot. "Do you mean to tell me that after being away over two years you decline to stay long enough even to have lunch with me? You're supposed to be my niece, aren't you, and at least Christian enough to take time to give me a few details of my own brother's last illness?"

"But I wrote——"

"You didn't even tell me the last words he uttered or what medicine he was taking! See here, Kate Fennigate, there are such things as fam-ily duties and I'll never forgive you if you don't perform at least a few of them. I want your promise this instant to stay here a month at the shortest, and then if you think you can't stand it you can——"

"A month, Aunt Daisy? I couldn't possibly——"

"Well, then, a week—to begin with."

"Aunt Daisy! I couldn't——"

Aunt Daisy stamped her foot again. "All right! Are you going to stay here for lunch or not? I want to know so I can tell my cook. Are you or are you not?"

"Well, for lunch, then, if you want me."

Aunt Daisy went out into the hall and shouted upward. "Mary!" she called. "Mary, come down and make Celia come in. Kate Fenni-gate's home at last!"

X

AT LUNCH, WHEN FOR A TIME AUNT DAISY DROPPED TALK-
ing for eating, Kate spoke to the smiling but thin and rather tired-
looking young man across the table. "I hope you didn't come home
to-day on my account—to welcome the wanderer—Cousin Ames. Or
are you usually here for lunch, anyhow?"

"Yes, I almost always am," he said, and the sound of his voice,
heard again for the first time since his hearty greeting of her in the
living-room, had a disturbing effect upon the inner sensations of the
returned traveler.

The sight of him hadn't done that. Looking upon him again had
renewed only an old warm friendliness; but his voice, cheerful above
undertones of patience and melancholy, was a long unheard music
unexpectedly heard again. Faces may be civilized into masks; but in
the very quality of even the most conventionalized voice there is revelation of what manner of man speaks. Ames Lanning's voice suddenly
brought him back to Kate not as something familiar-unfamiliar but
as wholly familiar. Her breath quickened and she seemed not to have
been away at all.

"It's only a mile walk from the offices of Caldwell, Hardy and Caldwell," Aunt Daisy said. "The exercise is good for him. I suppose
you've picked up the European idea, Kate, that every American owns
an automobile and's forgotten how to walk?"

"No, Aunt Daisy. Speaking of exercise, Cousin Ames, how's your
tennis nowadays? Are you still in tournament form?"

"Well—no," Ames said; and Kate, receiving a blow upon the ankle,
comprehended not only that Aunt Daisy had kicked her under the
table but that this warning conveyed the message: "Don't talk to him
about tennis." No more was needed; women pass these informations

about among themselves with complete taciturnity: Aunt Daisy hadn't wished Mary to be "dragged about" to watch tennis matches or to let Ames appear to neglect his wife by going alone, and Mary always wanted to go if he did. Probably much had been said about the cost of tennis balls, clean flannels, rackets and carfare, and the end of it had been that Ames didn't play tennis nowadays. Mary had acquiesced; apparently her mother's ownership of her was now complete.

"How'd you come out in the battle, Celia?" Kate asked. "Did those boys get brave and come back after you chased 'em over the fence? Classmates of yours in school, are they?"

"No, they are not," Celia replied. Her tone wasn't affable. She was shy with Kate, avoided looking at her and held to the manner of a distant acquaintance suspicious of advances. At her age two years of separation from a friend often change everything. "They used to be in my class," she added gloomily. "They're 'way ahead of me now forever, the dirty dogs!"

"Don't use such terms, child." Aunt Daisy, too, looked gloomy. "Celia hasn't been given your advantages, Kate. She's had to go to the public schools, not Miss Carroll's, unhappily, and that's worked out all wrong, especially right now. We're expecting a call from the truant officer any day."

"Let him come!" Celia said. "It's a matter of uttermost indifference to my conduct of life. He won't be here to-day, because it's Saturday and anyhow they haven't found out I'm well yet."

"She's had the measles," Mary explained. "They lasted and lasted and now she's well she won't go back to school because she insists her class has got so far ahead of her it'd wear her all out catching up. It keeps going on and on this way from day to day and we just don't know what to do about it."

"I do," Celia said. "Haven't I told you a hundred thousand times? I simply decline to drop back a grade and there isn't a thing on earth can be done about it except let me read all the books I care to from the public library and educate myself. If a truant officer tries to busy himself in my life, my father's a lawyer, isn't he? He'd be supposed to know how to handle it, wouldn't he?"

"No," her father responded. "I wouldn't."

"Then listen," she said. "The least you can do'll be to give me that twenty-five cents I asked you for at breakfast this morning, because I've simply got to see 'The Fall of Babylon' this afternoon. It's an eight-reeler all full of the Bible and history and's got Belshazzar's Feast in it and teaches more education than a whole year's work at the tediousest school on earth. Every boy I know's already seen it and I'd rather die right here in this chair than put off going any longer. I've got to have your answer, Father. Are you going to give me that quarter or not?"

"Not," Aunt Daisy said. "Indeed he's not! Stop looking at him as if you're going to cry. He hasn't any quarters to throw away on movies."

"They wouldn't be thrown away!" Celia looked fiercely at her grandmother. "How do you know he hasn't any quarters?"

"Never mind." Aunt Daisy addressed Kate. "Ames is still with Caldwell, Hardy and Caldwell, I suppose Mary's mentioned in her letters to you. Not a very successful firm, unfortunately."

"No, perhaps not." Ames looked up mildly; but there was feeling in his voice. "However, Mr. Bortshleff told me last year, you remember, that if I——"

"Bortshleff!" Aunt Daisy exclaimed, and turned to Kate. "That horrible bellowing old Bortshleff was the attorney for the city when it robbed my husband of eight thousand dollars in taxes it had no right to in Nineteen-twelve. He's a disgusting man; but his firm's got most of the Roe Corporation's law business nowadays and Ames thinks they're grand. That old rascal of a Bortshleff showed some interest in him last year, and he thought it meant a chance to change over from Caldwell to the Bortshleff firm; but Mary couldn't bear the idea and Ames very wisely decided not to associate himself with a man that had been her father's enemy and robbed him. I think we'd better discuss more pleasant topics."

"So do I!" the quick Celia said. "Father, are you going to practically proscribe me out of seeing 'The Fall of Babylon' this afternoon? Do I get that twenty-five cents or don't I?"

"You don't, I'm afraid," Ames replied. "For one reason, suppose the truant officer happened to see you there. You don't want to get your mother and me in jail, do you? Did you see signs of the great American boom as you came through New York and across the country this side of it, Kate? Your letters were interesting about the poverty and depression abroad. That's going to begin to happen here before very long, you know. We've over-produced; especially we've over-built, and when the building trades collapse we're going to get it in the neck and over there they won't need to be calling us 'Uncle Shylock' any more."

"No," Kate said. "We'll be Uncle Lazarus. I'm afraid you're a good prophet, Cousin Ames."

"Oh, see here!" Aunt Daisy rapped the table with a knuckle. "I said pleasant topics! Old Joe Caldwell stopped me on the street one day to tell me he thought Ames had a head for business; but right when the whole country's fairly rolling in good times—except me and my own household—he's nothing but gloom, gloom, gloom! I'd like to hear a little more about what was really the matter with Malcolm, if you please. Did he know he was going, Kate?"

Kate flinched. "I—I'll try to tell you another time, Aunt Daisy. Mary, I've been trying to find out about boarding-houses and——"

"No, no, you mustn't, Kate. Mother expects you to stay and we all want you to. Promise you'll——"

Celia interrupted. Perceiving that her father was about to rise from the table, she made outcry. "You wait! You got to listen! I told you I'd rather die in this chair than not go, didn't I? In all my days and whole life I've never done a solitary act I didn't get interfered with and it's about time I was permitted a little harmless freedom. Are you going to go back to that office without giving me my quarter?"

Ames laughed, as he rose. "If I can make it I am. At least I'm going to try." From outside the doorway he waved a disappearing hand. "It's great to see you again, Kate!"

Celia angrily scrambled after him and could be heard in pursuit down the hall. "You wait! You stop! I don't care if it's the last quarter on this earth I've got to have it! I've *got* to! You can't leave me in the lurch like this. I'm your only daughter and I *demand*——"

Mary said, "Oh, dear!" rose and followed through the hall.

"He probably hasn't got even a quarter," Aunt Daisy said to Kate. "I've often known him not to. Fred Bishop was in love with Mary and I begged and begged her to wait. I told her she wasn't old enough to know what she was doing; but no, nobody ever listens to me and she must have Ames or die. Everybody says Fred Bishop's made over two hundred thousand dollars in the stock market just these last three months. Everybody gets rich except us. He can't buy her even a Ford."

Mary returned to the table, sighing. "He had to give it to her. I think she gets her determination from you, Mother. She'd have run after him half way downtown if he hadn't given up and let her have it. He's very anxious to go to the Bill Jones party to-morrow night, Mother, and now that Kate's here you wouldn't be left alone with Celia, so you won't object to our going, will you?"

"I most certainly shall!"

"But, Mother, our every-other-Sunday suppers with the crowd are about all he enjoys nowadays. Please——"

"No!" Aunt Daisy was emphatic. "In the first place, I don't approve of Bill Jones and you wouldn't get anything fit to eat at a bachelor's apartment supper. You're not strong enough and Kate hasn't said yet that she's willing to stay here even over Sunday. If she won't I'd be left alone with Celia and I'm not up to fighting her about what's her bedtime or stopping her yelling if she has one of her nightmares. I think she puts the whole thing on; I don't believe they're genuine. By the way, she didn't finish her lunch. Where is she?"

"She's gone, Mother, and I don't suppose we'll see her again till evening. I haven't any influence with her at all."

"Don't look at me!" Aunt Daisy said. "I haven't any influence with anybody. Can't even get my own niece to send for her baggage and spend a week with me—after she's been away for more than two years!"

Mary put a sallow hand upon Kate's arm entreatingly. "Oh, surely, surely, Kate, you'll stay at least that long with us. Please, please, say you will! Only a week? Won't you?"

Kate knew that she wasn't deciding to stay "only a week".

XI

Aunt daisy had counted successfully upon her niece's driving urge to set things aright wherever they were askew. Some women can't see a slovenly room without cleaning it, no matter whose it is. Mary's increased fragility and Celia's perilous intractableness had been advantageously displayed; but more had been shown to the niece than the aunt realized. Thus far in her life Kate had seen no man flatter beneath his mother-in-law's heel or so ill-protected by his wife or worse bullied by his only child. He was in the hands of the enemy; they had him down, a man of large possibilities, and he might stay down.

It would have been easy to think him stupidly weak for not freeing himself, and Mary too, from Aunt Daisy long ago; but a man with a sickly wife is peculiarly vulnerable to the wife's mother, especially a good man, chivalrous and still youthfully blind to the devices by which women apply controls. Ames was such a man—permanently no match for women—and, although if Kate had found him victimized by selfish and adroit men who played upon his simplicity she might have thought him too simple indeed, the fact that his misusers were of her own sex roused championage within her. There is a gallant type of woman always impelled to come to the defense of a man who lives helplessly in female hands, and Kate belonged to this type. That recalling quality in Ames Lanning's rich and pleasantly sad voice might have decided her for her own sake not to risk staying; but what worked upon her was the plight in which she found him.

Her first day and a half made at least a beginning. Mary came drooping into her room late on Sunday night after Bill Jones's party. "I saw the light under your door, Kate. Am I interrupting your reading?"

"No, I'm just glancing over Celia's textbooks to see if——"

"Oh, do you think you can?" Mary expressed a strong hope in a weak voice, as she dropped into an old mahogany and green plush easy-chair that had been retired from service downstairs. "It would simply be God's mercy, Kate, if you *could* get her back to school again in her own class. You're so clever I'm sure a little of your tutoring would do it, dear. I do hope she didn't have any of her nightmares and wake Mother up. Did she?"

"No, Mary. She had one; but I stopped her in time."

"Was she dreadfully nervous afterward?"

"Not very! Indignant, I think I'd call it. Indignant with me—until I got her to laughing."

"Laughing?" Mary was puzzled. "You say you——"

"Yes," Kate said. "Your mother's right about her, Mary. Probably Celia used to have bad dreams that'd wake her up yelling; but I don't think that's happened for quite a long while. She enjoyed the effect, though, and now when she wakes up she puts on an act instead of going to sleep again. It entertains her. She was furious with me tonight when I told her so; but I kept on laughing until she laughed too, and we began to get really acquainted again. It was quite a success."

"A miraculous one!" Mary cried; and Kate didn't tell her how Celia, becoming merrily confidential, had uttered a self-congratulatory exclamation that revealed the motive behind the supposed nightmares: "Golly! How I've always hated Grandmother!" Mary, content to be pleased, didn't need details. "Then you really think you can manage her a little, Kate?"

"Well, at least Celia and I seem to be back on our old footing."

"Kate, you're an angel! I've often more than half believed Celia was doing just that; but I simply didn't know how to meet it—and now if we can manage to get her back into school, too, what a relief! I'm pretty much a broken reed; but I'll help all I can. Kate, you will postpone going to see old Mr. Roe, won't you?"

"No, I'll go to see him to-morrow; but I'll ask him if I can't postpone the job with him a while, if he still has it for me. There's something besides getting Celia back to school that needs help here, Mary. Ames was anxious to change into Mr. Bortshleff's office and it's pretty plain that he still wants to. If you'd back him up——"

"No, no!" Mary looked frightened. "You mustn't try any of that, Kate. It's not to be thought of. Mother hates that firm. She's always hated that old Bortshleff almost more than she hates anybody else in the world."

"In the world, Mary? I thought she always hated William Jennings Bryan the most, though I remember she seemed to let up on him some when she heard he was an anti-evolutionist."

"Well, anyhow," Mary said. "It's especially Mr. Bortshleff now because she's been brooding over what she could do in the stock market if she only had that eight thousand dollars he cost Father in taxes. It really won't do to talk about Ames's going into that firm. Once Mother's will gets set, Kate, you know as well as I do it can't be broken, and myself I really don't think it *would* be right for Ames to associate with a man who did Mother and Father such an injury. You mustn't bring up the matter, dear."

"Ought it to be left to her?" Kate asked.

"What?" Mary's lifeless voice showed that she didn't hear the question, and couldn't.

"Nothing—only something else that'll have to be postponed a while," Kate said. "Was it a pleasant party?"

"Yes, I suppose so. Ames seemed to be having a good time. He loves the evenings with our crowd and of course he's had fewer and fewer of them these last years. He loves to be lighthearted, you know, and to get at a piano and play accompaniment chords and sing with the bunch. By the way, an old friend of yours was there, that girl you always seemed so inseparable from."

"You mean Laila Capper?"

"Yes. Bill Jones and Gilpin Ames are crazy about her. Bill invited her and seems to be trying to work her into the crowd. I'm sorry to say I never did care for her very much; I hope you don't mind. Mother's always thought her rather ordinary and now she seems to be putting on a good deal of side. Artificial and very affected, I thought; but of course she's remarkably beautiful and very lively, so the men don't seem to mind. She asked about you. She'd heard you're home again. She asked me to be sure and tell you that she'll be coming to call as soon as she can possibly find a moment's time. Well——" Mary rose, helping to lift herself by pushing forcelessly on the arms of the chair. "You're being my saviour with Celia, Kate; thank heaven you're here! I'll be dragging to bed now, happier than I've been for ages. Goodnight."

Kate's response was absentminded; she was thinking how little she'd lament if Laila Capper never found the moment's time for the promised call. Laila's engagements weren't that continuous, however; but weeks elapsed before she made her appearance. By that time Kate was regarded as a fixture in the house of her grandparents; and she'd fully comprehended that her long previous suggestion to Aunt Daisy —that Celia be provided with a nursery governess—had at last been accepted. Aunt Daisy had also provided herself with a housemaid and Mary with a skilled attendant. Mr. Roe's salary list had not been in- creased and neither had Aunt Daisy's. Kate had insurgent hours— "Why do I go on wasting myself?"—but the bitterest of these insur- rections didn't overset the rule of her own nature. She'd found her task—or it had found her—and so she stayed.

When Laila came she thumped down a bag of golf clubs in the hall; but Kate retained the feather duster she'd been using. They didn't kiss. They went into the gilt "reception room", and Laila continued the chatter she'd begun at the front door, exclaiming that she had a thou- sand things to tell. She was unaware that there might be anything to hear.

More beautiful than ever, she wore heavy tweed "sport clothes" that looked New Yorkish, or at least like the New Yorkish pictures, and her pronunciation of words had more than traces of what was once here and there called an "Eastern accent". That is, she often broad- ened the first of the vowels, but sometimes didn't; she sometimes remembered to blur the consonant R and sometimes didn't. She pro- nounced "been" sometimes as "bean" and sometimes as "bin"; earlier in life, before she went to Miss Carroll's School, she'd said "ben." She'd been too wise to emaciate her fine dark eyebrows. Her lips, however, were over-emphasized with a coral grease, and for a time her

facial expressions also seemed laid on, intended to imply her occu-
pancy of a high place in the world. There were intervals, of course,
during which she became almost too natural. Kate had seen other
Midland girls undergo such a phase; most of them recovered but
some never did.

"It's a dreadfully ully hour to drop in on you," Laila said. "I had
to come so ully in the mawning because I'm dated for every moment
of the whole rest of the day. No wonder you're dusting, you paw
dolling. The grime in this dreadful old neighborhood's simply appalling. Of coss you knew *we'd* moved ages and ages ago; we're miles out
now in a rathuh nice spot. I've never happened to be in this house
before." She looked about her amusedly. "Shawly it's one of the queer-
est old Victorian left-overs in town—all these doodads! You don't
look a bit changed, Kate—still about sixteen—but tell me: How do
I strike you?"

Kate laughed. "Even better-looking than when I left, Laila, and
that's saying a lot."

"Oh, that," Laila said. "I suppose we might rathuh take each othuh's
looks for granted. I was thinking of something rather maw significant.
You wouldn't know, I suppose; but I'm a pretty different person from
the gyell you used to know, Kate. When I look back I positively
mahvel how I could ever have been that unsophisticated raw silly little
gyell who used to live on East Cherry Street. What hotel in New Yawk
did you stop at?"

"On my way home, you mean? Not at any. I was only there a day
and a half—in a boarding-house near the Museum of Natural History."

"Near the what?" Laila asked; but didn't pause. "Mom and I
stopped at the Plaza when we went on for our winter things this
year." Here Laila became more like herself. "Listen, did I have a
whirl? Boy! I'll say! Mom too. I bet if her old Barnesy'd seen her some
o' those nights he'd 'a' cut her head off!" She laughed loudly; then
glanced again about the room. "How do you stand living in this
house, anyhow? I bet that old aunt of yours'd drop dead if you suggested putting in a bar! Everybody's doing that nowadays, you know,
Kate. Doesn't the place give you the willies? Why didn't you show up
at Bill Jones's party with your cousins? Oh, I forgot! I suppose you

thought it was too soon. I'm sorry about your father. How long's it been, dearie?"

"Four months, Laila."

"I'm so sorry," Laila said. "You'd have enjoyed Bill Jones's party. That Lanning man, you know, is really quite fascinating; I don't mean he tries to be, so that's probably the reason he is. By the way, do you know who's that red-headed man he seems to be so thick with?"

"No, I don't think I know any red-headed man who'd have been at that party, Laila."

"He wasn't at the party," Laila said. "I think he's only been in town the last few months or so; but I've seen him on the street several times and he's got a face that intrigues me and always wears the right clothes. I'm pretty sure he's from New York. His hair's that orange red, you know; you can't help seeing him. I think he lives right across the street from you here because twice as I've been driving by I've seen him come out of that apartment house. Be a sweetie-pie and try and find out who he is for me, will you?"

"You say he's a friend of my Cousin Ames Lanning's, Laila?"

"Yes, because only yesterday afternoon I saw them downtown walking along together and they were laughing and talking the way men do that know each other terribly well. You can always tell. I don't mean I've got a complex for red-heads; but really he intrigues me quite a lot, so you find out about him for me and give me a ring and I'll do something for you some day." Laila rose and reverted to the opening elegancies with which she'd begun her call. "I must trot, dolling. We're playing golf all winter when there isn't snow or a thaw and I've got a female fawsome. Baw but keeps one's hand in. Anothuh time you must tell me all about yourself, what intrigued you most on the othuh side and if you got engaged to anybody and all that. No, of coss you didn't, though. You'd have just poked about museums and things being feffly intellectual. You see I remember your style peffectly. We're going to be as great pals as ever, though, aren't we? 'Bye-bye. Don't forget our precious red-headed friend and to give me a ring when you find out. It's lovely to know you're in town again."

Musically laughing, moving with grace, chattering, Laila recovered her bag of golf clubs and went forth to the "convertible" she'd left at the curb before the house. Kate, wryly amused by Laila's new style and the object of the call, continued her dusting; but at lunch she was curious enough to ask Ames about his red-haired friend.

"If he's not already too vain you can tell him you're asking on behalf of a girl who wants to know."

"Vain, no," Ames said. "Old Tuke'll be flattered."

"Old who, Ames?"

"Old Tuke. His name's Tuke Speer and he's old because he's almost as old as I am. He's twenty-nine. He's from Centerville and was a sophomore at college when Mary and I were seniors; but we knew him pretty well and liked him. Sam Augren spent most of last year scouting over the country, picking up the best men he could find for Roe Metal Products, and Tuke's one of the dozen or so young technical wizards the corporation's brought here. Who's the girl that's so excited about him?"

"Laila Capper. It seems principally about his hair."

"Laila Capper?" Ames didn't immediately remember. "Oh, yes! That tall, very pretty girl who was at Bill Jones's party. I must tell Tuke; he'll be flattered indeed! She struck me as a very superior type."

"'Superior'?" Mary echoed in simple astonishment and looked helplessly at Kate. "Aren't men the strangest things? Ames, you'd better tell Tuke to send Miss Capper a lock of his hair, since that's his attraction for her, but to keep away himself."

"A lock of his hair?" Ames looked puzzled. "Why?"

"Nothing," Mary said. "It might be more to the point if you'd give him the chance to meet Kate, because she really is superior and it's about time for her to be meeting somebody like Tuke Speer. The boys she used to know here are most of 'em probably too young for her now; at any rate she doesn't seem to find any of 'em of the slightest interest—and there's Tuke living right across the street. I ought to've thought of it, myself, long ago. Don't you think you might——"

"Why, of course!" Ames looked at Kate surprisedly. "I'll see

what he's doing this evening. Somehow I never happened to think
of—— I mean that with Kate it doesn't occur to one that she—— I
mean——"

Kate laughed at him forgivingly. "Don't explain any further,
Cousin Ames, and don't drag your red-haired friend across the
street by force. Don't I seem cheerful enough as things are?"

XII

AMES, VAGUELY AWARE THAT HE HADN'T BEEN VERY
complimentary, though he didn't see just why not, said that indeed
Kate did seem cheerful enough; and he was right about that seeming.
Outwardly she was sunny; inwardly she was determined. She had re-
solved that the tragedy of Malcolm Fennigate's thrown-away talent
shouldn't be repeated in Ames Lanning.

Artful suggestion touched nothing in Aunt Daisy, and nobody ever
persuaded her to do anything: the stronger the persuasion, the happier
grew her pride in her refusals. Therefore, one way or another, Ames
had to be roused out of his subjugation; and, after Kate had known
and warmly liked his friend, Tuke Speer, for a week or so, she spoke
to him about this.

"It ought to be easy," the responsive young man said. He was a
confident soul, mentally and athletically lively, as gay in disposition
as in the color of his hair. At first sight Kate had heartily approved of
his comely outdoor pinkish face and they'd reached an easy congenial-
ity within an hour. "Of course you're right about Ames," he added.
"I'm already beginning to think you're right about—well, about everything!—and certainly he ought to jump at the chance to get in with
the Bortshleff outfit. Of course I haven't lived here long; but I've seen
this much: Roe Metal Products is the heart of this city's industrial
life and Mr. Roe's head lawyers are the top of their profession. If

Ames has the chance to join up with them, even without his name on the door, he ought to leap for it, mother-in-law or no mother-in-law. Why don't you just tell him so?"

"He knows it, without," Kate explained. "If I urge it upon him it will only look like an underhand opposition to my aunt and to Mary. You've seen that poor Mary's always been deathly afraid to let him do anything against her mother's wishes, haven't you?"

"Yes, of course. It's been scaring me for some time. A man doesn't know what kind of jam he's getting into when he turns into a husband. Anyhow, though, Ames is really a big sort of fellow; we all knew that long ago in college. He ought to be able to——"

"Well, he isn't," Kate said. "I think perhaps you're the sort of man that'd stand up against the will of women who'd try to control you, no matter how they'd wear you down; but Ames was never born to do that. My aunt has always believed that her own feelings and wishes are the moral law. Of course that isn't a rare conviction in people; but she's always had it so powerfully that she's put it over on Mary completely. Ames can't fight women, especially not an ailing one; but if he had another man, a husky-minded friend, to back him up and talk right out about what he ought to do, maybe he'd see that if he did it he'd be improving his wife's condition as well as his own. Wouldn't you try?"

Tuke looked at her with an amused curiosity. "You do go at things! I get the idea you've been straightening out your world the whole of your young life. No, I can't talk to Ames—I mean not the way you really want me to. About the only reason I can give you why I can't, it's that men don't. I mean the sort of men that Ames Lanning and I are."

Kate was downcast. "No, I suppose not. You're both too masculine."

"Don't droop," Tuke Speer said. "Don't think I mind your wanting to use me, either. I like your letting me in on it. Shows I'm making headway with you, doesn't it, please? Fact is, I'm probably about as big a rube with women as Ames is, himself, though as you say I'd at least put up a fight if they tried to get me down. I have the feeling that you wouldn't want to get me down—or at least that you'd never let me know it if you did it. That isn't all the feeling I've got about you, Kate Fennigate."

She laughed. "What's the rest of it?"

"You'll say it's rather sudden," he admitted, laughing too. "Our fathers and mothers—or maybe it was our grandfathers and grandmothers—used to talk about 'Platonic affection', I think I've heard. No, I believe they called it 'Platonic love'. I mean to say I've got a most awful crush on you along that line. Do you think I could hope it might ever become reciprocal?"

"Yes, you could!" she said, and, although she blushed unplatonically as they both laughed again, she knew that his appeal was as simply honest as he was, himself. "Now that we've made this pact," she added, "let's get back to arguing about what we were arguing about yesterday—Nietzsche and Napoleon."

As requested, she had telephoned to Laila, though with slight information. Kate's treacherous thought was: "Keep your hands off, he's too good for you"; but Laila's response was airy. She'd forgotten all about the red-haired new man in town, she insisted. Had she actually asked Kate to find out about him? Really, if she had she must have been dizzy; she couldn't recall having given him a thought. New men were always turning up nowadays to go into Roe Metal Products; one couldn't keep track of them. She'd met faw or five of 'em within the last month or so, all feffly stupid.

"One of 'em's rather a handful, at that, my dear," she said. "Dogs me day and night. Quite a swanky boy; but I'm in no need of an extra shadow, thank you. Feisty, too, with the others he is, and of all annoying things I do despise jealousy, don't you, dear? Good of you to give me the ring about Mr. Orange-top; but really and truly I've forgotten all about him. If he knows I asked, you tell him so— tell him I said it was ever so long ago and I've forgotten all about him. Be shaw to say I couldn't remember him, dolling. 'Bye-bye. I'm neglecting you horribly; but I'll be trotting in to see you almost any day, old thing. Lovely to know you're in town again."

"Of all the pinheads!" Kate said to herself, and put her mind upon more serious matters.

She didn't like to waste effort but couldn't forever resist the constant temptation to try to work upon Aunt Daisy. As prelude to one such attempt, "Those new leaks in the roof aren't improving any," she said suggestively after two days of spring rain. "The pans I put under 'em in the attic overflowed, and one of the old leaks dripped almost a bucketful, too. It——"

"Yes, I know which one," the aunt interrupted. "I thought it would. It's the one Ames bragged about because he got up on the roof one Sunday with some pieces of slate and claimed he'd fixed it. I told him he couldn't because he didn't put tar-paper under the slate. I used tar-paper that way, myself, for three of the oldest leaks one day, with every window of that horrible apartment house across the street full of faces goggling at me up there, and none of them have dripped a drop since I did it."

"Yes, they have, Aunt Daisy. Some drip more and some drip less; but they all drip. Mr. Paulus, the slate man, told me——"

"Who?"

"Mr. Paulus, the slate man. I had him look over the roof yesterday afternoon when you were at your Church Fellowship Committee meeting. Mr. Paulus——"

"You must have been crazy! He's the most expensive in town. I'd never in the world think of——"

"I only asked him for an estimate," Kate explained. "Just for repairing the leaks. But he told me patching here and there'd be practically thrown away, the whole house ought to be re-roofed. You don't need to tell me again that you can't afford it; but it seems to me that Ames could if you managed better about him, Aunt Daisy."

"Managed better?" Aunt Daisy repeated in frankest astonishment. "Managed Ames better?"

"I mean," Kate said hurriedly, "I mean about his being more prosperous. I mean of course he's settled down with Caldwell, Hardy and Caldwell and seems contented just to be in a rut there; but if you could only somehow stimulate him to try and get with a more important firm, where maybe he'd have a percentage and——"

Here she was stopped. "Come with me!" Aunt Daisy gave this as a command and preceded her niece into the dark little room called "the

library". Aunt Daisy pointed to a portrait on the wall above the narrow glassed book-case that gave the room its name. The portrait was
of a Vandyke-bearded gentleman rigid in a winged collar and black
frock coat, with a silk hat on the table beside which he stood. "Look
at that picture," Aunt Daisy said. "My husband, John Cunningham,
gazes down upon us. What do you think he's saying?"

"I don't know, Aunt Daisy. I'd be afraid to quote what the dead
say; they mightn't like it."

"Smart, aren't you?" Aunt Daisy retorted. "He was my husband and
I know what he's saying now as well as if I heard his voice. He's
saying, 'Take care! Be on your guard, Marguerite. If you're not watch-
ful you'll be caught in a web and find yourself consorting with an
enemy who cost us eight thousand dollars that might very well make
as much as forty thousand for you now, if you had it, Marguerite Cunningham.' That's what he's saying to me, and he's speaking to you
too, Kate Fennigate; he's telling you that you needn't waste your
breath on traps and insinuations that are clear as day to a woman of
my age and experience. Leaks in the roof, indeed! I'll keep pans under
'em till Kingdom Come before I'll let my daughter consent to her
husband's betraying this family by consorting with Oscar J. Bortshleff.
I hope you understand *now* what your Uncle John is saying to you,
Kate Fennigate!"

Kate was meek. She hadn't really expected to accomplish anything,
though. She was sorry for her Uncle John. If he'd been alive, she
thought, he very likely would have said what Aunt Daisy said he
would; Aunt Daisy'd have made him. Cousin Roberta Gilpin had told
Kate that Uncle John sometimes drank a good deal and would be away
from home for as much as a week, no wonder. Kate wasn't sorry for
Uncle John only; she was sorry for all men. They seemed to her to
have a pretty hard time—except those that avoided domestication. On
the other hand, old bachelors and old widowers appeared to live in a
dusty sort of loneliness; they didn't even know what not to eat or
when to have their hair cut and plainly lacked both care and guidance.
Then, too, a domesticated man had compensations: Ames was often
delighted by young Celia, especially since she'd become interested
in her studies.

Talking over these thoughts with her confirmed friend, Tuke Speer, Kate made him laugh aloud. "Mrs. Cunningham's too much for you, I'm afraid," he said. "I gather you conclude a man ought to marry at about sixty; but I've known mothers-in-law who were charming. You're a funny girl."

"Am I?"

"Yes. For instance, why don't you like to go about more? Of course I understand that for a good while after losing your father you didn't feel like it; but now it's different, isn't it? You seem to be burying yourself in this house. When you do go out anywhere you have the air of a girl who's thinking about trigonometry and's going to wear nose-glasses pretty soon. Of course the boys like you but——"

"Yes, 'but'," she said, as he paused. " 'But' indeed! What you mean is that I'm convenient to talk to but by no means would any of 'em ever fall in love with me. Not they, and nobody else. Nobody ever did or will, and I'm not deeply concerned about that."

"Perhaps that's the trouble," he suggested. "I mean your not being deeply concerned about it. You always look as if you weren't, and it sets up a barrier—like one that surrounds a settledly married woman. Now that I think of it, it's much more like that than like trigonometry. Nobody'd ever try to make love to you any more than he would to a girl he knew to be engaged—engaged, betrothed and unalterably plighted to marry some man on the other side of the world. You aren't, are you?"

"No." Her color heightened but so slightly that he didn't perceive it.

"Well, then, maybe it's trigonometry after all, Kate. Anyhow, there's a preoccupation. Maybe it's trying to get good old Ames where the stuff he's got entitles him to be. By the way, Ames ought to be in the Carlyle Club. They very kindly put me in a while ago and it's a pleasant institution. I think Ames would enjoy it, don't you?"

"Yes—yes, he would."

"You don't think he could afford it?"

"Not as things are, probably; but if he could—well, it would be difficult."

"I see," Tuke said. "He wouldn't be allowed to. Mussolini would

envy your aunt. Too bad; the men at the club all think Ames is a
great fellow. By the way, the noisiest of 'em, Bill Jones, claims to know
you; says he always has."

"Yes, I suppose so. He knows everybody, doesn't he?"

"Certainly seems to," Tuke said. "That reminds me, the other night
he took me to see that girl Ames told me you said inquired about
me because of my terrible hair. Remember? It was months ago, 'way
back when you and I first began to know each other and——"

"Laila Capper." Kate spoke the name in a low voice, thoughtfully.

"Yes," Tuke said. "She's a lustrous-looking creature. There were
half a dozen competitors of Bill's there—he seems fairly overboard
about her in his own whoop-it-up way. Her talk was just personal
gabble, kidding, gestures and everybody-come-hither. She tried to
fuss me about you, because somebody'd told her you and I were at
those Chamber Music concerts together last month. Went on to say
you'd been her most intimate friend for years. I couldn't imagine it.
Were you?"

"Well—probably I was."

"So? Then you can tell me if I've sized her up right. No talk, just
gabble and razz and whose-baby-are-you? Isn't that about all there is?"

"And her beauty, Tuke."

"Plenty," Tuke said. "Plenty; but what of it if it's only a dumb-
head's coating? I did think, though, that she's jolly and good-natured,
glad to give everybody a good time. Well, after all, what more does
any girl need?"

"Need for what, Tuke?"

"To be a dazzler," he replied. "I'm not talking about your kind of
girl, of course, because you really are non-personal. I was saying
Miss Laila Capper's got what gets 'em. Holler all you like; but beauty
is and's always been what goes places. Beauty's got to have animation
with it, that's true; but it doesn't much matter what kind of animation, so what more does this girl need than what she's got?"

"What indeed, Tuke! Entirely he-man, aren't you? Women are
designed by Allah as accessories. 'Escape' would be the stylish new
word for it, wouldn't it? Women are born to provide escape for men?"

Tuke looked slightly annoyed. "You know that wasn't what I meant and that I wasn't talking about myself. I'd look for something I don't see any symptoms of in Miss Capper."

"Yes, of course," Kate said. "I didn't mean I thought you were the kind who'd fall for just make-whoopee and Turkish Delight. I'm sorry."

" 'Turkish Delight'?" he repeated. "Well, she isn't fat, you know; and all the same I did get another impression of her besides what I've mentioned."

"A more admiring impression?"

"It was this," Tuke said. "She's not my style, of course, and I can't imagine her ever saying anything an undazed man could listen to; but she *has* got a frank, outspoken, straightforward look that's attractive. I mean you can see right away that she'd never let anybody down, that she isn't the slightest bit tricky or catty, wouldn't ever do anybody dirt to get an advantage for herself and that she truly is just what she seems to be—an up-to-the-minute, been-everywhere, smart-crowd Beauty but a darned good sport and completely on the level."

Kate was able to look at him scrutinizingly, for, absorbed in his analysis, he gazed frowningly at the wall. He was wholly in earnest; and, although she had a severe temptation to gasp at him, "You didn't even notice her accent?" the impulse had to be downed. Tuke's revelation of his simplicity, she knew, was only another instance of the ancient and modern but always dumfounding incompetencies of men in their witless relations with women.

XIII

SHE LOOKED AT HIM LONG. HE KNEW NOTHING OF HER gaze and, in spite of their intimate companionship, he knew almost as little of herself, Kate thought. He took it for granted that she (being "non-personal") agreed with him about Laila's good sportsmanship and straightforward character, and when he spoke again his topic had changed. He began to talk of the still wildly soaring stock market and Mr. Roe's foresight in providing buffers for Metal Products when the ultimate certain crash should come. The two friends often spoke of Tuke's work, of Mr. Roe and of the second big Plant Metal Products had built, and usually Kate was interested; but now she was absent-minded. She'd already begun to wait with a prophetic sickishness for Tuke to mention Laila Capper again.

She saw him almost every day, walked with him through twilight, sat many evenings facing him under Uncle John's portrait in "the library", as they explored the "expanding universe", new chemistry, old religion, American business, Mr. Roe, Tuke himself, and Ames Lanning. Tuke didn't speak of Laila again for six weeks; then all he said was, "Bill and I were out at your friend Laila Capper's again last night. She asked me to shoot a round of golf with her Sunday morning." Kate said, "I'm sure you'll enjoy it" and they went at once into a political argument.

At the dinner table, a fortnight after this, Aunt Daisy, always ruthless, made a pertinent inquiry: "What's become of your redheaded Speer man, Kate? I was beginning to think you and he couldn't live without seeing each other at least once a day; but I don't seem to have seen him around lately. You oughtn't to mind, because he's just a beginner at that ordinary old Roe's Works and I bet he's as poor as a Unitarian churchmouse. What did you fight over?"

Ames interposed mildly. "He isn't quite so poor as that. At any rate, if he is, he won't stay so. He's one of the most energetic, up-and-coming——"

"Pooh!" Ames's mother-in-law often checked him thus. "He's a red-head, isn't he? Never saw a red-head yet that wouldn't fly off the handle at the slightest contradiction, especially in hot weather like this. What did you fight about, Kate, or has he got another girl?"

Ames again tried to be of help. "Mary, do tell your mother that even after we were engaged and before the war there were times when I was so busy that we didn't see each other for several——"

"I'm afraid I couldn't quite say that, Ames dear." Gentle Mary
looked distressed. "I mean I don't think we went without seeing each
other so long as this. I mean I don't think you ever stayed away quite
so long as Tuke's been——"

"Hold everything, please!" Kate recovered a momentarily lost
composure. "I'm not a complete wreck, ladies and gentlemen. Don't
look so sympathetic, Ames! I'm very, very fond of Tuke Speer; but
we haven't reached the point where we confide everything to each
other, so he hasn't told me why he fails to find me a daily necessity
of late. Maybe he's just tired of looking at me—such things do happen
—but I'm still able to make Celia keep her hair brushed, amn't I?"

"Blast you, yes!" Celia said precociously, and the inquiry was over;
but the next day brought an answer, an expected one, to the person
most concerned.

In the afternoon Kate had finished her daily task as a masseuse.
She'd given Mary a "rub" and was darkening the patient's bedroom
for the rest old Dr. Powls had prescribed to follow the treatment.
Aunt Daisy came in exasperated by a back-door argument. "It's that
upstart negro, Wilberforce," she explained. "I never was so provoked!
The politicians spoil 'em. They don't stop at merely buying their
votes on election day for two dollars; they spout speeches to 'em that
make 'em believe they're the sultans of this earth. Wilberforce used
to cut my grass once a week for seventy-five cents and only too glad
to get it. He's been grumbling all summer, hasn't been around for
over two weeks and *now* what do you think he has the face to ask me?
Said he couldn't think of it under a dollar and a quarter! Kept telling
me over and over, 'No, ma'am, I couldn't think of it for less. I simpully
couldn't consider it.' I told him to get off my back porch and never
dare set foot there again. Well, Mary, that settles it."

"Oh, dear!" Upon the bed Mary became murmurous. "You think——
Couldn't it go a little while longer without being mowed? These hot
days he—he looks so tired when he comes from the office, Mother."

"Tired, does he? Tired of being a failure maybe. Always babying
him, Mary! He's supposed to be an athlete, isn't he? I guess it won't
hurt him to cut my grass. It might put a little gimp in him, enough

to make him decide to cut some ice in this world and *be* somebody!
I'm going out on the street-car to see what Roberta Gilpin's doing
for her sciatica—I'll bet it's wrong—and I won't be back till dinnertime. Ames'll be here by the time you get up and you can tell him
you want to give me a surprise, wouldn't it be nice if he'd have the
lawn all shipshape again to give my eyes a treat when I get back."

"Oh, dear! Mother, do you think it really needs to be——"

" 'Needs!' Why, it's a disgrace! It makes the whole place look shift-
less. I should think Ames'd be ashamed to see it; but of course if you
want to go on babying him and letting him wander through his whole
life with his head in the clouds and no shine on his shoes——"

"No, I'll tell him." Mary's hand, lifted in protest, dropped limply
upon the coverlet. "I'll tell him, Mother. He'll do it."

Kate left them, waited until Mrs. Cunningham had gone forth;
then went to the anomalous old brick stable behind the house,
dragged out the lawnmower and began to cut the grass. The lawnmower was a heavy, old-fashioned one, Wilberforce hadn't left it
sharp, the grass was long and tough, and indoors thermometers in
this part of the city had pushed their threads of mercury to the discouraging figure ninety-six. Kate toiled determinedly, wiping her face
with bared forearms, pausing to get her hair out of her eyes or to
mutter fiercely at the lawnmower when it jerked and balked. The
swathes she cut were interminable in length, and, when she'd worked
an hour, the area of mowed lawn seemed a trifle compared to the
vast shaggy spaces still untouched.

An hour for half the front yard! At this rate she'd have the vile
grass cut, not by the time Ames came home but at about midnight!
Aching in ankles, knees, back and biceps, hating the sound of the
mower in her ears, itching from grass inside her stained canvas shoes,
she rested two minutes; then seized the machine's handle again, a
shabby small figure at an angle of forty-five degrees pushing savagely
in a rage with the grass, the heat and the dull blades of the mower.

She'd turned at the end of a swathe and started upon a new one
when the lawnmower jammed, her fingers slipped from the wet
handle, she stumbled, tearing her white cotton skirt, and went down
on knees and elbows. This was her posture as Laila Capper's passing

"convertible" abruptly swung to the curb and stopped. Tuke Speer and Laila jumped out, and Tuke ran forward. "Let me help you up!" Kate wasn't gracious. "What for?" she asked, as she got to her feet and cleared her eyes of damp hair.

"Well, I only thought——" Not at all at his ease, Tuke began to explain. "I—I thought maybe you'd hurt yourself. Laila's giving a woods picnic and picked me up at the Plant. We were just on the way to—— I mean we saw you fall and——"

Laila, cool-looking in lilac linen, came up laughing. "You looked so funny!" she exclaimed. "I hope it didn't hurt you, but the way you flopped it was just like some terribly funny animal looking for its hole! You mustn't blame us for laughing, you dear little Kate; but really——" Overcome with mirth, Laila was unable to continue.

"Please don't think I did any laughing, Kate." Tuke's embarrassment made him awkward. "I—I mean Laila's sense of humor is always with her; but I——"

"Never mind, Tuke." Kate brushed at green stains, and, with forearms to which blades of grass adhered, wiped her moist red face. She looked down at her bedraggled skirt, and laughed too. "I must still look pretty funny, I should think."

"Oh, no, not a bit! Indeed you don't—no, indeed——" Tuke seemed to feel that he ought to reassure her; but he was interrupted. Ames Lanning, languid after his hot day's work, turned in from the sidewalk and came across the raggedly mowed stretch of lawn.

"Hello, hello, hello!" he said. "How do you do, Miss Capper. What's up, Tuke? Kate, what on earth have you been doing?"

Laila took Tuke's arm. "How's Mr. Ames Lanning's elegant baritone?" she asked, with the slightest inflection of coquettish impertinence. "Singing at any more parties these days? I'd hate to think I was missing it. Your poor dear cousin here stepped on her skirt and gave us an imitation of a woodchuck in the grass, so we stopped to see if she needed help. She didn't, so we'd better be on our way. Adios! Tuke, we'll be feffly late."

Tuke would have turned toward Kate again; but Laila gave a possessive tug to his arm, released it and ran lightly toward her car. He had to follow. Ames looked Kate over. "She meant you'd fallen down? Yes, look at your knees and that skirt! Why, it's all rags! You mean to tell me you were trying to cut this grass? Where's Wilberforce?"

Kate was redder than ever. "He's resigned—in person," she said, and grasped the handle of the lawnmower again. "If you'll stand out of my way, please——"

"No." Ames glanced at the departing car, then at Kate; and, with a deeper anger, she saw that his eyes held compassion.

"Get out of my way!" she said between her teeth. "I started it and I'll finish it!"

He took off his coat, threw it upon the ground, forcibly removed her fingers from the handle, and laughed; but she thought that even the half-mirthful sound he made held pity for her. "You'd better run indoors, Kate, and get yourself ready for dinner. I can finish the yard by then. I ought to've done it before; but I never dreamed you'd——"

"I've got a right to, haven't I? I seem to be living here permanently, damn it, don't I? So I've got a right to cut the grass if I want to! Do you think I care what I look like?"

"Now, now, Kate," Ames said gently. "People can't keep dressed up all the time; anybody knows that. Don't jump to conclusions, either. I don't think it means much. Just driving around with a pretty girl now and then wouldn't necessarily mean that good old Tuke is——"

"Oh!" Kate's gasp was so loud as to be an outcry. Her widely opened eyes showed him an anger so flashing that he was disturbed as if by the sudden presence of a stranger in the midst of a domestic scene. In that furious instant he felt wholly unacquainted with his Mary's Cousin Kate, a familiar and agreeable part of his daily life. "You let me alone!" she cried, as she whirled from him and ran to the house.

She apologized to him after dinner. He was alone in the living-room and had begun to fan himself with the newspaper he'd finished reading. When Kate came in she stopped not far from the doorway and stood, her eyes downcast.

"I've wanted to say I'm sorry, Cousin Ames. I hate to be rude and I beg your pardon."

"Good heavens! What for, Kate?"

"My behavior this afternoon when you took the lawnmower from me. I was outrageous."

"Not at all, not at all! If there's any apology it's due from me, not from you. I'm afraid you felt I was intrusive."

"No, you were only being considerate, Ames. You see I have so few affairs of my own I suppose I'm rather jumpy about keeping them to myself; but I ought to've understood that you just wanted to make me feel better and not to realize what I looked like by—by comparison— and not to think I'd wholly lost a friend because he sees something of other girls. That was kind of you, Ames; but it wasn't needed, so I was silly enough to get into a temper."

"Well, you did," he admitted. "I never saw you in one before, so it was quite a surprise; but that makes the case clear, doesn't it? I ought to be the one to apologize for upsetting you."

"No, I was ungrateful. When people get too busy feeling things themselves they haven't sense enough to understand how the things other people do are meant. That's why I'm asking your pardon, and my explanation of my conduct is that I don't need—or care for— other people to be sorry for me about Tuke."

"No, no—of course not!" He spoke hurriedly.

"Well, then, that's all." Here she looked up and smiled. "You see?"

"Yes, of course."

She smiled upon him again, took a book from a table, went to a chair beside an open window, sat and read. He fanned himself, lighted a pipe, smoked, and from time to time glanced at her covertly. He'd have liked to tell her again not to mind about Tuke and that she was only twenty-one, she'd get over it and there'd be plenty of others in time. Tuke was foolish, Ames thought; Kate was a fine girl. Still, of course, it was easy to see how a man could lose his head over a grand-looking creature like that beautiful, tall Miss Capper. Poor Kate!

XIV

Mrs. HERBERT GILPIN, GETTING A LITTLE THE BETTER OF
her sciatica, because she hadn't followed Mrs. Cunningham's advice,
gave way to a philanthropic impulse. "Sometimes I just can't bear
to think of it!" she said to her granddaughter, Martha. "Daisy Cunningham's simply using her—yes, without a qualm! She'd sacrifice
anything and anybody for Mary and to keep that ugly old house
going. It's on my conscience that I practically suggested to Daisy to
get Kate there, though Daisy'd already thought of it, herself, I
could see. I didn't realize what a slave the child would come to be.
I declare, after all, I believe it would have been a lot better for her
if she'd got a position with Mr. Roe and lived by herself! Daisy says
she's been having a beau, though."

"What? Kate? How much of one, Grandmother?"

"Not so much as to've really worried Daisy, apparently," Mrs.
Gilpin said. "Anyhow, she laughed when she told me, so she's certainly not much afraid of losing Kate. Said something's happened
between 'em, she doesn't know what, and he hasn't been around
for quite a good while; but from what she'd heard of their conversations——"

The granddaughter interrupted. "Heavens! How much and how
many of their conversations do you think Cousin Daisy's overheard?"

"All she decided to, Martha. Well, anyway, she didn't mention who
the young man is but said everything was on a high intellectual basis,
the way it would be with Kate of course, and so probably it didn't
mean anything serious."

"No—except for Kate maybe, Grandmother. She'd never let anybody see it, though, of course."

"No, she wouldn't," Mrs. Gilpin agreed. "She's always been the most bottled-up child we've ever had in our whole family connection. Well, anyhow, what I want, Martha: when she comes to lunch to-day, you get her away from the family afterward and up to your own room and see if you can't persuade her. Be very tactful; but press it upon her that it's really almost a year since her father died and nobody's going to criticize her for being in a wedding party."

"I don't think it's that, Grandmother. She's already gone to two or three dinners. I think it's probably the expense."

"That's what I've been thinking, myself!" the old lady grumbled. "It'd be just like Daisy to let her be without a single cent to her name. Well, you be tactful; but make her understand that I'll see to it. It won't be much—just her hat and dress and slippers and I suppose there'll have to be some sort of little present for the bride, a silver card-dish or something. You make Kate say she'll let me do it for her."

"I certainly will!" Martha said; but after lunch, in her own room with Kate, found that the promise couldn't be kept. Against all urging, Kate shook her head.

"No, and it won't matter, Martha. It's sweet of Adele to want all the bridesmaids to be from our Carroll class; but she'll easily find somebody else to take my place and fill out the eight she wants."

"No, she won't. Not unless she takes Laila Capper. That'd be a pill for all of us, especially Adele, because Laila'd hog the show— even from the bride. I'd hate to see Laila have the satisfaction of being in a wedding, all Carroll girls. She makes great play these days of having been a Carroll girl, herself, now that she's pushed in with almost everybody. I suppose of course you know the story she finally got going around about why she didn't graduate?"

"No, I never heard it."

Martha laughed. "The rest of us are supposed to have ganged up in some mysterious way during exams. Laila was the only one that wouldn't cheat! How's that for a pretty? Of course you know I've never believed she was as great a friend of yours as she gave herself out to be. Who's that red-headed older man she's around with every-where lately? Do you know?"

"Yes, Tuke Speer. He's in Roe Metal Products and a friend of Ames and Mary's."

"She's certainly got him," Martha said. "He looks attractive, too. She trails 'em after her, all ages. Kate, listen to me: of all the Carroll girls of our crowd that aren't already married, and outside of some that just wouldn't look right at all, there are only eight including you, and you'll simply have to write another note to Adele and tell her you've changed your mind, you'll do it. Grandmother told me to be tactful with you; but I never was good at that. She wants you to have a little fun and be bridesmaid for Adele, so she says she'll see it won't cost you anything. She'll take care of all the bills for your dress and everything and a piece of silver for Adele. She wants to. You'll let her, won't you?"

"No. Cousin Roberta's a dear to think of it; but I couldn't."

"Why not? Grandmother was your father's first cousin, wasn't she? It's all in the family, isn't it? So why not?"

"I couldn't."

"Too proud!" Martha leaned forward, pressing the question. "Kate Fennigate, answer me this: Why do you keep on staying in that dismal place?"

Kate smiled. "Why—I suppose because I like to."

"You couldn't! Here you are too proud to let even Grandmother give you a few days of show-off and good times—the wedding party's to have lots of dinners and things—and you won't take it! Well, if you won't let anybody do it for you, why don't you do something for yourself? Why don't you break away and take that position with Mr. Roe? You'd probably earn money enough to do lots of pleasant things you won't let your own family help you do. Why do you go on letting old Cousin Daisy make a perfect victim of you? I want to know what *for*?"

Kate smiled again. "The line of least resistance, Martha."

"Not you!" Martha Gilpin said. "You've always batted your head on the line of hardest resistance. Well—no use saying anything more about Grandmother's offer?"

"No." Kate rose. "I'll go and thank her."

"You can't. She's taking her nap. Sit down. I want to ask you about your suitor. Who is he, Kate? Grandmother says Cousin Daisy told her——"

"Goodnight!" Kate exclaimed. "I'm off! If we begin to talk about what Aunt Daisy and your grandmother tell each other, where'll we end?"

Martha went with her all the way to the gate, where they parted, one still murmurously protesting and the other still laughingly evasive. Martha supposed Kate was on her way to take a 'bus at the next corner of the comfortable and almost smokeless semi-suburban street, but Kate didn't. She walked, though she'd have preferred the 'bus in order to spare her shoes. These, like everything else she owned, were wearing out; but she hadn't the money for a 'bus fare. For more than a month she'd had no money at all, a condition involving various difficulties and embarrassments even when food and lodging are secure.

Aunt Daisy knew it, because she'd put a new can of toothpowder in the bathroom Kate used; but that was as far as Aunt Daisy intended to go. The can of toothpowder spoke its message clearly enough: "Yes, you *would* sell that house and drag your father away to squander every cent of the money on foreign travel! How often did I tell you not to?" Kate didn't wish an allowance from Aunt Daisy; but it should have been offered and she resented the toothpowder every time she used it.

She had a light step. She walked the three homeward miles trying to make it lighter for the sake of the thinning soles of her only pair of brown shoes. Tuke Speer came out of the apartment house across the street and joined her as she reached Aunt Daisy's front door. "Spare me a few minutes, Kate? Half-holiday at the Works; running light this month. If you're not too busy——"

"No, of course not. Come in."

"Thanks, but couldn't we just sit here on the steps? Laila's coming by to pick me up and perhaps I'd better——"

"Of course, Tuke." They sat upon the top slab of the grey limestone steps, and Tuke looked toward downtown, watching expectantly. "You want to talk to me about her? Is that it, Tuke?"

"Afraid so," he said, and laughed apologetically. "You're a pretty shrewd girl, so I daresay you suspect I'm not able to talk about much else nowadays, except when I'm on the job at the Plant."

"Yes, of course, Tuke." She laughed, too, companionably.

"Well, the first thing I want to say——" He gave her an instant's sidelong glance; then returned his gaze toward down the street. "I don't want to seem fatuous but——"

"Fatuous? I'd never think it. Get ahead!"

"Well, it sounds stupid," he confessed. "I've been wanting a chance, though, to say something to you. It's this: A man's friendship for one girl doesn't necessarily change, no matter how he might happen to feel about some other girl, does it?"

"I don't know, Tuke."

"Well, I do," he said with earnest emphasis. "I know I'd never change about you, Kate, never!—and I hope you wouldn't about me. You haven't, have you?"

"No, certainly not."

"Thanks," Tuke said. "I guess we're neither of us the kind of people that change much—inside. I know I'm not, and that's why I think I'll never change about her, Kate. I know you guessed I was falling for her. Well, I did—hard!—and unless I'm fooling myself about myself, and I don't think I am, that'll never change either. If you could let me just bust out to you about her a little——"

"Why, of course. Why not?"

"Kate, there's something glorious about her!" Tuke's pink face grew pinker; he gripped his knees with his hands and Kate thought that he trembled. "Glorious! I can't look at her without seeming to see a glory all about her—something vibrating that she radiates. I can't think of her except like that and I think of her all the time. I never dreamed I'd be this way about anybody, never thought it was in me to." He relaxed; then shook his head ruefully. "They say it always bores a woman to hear a man rave about some other woman; but it'd be a help to me if you could stand to let me do it sometimes, because I just can't keep it in."

"Why should you—with me?" Kate asked in a gentle voice. "It isn't 'fatuous' of you to think that I've valued our being friends. We both have, and we both know it. Well, it goes on. Come and talk to me about her when—whenever you have time. Yonder she comes, Tuke."

"Where?" They both jumped up. Tuke, though he was gazing down the street, didn't recognize Laila and her car as soon as Kate did. Another figure was beside Laila's, and Tuke had expected her to come alone. "Yes, so it is," he said. "She's got that curly young Patterson boy with her. Of course he's a nice young fellow. Well— thank you, Kate, and good-bye."

Laila and the curly Patterson boy were both waving jovially as the car stopped before the house, and Kate, glancing back from the front door, with her key in the lock, thought that Tuke's shoulders expressed discontent. She needed no special prophetic inspiration to be sure that Tuke would ere long confide to her impressions he'd have of Laila other than her gloriousness.

. . . In the hall, approaching the front door from the direction of the living-room, were Aunt Daisy and a stiff-collared, spectacled, middle-aged man in "pin-striped" dark grey, almost the uniform of a serious business man. He closed a black leather brief-case as he took his hard straw hat from a table; then shook hands with Aunt Daisy whose nose-glasses, faintly gleaming ovals, seemed to denote excitement. "Your judgment's certainly proved good so far, Mrs. Cunningham," he said. "I don't see any reason why we shouldn't depend upon it for the future. I admit some very good heads think that this can't last; but others——"

"Others are sure it will." Aunt Daisy took the sentence from him. "They are the smartest ones, Mr. Lucius. You remember my niece, don't you? Kate, I think you've met Mr. Frank Lucius?"

Kate bowed; Mr. Lucius said, "Miss Fennigate. Oh, yes, indeed, of course," and departed. Aunt Daisy was unmistakably in a state of elation, something so rare with her that it was almost shocking. She gave Kate a pat upon the shoulder, a slap of joy apparently.

"Kate, you may be glad yet that you happened to be born my niece. We'll see, we'll see! That Frank Lucius is a very, very unusual man. He's a splendid example of what the sound, clear-headed American business man can rise to be. When he was just beginning, your Uncle John had business relations with him and never was disappointed."

"He's a broker, isn't he, Aunt Daisy? I think I've heard so."

"And banker," Mrs. Cunningham added. "Beaton and Lucius, Bankers and Brokers, the best in this city. They've always looked after the poor few little securities I've had to skimp along on, and he's just been telling me that things look a little better for me. Only a wee bit of course, Kate—I mean just the slightest, tiniest bit better of course—but anyhow that's something. It'd be a wonderful thing if they got even better still, wouldn't it?"

"Yes, it would, Aunt Daisy."

"Well, we'll see, we'll see!" Aunt Daisy, in her exhilaration, couldn't help looking gayly mysterious. "Stranger things have happened. We might be able to put a whole new slate roof on the house yet, dearie. Who knows? Oh, by the way——"

"Yes?" Kate, who'd been moving toward the stairway, paused.

"Mary's waiting for her rub; but it might be just as well if you didn't mention Frank Lucius's being here to her, Kate. She doesn't mean to; but she's forgetful and sometimes she tells things to Ames —even things I've asked her not to."

"Ames doesn't like Mr. Lucius, Aunt Daisy?"

"Oh, certainly he does." Mrs. Cunningham laughed lightheartedly. "I only mean that what Ames doesn't know won't hurt him, the old croaker."

"'Croaker'? Ames? That's the last thing in the world I'd call him. What makes you——"

"Because he thinks the end of the world's coming, Kate. Here's this country enjoying such prosperity as it's never known, soundly on its feet at last and all the best minds certain that only greater and faster progress is ahead of it—and what's my deep-thinking son-in-law got to say about that? Why, you've heard him yourself a dozen times. 'Over-production!' 'It can't go on!' 'Sure to be a collapse in prices!' You don't call that croaking? Fiddle-de-dee!"

"Mr. Roe thinks so, too, Aunt Daisy. Tuke Speer told me Mr. Roe thinks——"

"The same as Ames Lanning?" the aunt asked, her high spirits only higher. "You and Mary probably think Mr. Roe consulted Ames. My soul! Henry L. Roe never heard of Ames Lanning's existence. They're both boneheads, though, for that matter."

"Aunt Daisy, you——"

"Don't 'Aunt Daisy' me!" Kate received another slap on the shoulder, accompanied by a cackle of hilarity most untypical. "I know what I'm doing, thank you, and I don't care for any advice from my poor Mary's husband. Just let him attend to his own affairs—or begin to get some to attend to. You trot upstairs and give Mary her rub."

XV

IN A MATTER OF DAYS KATE'S INTERPRETATION OF THE discontent expressed by Tuke Speer's shoulders proved correct. He came in, looking driven, and they sat again by bulb light under the late John Cunningham's portrait. "I don't know whether you can advise me or not," Tuke said. "You're so different from her maybe you wouldn't know what'd affect her. You're a girl, though, and she's a girl, and so I ought to be able to get a little something out of you. More than I can get out of myself, anyhow. I want to know how to treat her."

"Not in particular about the curly young Patterson boy, is it, Tuke?"

"No, about all of 'em—and something else, too." He gave Kate an impatient look; then stared at the glistening narrow glass doors of the book-case. "Me! I never thought I'd come to this. Why should I be so rottenly upset about practically nothing? Didn't even telephone me herself, had her mother do it. There was a kind of cheapness about that—getting her mother to do it—and I hate it."

"What did she get her mother to tell you, Tuke?"

"Called me up at six o'clock," he said. "Mrs. Barnes told me Laila was awfully sorry but just too rushed even to come to the telephone to tell me not to come out there to-night. Said she'd got in a jam, had to go and see some other girl about what to wear this evening at

a dinner for a wedding party that she'd just found she couldn't get
out of. A dear old schoolmate of hers named Adele Something's going
to be married, and Laila'd told me two weeks ago she'd been asked
to be a bridesmaid but had declined because there were going to be
lots of things given for this Adele's wedding crowd and if she accepted it'd interfere too much with her being with me. Well, after
telling me that—making me feel all lit up about preferring me—here
she leaves me standing out in the cold. What do you make of it?"

Kate made enough of it, but didn't say so. Laila, in her pose as
"a Carroll girl", had thought that Tuke, among others, might hear
of the wedding or read of it in a newspaper—"the bridesmaids all
former Carroll School girls, classmates of the bride." There could be
invidious wonder: Why was the conspicuous Laila omitted? The
bold little lies of a climber must needs be a myriad; nobody'd know
how many people Laila'd told she'd been asked at the outset to be
one of Adele's bridesmaids. Kate gave way to a small curiosity.

"Did Mrs. Barnes say why Laila'd so suddenly changed her mind?"

"Yes, and it sounded like guff. She said the bride had coaxed and
coaxed till Laila just didn't have the heart to refuse any longer. Said
Laila'd had to decide it was her duty: when a dear old classmate asked
such a thing of her so insistently it simply wouldn't be right to keep
on saying no. I'm not too crazy about Mrs. Barnes, you know. It
sounded phony to me."

"Mrs. Barnes did, Tuke?"

"Yes; but I mean the whole thing. Why didn't she call me up,
herself? Afraid she'd give something away? I think so. Laila knew
I'd ask her why she'd changed her mind all quick like that and she
knew she didn't have any answer that'd go down with me. She knew
that no matter what she'd tell me I'd have my own theory."

"Yes, you'd always have your own theory, Tuke. What's this one?"

"New man," he said, still staring at the light's reflection on the
book-case doors. "You see I'm beginning to know her better than
I did. She's a collector. Well, I've had my turn at being new man.
Here's my bet: when she was first asked to be a bridesmaid she
thought the ushers'd all be lads she already knew and was used to;
but now she's heard that some of 'em'll be from out of town or any-

how not on her list of previous captures. So she thought that'd give her a bigger time than sticking to the honey hooey she'd handed me about staying out on my account. Well, that's a hell of a thing for me to be thinking about her." He turned his head to look at Kate. "Can you see it any other way?"

It was her turn to stare at the glass of the book-case doors. The petty truth would cheapen Laila in Tuke's eyes; but it wouldn't help to cure him and he'd feel distaste for the teller of it. He had a good mind; but he was a passionate man and he was in for it. In for it indeed, because when a girl like Laila begins to have her mother do the telephoning, the lover at the other end of the wire will best seek elsewhere.

For some moments, staring at her hungrily, Tuke waited; then answered himself. "No, you can't see it any other way. You know it's true, so you needn't tell me. You can try to advise me, though, can't you? When a man's treated like this, what's the best thing for him to do? I want to know how to behave so that she doesn't do it again and so that I won't be dropped into the discard."

"There's an old prescription, Tuke. It's supposed to work with certain types; but it has to be used with a good appearance of cheerfulness. Stay away."

"As simple as that?" he asked. "Make her wonder if I'm not having myself a grand good time without her?"

"Yes, that's the idea."

Tuke shook his head. "Not for me. I've got to look at her, Kate; I've got to! I've had several suspicions that she isn't the grand and noble being I first thought she was. I mean in her spirit and her mind. Her mind, in fact, I haven't thought much of from the start; but I had lots of imaginings about her spirit. Well, I've found that I don't care any more about her spirit than I do about her mind. It's she herself I'm in love with, I don't care what she is or what she does. I don't care if she's noble or ignoble; I don't care a damn! Well, what's to be done?"

"You've come to the wrong person, Tuke; I don't seem to be an expert."

"No, I suppose not." He got to his feet, despondent. "I suppose that's because you've never been in love and aren't likely to be. Anyhow it's a relief to sputter my drivel out to you. You'll let me do it again—if I have to?"

"Yes. Maybe you won't have to."

"Fat chance!" he said, as he turned to the door.

. . . Laila didn't find a "new man" in the wedding party, at least not successfully, and, within the hour of the honeymoon departure, she began to soothe Tuke. He came across the street, in the dusk, to where Kate sat pensively on the front steps watching the lights of the cars that went south to the movies and of those that encountered and passed them, streaming northward for an evening drive in the country, out of the city's August heat.

"Sit down, Tuke, won't you?" she said. "If you need cheering up, why, so do I. It's unreasonable, but progress makes me sad. When I was a child in this neighborhood we'd see one automobile where now there are a hundred. At this time of the evening I used to sit and watch the lightning bugs coming out. Aren't any nowadays—instead, these machines and their glares coming out. Fireflies swearing at everybody ahead and leaving ugly smells behind 'em. You won't sit down?"

"Thanks, but I'm on my way, Kate. Just stopped a minute to tell you——"

"You needn't. I see now your shoulders look jaunty and I think you're smiling, aren't you?"

"Yes," Tuke said. "I am; but I ought to be laughing—laughing at myself for having been such a squirrel the night I came over here to complain to you. I was dead wrong about that whole affair, so please forget it. Laila was only being good-natured and loyal to a classmate, doing what she thought was right, and I was just a suspicious idiot. I'm ashamed to tell you what I was crazy enough to do."

"When, Tuke?"

"Yesterday noon. Dressed myself all up and went to the church part of that wedding without an invitation. When she came down the aisle I thought I'd die of misery. She looked like dawn on a hilltop with the London Philharmonic playing 'Pomp and Circumstance' to it. That glory I was blatting to you she radiates—well, it filled the church! I couldn't see anything else; nobody there could, either. Worse for me, she looked unattainable, foreverly so. I walked away from there in hell, and about four o'clock she called me up at the Plant. Kate, it's all right; she's a darling!"

. . . The rhapsody within him wasn't durable. The next time Kate saw him, three days later, he was just from his work and began by saying that he hadn't been able to keep his mind upon it. "That's a bad sign," he added. "She's got me so far down I don't like the looks of it. I seem to remember reading in some schoolboy romance that being in love is exalting and the lover does everything twice as well because of it. That must have been hooey. I like this job I've got; I've been absorbed in it and felt I could do great things with it; but I'll not get very far if I let it become just routine I do mechanically because I can't put my head into it. Well, how can I while I'm being bedeviled?"

"How bedeviled this time, Tuke?"

"This time?" he repeated, and groaned out a laugh. "Yes, I see it begins to look like a habit. Well, what she's done isn't anything she hasn't done before—lets me think I'm high man for an hour or so; then puts some other fool there and drops me to the bottom of the class; then puts me up again, and down again. Plays 'I'm Utterly Thine' with a look or a touch; then you catch her being utterly thiner with even that souse, Bill Jones. When I show it turns me sour she goes noble on me: nobody but a cad could doubt her because her knee was against Bill's under the table, I must be full of poison worms. You tell me, 'Stay away!' and I tell you I can't! Aren't you a good enough friend to think up any other advice?"

"Only this," Kate said. "You've got something—caught something—that'll have to run its course. Every kind of fever does that; but in time there comes——"

"Convalescence!" he interrupted, in angry mockery. "Yes, if it doesn't kill you first."

This was his parting word, and the next twilight, finding her upon the steps again, he was back for another brief rapture over the heavenliness of Laila who'd given him a whole evening of beauty,

alone with him. Even her mind, he had discovered, was more than
he'd thought it; there were depths in it he'd been too dull to discover
earlier. She really thought about certain things worth thinking about
and with a divine sort of gentleness agreed with most of the important things he thought he himself thought. Kate didn't see him
for a week after this—a week assumably of more beauty—then he
telephoned from his department at the Plant that he must talk to
her at once.

When he came she took him quickly into the library; he shut the
door and began to pace the small area of red-flowered old carpet.
"Why in hell can't you tell me something about women?" he wished
to know. "You *are* one, aren't you? So far as I'm concerned you're
a man, might be my brother; but it stands to reason you've got some
of the attributes of your sex. You must know what makes them fall
in love with men and how men ought to treat one of 'em who's true
to him one hour and false to him the next. Are women like Laila
Capper sadistic? Is she merely a born devil who wants to see a man
writhe just to feel her power over him? Is she——"

"No, no!" Kate protested. "Pretty much everybody's out to get
what he wants, isn't he, and doesn't really care much about anything
else? Laila's like most people, not very subtle, so her works get
exposed. That shocks you and you're furious at the sight of 'em; but
she's not unique. There are plenty of Laila Cappers, Tuke."

"I don't believe it! There couldn't be. God wouldn't have been
mean enough to make more than one. Do you know what she does?
She lets me believe I'm practically engaged to her—yes, and with all
that goes with it! Then she doesn't just break the engagement. Oh,
no! She claims she'd never meant anything of the kind—I'd misunderstood. Misunderstood? Good God! I believe she does exactly that
with the others, too, when they get far enough along with her. I do!
I swear I believe it!"

"Poor Tuke!"

"But that's vile!" His voice was loud, his gesturing extravagant.
"It's a vile thing to believe! Yes, and to be in love with a girl I could
think so vilely of! Why don't such thoughts of her make me through
with her forever? Why don't they cure me? They don't, that's all I

know. They don't. She's got me and it's going to last; I'll never get over it. Despising her doesn't keep her from seeming glorious to me. Nothing can ever drive me away from her, nothing she does or anybody else does. If she marries any other man I'll be the finish of the three of us, one way or another. I'll never let her——"

"Tuke!"

"Yes, I hear you!" he cried. "You don't need to tell me I'm talking crazily. Certainly I am; she's my insanity. She tears all my self-respect out of me. She doesn't even leave me decency enough not to come here spilling my craziness out on you like this. I'm not even a gentleman any more; I'm just a babbling, frothing——"

"Don't worry about what you are," Kate said. "It doesn't matter, because nobody'll know it but me and I won't think differently of you. All I see is just that you've been hurt. Go on—say all you'd like to."

He was quieter after that, though not less desperate. Kate was mistaken, however, when she'd said "nobody'll know it but me." At the breakfast table the next morning Mrs. Cunningham looked reticently amused.

"Our friend from across the street seems to be quite attentive again, doesn't he, Kate? I happened to glance out of my window just before dinner yesterday evening and——"

"Yes, that's when he left, Aunt Daisy."

"A little bird's been telling me something about him," Aunt Daisy resumed; and Ames Lanning sighed heavily, though only to himself and his coffee. He'd had many a nip from his mother-in-law's little birds' little bills and he feared that some day when she'd refer to this source of information he'd say or do something that wouldn't be good for poor Mary's heart. "A little bird told me," Mrs. Cunningham repeated. "A little bird that flies all around, 'way uptown and everywhere. It told me Mr. Tuke Speer's in quite a state about somebody and better look out. It told me if he isn't careful he'll get it where the chicken got the axe." This, for Aunt Daisy, was so frolicsome that Mary looked up.

"What ought Tuke to be careful about, Mother?"

"About getting married, Mary. He'd better look out or it'll happen to him and he'll be sorry forever after. The little bird told me he's been spending much too much time with that ex-Mrs. Capper's showy daughter. Murder! Did anybody ever see such awful changes as have taken place in this town? One of Adele Rowan's bridesmaids! I never saw anything so brassy bold as the way that Capper girl came down the aisle—and the newspapers afterwards, you'd have thought those silly photographers couldn't see anybody else. Probably slipped 'em a few of her stepfather's ten-dollar bills. You'd better look after your friend Speer a little, Ames."

"I doubt if he's in much danger."

"Oh, you do?" Mrs. Cunningham's tone was sarcastic. "This little bird told me the Capper girl's got him where he doesn't know if he's upside down or on his feet. That's why I say he'd better look out or she'll marry him."

Mary and Ames were both all too plainly sorry for Kate again. "But no, Mother," Mary said. "When you got home from the wedding you told me, yourself, everybody was saying she's caught the catch of the town, that little Harris Patterson. You told me his mother's worried to death he's so out of his head over Laila Capper. You told me——"

"Maybe I did," Mrs. Cunningham interrupted. "I didn't say he was going to be allowed to marry her, though, did I? His mother's got every cent of the Patterson money, hasn't she? Yes, sir, and money marries money, doesn't it? If that ordinary old Roe's girl grandchild were out of the kindergarten—I hear she's a defective—Molly Patterson would marry her little Harris to her like falling off a log. No, sir; rich boys may play around with the Laila Cappers and even want to marry 'em, but they don't get to. Laila Capper'll find this out, you see if she doesn't; and that's when your friend Tuke Speer'll come in handy, Ames, the poor ninny!"

Ames couldn't accept this with his habitual docility. He was hurt for Kate, angry for his friend Tuke and to some extent revolted, too, by his mother-in-law's coarse handling of Laila Capper who seemed to be a superior sort of girl. With a noticeable abruptness, he rose from half a breakfast, and, for all of his farewell, touched his wife's thin shoulder as he passed her on his eloquent way out of the room. Performed by a son-in-law so long subjugated, the action was an outright rebuke and had a strange effect of harshness disproportionate to its cause. He was late in turning rebel and might better never have become one; for this was September of the prophetic year Nineteen twenty-nine, and Aunt Daisy's time of agony approached.

XVI

AMES LANNING, SUBMISSIVE TO YEARS OF HENPECKING, was by no means so meek in disposition as might appear. He was henpecked not by but through his ailing wife, and always when he dared try for a bit of independence or to reason with his mother-in-law, Mrs. Cunningham had never needed to fall back upon last resorts for the conquest of him. She had only to ask solemnly, as she did whenever she felt it useful, "Ames Lanning, are you deliberately trying to kill your wife?" Mary, sincerely intending nothing, supported this every time, even when she didn't overhear it; she was unable to bear any disturbance of peace. Herself without power to dispute anything, she was sickened by sounds of dissension, faded visibly when she heard them, no matter where justice lay.

Good old Dr. Powls, friend to the family as well as its physician, had long ago placed a rock foundation under Mrs. Cunningham's feet. Dourly grave but inwardly triumphant, she was charmed with him when he told Ames in her presence that Mary positively must at all times be kept cheerful. Thus the mother-in-law had professional authority to back up the fatal question, "Do you wish to kill your wife?" To that she could add, "Don't forget I was there when Dr. Powls told you that if you got Mary agitated or let her worry about anything she might drop dead at your feet and you'd be responsible, Ames Lanning."

Brought up to be chivalrous, he was devoted to his wife out of long habit now, and most tender of her fragility; but he trod the consequent path of failure, knowing irksomely that he did so. The powerful Bortshleff had renewed his offer. Ames, in admiration of the Jovian manner in court, had somewhat assumed it himself during an argument Caldwell, Hardy and Caldwell had allowed him to make, and the imitation, though it lost the case, had pleased Mr. Bortshleff who was present in opposition.

"I like your style, my boy," he said cordially, afterward. "Most of you younger fellows only squeak and scratch; but I see you remember there are such things as forensic force and dignity. Any time, as I told you before, any time you care to come over to our office for a little business talk we'll see what we can do for you."

Ames dared only to thank him. The offices of Caldwell, Hardy and Caldwell, slumbrous, were seldom disturbed by the voices of new clients; old ones died and the firm did little except the dull business of settling estates. Ames felt the dust drifting down upon his professional life, a glum affair for a man just moving into his thirties, conscious of ambition and believing that he had powers. At home he was no more than a part of his mother-in-law's routine to preserve her two worshiped possessions, her daughter and her house.

So thoroughly routined, in fact, had become his own perceptions that he failed to realize to what degree his life was gradually being made more comfortable, and at times even livelier, during the months since Kate Fennigate had set herself to change Aunt Daisy's routine as much as might be. He didn't know, for instance, that his clothes were kept brushed and in repair; though he did indeed comprehend that the intractable Celia was no longer a worry to him but often, on the contrary, a source of actual pleasure. He was aware that he had Kate to thank for this and he tried to make his gratitude known to her, speaking also of another thing he felt he owed to her.

"It's providential for Mary and Celia that you're their cousin," he said. "They happen to be my wife and my child so I benefit, too. For Mary you're as good as a doctor and a nurse combined, and I hope you understand we're both going to appreciate it all the rest of our lives. The change that's come over Celia since you've lived here—well, it's a mystery to me how you did it; but it's happened, thank heaven, and you'll never know what a relief it is. How's anybody ever going to repay you?"

"Well—stand up to Aunt Daisy sometimes. I mean of course when Mary isn't looking."

"I can't, even then," he said, and laughed. "Me stand up to her? No, the best I can do is to leave the room, as I did the other morning when she was gibing at poor Tuke. You're the only person I ever knew who could stand up to her and even you don't get away with it very well unless you keep her from seeing it's what you're doing. Queer how we both let ourselves be so buffaloed. We've both got tempers."

"Have we? I haven't seen many signs of your being furnished that way, Ames."

"Oh, I've got one!" he said ruefully. "As for yours, though, I suppose I'm the only person in the house who's seen it flash. Since then I've been wondering—well, sometimes I've been afraid you'd leave us, Kate. I hope you're not thinking of it."

"No." She was meditative. "I couldn't anyhow, not just now."

"I certainly hope not," he said. "Not for a good while longer, I do hope, speaking in pure selfishness. I'm afraid it involves some sacrifice on your part, because I can't imagine your not preferring to have that job with Mr. Roe and be out on your own. Of course for a while I thought there were going to be compensations for you here because——"

"Compensations for me, Ames? You mean Tuke Speer's living just across the street?"

"No—oh, no!" He was hurriedly emphatic because this was what he'd meant. "No, I only meant I thought conditions might get cheerfuler for you generally, so to speak. I only meant——"

"Never mind, thanks, Ames!" She said it sharply, and, turning back from the front door, whither she'd accompanied him after lunch, walked away quickly.

He stared after the small figure as it went down the hall and then swiftly ascended the stairway. Kate's back, he thought, was graceful but strongly expressive of sudden dislike, and he sighed, feeling that he must always be inept with women because their inwardnesses could never be anything but mysteries to him.

What in the world was the matter with Tuke Speer, Ames wondered for the hundredth time. Here was a girl who'd be a devoted, splendid wife to any man, and Tuke was missing his chance, since it was sadly plain he could have her if he would. Ames didn't think, as Tuke did, that Kate was the sort of girl who'd never be really in love with anybody; Ames's strong impression was that she had profound capacities of this order and that she was bravely suffering because she'd wasted them on Tuke. Laila Capper was an attractive girl, of course, and no doubt a fine person; but Ames understood that the competition there was heavy. Probably Tuke wouldn't win and it would be too bad if he then returned to Kate with nothing better to offer than a heart on the rebound—second choice! Kate might have too much pride to accept it, and, if she did, wouldn't there always be a kind of soreness somewhere? Ames walked down to his office certain that Tuke didn't know what was good for him.

Something that Kate had said a few minutes earlier passed unnoticed, and her haste in ascending the stairway after lingering with Ames at the door wasn't all caused by anger with him. When she'd said that she couldn't leave her aunt's house "just now" the last two words were the significant ones, and when she hurried upstairs it was to attend upon her cousin Mary as a nurse. There'd been a September change in the weather; Mary'd caught a slight cold that didn't stay slight. A crisis in the lives of the occupants of Aunt Daisy's house was upon them, and the end of one of those lives, the frailest one.

On the day after Kate hurried upstairs, Dr. Powls saw Mary three times; and, at four o'clock in the morning of the second day after that, Kate came out of Mary's room to speak to Aunt Daisy, but Aunt Daisy ran down the stairs screaming.

She reached the telephone and used it before she fainted. When Dr. Powls got there he did nothing and only said he hadn't expected Mary's heart to hold out as long as it had.

It was well understood, even by the recurrently sobbing Celia, that Aunt Daisy was the chief personage in the mourning. After her collapse she was inhumanly quiet, wept not at all, spoke almost not at all; yet was so strange that she frightened Celia.

"Isn't Grandmother ever going to sit down again?" she asked Kate, the next day. "I don't like it. She keeps standing up. You can't go into a room in the house that she isn't there, all black and just standing there. She doesn't say anything, she doesn't look at you, she doesn't do anything. Can't you get her to sit down?"

"She will, Celia, after——" Kate paused.

"After Mother's funeral?" Celia sobbed. "I bet she won't, Kate. She acts as if she's never going to sit down again; she'll just be standing up so tall and black all around everywhere the rest of our lives, making us feel we ought to be dead instead of Mother. I can't bear it!"

Kate, too, was daunted by the dark apparition of her aunt, speechless and erect. This was a shock of grief that awed the beholder: Aunt Daisy had evidently believed that her invalid daughter was going to live forever. For the others the fading Mary had been a gentle-spoken, pale picture, a part of their daily lives yet a faint part. The young widower wept and his daughter sobbed; but they could sleep, they could sit—presently they could sit and talk and even smile. Mary had been and now she was not; there was no stabbing emptiness in the house after she'd been borne from it. Before long the fact that there wasn't an acute vacancy became itself a hurt, a guilty one. Again it was Celia who vividly expressed the feeling.

"I'll have more nightmares; I know I will!" the little girl whispered, pushing herself up in her bed. "Don't put out my light yet, Kate. I'm afraid. I mean I'll have true nightmares again, the kind I *really* had. Sit down on the bed close to me, won't you, and talk to me?"

"You mean listen to you," Kate said; but complied.

"No, no. I mean talk to me." Celia clung to her, and continued the whispering. "I'm afraid to talk, myself—anyhow, to speak out; she might hear me. She's so still, herself, it scares me all the time to say anything out loud. She makes me feel wicked, Kate. I bet she does you and Father, too. Doesn't she?"

"Makes your father and me feel wicked, Celia?"

"Yes. Like me. Wicked for not feeling sorrier my mother's dead.

I do feel sorry. I feel terrible about it. I do indeed, Kate. I do, I do!"

"I know, Celia. Of course you do."

"Yes; but now it happened last month I don't remember it all the time, Kate. I keep forgetting it, especially when I'm outdoors or in school, and then when I see Grandmother I know it was wicked to forget. At first she wouldn't look at me; but now she does sometimes and I know she's thinking I'm wicked for ever forgetting it one second. She never will, herself, never, never, never, will she, Kate? Well, we can't stand it, can we? I just know I'm going to have my nightmares again!"

"No, you aren't. I'll sleep on the sofa here to-night if you'd rather."

"Oh, Kate, would you? Then maybe I'd not have to think about Grandmother while I'm getting to sleep."

This was October of that year, the month that brought the second of the only two blows with which life was capable of demolishing Aunt Daisy. Bodily she was so unfortunate as to survive them both; though, even before the second fell upon her, there appeared to be evidence that her mind tottered as a result of the first. Kate was convinced of this; but Ames wasn't.

"No," he said. "She's got the house to fall back on, you see, and it's begun to occupy her again. Only yesterday I saw her rubbing at that terrible old green marble parlor mantelpiece with a dust cloth."

"Yes, so she did, Ames; but she dropped the dust cloth on the floor and didn't know it. She went up to Mary's room and just stood there, the way she does. No, there's something gone, I tell you, and it won't come back. I think you ought to take Celia and find an apartment or a boarding-house somewhere and——"

"What about you? Aren't you ready yet to ask Mr. Roe if he still has that place for you?"

"No. I mean of course I couldn't go just now, couldn't leave her in the state she's in. I'll have to wait till——"

"Then so'll I, won't I?" he asked. "It wouldn't exactly be decent of Celia and me to clear out and leave you here alone with her, would it? No, I suppose we'll all three have to stay—for a while anyhow. You seem to have got Celia quieted down and cheerful again."

"Maybe we can keep her so," Kate said; "but there's one thing that ought to be done right away—a change, I mean. You can do it now, Ames—without hurting anybody."

"Mr. Bortshleff?" He rubbed his forehead, doubtful. "I think he'd be glad to take me, yes, Kate; but—but doesn't it seem—well, a disloyalty?"

"To Mary? No! She had only one reason for not wanting you to do it. That was her fear that it would hurt her mother. Well, that's over because it won't hurt Aunt Daisy now."

"Why won't it?"

"Because it wouldn't seem of any consequence to her. When you're stabbed through the heart, lesser wounds don't signify. What's more, Ames, you could join the Bortshleff firm and have it headlined in the papers to-morrow and I doubt if Aunt Daisy'd know it."

"You're really sure I ought to do it? I admit I hesitate. It rather worries me to think she might——"

"No, no!" Kate was sharply urgent. "You've got to get out of the habit of worrying about such things. It's a long time since you made any important decisions for yourself. You've got to get back to the habit of mind that decides questions and isn't timid with 'em. Don't you see that?"

"Well—I suppose I do. Then you think——"

"I'll tell you what I think," she said with vigor. "I think that when you come home to-morrow evening you'll be able to tell me that you've seen Mr. Bortshleff and notified the Caldwells your services with them terminate at the end of the month. You'll do it?"

"Well, I——"

"Well nothing!" she said sharply. "You've been putting off your future long enough, haven't you? I want to hear you say you'll do it."

He laughed feebly. "Well, if you think so. Yes, I will."

"Atta boy!" Kate Fennigate cried.

XVII

In new york a stockbroker leaped from a window as high above the ground as had flown the wares in which he dealt. The wares did worse than fall; being made of airy vapors, they dispersed themselves—and other brokers jumped. These things were not the causes of the historic long Depression that was to last ten years; they were only surface symptoms betokening men's finally forced perception that Prosperity had been overplayed. The whole country sank, all property lost its rated value and those who believed they'd owned it cursed the stock market, like sailors in a hurricane damning the barometer.

One bereft old woman, however, Marguerite Cunningham, didn't swear at the market; she hadn't understood what its romancings had done to her. Mr. Frank Lucius came to see Ames Lanning in the small room Ames occupied in the Bortshleff suite of offices and there followed a gloomy long talk over the contents of the brief-case Mr. Lucius brought with him.

"Yes, you'll have to take it up with her," the caller said, in conclusion. "Of course I want to be considerate in a time of bereavement; but these matters can't wait forever, you know. I've tried and tried over the telephone to explain to her why they can't and she won't even make an appointment to see me. She seems to be listening and then just says, 'I don't know what you're talking about' and rings off. I'm afraid her daughter's death has almost unseated her. I beg your pardon for mentioning it again; I'm sorry. Well, this thing's gone on and on until I didn't know what to do except put it up to you to make her understand, if you can."

Ames shook his head unhappily. "Yes, I will—if I can."

He went to Kate for help to make her Aunt Daisy understand. "You see, she's considerably worse than just broke," he explained. "Even with the house and everything else thrown in, Beaton and Lucius are going to have to take a loss because it was really they who let her have most of the money. I declare I couldn't have believed it of her if he hadn't shown me the stuff. We don't even know the people we live with day by day and year after year, do we? Who'd have thought that a woman as close as she is and with such a tight grip on everything she owned would have turned gambler in her old age? Of course it was a contagion all over the country with the most unlikely people catching it; but Lucius tells me she began about three years ago. He's really sunk that he didn't advise her not to; but they'd caught the disease, too, by that time. Beaton and Lucius are in a pretty bad hole themselves."

Kate looked frightened. "The house too, you say——"

"Oh, certainly! It's swept away the house and everything, Kate. Talk about secretive! The trouble was, she got the fever, tried a shot or two and found herself winning. Some people can't stop when they're losing; but she's the kind that can't when they're winning. So after winning quite a little she went all out for a big clean-up. I don't suppose she ever dreamed she might lose the house; she didn't know what she was risking, because she'd become convinced that there no longer was any risk. She was like Napoleon up to Eighteen-twelve; she thought everything was just win, win, win."

"But the house!" Kate said. "The *house!*"

"Yes, I've told you. They'll do what they can to spare her, and the simplest way to handle it's just a deed of the property to Beaton and Lucius; but it'll have to be done pretty soon. They think they've got an Armenian rug dealer interested in the house; but he's looking at one or two other places and they don't want to lose him. Of course she'd have to let him come in and look over everything. We ought to talk to her to-night. I mean right now, Kate. Do you think you could see her a few minutes first and prepare her for what I'll have to say?"

"No." Kate glanced upward. They were in the living-room after dinner and sat leaning toward each other, speaking as if they exchanged grave secrets. "If I try to prepare her she'll know what's coming and I don't think she'll listen. We'd better go and find her. Then tell her what you have to as quickly as possible, Ames."

"You don't need to." Aunt Daisy came in through the open doorway and stood before them stiff and still in her black dress, her face apparently emotionless. "You don't need to go and find me; I've heard every word you said."

Kate cried out pityingly. "Oh, Aunt Daisy! Please——"

Aunt Daisy paid no attention to her. "It'll take better men than you and that fool, Frank Lucius, to scare me, Ames Lanning," she said. "He holds securities of mine that more than cover everything he claims I've lost. His chicaneries may strip me of them; but he can't touch my house. Do you dream I was crazy enough to put a mortgage on it? On my *house?*"

Ames tried to begin an explanation. "No, you didn't; but you see it isn't a question of——"

She declined to listen. "This house of mine cost my father over forty-eight thousand dollars to build when labor was cheap and it's increased in value ever since. You couldn't build a house like this now for three times the money—no, not for four times. The lot has a hundred and seventy-one and a half feet frontage on National Avenue, and it's three hundred and three feet deep, back to the alley. I could have sold it two years ago for I won't tell you how much if I'd been willing to see a horrible automobile warehouse and salesroom building take the place of my house. If Frank Lucius claims he can throw me into bankruptcy through his chicaneries I'll sell eighty feet off the side yard and he can grab the money if he's sunk that low. Eighty feet off the side yard would be more than ample to——"

Ames tried to interrupt. "No, I'm dreadfully sorry, but I'm afraid not. Real estate values are probably getting hit harder than almost any others and for some time back there's really been no market at all for——"

"That'll do for you!" Aunt Daisy neither raised her voice nor altered the inscrutable look with which she confronted the troubled Ames. "I've told you I heard your mumblings and I know what you want me to do. I know more than you think I do—for instance that my daughter wasn't cold in her grave before you went over to her

father's enemy. Do you think I'd take advice from an employee of
Oscar J. Bortshleff's? You seem to have changed in quite a number
of curious ways since my daughter died."

"I——" Ames was as hurt as incredulous. "You mustn't say that."

"Mustn't I? What about lunch? After my daughter died you suddenly found out you could afford to lunch downtown. Since she
was taken from me you seem to feel you're entitled to branch out in
a lot of new ways. You seem to have recovered a great deal of
your——"

Kate strove to intervene. "He hasn't! It was I who told him to lunch
downtown. I thought it would be—better. I——"

Mrs. Cunningham continued to address herself to Ames. "You and
Kate Fennigate, my own niece, think my mind went into the grave
with Mary—oh, yes, I know you do!—but perhaps I'm a little too
smart for you yet. You go back and tell your new client, the strictly
honorable Frank Lucius, that I don't recognize you as my attorney,
Mr. Lanning. When I want legal advice I'll go to my own lawyer,
Mr. Joseph Caldwell. He'll be summoned to my house to-morrow to
go into these matters and I expect he may have something to say
that your new legal and banking friends may not relish."

Kate tried again. "Aunt Daisy, Ames knows how terrible this is
for you. He only wants to do everything he can to——"

"So you say." Aunt Daisy turned slowly toward the door. "My
mind may lie buried with Mary as you two believe; but I don't
think anybody is going to get my house away from me. You may be
a little surprised when you hear what Joe Caldwell has to say about
that to-morrow."

. . . She left them and they sank wretchedly into the chairs from
which they'd risen. "It may be a good thing, though," Ames said, after
a time. "When she gets it from Caldwell maybe she'll begin to see.
Well, when she does, what's to be done?"

He meant what was to be done by the four of them, Kate, Celia,
Aunt Daisy and himself. Kate shook her head. "I don't know. She's
beyond me; I didn't think she realized what was going on at all.
What can we do except fall back upon, 'Don't cross bridges till you
come to them'? We'll have to take it step by step."

The talk between Aunt Daisy and her lawyer seemed to be the next step. Kate kept out of the way when he arrived; but later turned eavesdropper so far as she thought respectable. She sat tensely in the gilt "reception room" while Joseph Caldwell talked to Aunt Daisy in the living-room on the other side of closed sliding walnut double doors that let Kate hear the tones of the two voices sometimes, though not the words uttered.

Kate heard her aunt speaking steadily and calmly as in opening explanations; then, after apologetic coughing, the lawyer's voice seemed to be dissenting persuasively. He talked on and was interrupted only four or five times, though he spoke for almost an hour. The interruptions were quiet, sounded like questionings; and Kate, who'd expected to hear vehemence, outcries of protest, was dumfounded. She couldn't believe her ears when she heard the lawyer in the hall, departing, and Aunt Daisy's footsteps on the stairway, ascending. Kate stopped Caldwell at the front door and spoke to him in a hushed voice.

"You didn't tell her? I mean you didn't go into the——"

"Oh, yes, certainly," he said, keeping his voice down, too. "She's perfectly reasonable. I own I didn't expect it. She's a surprising woman, very. I've known her to get ten times as excited when I've had to persuade her not to sue the city over an assessment for street paving. She took this as quietly as you please; I couldn't see any change in her expression—not even when I said we'd better get things done as soon as possible. She told me she was ready to affix her signatures to-morrow or any time I'd bring a notary. She only asked that Frank Lucius shouldn't be present. Evidently she never wants to see him again." Caldwell chuckled just audibly. "That's understandable. Poor old Frank, though, I expect it's mutual. I'll try to get around for the signatures by Friday, Miss Fennigate. Fine day!"

Kate ran upstairs and found that Aunt Daisy was already locked in her own room. "Go away, please!" was the only answer, a quiet one, to knocking. Later the colored cook, Morella, was admitted with a tray, Aunt Daisy having stipulated through the closed door that Morella, not Kate, should bring it. Neither Kate nor Ames saw Aunt Daisy again until Joseph Caldwell arrived with a notary on Friday morning. Aunt Daisy came downstairs, didn't examine the papers they put before her on the library desk, and meekly wrote "Marguerite Cunningham" in a neat hand wherever Ames or Caldwell indicated that her signature was necessary.

"Is that all?" she asked, as meekly, when Caldwell began to fold up the papers; and, being assured, more in a doctor's voice than a lawyer's, that it was, she rose stiffly from the desk and returned to her room.

At the foot of the stairs that evening, just before Celia's bedtime, the little girl was excitedly describing to Kate a schoolroom episode. Ames stood in the living-room doorway listening amusedly as Celia's voice grew loud. "And then, Kate and Father, what do you think that awful boy said to the teacher? He told her—he actually did—and the whole schoolroom was prackly deafening it was in such a crommotion—that terrible Georgie Cooke simply bellowed, 'I'm not any dumber than you are, yourself, and you better look out because my Uncle Elmer's a member of the School Board!' He did, Kate, and he shouted at her, 'If you dare to call me dumb again'—— Oh!"

Celia stopped abruptly. Aunt Daisy was upon the dark stairway landing above their heads. Celia gripped Kate's wrist and all stood rigid.

Aunt Daisy said, "Yes, I see. I suppose you three will leave me now." Then she turned and disappeared upward into shadow.

At the moment they had no answer; but when Celia was in bed Kate went to the locked door in the upper hall and called through it, "Aunt Daisy? Won't you let me come in to talk a little while?"

"No."

"I just wanted to say," Kate said, "you mustn't believe it. I'm not going to leave you, Aunt Daisy. You mustn't think——"

"Please go away."

Kate didn't go at once. Head bowed, hands hard against cheeks, she stood in the dim hallway thinking strickenly of the mortal hurt enclosed by the shut door and of her own kinship with the sufferer. Aunt Daisy had been a determined and dominating woman; and, in an anguish of sympathy for the aunt, the niece felt herself to be of the same family stock. She, too, was determined and dominating. Now

Aunt Daisy was virtually dead because she'd forever lost what she had made the whole fabric of her life and it was through this dreadful liquidation that Kate had her own way. She couldn't have had it otherwise; but she had it. Ames Lanning had made the change she pressed upon him, and already, as the beaten Aunt Daisy had wanly perceived, there were symptoms of change in the man himself. His voice even at home was firmer, his step more decisive, his manner a little more authoritative. So now as something of new life seemed aglow, however faintly thus far seen by the three who were to possess it, the fourth accepted her compelled obliteration, became a shadow and passed from the scene with the passing of her generation.

Kate's voice broke as she spoke pleadingly, "Aunt Daisy, won't you please, please——"

"No. Don't stand at my door. Be kind enough to go away."

XVIII

THERE WAS A DAY OF HEAVY RAIN, CHOSEN SHREWDLY BY the Armenian rug merchant for his view of what had been Aunt Daisy's house. "When I go to buy something or maybe lease," he explained to Kate, "it's useful it looks as worse as can happen to it." He laughed agreeably, let his dark eyes dwell upon her with a tender favor. "It's like as if I'm going to be married and first see the lady dressed like you with apron on and clothes not so new maybe. Then if she shows up still looking good in spite from what she looks like, I get more confidence I'm going to like her so much I'm going ahead. You see, Miss?"

"Nothing could be clearer. Will you start with the cellar?"

"Attic first, please," he said. "Cellars last, so if I become tickled by nice rooms between I'm going to feel so discouraged by old cellars on such a dark early winter wet day the last thing before I go out, then the face I show Mr. Frank Lucius it's full of sincerity when I start beating him down he wishes to ask from me ten times too much."

She took him up to the attic where the rain was noisy above them and water found its way, here and there, to pans and buckets beneath the leaks. "Oh oh!" he said reproachfully and glanced at a ladder slanted up to a trap-door overhead. "By rights I should climb to look at your naughty roof from on top, Miss. No, I won't be so wet, I'll just be more discouraged. How many leaks? I'll count." He began to walk about. "One, two, three, four. Oh oh, here is another—five—and over there——"

Kate stopped him. "Please don't go there. It's just above my aunt's room. She's ill and I hope she's asleep. The sound of footsteps over——"

"Yes, yes, I understand; it's Mrs. Cunningham, no? They inform' me she's the owner previous and stays maybe one two weeks more, not disturb her. Oh, what a roof!" He went to one of the low half-moon-shaped windows and looked down. "These old houses, how high they builded them! Tall, tall ceilings, long, long staircases where you lose your breath and you wear out your back climbing up and down. It's very bad, Miss. Look, what's this?" He pointed with his shoe at some fragments of slate upon the floor. "The roof begins to fall into the attic?"

"No, not yet. Mr. Lanning tried to make some repairs. Have you seen enough of the attic?"

"Oh, too much. Drip, drip, drip, it's terrible. Oh, what old broken furniture, broken looking-glasses, trunks, trunks, trunks, old boxes, boxes, boxes! When you move out, Miss, how can it ever be done? Oh, my, lead me other places, please!"

They descended to the second floor, and Kate began to show him the bedrooms. "When we pass my aunt's door please walk on tiptoe," she said; but when they came to that door she was surprised to find it ajar. She stepped within the room and before she could stop him the rug merchant followed her.

"Everything clumsy old-fashioned," he said. "Lady not here. Not so sick, no?"

The house, never bright within on a sunny day, was dusky twilight
From low clouds the rain ran heavily down the long and narrow
windows. Kate had thought to keep from Aunt Daisy any knowledge
of the Armenian's visit, but now suspected that Aunt Daisy knew.
As the tour continued a presence unseen and walking soundlessly
seemed to follow from room to room, listening spectrally. Kate hurried when she could and got Mr. Billi Berriam (he gave her his card)
downstairs as soon as possible. He complained of the windows in
the "reception room" and the front parlor.

"Too long. Too high. Too thin," he said. "If I put my most beautiful
rugs close to these windows so the people on the street and sidewalk
should see, how can they? Look, Miss, even when the sun shines who
sees my rugs through such windows? I will got to tear out front walls
to make display windows. Big thick brick walls, it's expensive, it's
terrible! Now, the cellar. I am sure I am feeling bad enough already;
but the cellar too, please, Miss."

He couldn't have asked for more despondency than the cellar
brought him, and, at the end of his inspection in the room beneath the
kitchen, he moaned continuously. "Oh, my, my such a place! How can
I make myself a sales talk that will sell myself such a house? My, my,
that furnace you showed me, Miss! Cellar with stone walls, yes; but
sweating water and spots wetness on the floor, oh, my! Oh, Miss, no,
I couldn't."

Kate wasn't listening to him. Overhead in the kitchen there seemed
to be something like commotion; she thought Morella protested
spiritedly and that Aunt Daisy responded in anger. "Losing another
cook?" Kate wondered sadly, then was more practical. What did it
matter if the cook went when the house was going too? "I beg your
pardon, Mr. Berriam, I didn't hear what you said."

"No. Peoples quarrel upstairs, Miss, so maybe you couldn't. Now
they stopped I'm telling you, What's the use? I seen it all, thank you
for your politeness, but such a house I couldn't. I got my sister's
family to take care of, they could sleep in the bedrooms, yes; but what
a talk my nephew gives me he's expected to help in the shop and at
the same time work such a furnace. No, and if I must cut display

windows for those two front rooms upstairs both sides the middle
hall——"

"Listen, please!" Kate said.

"Miss Kate! Miss Kate! Miss Kate!" Morella's voice was heard from
above.

Kate stepped out into the basement hallway. "Yes, Morella?"

The cook stood in the open doorway at the head of the cellar stairs.
"Miss Kate, please come; I think you better. Your aunt gone up to
mend the roof, I couldn' stop her."

"What!" Kate was already ascending.

"Yes'm. She had couple pieces slate in her hand and come in my
kitchen fer hammer'n nails on that cupboard shelf and tuk 'em. I tell
her nobody can't mend slate roof that-a-way, tell me *she* can. I say
she catch pneumonia, she say don't talk to her. I hollered at her all
the way through the front hall, can't stop her; she gone up there.
Miss Kate, she oughtn' never be allowed out on that slippery roof in
all this rain and wind and—— Yes'm, you go stop her!"

Afterward Kate realized that she'd known she couldn't stop Aunt
Daisy. Out of breath with the rush through hallways and up three
flights of stairs, Kate reached the top of the third and had seen the
rain beat through the open trap above her before she heard faintly
Morella's loud scream from far below. In the dining-room Morella
waved open brown hands on high, jumped, prayed and swayed.

"Something black!" she babbled at Mr. Berriam. "Something like a
big black bird flew down pas' the window! Saviour save me! I heard
it hit the ground! Oh, my Saviour! I ain't go' look out that window;
no, Saviour, I can't! Man, you go see whut layin' on the ground outside that window! Go, man, go!"

So it befell that Mr. Berriam, the rug merchant, carried Aunt Daisy
into her house the last time she ever entered it. Interested, he stayed
until after both Dr. Powls and Ames Lanning had arrived, and he had
a final talk with Morella in the kitchen. Morella was calmer but
maintained that the fall was not an accident. Mr. Berriam held that
it was.

"Listen, Miss," he begged. "Haven't I got any rights to speak? That
roof's in such a condition anybody could get scared the water will

come through ceilings enough to spoil their rugs. The son-in-law he says himself she tried on the roof with slate before, so to-day she's desperate with all the water, she goes again and it's slippery up there and the wind's blowing and——"

"Don't tell me, man!" Morella was certain. "Look all these pieces in the paper! People th'ow themselves off the high places, one catch it from another; they get the jumpin'-off fever. You the very person put it in her head to do it."

"Me? Miss, I never saw the lady in my life till I went out to bring her in!"

"She seen *you*, though, man. They try to fix it she don't know you're comin'. She fool 'em! She hear you trompin' round and she know it's you. She only make believe she go' fix that roof. She gone up there to do whut she done!"

"Please, Miss!" Mr. Berriam besought her. "Never in my life was more unjustice! If she does such a thing she does it so she won't be alive, won't she? You can't say I'm responsible. She's alive, ain't she, the doctor says so, please answer?"

The argument continued, and it prevailed elsewhere, though short items in the city's newspapers mentioned that Mrs. Marguerite Cunningham, an old resident and formerly well-known, had been seriously injured by an accidental fall at her premises, 1072 National Avenue. Ames Lanning held this view, urging it upon Kate.

"Why not see it so?" he asked. "That passion for the house itself—yes, even though she knew it wasn't legally hers any longer, she'd still have that lifelong urgency, wouldn't she? She'd still want to keep the place patched up just the same. A mother might let her child be adopted; but if he scratched his face she'd run with a lotion for the scratch. It was a crazy thing to do on such a day; but we both know that she hadn't been herself for a good while. Perhaps, as you believe, she heard you and that man walking about the house and maybe she did follow you and listen. That wouldn't mean she didn't get the idea of going up there to stop the leaks if she could. I don't see why you insist——"

"I don't," Kate said. "I just know. Aunt Daisy was finished and what she did was her recognition of it. I think she heard some of the things Mr. Berriam was saying and she thought the house must be dead, too, since it could be so insulted." Kate tried not to sob. "She and the house were both gone out of life; she didn't see why her poor old body should survive."

"But it does," Ames pointed out, with a response like Mr. Berriam's to Morella. "She wouldn't have taken a way that could fail. She'd have done something else. The answer to your morbidness is that she's still alive."

Kate didn't think this the answer; but he was unhappily right about Aunt Daisy's still being alive. She lay month after month in her old Eastlake bed upstairs. After her fall she never again spoke intelligibly. No one knew what she thought.

XIX

ALTHOUGH IT IS TRUE THAT NOTHING EXCEPT CHANGE IS permanent, the changes seem to move at such variable gaits that sometimes their motion isn't perceptible to us and we believe ourselves to be stabilized, living in a static world. After the great jolt that ends such a delusion we look back, and, always pressing for lingual definitions, say that we were living in an epoch. For some reason this seems to satisfy us, even though we cannot fail to perceive that the epoch was itself anything but static—on the contrary, a rapid slide toward the jolt. During the hours, days or years of jolt we know all too well that we're in extremities of motion and often desolately wonder where we shall come down when the explosion that hoisted us shall have expended its force.

The dispersive concussions of Nineteen twenty-nine were accelerated through the year Nineteen-thirty; Kate Fennigate, unusually steady-headed for her age, twenty-two, wasn't at all sure where she or anybody else was to come down—though she made an exception of old Mr. Henry L. Roe. She spoke of this to her friend Tuke Speer as they sat again in the faded library under Uncle John Cunningham's portrait, where Tuke hadn't been for a long time.

"He's an unbeatable old marvel!" she said. "Went ahead and finished his Equitable Trust Company building, nineteen stories, according to original plans just as if nothing were happening. Everybody said it would be a case of Roe's Folly and the whole building'd stand vacant; but look at it! Uses the four top floors for the headquarter offices of Roe Metal Products and of course the ground floor and second and third for the Trust Company. Well, there are about six floors of doctors and surgeons and specialists because he got the Wilson X-ray people to bring their laboratories here, just over 'em. Quite a lot of the rest of the building is rented, too—it'll pay its taxes. But you'll see it to-morrow."

"Yes, we're putting our conclusions before the Old Man in the morning." Tuke had been away five months, engaged in work for Roe Metal Products. "Of course I've been only a junior technical member of the squad he sent East; but I've had quite a hand in drawing up our report. Our recommendations are going to be in line with the policy he followed in putting up that building. They're to the effect that Metal Products is strong enough to organize an Eastern Division right now, Depression or no Depression. Everybody else is retrenching, nobody's buying anything; but Roe makes some gadgets that save people money and we've found him some empty factories that he can buy for nothing and re-vamp. Talk about economic revolution—our report favors expansion on a falling market. How do you think he'll take it?"

"All right, Tuke, if your squad keeps reminding him that it's his own idea. I'll put in a word for you with him if I ever get the chance."

"You're that thick with him, are you?" Tuke laughed.

"You'd be surprised! Anyhow since you went East he's put me in his own office, and every now and then he asks me questions you'd never believe. That doesn't mean I quite dare to thrust my opinions upon him."

"No," Tuke said. "You mean you don't thrust 'em on him yet. Up to now they've probably been shown to Mr. Roe in much the same way your opinions about my private affairs have been shown to me. You don't suppose I've ever been really in the dark about your opinion of Laila Capper, do you? Or of what you think of me for being in love with her?"

Kate looked down at her hands, small and quiet upon her lap. "You say 'being' in love with her, Tuke. Then your absence hasn't——"

"I didn't write a single word to her. The night before I left I told her I wouldn't, I never wanted to hear of or from her again. She wrote me four letters I didn't answer. Well, I got off the train at five o'clock this afternoon and didn't call her up; instead I went to the club. By the way, I was pleased to see Ames there. I had a drink with him and Sam Augren in a corner and he told me you were well and enjoying your work. Said I'd find you here in the old house if I looked in any time after your office hours."

"He did? Ames suggested your coming to see me?"

"Naturally I'd have come pretty soon anyhow," Tuke said. "I'd certainly want to say hello, wouldn't I? Ames didn't say how you still happen to be here. When I went East the place had already been on the market four or five months, hadn't it?—everything to be sold and——"

"It still is," Kate informed him. "Everything still is to be sold or leased. Unfortunately for Mr. Beaton and Mr. Lucius they've never had but the one really serious 'prospect'—that rug dealer who was here the day of my aunt's accident and didn't come back. Nothing's changed since you left: we're still here, at Mr. Lucius's request and a nominal monthly rent—just to have the place looking as if it were 'a little kept up,' he says. Our agreement to show 'prospects' over the house if any turn up hasn't burdened us much."

"'Our'? 'Us'?" Tuke asked, and for a moment looked as if a new thought about her began to puzzle him. "You and Ames?"

She caught his look but didn't show that she understood it. "Oh, there are other people here, of course. There's the cook and Mrs. Ferry—Mrs. Ferry's the woman who looks after my aunt—and except in school hours there's Celia, too. Celia's become quite a responsible person since she's been at Miss Carroll's, you know." Kate's voice changed a little, as it always did when she mentioned Miss Carroll's School; but Tuke didn't notice this wistful slight alteration. Kate hadn't presented Celia at the school; she'd arranged for Martha Gilpin to do that. "My aunt sleeps, or seems to, most of the time, Tuke; so when the cook's out and Celia's in school Mrs. Ferry's usually available."

Kate continued to speak casually of these domestic arrangements but omitted some that were more intimate. She had tried to persuade Ames to move to an apartment with Celia—yet was never to be sure that she'd tried as hard as she could. A surreptitious remorse sometimes beset her and she nagged herself for not having got them out of the gloom of the house that still contained the living-dead Aunt Daisy in the room where Cousin Roberta, when she came, only whispered with Kate or Mrs. Ferry. A consciousness of that room pervaded every part of the house; Kate pressed this upon Ames as a reason for taking Celia out of it. He said no, he and his daughter were more in duty bound to see it through than a niece was; and Kate, yielding guiltily she feared, took up financial questions with him. She paid half the "nominal rent", also everything for Aunt Daisy, including Mrs. Ferry, and half of the monthly bills. Otherwise Ames couldn't have sent Celia to Miss Carroll's and joined the Carlyle Club, necessities upon which Kate insisted. Mr. Roe had been liberal; but Kate still had to step lightly to save the soles of her shoes.

As she went on talking, telling Tuke nothing of these matters but becoming uncharacteristically voluble upon others, his new thought of her reappeared in his expression. It became one of surprised curiosity. "I think I get the picture," he said finally. "In the evenings after you've spelled Mrs. Ferry you go over Celia's school work with her; then if Ames is at home you and he get out the chess board. You've got him started going out again, though, quite a little, I seem to see—the club or now and then a party with his married crowd. You don't go with him to the parties?"

"Why, no, of course not; there's too much to do here."

"Yes, I suppose so." Tuke looked reflective. "Your account of things

--really almost entirely about him—well, I wonder if you realize, your-self, Kate, what a domestic scene you paint."

"What?"

"You don't know it?"

"No!" she exclaimed, and her angry blush was deep. "What's 'domestic' about my sticking to a paralyzed aunt, the nearest relative I have—or about Ames and Celia's feeling they couldn't decently abandon her, either? Celia's only a child and a nervous one; but she's at least able to think of such things and want to do her share. She's——"

"Yes, I'm sure she is." Tuke was amiably amused. "Kate, you seem rather flustered. In fact, I don't recall seeing you more so. Of course you know I'd never be intrusive in your——"

"You may, though!" Kate had her poise again. "You may be as intrusive in my private affairs as you like, because I haven't any. Let's get to something more exciting. I mean *your* private affairs, Tuke. You say you didn't call Laila up this afternoon but went to the club instead. It's ten o'clock now and you got here about nine. You stayed all that time at the club—four hours?"

He laughed, seeing how keenly her eyes were fixed upon him. "You should have been a criminal lawyer. You think I've gone back on everything I swore to myself, do you? You think I've seen Laila?"

"Of course."

"You've got me," he admitted, smilingly rueful. "You're too much for me. I didn't call her up; but she called me at the club. She must have had scouts out because she knew I'd got back this afternoon. I haven't a chance on earth, Kate; I couldn't get out there fast enough. Gave me just one look and I made it all up with her. Everything's angelic again and I'm rolling in silly bliss. No Patterson boy, no any-body. Nobody but me. That is, of course there are some old stand-bys, and Bill Jones grabbed her after dinner for something she'd promised and couldn't get out of. Dinner itself strictly family—just her mother and stepfather and Laila and me. Mr. and Mrs. Barnes didn't give me their blessing in so many words; but they had a melancholy air of sanction of me. Laila laughed about that when we were alone after-ward before Bill came."

"Did she?" Kate asked. "About their melancholy sanction of you?"

"Yes. She can be pretty fascinatingly humorous sometimes. She said they reminded her of a kind old couple who were going to the poorhouse and couldn't take their pet canary with 'em but thought they'd found it a fairly good home—not what they'd hoped for the poor little bird but anyhow somebody who'd do his best to buy enough birdseed. Not laughing, Kate? You'd heard Mr. A. Villrid Barnes got badly caught in the big collapse, hadn't you?"

"Yes, Tuke. Looking over the town one doesn't ask who's gone under: one asks who hasn't. I've wondered what Mr. Barnes'd do. I even wondered if——" She paused.

It was Tuke's turn to be shrewd. "You even wondered if Laila'd go to work?"

"Well, almost. I mean I almost wondered that; but not quite."

"No." He spoke earnestly. "She was never meant for it. She was just meant to be beautiful, Kate—beautiful and worshiped. Some things are created to live on high. The Acropolis oughtn't to be turned into a factory, ought it? There I go, making you think again that I'm a fantastic ass. To get down to earth, I don't mind telling you I think it's about settled. Her flashy old stepfather—I oughtn't to call him flashy any more because the poor berry's down on his luck and looks it—but anyhow, he mentioned that he thought he had an opening on the coast, Seattle or somewhere, and he and Mrs. Barnes are talking of moving out there. Laila told me she couldn't bear the idea and absolutely wouldn't. She hasn't promised in so many words; but I think, Kate—I really do believe so this time—I think she's going to stay here—with me. Unless I'm the worst fooled man alive, my going away really did some good. Well, being pretty sure of your true opinion, I suppose if I'm able to drag her into a Justice of the Peace's office one day before long I'll have your condolences. Will I?"

"No, Tuke, I'll keep those for myself. Of course I pretty well lost you long ago when she first laid hands on you; but after you're married I shouldn't expect——"

"Don't jump so far," he said, smiling. "Married? With Laila, a man couldn't entirely believe that till the deed were done. It does begin to look like it, though, Kate. Well, I've hoped that maybe it wouldn't interfere with you and me—that maybe I'd even see more of you than I have during all these fracases and make-ups I've had with her. Laila as a married woman would be an awful lot improved by your influence, Kate. No, don't stare; she would. I've thought maybe you and she could be as thick as you used to be. I've hoped so. She talks a lot about you, you know. She was asking me all about you to-night. I——" Tuke hesitated timidly. "I told her I wished you and she saw more of each other nowadays. Could you—could you stand it, Kate?"

His earnestness and that timid hope of his were touching; Kate was easily reached that way. She told him she could stand anything for him.

Deeply pleased, he showed great feeling; and, in these moments of emotional friendship, neither of them realized the extent of what they were implying about Laila Capper.

XX

It was apparently something like a new Laila who came to please the most constant of her lovers by renewing an old intimacy. At the top of her beauty and in the hour of its compelling radiant full bloom she seemed anxious to be ingratiating. She'd simplified herself and announced to Kate that she'd discarded her affectations; she had the grace to laugh at them.

"Oh, yes, I'm onto myself these days!" she said. "Tuke's tough medicine to swallow. Every time he thinks I'm putting on side, dropping my R's and all that, he burlesques it, gives me a horrible imitation of myself. I can hardly stand him most of the time; but anyhow I'm through being anything but natural. Guess I've been going through sort of a raw period; but I'm not the only girl that ever caught it. He's always talking about you and it makes me sick; but he might be right at that, old girl. Looking back over my life, I've often thought you're the only real friend I ever had. Mom's all right; but she can be a hellion to me too when she feels like it, you know."

"I've had the idea she was always jolly with you, Laila."

"So? You ought to've seen her a few times when she'd get jealous of me about her old Barnesy! When he gave me that car—whooee! Anyhow, though, Kate, I think Tuke's correct about you, and I'm pretty crazy about him right now. I don't know if you still like me as much as you did; but I'd be glad if you do. I think he kind of hopes we'll make it a foursome."

Kate didn't immediately grasp this. "A what?"

Laila's tone became cozy. "Well, you see, Tuke's so devoted to Ames Lanning, and you and I used to be such good friends, too, so if we were that way again—why, I think Tuke feels it would be pretty nice all round. You know what I mean: bridge and golf and little parties like all four dining at restaurants together sometimes, and all that."

"It's Tuke's idea, Laila?"

"Well, of course he didn't put it just exactly that way, Kate; but——"

"He knows I couldn't," Kate said. "I'm at the office all day and the rest of the time I can't go out anywhere, particularly not in the evenings."

"Just on account of your aunt's condition?" Laila looked arch for a moment; but let the look be the extent of her badinage. "Well, of course that isn't going to last forever," she added. "Listen, does she just lie there all this time? Somebody told me she couldn't speak and couldn't move, except one hand. Does she—does she recognize anybody? You, for instance?"

"I'm not sure, Laila. She tries to speak sometimes, a little—and I'm afraid she thinks I'm Mary."

"Golly, Kate! Well, cheerio! We'll hope Tuke'll get his way about the foursome before so very long, and in the meantime I think you're the same dear little thing you always were and aren't going to mind my giving you a big rush to please him and improve my character— on his account!" She laughed and took Kate's hand affectionately. "Okay, girlie?"

Laila, anomalous in such a scene, was like a lighted candelabrum of crystal and silver.

She was gay and easy, though at times a hint of her previous girlish elegance might have been detected in a slightly blurred R or broadened A in a wrong spot—she said "ond" for "and" once or twice. She recalled to Ames that they'd once bumped each other at a Carroll School dance, said she'd been "quite in despair for weeks afterward" because he'd frowned at her so fiercely during the bump. Then, to his evident pleasure and amusement, she prolonged her insistence that the frown had "completely withered" her.

"Oh, yes, you can't imagine! You were one of the 'older men', you see. No one knows the depth of a schoolchild's agonies over a blow like that. You'll have to be terribly nice to me, Mr. Ames Lanning, if you expect to make up for it; but even at that I doubt if you could ever quite wipe it out."

Celia, fascinated, seldom took her gaze from the guest, and Ames was roused to be more jovially communicative than usual. The large-eyed Celia mentioned this.

"I guess it's a good thing we're entertaining some company at last, Father," she said. "I haven't heard you laugh and talk as much as this since practically I was a little girl. It makes you look handsomer, too."

"Well, well!" he responded. "If it does all that I'd better keep it up."

"You needn't bother." Celia remained grave. "You're plenty good enough looking—for a man anyhow. Wouldn't you think so, Miss Capper?"

The others laughed accommodatingly, and Laila, without looking at Ames, answered in a voice just perceptibly shaded by a warmed significance, "Yes. I always have."

When they left the table Kate went to do the telephoning, prompted by Laila. Tuke consented to spare a few minutes before going forth for the evening's wooing; but Kate didn't go back to the living-room then. It was time to help Mrs. Ferry feed Aunt Daisy.

When that was done Mrs. Ferry took the tray away, Kate sat beside the still figure on the bed, and for an hour read passages from the New Testament and from the Psalms of David. This was routine. A translation of mumblings and of gesturings with the one movable hand had seemed to indicate that it was the invalid's nightly desire. Celia was shouting from downstairs, calling Kate imperiously, before Mrs. Ferry came back to relieve her.

Celia, alone in the living-room, was reproachful. "You've been almost two hours to-night! What's worse, you had visitors—and if you ask me I'd call it pretty rude. I don't care about that Miss Capper, though I love to watch her; but Mr. Tuke Speer's awfully nice and I heard you myself asking him over on the telephone and when you weren't in here he didn't like it a bit himself. I could see he didn't."

"Where are they, Celia? Where's your father?"

"Gone. What do you expect?" Celia said. "Think people are going to just sit around forever? Oh, I know you have to look after Grandmother every evening; but not as long as this! Mr. Tuke Speer didn't like it at all, I can tell you!"

"How do you know, Celia?"

"From his face," the observant girl replied. "First he seemed right surprised and pleased, because that Miss Capper made us let her go to the door and let him in. So then they sat around a while and she and Father did practically all the talking and she was laughing and moving her arms and feet and telling Mr. Tuke Speer how the first time she ever saw Father she bumped him at a dance and he hated her for it—and all that about how Father'd haf to be nice to her all over again. Then after a while she said it looked as if you were *never* going to get downstairs again, there was such a splendid movie, all about a triangle in India, at the Monument Theatre, so why didn't they dash off to it, her car would hold three and they just had time to get in for the second show, I could tell you goodnight for them and say they *did* wish you were going too; so then they——"

"Wait! Take a breath, Celia?"

"Good heavens, I do!" Celia said. "I would have offered to go up and try to get you out; but I remembered nobody's ever supposed to go disturbing Grandmother's room; so after they'd gone I sat around with these darned French verbs as long as I could stand it until I just couldn't help letting out a kind of a chirp for you. I tried to make it soft so you'd hear it but maybe Grandmother wouldn't; but maybe it got up a little bit loud before I heard you coming out and quit. You ready to go after these irregular verbs with me at last?"

Kate was ready, though absently. She heard the lessons; and afterward, when she'd got Celia to bed, went again to her aunt's room, whispered a while with Mrs. Ferry, then both came out, closing the door for the night. Kate went down to the living-room, sewed and waited. The movie must have been a long one, she thought at midnight, when she heard Ames's key in the latch of the front door.

"Hello! Hello!" he said, smiling and bright-eyed as he came from the hall. "Still up? I suppose some ladies never do finish mending their stockings, though. Wish you'd been with us. I don't care a lot about movies usually; but this was one I'd be willing to see all over again. Wonderful pictures of tropical jungle and of English life in the Indian cities. Romantic of course; but a little of that now and then's not so bad. Really it's worth seeing; I hope you'll find a chance to go before they put on something else. You ought to get out a great deal more than you do, Kate."

"Ought I? She brought you and Tuke home, did she, Ames?"

"No." He sat down genially, looking talkative. "I drove out to her house with her and came back on the street-car. She'd have had to put her car away alone in the garage behind the house, I discovered, and I thought she'd perhaps better not do that all by herself so late. She didn't want to let me; but I insisted."

"Yes, of course." Kate seemed preoccupied with her sewing. "Then altogether you had a pleasant evening, did you?"

"Yes, very," he said. "Really very." From the drawer of the table beside him he took a briar pipe, smiled upon it affably, filled and lighted it. "You know, I think I've rather been inclined to under-rate this attractive friend of yours, Kate. For instance, I like her not pretending to be an intellectual type. She seems to have no pretenses at all, just to be what she is—a frank, gay, open-hearted girl and of course pretty overwhelmingly good to look at. In that line she strikes me as——" He regarded his pipe admiringly. "In fact, wouldn't you say, Kate, that she's just about the handsomest girl you've ever seen?"

"Yes, I would."

"Yes," he said. "Another thing, Kate: Don't you like that way she has of looking you straight in the eye suddenly and then looking down so you can tell she's really thinking about what you've been saying? Yes, there's something really stimulating about her. You feel she'd always be a truly good friend and a good sport into the bargain, too. Oh, yes, and another thing, Kate: I think I had quite a wrong impression about her and Tuke."

"What wrong impression, Ames?"

"I'm afraid I thought she was playing him." Kate glanced up then and saw that he was looking at her with smiling benevolence, the expression of a kind well-wisher about to impart good news. "It shows how mistaken anyone can be who judges from distant appearances," he went on. "This closer view of those two to-night rather changed my mind about both of 'em. In the first place, I'm satisfied there's nothing like an engagement between them, Kate. In fact, on our drive home she as much as told me there isn't. She said she had real fondness and affection for Tuke and was getting worried about him because he's so morbid sometimes. She said she thought he ought to marry some nice girl who'd be wholly devoted to him and keep him cheered up so he wouldn't get these morbid spells of his."

"Yes? When does he have them, Ames?"

"Well, to-night for instance," Ames said. "I haven't thought of Tuke as morbid, myself; but of course women see things that men don't. I did notice, though, that he got a bit testy and frowning even before we went off to the movie. He——" Ames hesitated; then his kindness prevailed over caution. "You're always pretty jumpy over my intrusions with this subject, Kate; but I must say it struck me I saw a pretty good reason for his being almost openly ill-tempered. You never came down, you see."

"No; so I didn't." Kate gave him a look as ill-tempered as any that either he or Laila'd had from Tuke Speer in the darkness of the movie theatre. "I see what you mean. You and she have decided that Tuke has morbid spells, and your own interpretation is that he had one to-night because he missed seeing me. That was morbid of him, was it?"

Ames, confused, made an appeasing gesture. "Why, I only thought——"

"Yes, of course you did," she said. "What else morbid did Tuke do after his crossness because I wasn't downstairs? You didn't both take Laila home, I've gathered. What happened to him?"

"Tuke? He didn't like the movie," Ames explained, in good faith so plain that in all the world, Kate thought, no other except this inexperienced young widower could be capable of it.

"Why didn't he like it?"

"Oh, he said he was sick of triangles in the tropics or something. Said he already had one indigestion and the picture gave him another, he couldn't stand it. He went home before it was more than half over."

"But you and Laila liked it and stayed?"

"Yes. Tuke was all wrong to go, because the best part of it came after he left. It got more and more interesting all the way to the end."

Kate put away her needle and gathered the mended stockings into her work-basket. "Yes, it would. Are you playing golf with Laila next Sunday, Ames?"

"No. Why?" he asked, surprised; then added cheerfully, "I imagine we'll see her to-morrow, though. Just before she went into the house she told me she was having a dreadful row with her parents because they're moving out to the west coast before long and she won't go with them. She said you were her only refuge from table arguments, so not to be surprised if she invited herself to dinner here again. She said several times that you were her only refuge, Kate, and, though she laughed, I'm sure she meant it." He beamed upon Kate fondly. "Men are always pulling the stale old cracks about female friendships; but I think it's pretty pleasant when two girls feel this way about each other."

Kate's response was merely, "You'd better go to bed, Ames." Her voice was somewhat muffled; he caught from it no ulterior significance.

XXI

OTHER GIRLS SAID OF LAILA CAPPER THAT HER WORK WAS
always fast on the follow-up, but that for a time nobody could tell
whether she was just briefly amusing herself with some poor dumb
boob or meant to pamper herself with a heavy affair. Exquisite in a
different type of evening dress each time, Laila invited herself to dine
with Ames, Kate and Celia again that week, twice; but, after that,
seemed to feel no need of so much exertion or of continuing her
"rush" of Kate Fennigate.

Ames, cheerfuler than for years, as Celia often observed, began
to "change" for the evening meal. When his dinner coat wasn't worn
at the dinner table Kate and Celia understood that he would remain
at home; but this was seldom. His high spirits were evident in his
face and voice all the time, though most emphatically when he was
going out. "I ought to've stayed at the office and dined on a sandwich,"
he informed Kate on one of these livelier occasions, just before he left
the house. "The firm's got behind on a long case and Oscar J. a little
more than hinted that night work was needed from all of us, so of
course I ought to be down there right now using up my eyes to
please him. Not me!" He laughed and touched Kate's cheek with a
forefinger. "After all, as the bar-flies say, we only live once. Righto,
what?"

"Maybe. I don't know, Ames." She brought his overcoat from a
hall closet. "Possibly some of us lead several different kinds of lives
all at the same time."

"Oh, of course, of course." He got into the overcoat. "Our friend
Laila, for instance." He had the air of a discoverer. "Out with
people she's one sort of girl but alone with you she's somebody

totally different. Then with her mother and stepfather she's still another girl entirely. She teases them you know, gets them laughing in spite of themselves. That row she had with them, for instance, about not going west when they do—the stepfather seems upset about it sometimes; but her mother's altogether reconciled to it. They're rather queer, those two, don't you think, Kate? Strange thing, isn't it?"

"Strange? What thing, Ames?"

"Why, a girl like Laila being in such surroundings, being born of such people, though of course Barnes is only her stepfather, I'm glad to say."

"I see." Kate's tone betrayed no animus, no mockery nor anything else that she felt. "It's like the beautiful flower growing out of the muck heap, you mean, Ames."

"Yes," he said. "It's an old comparison; but it seems to fit and sometimes the old ways of saying things are the best. She does seem like that. Of course her mother must have been much more attractive earlier—I don't mean that Mrs. Barnes is vulgar precisely—but Laila's so fine, Kate; there's such a fineness about her—I mean you see it, underneath, in everything she does——"

"Yes, underneath, Ames."

"Yes," he said, not listening. "And such a grace—such a——"

"You've got your key, Ames?"

"Key?" He felt in a pocket. "Yes. Oh, yes! Don't sit up for me."

"No, not necessarily, Ames."

She did, though, thus giving herself the useless experience of hearing more about Laila's fineness when he returned.

Martha Gilpin came as a proxy for Cousin Roberta whose arthritis confined her. "Grandmother thinks it'll be a great mercy," Martha said. "Old Powls told her yesterday he believes your long trial's about over, Kate. Not more than a month longer at the utmost, he thinks. Grandmother's worried about you. She feels we ought to've been more help to you in all this, and of course we should have. She thinks you've had a really rotten hard time of it, Kate. Nothing but sickness and death and debts around you ever since you were a little girl—and your poor father's drinking and now this long, long drawn-out awfulness in that room upstairs—and——"

"No," Kate interrupted. "Cousin Roberta doesn't understand. I didn't plan to come to live at Aunt Daisy's and I didn't want to; but I've had a happy enough time here, Martha."

"Happy? Good Lord! How?"

"Well, Celia's always great fun for me and—and there couldn't be anybody pleasanter to live with than Ames, you know."

"Ames! Oh, dear!" Martha uttered the brief sibilances that indicate lamentation for naughtiness. "That's worrying Grandmother simply to death, Kate. She insisted I tell you she wants you to do something about it. She says it's just got to be stopped, and indeed we all feel so, too, Kate. Everybody's talking about it—horribly afraid that he'll actually *marry* Laila Capper! Grandmother says she can't see why you ever let him get started."

"Let him? Let him?"

"Oh, *you* know!" Martha said. "Grandmother says you've nearly always seen how to manage things, Kate. Yes, you have; you needn't deny it! Well, why have you let this go on? You know darned well all you had to do's tell him what Laila's really like!"

"That's all I had to do, Martha? Just to tell a man that some people don't approve of the girl he's in love with? Did you ever try it?"

"No, but——"

"Neither have I," Kate said. "I've never tried, either, to put out a fire by blowing on the hot coals."

"He's got it that bad? How awful! It'll make Grandmother sicker; she's always admired him so and had such faith he was going to amount to something—and, after his having such a spiritual, gentle wife as Mary, then to go and——" Martha paused, then absently said more than she intended. "Of course we'd all rather supposed that naturally—— Well, you and he and Celia being settled down here this way together so long, you know, and——"

"No!" Kate cut her off brusquely. "Not at all! Please tell Cousin Roberta I don't care for that sort of supposing."

"You needn't take my head off, Kate. We understand perfectly that we were mistaken and there was nothing in it, though it really would

have seemed appropriate. Sit still; I'm not saying any more about it!
By the way, what of Mr. Tuke Speer? Hasn't Ames any qualms about
coming out as his great friend's rival?"

"No, I think not. I gather that Laila's convinced him there's no
rivalry, because Mr. Speer could never have been anything to her
except a dear old friend."

"Then she's some convincer!" Martha exclaimed. "What about Tuke
Speer himself, though? How does he take it, Kate?"

"I can't say. He hasn't been near me."

"He hasn't?" Martha cried in surprise. "Isn't that pretty queer,
since he really is *your* dear old friend?" Kate said nothing, and
Martha, after staring at her calm face for some moments, gave way to
expressions of perplexity. "What a mess! I should think you'd be the
very one he'd——" She interrupted herself sharply. "Oh, see here,
Kate! Don't you ever tell anybody anything? Don't you *ever?*"

She had to return to her grandmother with only the information
that Kate Fennigate was a bottled-up little Sphinx, which Mrs. Gilpin
defined as redundant because everybody knew that and had been
saying it ever since Kate was born.

"It's a really improper situation," the old lady went on fretfully. "I
don't say it's immoral; but it's certainly unconventional, their not
getting married to each other after going on living in that family way
all this time. If it were anybody but Kate Fennigate it would injure
her reputation because of course everybody knows that Daisy Cunningham's in no condition to be a chaperone and Ames is only a
cousin-by-marriage. Did you ask her if she'd told Ames he'd better
think a little about what kind of a stepmother he was proposing to
hand over his daughter to?"

"No, I didn't, Grandmother. She was so—well, so unreceptive—I
thought I'd better not go into that."

"Somebody'd better," Mrs. Gilpin said. "Somebody'd better go into
it. I'd do it myself except I'm not able. I even doubt if I'll be up to
going to the ceremony for Daisy when she passes on. Of course Kate
knows she must have Plaestro and Son. We always have. I suppose
she does know because she had them for Mary, and she made all the
arrangements then. She handled it very well; but I certainly won't

attend if I have to go in a wheelchair. I hope she understands she and Ames can't go on living there like this after Daisy's taken away. You think she does, Martha?"

"You don't have to worry about that, Grandmother, do you? Not if Ames marries Laila Capper."

"Oh, dear!" Mrs. Gilpin made herself moan with the thought and by impatiently trying to shift her position in bed. "Ouch! He may have a right to throw himself away like that if he's bound to; but what on earth will become of that poor little Celia if she has to have such a stepmother? Widowers never, never ask themselves that question. In all my life I never knew one that gave it the slightest iota of consideration."

Ames Lanning, in spite of Mrs. Gilpin's conviction, had given the question frequent consideration, always favorably. His face was bright with tenderness and hope, yet held a kind of solemnity, too, when first he approached the subject with Kate. The full year of widowerhood had passed; he'd dressed for the evening and was going forth once more to a "Sunday supper" with the lively "young married" friends who'd been his and Mary's intimates. Kate's door was open and he came into her room on his way to the stairs. "I just thought——" he began.

"Yes, you're all right," she said. "Your tie couldn't be better and I'm glad you got the new dinner clothes. The others weren't going to hold out much longer. You couldn't look nicer, and neither could anybody, Ames."

"Thank you." He sat down, smiling absently. "Ah—there's a matter I thought—— Well, I—it seems about time for me to take it up with you, Kate."

"Does it?" She lost her breath, but only in one suppressed gasp. "Laila's going with you to-night, is she? You—you've asked her to marry you?"

"No." His smile became gentler yet brighter. "Not yet. I've known that you understood about it, Kate; you always do get things so easily. No, I haven't put it directly to Laila; but she's another who gets things easily and of course she knows I'm going to and—— Well, she's so true blue that I'm sure I'm not flattering myself when I say that there isn't a doubt about her answer. She's shown me—— I mean I—I know she cares for me—very, very beautifully, in her own charming lighthearted way, Kate. It's a precious thing to come into a man's life; nothing dearer and lovelier could happen to me in this world. Of course it means a change in our two lives, yours and mine; but I hope that need be only a surface change. Don't you think it will?"

"Do you?" She sat expressionless, looking full at him.

"Indeed I do!" he said confidently. "She's almost as devoted to you, Kate dear, as I am, myself. It's sure to be all right. Another thing that'll be all right, too, Kate—I've thought and thought about it and I'm certain I'm not mistaken—it's the change with regard to Celia. Of course in a certain way it involves some little separation between you and Celia and—— What's the matter?"

This break in his thoughts was caused by a glance at Kate, a glance that abruptly supplanted affectionate complacency with alarm. Kate's face had suddenly become contorted into shapings he'd never before seen master it. Not the face of Kate Fennigate seemed before him but strange features convulsed by horror and pain.

"What's the matter?" he asked again. "Kate, what on earth——"

"Nothing." She was as before, and produced her handkerchief. "Haven't you ever seen anybody who's about to sneeze? No—false alarm. I'm not going to. Go on, Ames. About Celia you were say-ing——"

Much relieved, he laughed. "I hope you don't do it often. Yes, about Celia—it's been pretty gloomy here these years for a child, Kate. I'm sure that living with anybody so lighthearted and lively as Laila will get Celia all brightened up and keep her that way and have only the very best of influences upon her. It ought to make a very gay little household, Kate, don't you think? Of course I know that above all things Laila will want you to see as much of Celia as you can and advise about her education and bringing-up generally, just as you always have—or almost as much, anyhow. It would be nice if you'd have an apartment near us. I thought I'd see if I can't afford a four-room apartment for Laila and Celia and me; Laila'd like having one with quite a good-sized living-room for little parties, don't you think?"

"Yes, I think she'd almost insist on it, Ames."

"Well, we'll see, we'll see." His eyes had been frequently upon his watch; now he rose springily. "Of course we'll have to begin pretty modestly; but she'll make all that great fun if I know her and I think I do! I don't need to ask you if I have your blessing, do I, Kate?"

"No, you don't need to ask that."

He'd been gone from the house five minutes when Tuke Speer rang the bell. "I'd been watching to see him go," Tuke admitted, in the library. "She told me this afternoon he's taking her to-night. She slid that in just as I rang off. You see she calls me up rather often, when-ever I show her I can stay away from her; but I make my end of it pretty brief. I've been keeping away from you as well as from her because I haven't wanted to talk to either of you. I'd like to talk to Ames, though, if I could—alone."

"I think you'd better not, Tuke."

"Yes, so do I," he said. "I think I'd better not, too; but that doesn't mean I wouldn't like to, does it?"

XXII

"No," KATE SAID. "I'D LIKE TO, MYSELF. WHAT WOULD you tell him if you talked to him?"

"The same thing you would. I'd tell him he'd better save himself a lot of experience by not going through what she's put me through. She lacks inventiveness; she plays it the same with one of us after another. Sometimes she makes it short, sometimes she makes it long; but it's always the same. First you're high man with her, then you're low man; then you're high again, then low; then she gets tired and either slides you out altogether or else strings you along just for num-bers. When you're low man she loves deviling you with whoever's high man; but I haven't fallen for that with Ames. I've fooled her by simply staying away. I haven't let her make me jealous of him—I'm not, probably because I know what she'll do to him before long."

"No." Kate shook her head slowly. "I don't think so."

"What? Why, of course she will, Kate."

"I don't think so. She's twenty-three, Tuke, and she knows she's had about all that sort of fun the law allows. She's always had a kind of ambition. She's always looked forward to climaxing with a fanfare of trumpets, marrying prosperity, prominence, big parties and Sunday column headlines."

"Don't you suppose I know that?" Tuke asked bitterly. "It's exactly what poor old Ames is going to find out when she——"

"No, I'm afraid he won't, Tuke, because——"

"Because she'll marry him?" Tuke's interruption was mocking. "You've just said she'll only take a Big Shot. That doesn't fit Ames very closely, does it?"

"Ames hasn't any money," Kate admitted. "It's true he's not much more than started in his profession; but he does have a kind of prestige as a person and because his family and connections were respectfully known in the earlier days of the city—something Laila's always been impressed by and probably envied more than you'd guess, Tuke, even as well as you know her."

"Oh, I've seen it!" he said. "She's a climber of course. Look at the campaign she made to get into the Junior League. It was almost funny. Climbing's only part of it, though. She's luxurious; she wants even more—yes, a lot more—than her stepfather supplied her with while he had money. She wants a thousand times more than Ames Lanning can give her, Kate."

"Where's she to get it?" Kate asked. "The Depression's smashed quite a few eligibles, Tuke, and I don't know any of the survivors who are taking an interest in Laila Capper. Her mother and stepfather are on the point of disappearing over the horizon and she won't go with 'em; so it's either work or a husband. What husband? Well, for scarcity of worldly goods you're about where Ames is, aren't you? You're just getting started, too."

"Am I? It's being a pretty fair start, Kate. I've had three raises, and the last one, after the eastern trip, amounted to really quite a little something. I probably owe it to you, at that—the good word you were going to put in for me some day with the Old Man. Anyhow, somebody he listens to must have told him I wrote most of that report. You, wasn't it?"

"No, not directly, Tuke. He had me make some copies of it and muttered something about the report's being very thorough and clear."

"Yes, go on," Tuke said. "What did you say then?"

"Nothing—except that I wondered who wrote it."

"I can hear you!" Tuke said gratefully. "Just murmured that musingly, didn't you?—so he looked it up and I got my nice little jump. I thought I had you to thank, and I do. It doesn't put me out in front in Roe Metal Products, and with the Old Man I'm still small potatoes, of course; but at least it does give me an edge on Ames, doesn't it? You seem to have it all set that it's to be Ames or me—though I think you're forgetting something, Kate."

"What am I forgetting?"

"Her looks and a few other things about her," Tuke said. "She could go out and take just about any man on earth she wants."

"Yes, I know you think so." Kate spoke gently. "I'm afraid there are only the two of you in sight just now, Tuke."

"I wish I could hope so," he said. "She knows she wouldn't get her luxuries from me, not yet; but she's heard rumors from the Works that I'm expected to do pretty well there in time. Ames used to be thought to be going to cut quite a swathe; but that promise hasn't exactly flowered, Kate, you might say. Don't you suppose she gets all that? His only real advantage over me is that he's newer to her than I am—an excitement that precious soon wears out with her. Ames is fun at a party; but outside of that he's a placid, dreamy soul and she wants something always doing. He's the most guileless young widower that ever tied himself down to a law office, and when he marries again he'll want to stay home evenings. On top of that, do you suppose she has any intention of bringing up a stepdaughter—a mousy-eyed child that'd take up room in an apartment and get wise to everything Laila did?"

"Ah——" Kate's forehead was covered by her two hands. "I can't think of that!"

"Laila can. She'd never stand for it," Tuke said. "No, she's just playing him. If it's down to the two of us, as you say, it's true she might have wanted to look him over; but it won't last long. Ames doesn't look like going big places any more. He's the best fellow I know; but in a worldly way he begins to smell of failure. Laila's smart in her own dumb way; she'll never take him. Don't give up, Kate; you'll have him back."

"What?" Kate's hands dropped to her lap and she stared, frightened.

"You didn't know I'd got on?" Tuke was compassionate. "One reason I've been keeping away from you, I was afraid I'd blurt out something like this and it'd distress you. Well, I've done it; I know your secret, Kate."

"You don't!" Her voice tried to be firm; but it failed. "I haven't any!"

"Poor child!" he said. "I had a wooden head about you for a long time. Like everybody else, I was fooled. You've always appeared to be the kind of girl nobody expects to have anything except a sense of duty and the Sunday-school virtues or to feel anything but a spinsterly maternalism. You're expected to do all the messy little jobs around the house for everybody; you're the one to clean up the picnic supper and get everything back in the baskets while the other girls trot off in the moonlight with the boys. You're supposed to like to do the chores, to prefer that."

"Am I?" Kate was pale, her voice just audible.

"Well, aren't you?" he asked. "Don't you know you're absurdly believed to be that sort of girl?—not to have emotions and to enjoy living usefully in the background? No woman could imagine being jealous of you about a man, and no man or woman either could imagine your being in love. I held that view of you myself until lately. I'm almost sorry I know better now, Kate."

She made a gesture forbidding him to speak further. "You do not! I'm tired, Tuke; I don't want to talk any more."

He stepped toward her, but turned away submissively as she rose with her face averted from him. "All right. I'll let you alone."

When he'd gone she didn't yield to the tiredness that had come upon her so suddenly. She walked about the house, moving rapidly, went from room to room, paced up and down the dim front hall. Not knowing why, she went into every room downstairs, turned and went swiftly out again. This was mere confusion, the panic of a distracted creature that can only run from blind corner to blind corner and is bereft of all but fear. The panic was useless since what she feared had already happened. Tuke knew the secret she had so long and so profoundly buried that she had thought no living soul except herself would ever know it. She had not looked upon it as a treasure; but no miser could have seen his cask of gold thrown out upon a crowded street and suffered greater desperation.

More than twenty minutes passed before she had a grasp upon her thoughts and checked her almost running feet and fluttering hands. "Stop it! Stop it!" she said, whispering to herself. "Stop being a caught rat! If you're caught, you're caught; but what good's running into corners do?" Tuke's knowing would do her no harm, nor do Ames any harm, nor anybody; but his knowing had brought the hidden thing into what seemed the glare of day. It had been hidden with such long, infinite care to keep it in the dark that light upon it had brought the terror. Steadier, she comprehended and was able to examine her own agitation.

"Why, I'm like—I'm like Robinson Crusoe on his desert island," she thought. "Now I understand what he felt when he first saw Friday's footprint in the sand."

That was precisely what had hurried her aimlessly about the house, an utter startledness, and poor unhappy Tuke was her Friday. As a companion on her lonely isle he wasn't wise, though, she thought; he couldn't be wise about Laila because he was too dreadfully in love with her in spite of his cynical knowledge of her. It had been pitiable to hear him urge his view that he had a chance against Ames. That was hope, not conceit; his hope couldn't let him see that no girl, not even dumb Laila Capper, would ever hesitate an instant between

Tuke Speer and Ames Lanning—not unless Tuke had prospects of gold to shower, and he hadn't.

Tuke counted on Celia as a deterrent; but that wouldn't weigh with Laila, who'd be sure she could dispose of such a matter easily, though never by leaving Celia with Kate. Ames had meant that to-night he'd ask Laila to marry him. Then Laila was saying yes to him to-night—perhaps now while Kate tiredly trudged up the stairs to help Mrs. Ferry feed Aunt Daisy.

Celia came home at eight o'clock, gay after a long Sunday at Cousin Roberta's where she'd had candy and gift-shop presents. Then, after she'd talked herself to bed, Dr. Powls arrived and told Kate all about new treatments for anemia and bad gall-bladders before he went up to see his patient. He stayed a long time, came downstairs yawning absently and said, "I don't see any change since Friday. You can't call it sinking because she's already sunk. Oh, perhaps another week or so. Nothing to do, you know, nothing at all; so goodnight, young lady."

" 'Young lady,' " Kate thought, as the front door closed. "Do I still look like one?" She felt that she couldn't believe it when so grotesque a thing was happening: Ames Lanning was asking Laila Capper to marry him.

At midnight the only light in the house was the porcelain-globed fifteen-watt bulb atop the high ornamental brass fixture upheld by the carved mahogany newel-post at the foot of the dim stairway. Almost no light extended within the rooms opening from the hall; but Kate Fennigate was again walking hurriedly into those dark apartments, then hurrying out and pacing up and down the hall. This time her excitement wasn't caused by the discovery of Friday's foot-print; something long governed within her was at last ungovernable, finding expression and striving to wear itself out so that she could "get hold" of herself again. Aunt Daisy's treasures in the ugly rooms might have been thought to brood morbidly, invisible in their shad-ows and witnesses of a strange passion, the only listeners to half-uttered faint cries and gasped whisperings. "Bottled up," Kate's rela-tives had been calling her all her life; but inner pressures too long pent may crack the glass at last.

At half past one the light of the street lamp at the corner of

National Avenue and East Cherry Street disclosed the tall figure of
Ames, his overcoat open and blowing back from him, his arms swing-
ing as he came briskly home. From a black front window of the
"reception room" Kate watched him, held her breath as he strode
through the hall and up the stairs; then she came forth, picked up the
overcoat and hat he'd tossed upon a chair and put them into the
closet where they belonged. She looked fixedly at the feebly luminous
globe that held the fifteen-watt bulb. "Didn't even put out the light,"
she said half-aloud. "No, he wouldn't. Not this night!"

Standing on the second step of the stairway and stretching her arm
to its utmost, she turned the key of the bulb; then she ascended on
tiptoe and at the top of the stairs heard sounds that tore their way
from her ears to her heart. In his room, with his door carelessly ajar
enough to show a wide long crack of light, Ames was singing softly.
Kate thought he would be removing his tie, looking at himself in his
mirror. His voice was hushed; but rich baritone notes of it came
clearly as he sang:

> *"Who is Sylvia,*
> *What is she,*
> *That all her swains commend her——"*

The manly voice, suppressed but vibrant with new happiness, followed Kate into her own room, and, though the closing of her door
shut away the sounds, she knew that Ames was still singing of Sylvia
—a Sylvia who was Laila Capper and had promised avidly to marry
him.

The walls of that old house were thick, the partitions of solid brick,
closing off the occupants one from another as immutably as their
separating lives did; and so the house was like the planet on which
it stood, where the millions of lives go on close together yet walled
apart and all in solitary.

In Celia's room the child lay smiling in her sleep because beneath
her pillow were new gifts, a silver pencil and a tiny sewing kit in a
box of soft red leather. At the other end of the hall Aunt Daisy's
stony body was less and less stubbornly resisting her long effort to
make it die; and in the adjoining room stout Mrs. Ferry was wakeful,

not on account of Aunt Daisy but because of money troubles. Four
months earlier Mrs. Ferry, weakened by cajoleries, had lent her small
savings to her nephew, Albert, to pay an instalment on an automobile,
and only yesterday Albert's wife had telephoned that Albert really
would repay the loan next month but in the meantime if he couldn't
raise enough for another instalment right now he'd lose the automobile for good and all.

Kate's room was between Celia's and Ames's; and Ames, not displeased with his mirror, was singing of his new love. "Sylvia", he
called her, and she'd been kind; so he sang and saw before him only
years of happiness and silvery age glorified by a good and beautiful
woman's companionship. Never would he know that upon the other
side of the wall on which his mirror hung, two clenched fists were
beating, pounding that old wall convulsively in rage and grief that
had the mastery at last.

"You fool! You ruinous fool!" Kate Fennigate sobbed at him, beating his wall. "Fool—boob—idiot—you crazy, crazy, crazy muddler and
fool!"

XXIII

"SHE'S DONE TOO MUCH TO ME!"

This was Kate's plaintively fierce thought of Laila Capper; and in
the background of the picture was the shadowy figure of Laila's carelessly laughing and somewhat wanton mother. Kate had never wished
any of the Capper family to be a part of her life; nevertheless, both
the daughter and the mother had recurrently pushed upon her, altered
her course, threatened and damaged her. In a sense she was nothing to them, and for herself she asked only to keep out of their

way; but she repeatedly found herself in it and involved with them.

That was no uncommon experience, she knew. People who should have remained strangers to one another become entangled; whole intimate neighborhoods are made up of variegated human beings who should never have come near one another, and almost everyone has undesired acquaintances who are repeatedly intruded upon the private fabric of his life. Kate could bear the common lot; but Laila Capper, with whom her mind and heart had no kinship whatever, had intruded too often—harmfully.

Not Laila's malice was the reason. Restless, she only roved, and, regardless of the cost to anybody, took from the wayside what her fancy wanted for her pleasure. She didn't like Kate Fennigate; but then, though she could fall in love for a while, did she like anybody? This was doubtful. She wouldn't be displeased, however, if her roving hurt Kate. She hadn't been displeased, years ago, when to help herself she'd made a long arm and finished Kate with Miss Carroll. Laila'd probably giggled to herself over Kate's companionship with Tuke Speer and what had happened to it. Once the two friends had talked blithely of a thousand things; but since Laila'd reached for Tuke, absorbing his life, all the discourse had been nothing but Laila, Laila, Laila! The friendship still existed, but all pleasure in it had departed; Laila'd made it into a stupid kind of painfulness. Now she'd stretched forth that careless long arm of hers again—for Ames and Celia—and it was too much!

"Her mother took my father—took him from my mother and helped to ruin him," Kate thought, not fair and not wholly clear-minded in her extremity. "Is this the shaping of my life, its pattern —always and always to cherish nothing that Laila Capper won't seize from me and spoil?"

Work was done absent-mindedly that Monday morning. "What's wrong with you?" Kate's employer asked crustily, finding fault with freshly typed letters she brought him to be signed. "Have I got to go back to dictating to you? You're the only girl I ever had that I thought I could just say four or five words to, 'Tell 'em so and so,' and they'd get a polished letter that said what I wanted. Well, up to now you haven't failed me; but look at these! They're a mess, Kate Fennigate!"

"Yes. I'll do them over."

"You'll have to, doggone it!" The objurgation, a relic of his bucolic youth, was Henry L. Roe's complete system of profanity. "It's a Blue Monday, everything wrong. Got nobody I can depend on for anything. My grandchildren's governess—only good one I ever had—gives me notice at breakfast she's going to get married. Pastor of my church to dinner with me yesterday noon after services tells me he's worried about Locksley Carmichael's salvation. Well, so am I! I've been paying Locksley a big salary; but he's living 'way beyond his means and when he goes to New York he runs after chorus girls. Oh, yes, and I've heard it from other people, too! I won't have it. Every time I pass the Carlyle Club I see his car standing in front. It's a bad sign."

"Why?" Kate spoke up. "He'd meet the best men in town at the Carlyle Club, Mr. Roe."

"I don't care." The old man left his desk and began to walk about the big office peevishly. "Don't talk back to me, either. Locksley Carmichael drinks too much there, and everywhere else; he's made a spectacle of himself three times this year now, and I know all about it. If that club's members are the best men in town what do they mean by going there for cocktails Sunday mornings instead of attending to their church duties? I'm glad to hear the Depression's cut their membership in two and people say that nest of iniquity's going out of existence entirely before long. I hope so. Half the ablest young men I've got in Roe Metal Products think it's an honor to belong to it and waste their time and risk perdition there. Got anything to say to that?"

"No, Mr. Roe."

"I am surprised!" he said. "Something must gone pretty wrong with you or you'd be arguing and telling me how narrow-minded I am again. Commenced arguing with me when you were only about nine years old and so teeny weeny it was hard to see you. Sometimes I don't know how I stand you at all! Well, are you going to find me another governess or aren't you?"

"Yes, Mr. Roe."

" 'Yes, Mr. Roe'!" He burlesqued her lifeless voice and spoke unreasonably. "Talk like a parrot! Maybe you can get me another governess; but you can't find me a man to put where I was going to put Locksley Carmichael. The day's coming when I'm going to throw Locksley out entirely. I won't have any of the heads of Roe Metal Products conducting himself like that and getting talked about and giving my concern a fast name. I was going to make him a Director in my Trust Company; I was even going to make him a Vice President in Roe Metal Products. I looked forward to the day when Locksley'd be the next man to me and take some of the burden off my shoulders. I haven't got anybody to lean on, not a soul. Where am I going to find anybody to put my responsibilities on? In three years I'll be seventy, doggone it. Who's going to be boss around here if I break down? You?"

"No, Mr. Roe."

He stopped his pacing and stood looking at her with some solicitude. "What's the matter?" he asked. "Are you sick? Want to go home?"

"No, Mr. Roe."

"Well, something's certainly gone funny with you," he said. "When you let me holler at you and don't talk back, it's a mighty queer day. Come to look at you, you're all pulled down and peekid. Need a vacation? I hope not."

"No, I don't."

"Go on, then," he said crossly. "Go on get those letters the way they ought to be and 'tend to your own business; it's none o' mine. That woman's going to get married in two weeks from now and she wants off five days before. You'll have somebody there?"

"Yes, Mr. Roe."

"All right; I'll forget it. Now do me those letters and do 'em right."

Kate did the letters and did them right, though all the while she thumped the typewriter there were thumpings in her head. A painful modern commercial and journalistic habit calls all houses "homes"; but home does not need to be even within a house Kate

Fennigate and Ames Lanning and his daughter lived domestically almost as if Kate had become actually Ames's wife and Celia's mother; and that life together as a family, even in the house haunted by the silence of petrified Aunt Daisy, was home for the three of them. Laila Capper was smashing it as irresponsibly as she would later lightly smash Ames and Celia. Mary had died and Aunt Daisy had jumped in order that Laila might acquire this privilege? Such, then, were the "patterns of life" arranged by an orderly Providence?

At three in the afternoon Mr. Roe testily told Kate to clear out and go home, he didn't want any hollow-eyed spectres dragging their feet around his offices. She declined, but gave up half an hour later, walked home stoopingly and found Laila's car before the house. Inside the front door Kate stopped short. Celia's voice, softened unusually, was heard from the living-room.

"Please, please don't go, Miss Capper. I'm enjoying this conversation with you lots and lots. I don't feel as if I ever got acquainted with you before and I do wish you'd stay."

Kate went into the living-room. Laila was moving toward the door, followed by a wistful Celia. "Darling chick, I really can't," Laila was saying, when she saw Kate and laughed. "Caught in the act, Kate! Making friends with little goodykins here. Ames said he did wish I'd get to know her better some time—he's so crazy about her, himself."

"Oh, Miss Capper!" Celia was rosy. "Do you really mean that? Do you really think he is? I never——"

"Why, of course." Laila patted the girl's cheek. "So am I, now we're getting to really be acquainted, young Brighteyes. I tell you what you do right now, though: you skip out a minute or two. I want to have a little talk with your Aunt Kate, since she's happened to turn up. Skip along, will you, cutie, and I'll bring you something you'll like next time I come!"

"Well, I'll go since you ask me to," Celia said grudgingly. "I don't call her 'Aunt Kate', though, Miss Capper. She's only my cousin. When'll you come again?"

"Soon. Very soon." Celia departed, walking backward to look the longer at the lustrous visitor, and Laila, serious, sat tentatively upon the arm of a chair. "Seems an affectionate child, Kate. Pretty gabby. She's been talking for the last half hour straight without stopping for breath. Does she always talk this much?"

"Yes, I believe so, when she's given a chance. The other times you've been here you——"

"Oh, I know!" Laila said. "I didn't particularly notice her; but lately I thought perhaps I'd better begin to."

"Yes, I see. You seem to have made progress with her. Do you like her?"

"Like her? Oh, well, kids are just kids, aren't they?" Laila seemed amused briefly. "I don't suppose her clothes cost anything to speak of, do they?"

"More than you might think, Laila. If you want to know exactly, I'd say they cost more than mine do, for instance."

"That oughtn't to be much," Laila said, intending no unkindness. Her thoughts seemed to be calculating arithmetically. "Do you think he's positively set about her keeping on at Miss Carroll's?"

"Yes, I know he is."

"I don't see it." Laila looked annoyed. "Of course you and I and the rest of us all talk a lot about being 'old Carroll girls'; but if you come right down to brass tacks what's the low down on it? What did I get out of it for all the expense my parents went to, keeping me there? I couldn't tell you where Kamchatka is or who was king after Henry the Eighth or President before Monroe if you burned me alive. Now really I ask you! That Carroll joint, it's the bunk. It's nothing but a silly old hole where little show-offs read Commencement pieces and their grandmoms cry with pride and then begin to try to get 'em married to rich little bums like that Patterson joke. You know what I think?"

"Yes, I believe so, Laila."

"What?" Laila was surprised; then laughed. "Well, since you think you know, what do I think?"

"You were wondering if Celia couldn't be sent to a cheaper school somewhere out of town, Laila."

"Mind reader!" Laila cried, still amused. "Well, why couldn't she be?"

"There aren't any," Kate said. "Out of town she'd have to live at the school, which would be more expensive than being a day pupil at Miss Carroll's."

"What of that?" Laila was gayly brusque. "I know he talks pretty poor; but he belongs to the Carlyle Club, sends Celia to old Carroll's and keeps up this big house, doesn't he?"

"Well——" Kate paused; then added, "Between us we manage somehow, Laila."

Laila appeared to ignore this, though she paused before returning to her plans for Celia. "I don't see why the child shouldn't be sent to some good school somewhere, not a high-priced one but anyhow as good as old Carroll's. I bet I could find one—maybe not so far away she couldn't come home on a Saturday or a holiday sometimes if he thinks he ought to be seeing her. You seem to think he couldn't afford it; but——" Laila broke off and giggled amiably. "Well, I hope he doesn't show you his florist's bill this month! I don't mean it's anything like as extravagant as some I've guessed at; but still! He's a dear sweet thing, Kate. Don't get me wrong; I know perfectly well he's far from being a rich man right now; but so's 'most everybody else. Old Barnesy himself says that if Ames Lanning ever gets a start he'll shoot straight up to tops."

"Yes, I think he might." Kate spoke slowly, looking down at her lap. "That is, if nothing stops him, and, as you say, if he ever gets a start."

"Sure!" Laila said readily; then looked reflective. "I hear your aunt's just about passing out, Kate. That might be a help with Celia, getting her off to school somewhere. Of course I don't suppose Ames'd be left anything in the will—just an ex-son-in-law—but Celia, being her only grandchild——"

"No," Kate said. "There won't be anything for Celia. There's nothing at all for anybody."

"Nothing at all? Oh, of course there's always a little something, Kate! I know the poor old thing hit hard times; but in these old families there's always more than people expect—maybe a few stocks and bonds and old family jewelry and suchlike. She used to cut quite a figure in this town. I bet if all the old locked bureau drawers were dug around in she'd turn out to have some nice things that might sell pretty well or ought to be looked after and taken care of for Celia until she's grown up."

"No, there's nothing like any of that." Kate was decisive. "Aunt Daisy never cared for jewelry and she hasn't any."

"What a woman! Well——" Laila pushed herself up from the arm of the chair upon which she'd been sitting. "Guess you won't shed many tears because it's about over and you can get away from the old dump at last. By the way, how's our mutual friend, that Tuke person, lately? Over here to sit with you just about every night, isn't he?"

"No. Hardly at all."

"Go on!" Laila laughed rallyingly. "Don't kid me! He thinks you're just about his mom. Bet he runs to you with every little thing! Thinks he's clever giving me the go-by for weeks and weeks every now and then. Bill Jones gossips around Tuke's already had another little raise in his Metal Products department so he's right on the road to be high man with the boss in a few years more. Piffle! What I care? He bores the life out of me. Listen, hon. You give Tuke a message from me when he comes to-night."

"He won't be here to-night. He very seldom——"

"Go on!" Laila again said merrily, as she drew on her driving gloves. "You tell him I said keep on hiding, the next message he gets from me's going to be a happy surprise for him because it won't be in my handwriting. It's liable to be engraved!" She whooped with laughter over this, as she left.

Kate went upstairs to lie down with a camphor-soaked handkerchief upon her forehead; but, as she passed the open door of Celia's bedroom, she was stopped. "Look here, Kate!" Celia called, and, standing before her old-fashioned mahogany bureau, pointed to its mirror. "I got something to talk to you about. Look at me in that looking-glass and answer me a simple question."

"Yes? What question?" Kate came in slowly.

"Why didn't you ever say I'm pretty? In my whole life I don't ever remember your so much as once ever telling me I'm specially good-looking or anything like that. Why not? Don't you think I am?"

"Yes, of course, Celia. If I haven't mentioned it I suppose it's because I've had the habit of taking it for granted."

"Well, it's pretty funny," Celia said coldly. "Here you've been living in the same house with me all this time and related to me and supposed to take a good deal of interest. Yet in my whole life up to this very day only two people ever told me I was getting to be pretty good-looking: Thaddie Boscowen at a party once and that beautiful Miss Capper this afternoon. She said a good deal. She said she thought I was the prettiest young girl of my own age in this whole town. I didn't ask her if I am; I didn't even hint. She just told me so. She said she was coming back here soon. When's she coming?"

"I don't know."

"I didn't like her at first," Celia said. "I was absolutely mistaken. There's something that draws you to her when you're with her. I been thinking—well, you know I told you Mamie Augren's been my crush at Miss Carroll's. I wonder if Mamie'd mind if I changed and got a crush on Miss Capper instead? When you look at Mamie beside Miss Capper, why, Mamie's looks look like zero and practically less than nothing at all and she hasn't got any comparison to Miss Capper's intelligence of mind. Don't you think it'd be all right to change, Kate?"

"I rather think you already have, Celia."

"I guess I have." Celia looked shy but happy. "I guess I'll tell Miss Capper so next time she comes. I guess she'd like it, the way she treats me now she's got so interested in me. I think my nose is a good deal like yours, Kate." The mirror was again absorbing. "Maybe it's in the family. I expect I better tell Miss Capper she's my new crush if she comes to-morrow. Father likes it, too, when she comes here; he gets all jolly. Don't you think so, Kate? Do you expect maybe she'll come to-morrow?"

There was no answer and Celia looked round inquiringly but found herself alone.

XXIV

KATE, UPON HER BED, WITH SPIRITS OF CAMPHOR STINGING her forehead but not relieving it, heard the closing of the big old front door downstairs as Ames came in carelessly, and she fancied that he hummed "Who is Sylvia?" while he forgot the hall closet and tossed his hat and coat anywhere. After that the house was still.

Bitter questions throbbed through the headache upstairs. When Laila'd said, "But he belongs to the Carlyle Club, sends Celia to old Carroll's and keeps up this big house," why hadn't the response been brave and rough? "You bonehead! I pay half of everything, the house costs nothing, and if you marry him you'll wear old clothes till you die—or till you leave him!"

The headache continued its persecutions. "I could have done it. Why didn't I hammer, hammer, hammer cold truth into that dumb brain of hers? She might have sheered off and let us alone!"

At seven o'clock Kate went to the "upstairs back hall" and called down the stairway to the kitchen, informing Morella that she wouldn't be at the dinner table and was going to bed. She didn't need to help Mrs. Ferry feed Aunt Daisy; it could no longer be done. Kate was free to lie thinking of Ames and Celia in the dining-room below —jolly at the evening meal, just father and daughter cozily alone together without any outsider at all. Celia would be eagerly chattering of the new crush, the brilliant new figure in her life—and with what delight would the father be taking such dulcet sounds into his ears!

No one tapped on Kate's door after dinner or later; no one came to ask how she was. Perhaps that was considerate—or was it because they were too busy talking, or because she was expected to be always such a hardy little person that of course nothing really bothersome could happen to her?

Ames had left the house before she came down in the morning; office work kept her late in the afternoon, and he had come home and gone out when she arrived. "It's a date with my crush," the elate Celia told her. "Isn't it grand he likes her so much? He has to go and take the sleeping-car on the train about twelve o'clock to-night with Mr. Bortshleff because they have a trial 'way off somewhere that begins to-morrow and'll take all week; so he took his suit-case with him so he won't have to come back home because that'll give him more time with Miss Capper on account he's going to have his dinner at her house and they'd like to have as long as they can together afterward, they get along so well and he going to be away anyhow up to Sunday. He promised he'd ask her to come see me lots while he's away or maybe invite me to her house if she's too busy. Won't that be lovely, Kate?"

Laila didn't come to see her young adorer, however; and didn't extend the invitation expected as an alternative. Celia, fluttery with agitations, waited until Friday afternoon, then used the telephone for a timid inquiry. "I was afraid maybe she was sick; but they were almost rude," she told Kate injuredly that evening. "A man just said Miss Capper was too busy to answer calls, ring off; and I could hear bangings and bumpings, and right when he was telling me she was busy this man stopped and hollered at somebody, 'Put that down! Get the piano out next!' When she was here she told me her family was going to move away so she'd be left without any family at all unless she could have me for part of it, so I suppose that was what they were doing, because the way this man talked it certainly seemed like everybody in the house moving out. Of course he didn't go and tell her it was me calling, so it wasn't exactly a rebuff. If you were me would you try again to-morrow?"

"No, Celia."

This wasn't the answer Celia wanted. She tried the telephone again, several times, the next day, and had no response at all. Hurt, she didn't mention this to Kate, who seemed pretty bothersomely busy anyhow, all that Saturday afternoon and evening, in and out of Aunt

Daisy's room with Dr. Powls and Mrs. Ferry. Kate read psalms at the bedside late after Dr. Powls had gone, and in the morning, on her way to church with Celia, she said that they must both pray hard for Celia's grandmother to-day.

Celia was willing, she didn't mind; she felt that she would never be so religious as Kate and hoped she wouldn't. It seemed to make people pretty stiff and gloomy, not lively in stunning clothes and something drawing you to them like Miss Capper. Nevertheless, the two cousins, beside each other in the church, prayed for the soul of Marguerite Cunningham.

Ames arrived at five that afternoon. A little while after she'd heard him come, Kate went down to the living-room, saw him standing looking out of a window and said, "She's just going, Ames. There's no question now. It's the blessing of the end for her at last. I haven't thought there was any reason for Celia to go in—or you." He didn't appear to hear her; she spoke more loudly. "Ames, Aunt Daisy is——"

"Yes, I understand." He turned to face her, and, though she saw his features somewhat indistinctly against the light of the window, in his expression there was grief enough to be strongly visible. "I'm sorry, Kate."

"Why, no," she said. "If ever any poor mortal soul has longed bitterly for freedom hers has. It's wrong not to be glad, Ames."

"I know. I shouldn't have said I'm sorry. I suppose I was only trying to say the usual thing."

He spoke stiffly, almost harshly, and she stepped nearer him. "What's the matter? You look——"

"I look all right," he interrupted.

"You don't, though. You look crushed." Not Aunt Daisy's dying could of itself so affect him, she thought; but, even though he was now in love with another woman, it could recall and freshen his grief for Mary. "Ames, these next few days might be too hard on you. Why don't you go down to the club and take a room? You'd only need to come here for the ceremony and it'll be short. Why don't you——"

"No. Why should I? I'm not in a state of helplessness. I'll be at my office in the morning, working as usual. I——" He seemed to remind himself of something, and from his inner coat pocket produced a folded sheet of notepaper. "Oh, yes. I mustn't forget to give you Tuke's message."

"What?"

"She gave him my address," Ames said. "He was so kind as to write to me. His letter reached me yesterday evening. You might read it."

The room was darkening; Kate took the letter to the window.

"Dear Ames,

Nothing has ever prevented me from regarding you as one of my best friends and I hope that nothing will keep you from looking upon me as one of yours. Laila is deeply troubled for fear that you'll not understand that we both think of you with the warmest affection, and she's asked me to write these few words expressing that for her. I thought she should do it herself; but she insists that I'd be better able to make you understand how greatly we hope that you'll always keep a kindness in your heart for us both. Please say to Kate Fennigate I hope that she too will not discontinue the comprehension and indulgence she's always shown to people less perfect than herself. I have a two weeks' leave from the Works and I hope you and I are going to shake hands heartily at the end of this short absence.

"Yours faithfully
"T. S."

Kate put the bit of paper upon a table beside the window, picked it up, read it again, set it down again, and, open-mouthed, stood looking at it.

Ames sat down, rubbed his face with his hands, as if he washed it. "She was different Tuesday night when I went there," he said. "She was so absentminded that she didn't seem herself. Her mother and her stepfather looked absentminded, too, all through dinner; and they sat the whole evening with us afterward. I didn't get to talk to her alone except for just a moment at the front door as I left and then she seemed embarrassed. I'd thought she was going with me to the train; but I saw she'd forgotten what she'd said about that. I—I felt pretty baffled and puzzled."

"Poor Ames." This was only a murmur and Ames didn't hear it.

"I couldn't put my mind on our case at all," he said. "I'm afraid Bortshleff was pretty annoyed with me; he told me he wished he'd brought young Hamblin instead. I couldn't help feeling that something had happened. You see, Kate, that whole last evening with her was queer. You see, I——"

"Yes, Ames."

"Well, you see, I—of course I understand now how my imagining had over-reached itself and how I'd counted on things I shouldn't have—I'd been ass enough to think that she and I were—well, in my mind I must have exaggerated a lot of things. Apparently she can't bear to be—to be discouraging. She—well, she says things that sound like more than she means them to. I see now the reason she was embarrassed was that she felt I'd counted too much on such things and she couldn't bear to tell me I had. Well, I was already upset; but I can't deny that Tuke's letter last night came as a—well, as rather a shock."

"You understood what he meant, Ames?"

"I tried not to. Made it harder for myself, I suppose. On the train to-day it was only the climax to a bad week when Bortshleff got the Sunday papers at a station and said he thought he'd heard I was a friend of Tuke Speer's, I'd probably be interested in the item. You saw it, Kate?"

"No."

"Laila and Tuke were married Friday," Ames said. "You didn't know it?"

"No. Not till now."

He rubbed his face again and stared down at the worn-out Brussels carpet. "Probably they decided on it pretty suddenly."

"Yes. That's evident, Ames."

"I think I knew," he said. "I don't mean I had any idea at all that it'd be Tuke; but I think that in my heart I knew all week she'd changed about me. Maybe I shouldn't say changed. I suppose the right way to put it would be to say that she really liked me, even was truly fond of me, and when she saw I was counting on more than that she was—too merciful to me! You see, she—she couldn't even bring herself to write the letter. She just didn't know how to say what had to be said."

"Yes." Kate had stopped looking at the letter and had turned toward him; but he didn't know it. "I don't think she did know how."

"Ah, well!" He thrust his hands into his trousers pockets, lifted his head and stared at the wall instead of the carpet. "I'm afraid I'd built up quite a lovely fireside future for myself. I must have been gassy in the head, Kate. Well, I don't suppose it's any use either of us pretending anything. We both hate self-pity, and yet here we are, both given over to it."

"No! You're mistaken!" Kate spoke sharply. "I'm not!"

"I understand," he said. "Well, I don't want you to be sorry for me, either; I can do my own."

"All right, go ahead and do it!" Kate's tone was rough. "Be as sorry for yourself as you like; but be kind enough not to worry for me! So far as I'm concerned, I'm glad Tuke married her. If she'd married you or anybody else he'd have spent the rest of his life hanging round her just the same. I think maybe that's one reason——"

"One reason for what?"

"One reason she married him," Kate said.

Amid a whirl of imaginings she saw Laila's mixed-up and contrary impulses swing her to the abrupt decision. Tuke had played her, forever persistent yet working on her with long deliberate absences. He tantalized her; but she'd realized at the final critical moment that he was more in love with her than any other had ever been or would ever be. Yes, that was one of Laila's reasons.

So here was Ames, rather shattered, but home again.

"I suppose we'll have to take stock of our two selves, Kate," he said resignedly. "We'll have to be practical. We've both come to the end of a part of our lives and we'll have to face some new arrangements. We've stayed on here from month to month because of Mary's mother's condition; but if that's now ending—well, I can't imagine either of us being willing to stay in this house. For that matter, it seems to be more or less going to pieces pretty rapidly and—well, it's always been rather a sad place to live in, hasn't it?"

"No, not for me."

He was faintly surprised. "It hasn't? Yes, of course it's your dispo sition always to make the best of anything on earth, so you would of this too. You'd always——"

"I wouldn't!" she said angrily. "I've asked nothing better for myself than being here doing just what I've done."

His surprise somewhat increased. "That's fine of you, Kate; I wish I could reach that height. To be glad that you've felt about Tuke as you have, no matter how it's ended. I think that's splendid. It's——"

"It's nothing!" she cried. "Do you suppose I've stayed in this house in order to be across the street from Tuke Speer?"

A sardonic despair possessed her; but not enough to let her wail at Ames, "Why *have* I stayed here, using up my youth in this dark house, fending Aunt Daisy off you, slaving over your clothes, praying for chances to make you use the powers God gave you? Why have I served you for years, glad that I could? What *for*? Haven't you any sense at all? Don't you ever see *anything?*"

Such outcries, urging passionately from within, did not reach her lips. What she sharply said was, "What do *I* care if Tuke's married?"

"You don't? You mean you haven't been——"

"*No!*" she shouted. "Never for one instant, and don't you ever let me hear a word of such nonsense again!"

Ames uttered a groaning sound of laughter. "I see I'm altogether incompetent in such matters; I can't tell when people are in love and when they aren't. I thought of course you—— Never mind, I won't say it; I see I was wrong. It only proves me one more kind of fool; but I'm glad it turns out so in this instance. Your not having cared for Tuke may simplify things."

"What things?"

"Well——" He sighed a long loud sigh; then slapped his knee abruptly and got to his feet. "Going back to what I said about being practical and making new arrangements, I admit I'm too shot for my head to be quite clear; but I've thought of something like a plan."

"A plan for whom, Ames?"

"For all three of us, Kate. Celia has to be considered pretty seri ously, of course."

"Yes, she does, Ames."

"All three of us do," he resumed. "Your not being brokenhearted over Tuke makes it easier for me to go into it with you. Of course I know you may feel it's only another of my absurdities; but I'm pretty sure it'd be a sensible thing to do. Anyhow I'm going to ask you to think it over. I know how foreign anything sentimental is to you; but here's the situation as I see it: we're all three used to one another and get along together just about perfectly. For years Celia's been really dependent on your care and in many ways I've been that, myself. Even lately when I've been looking forward to a happy married life I've always thought of you as an intimate part of it. I couldn't imagine getting along without your being around somewhere pretty near. Well, Kate dear, except for moving out of this house, things wouldn't be so very different. Do you think you could consider it, Kate? I surely don't need to tell you what my feeling about you is— and has always been—do I?"

"No."

"No," he said. "I don't need to be told what yours is for Celia and me, either. I have a strong conviction that the three of us oughtn't to be separated. If you haven't any other plans, would you be willing to think of it?"

Kate's face was inexpressive and so was her voice. "Ames, you're asking me to marry you, aren't you?"

"Why, yes, of course."

"You're proposing to me," she said, as if to herself in meditation. "You, Ames Lanning, are proposing to me, Kate Fennigate. You're proposing to me." Then she spoke up. "It might be thought pretty sharply on the rebound, mightn't it?"

He was troubled and humble. "Yes—yes, I know. It might seem so; but at that I haven't been able to imagine life without you. I admire you above anybody; you're inexpressibly dear to me and I——"

"Never mind." Her face still told nothing; but she gravely gave him her hand. "I think it would be sensible, too. Yes, I will."

. . . This was the proposal of marriage from the man Kate Fennigate had fallen forever in love with at sixteen, and in this manner she accepted him.

As she gave Ames her hand Mrs. Ferry stood in the dark doorway to the darker hall, solemnly inclined her head once and whispered the word "Gone." Then she looked to Kate for instructions.

"Yes, I'll come," Kate said. "Please telephone Dr. Powls and then Mr. Plaestro. I'll call Cousin Roberta and the others."

Mrs. Ferry's skirts rustled faintly, disappearing. Kate hadn't withdrawn her hand. "Ames, will you call up the bishop and ask him? Aunt Daisy always——"

"Yes, I know; I'll ask him." Ames looked down at her hand as it left his.

"Thank you," she said in a whisper.

"Why, no, it's nothing. I don't mind asking the——"

"I didn't mean for that."

She turned from him; but in the last half second of this movement looked up at him, and he was amazed. Such joy and bright anger, too, glowed in that one look as made him feel once again that he'd never before seen her. For that brief atom of time she was a dazing lovely stranger. The half instant's brightness remained in the dim room after she'd left him and gone to telephone all the relatives that Aunt Daisy was dead at last.

XXV

THERE IS NO NEATLY CLOSED FINISH, NOT EVEN DEATH, to any part of any life; but if there could exist such a thing as a portrait of Kate Fennigate done in music, then here, at this point, the second of the first two movements would be completed, the earlier having concluded with her return from Europe and the next one, now, with Aunt Daisy's funeral. At the opening of the third movement, the more somber orchestrations would cease to be heard. The

fundamental theme, Kate, would repeat; but the time would accel-
erate and, with this increase in activity, the mood would advance
toward liveliness. A fourth movement would be indicated to follow
as a consummation; but it is with the third that this interlude concerns itself.

Elements heretofore not stressed must take their place in the com-
position: Kate Fennigate's life with Ames Lanning now differs from
what went before. It is to be pressed that she's American and that
she was a factor in the growth of Roe Metal Products. The country
and the corporation, too, would thus need to be more emphasized.

The business of the country, enfeebled after over-production, had
begun its long droop before Kate Fennigate accepted Ames Lanning's
offer of marriage. The droop continued, and governmental efforts to
restore prosperity by too many devices only frightened and harried
the drooper. Here and there, however, shrewd heads were still erect
and among them were those that built the high fortunes of Roe Metal
Products. This adroit corporation rose while others fell, and so the
men governing it had to meet the trials that beset worldly success.
Such trials are the most perilous test of a man, for adversity tries only
his courage whereas success strikes at everything weak within him.
Intimate with him in poverty and believing that you know him, you
may not even recognize him in his success, which will have clapped
upon him a new face. Kate Fennigate was to look long upon such a
face.

Over the country riches crumbled, moderate comfort grew poorer,
and faintly, faintly from geologic depths beneath the soil rose sounds
of thunder. Of those who heard them, some refused to listen and
more announced, as if with certain knowledge, that the earthquake
forming in faraway continents could never shake our American solid-
ity. A great deal of sea water, they said, made it impossible for the
dreadful tremors to reach us.

These approached, however, water or no water, and Roe Metal
Products was aware of that fatal nearing. Because of it the colossal
enlargements of the corporation's Plant Three rose in the smoke of
the southwestern borders of the city; and, for comprehension of what
befell Kate Lanning, who in her way was one of the builders of the

great edifice, the fortunes of a youth who came to do his part in it are revealing. Until he arrived he was unknown to Kate, though her husband had heard of him and Mr. Roe was expecting him.

Returning, finally, to the perhaps over-forced comparison of Kate's portrait to a musical structure, the fourth movement would open with the young man's coming. By this time variations based upon earlier passages might appear to be as extreme as are the often startling changes a decade can produce in the exterior life of any group of people.

XXVI

April twilight darkened the upper grassy slopes where stood the long-roofed country club; but while the western windows still shot last sunset blazings across the river valley below, chandeliers and table lamps within the clubhouse, like an opening chorus of light instead of sound, began a festal night. Out of the great smoke smudge that betokened the city's presence five miles down the river boulevard, hundreds of twin headlights swam fast through dimness, and now and then certain of them, bearing to the right, entered the club's stone gateway and followed the curvings of the long drive that bordered the links. One of these cars carried onward to a new phase of his life a young man whose dispositional curiosity was at least tripled by the probability that his future depended upon people he was about to meet for the first time. It is to his credit that he didn't know how agreeable an impression his amiable hazel eyes and general good looks would make upon them.

"How long will you let me go on being a human question-mark, Mr. Augren?" he asked the middle-aged man who drove the small coupé.

"All you like." Mr. Augren was affable. "I'm supposed to act as a kind of governess for you these first few days. To-morrow I'll be breaking you in at Plant Three; but now we're on a purely social basis. My wife'd be better for that—getting you introduced around among the young—but she's away. This shindig to-night's for the orphan twins, Roe's only grandchildren. One of 'em's a girl and not very attractive; but you're an upstanding young feller from the romantic Southland and maybe you'd like to begin your career with Roe Metal Products as the gilded grandson-in-law of the Old Man."

He laughed as he spoke, and the youth beside him, Miley Stuart, amiably laughed too. "What's Mr. Roe like, Mr. Augren?"

"Probably the self-madest man in the United States," Augren said. "He's all right, that old bird; but I expect you'll feel more at home at this big party of his than he will, though you're a stranger."

"Why?" Miley Stuart asked. "You see I don't know anything at all about him or about what's happened to me except that I got kept out of the army because my arm won't salute without dislocating my game shoulder, and my great-aunt wrote to Mr. Roe for a job for me. So many of my age are beginning to be in uniform now I keep feeling I ought to apologize to everybody and explain all about how my shoulder got me rejected. I'll feel more that way of course if we should get into the war and——"

"Oh, I don't know," Augren interrupted. "You might be more use on our blueprints than you would with a gun, if it should happen that we do go in. Some of our head men think we probably will; that's the reason for all our new expansions. You were asking me why Mr. Roe wouldn't feel at home to-night at his own party."

"Yes. Why wouldn't he, Mr. Augren?"

"Well, I'll tell you," Augren said. "Henry L. Roe only came here about forty years ago and's spent all his time going to church and building Roe Metal Products into one of the biggest industries in the country. Of course a great deal of the prosperity of the city revolves round him now; but on the social side I doubt if he trusts himself. This party to-night, for instance, the list of guests, music, decoration, food and everything else, I suspect he's put up to Ames Lanning. Here's a tip for after you get into your job, young fellow: a good deal might depend on what Ames Lanning thinks of your work."

"Lanning, Mr. Augren? He's not too big in Metal Products to notice how an insignificant new hand like me gets on?"

Augren chuckled and shook his head, as men do over a never-ending marvel. "Sometimes you'd almost think Ames Lanning knows how every man on the total payroll's pulling his weight—or isn't. Likely one reason why Mr. Roe stays in love with him, I shouldn't wonder. Lanning's supposed to be Roe's head lawyer, you know; but really he's the Grand Vizier."

"I take it he's a pretty able citizen, Mr. Augren."

"Yes, we've all had to admit that," Augren said. "He's gone over the heads of the rest of us pretty fast. Roe didn't put him on the Board of Directors till 'thirty-six, only five years ago this spring, you see. It makes some of us swaller fairly hard; but there's no denying he delivers. You'd be surprised! I expect right now the Old Man'd take Lanning's say on whether to put out a new issue of preferred stock and also about the proper hair-do for the little granddaughter, Marjie Roe. What I mean, Mr. Stuart, is it won't hurt you to remember if Lanning likes you, why, Henry L. Roe is pretty apt to like you, too. It oughtn't to be hard: Lanning's a good approachable sort."

"I'm glad to hear that, sir."

"Maybe he used to be a shade more so," Augren added qualifyingly. "I mean maybe he used to be a little more folksy than his position lets him be now. Except socially, he wasn't much of anybody, you see, until his legal firm beat the government in a suit it brought against Metal Products. Lanning's name was just barely gold-leafed below the rest on his firm's door; but it was his work at the trial that won the case. Roe saw that and right there began to take him up in a big way. Of course some people think Lanning's begun to get a swelled head; but some people always do think that about successful men."

"Do you, in this case, Mr. Augren?" the young man asked.

"Me? I like him fine. I've known him since a good long while before he got started, and you can take my word for it he's all to the good. He didn't get where he is by bootlicking the Old Man; Mr. Roe's too smart and Lanning didn't need to and wouldn't anyhow. Call him

the Brains of the Board, and from Henry L. Roe down nobody in
Metal Products'll start much of an argument with you on that. Here's
where we get out."

The car stopped; and, leaving it at the tail of a long line of parked
sedans, coupés and "convertibles", the two made their way across
a hundred yards of sward to the clubhouse. There they entered into
a cheerful large confusion of voices and movement, and presently,
at the top of a wide stairway, were in the midst of more of both.

"Splendiferous, what?" Augren said, alluding to the elaborately
gay floral decorations, the full dress of the crowding guests, and to
the strains from a distant orchestra. "Must be upwards of three or
four hundred people here. Yonder's the Old Man and his family,
under the archway. Come do the polite."

To the young Southerner's first glance Henry L. Roe was an anti-
climax, a stout little grey-haired man who'd already mussed his white
tie. He was shaking hands with clustering guests, passing them along
as hurriedly as he could to the twin grandchildren, Marjie and Marvin,
who stood beside him. Miley Stuart had time to perceive that in looks
Marjie was more "unattractive" than Mr. Augren had intimated and
that Marvin was fully her twin. About twenty, rich, ugly and inoffen-
sive, they seemed nonentities except for the riches, and riches had
come to have swifter wings than formerly. Miley, a sensitive young
man, knew a flighty moment of compassion for Henry L. Roe—that
he had to try to make such a pair important.

Augren, however, was introducing him; and the President of Roe
Metal Products, giving him an unexpectedly bright look of comprehension, became briskly hearty.

"Right, right; you look all right," Henry L. Roe said. "Augren, he
looks all right! We'll put him through. Forty-one years ago, just
before I came to this town, his great-uncle, Colonel John Miley,
backed me without security, Augren. Never forgot it and never will.
Give your great-aunt my love when you write to her, Miley Stuart.
Here, Marjie; here, Marvin: this is Miley Stuart, a fine young man
that's going into our Plant Three to-morrow. Make him feel at home.
Wait a minute!" Mr. Roe had a second thought. "They can't do anything; got to stand here and shake hands." He looked over his

shoulder and called to a dark-eyed girl chattering with a group of young people. "Celia! Celia, come here, will you? Miley Stuart ought to meet the young folks; Celia'll do better for that than you, Augren." The dark-eyed girl appeared before him. "Here, Celia. Here's Miley Stuart, a fine young man from Down South that's just come to go into the business. You take care of him. Understand?"

Celia at once began capably to take care of the stranger. She conducted him first into the youthful group with which she'd been standing, made him known to its members; then took his arm and joined an irregular procession moving into a big room where tables were laid for the dinner that was to precede dancing. There were no place-cards, she explained; they could sit anywhere, and, from the small table she selected, they commanded, through an open wide doorway, a view of the still crowded club lounge whence they had come.

"There, Mr. Stuart," she said. "From here you can look over almost everybody and make up your mind which ones you'd like to meet later. Snobbishly I'd call it rather a mixed crowd, because it's a tactful concoction of Metal Products and old citizenry. That dear old Mr. Roe picked me for your Who's Who because I can tell you about both."

" 'Dear old'?" Miley Stuart repeated thoughtfully. "I'm glad you call Mr. Roe that; it's encouraging."

"I didn't just call him that; he is!" Celia said. "He's a dear; but he's datedly strict: everybody has to be terrifically good the horse-and-buggy way. You've noticed there are no cocktails, and the waiters'll bring us terrapin but there won't be any champagne." She waved a hand toward the other tables. "Don't you want to ask me about some of these people? I'd like to know which ones stand out to a stranger."

As she spoke, Miley had been looking through the open doorway into the lounge, and his interest was stirred by a man and a woman both tall, both dark, approaching the dining-room together. The man, whose hair still showed no grey, had a commanding and resourceful eye; and his air of distinction was partly an effect of the look of success he seemed to wear unconsciously and by no interpretation pompously. The woman, ten years younger, was at once notable, too, as Miley Stuart observed. "Those two tall people just coming in," he said. "That woman in the close shiny black with the gold necklace and gold bracelets—and goldish skin, too, as if she's been beach tanning in Florida all winter—she seems to be aware herself that she's a personage. Who's she and who's the Grand Duke with her?"

Celia laughed. "You tell me. Give me your notion of 'em first and then I'll tell you."

"All right, I'll try," Miley said. "Those two would stick out from the rest in any crowd. They're rather like the star and leading man in a play—and maybe they feel a little that way, themselves, particularly the lady. She knows how handsome she still is—I'd have to put in the 'still', wouldn't I? She looks pretty experienced—enough to be over thirty, I'd guess. I think she feels important; but there's a kind of eagerness about her—— Would you almost call it pushing, as if she'd like to be a lot more so?"

"Ouch for her; but good for you!" Celia was delighted. "What else?"

"I hope they aren't your cousins or anything," Miley said. "She strikes me as a woman well aware she's had a good many men in love with her."

"And expects they'll go on being that way—and that there'll be more of 'em? Proceed, stranger!"

"I like the man better," the young Southerner said. "He looks darned able and—and pleased with himself and the world and everything but pretty friendly—and a good squareshooter, too, I'd say."

"Right!" Celia's pleasure continued. "Anything else?"

"Is that red-haired hollow-cheeked pale man behind them with them or just lurking along? He makes them look more like play hero and heroine than ever—as if he's the villain of the piece. I suppose they're husband and wife and he's——"

"No, he's the husband." Celia laughed again. "The lady's Mrs. Tuke Speer, and he's Tuke. Metal Products. The one you picked for hero is Mr. Ames Lanning."

"He is? For me I'd call that good news because I've understood from Mr. Samuel Augren——" Miley stopped short. The party of

three, hero and heroine and red-haired villain, were passing close to
the table, and Mrs. Tuke Speer made her voice cut through the babble
of the crowd as stressingly as she made her looks press other women's
looks into background. The gold bracelets clinked with her gestures.
"Ames, where in the name of all that's commonplace do you suppose
the idea for this décor came from? White and green! White flowers,
white blossoming branches, green streamers, what could be more
banal? Now if they'd only thought of something a little fresh—a surrealist décor or——"

"Or what?" This was Mr. Tuke Speer's interruption, from the rear.
"Hell, Laila, the Old Man's crazy about it the way it is, isn't he?"

The three passed on; and the reddening Miley Stuart drew a quick
conclusion from the fact that Ames Lanning had smilingly tapped
Celia's cheek with a forefinger as he went by. "Lord! He's your
father!" the young man gasped. "Why did you let me——"

"Because I'd guessed you'd be intelligent about him. You were, so
don't worry." Celia'd stopped being amused. "Yes; I'm Celia Lanning.
The Speers and we are pretty thick together; but Laila's a monkey
trying to put it in Father's head that the decorations aren't so good!
They're lovely, and why the devil would anybody want to make a
Metal Products party into a horrible surrealist show? Hang grand-
father-clocks on the chandeliers? Oh, well! Ask me about some of
the others."

He laughed ruefully. "It might be safer if you'd point out all the
members of your own family first."

"Safer? I'm sorry. Don't shoot; the danger's over and there's only
one other, my stepmother. She hasn't come yet and she's a sweet
presh anyhow. She's been here all day working on this party, abused
decorations and everything else, and didn't have a chance to rush
home to dress till after guests began to arrive." Celia looked moody;
then she smiled again and said, "Don't you want to try some more?
Look about and tell me who——"

The tête-à-tête was interrupted and the two unoccupied chairs at
their table were filled. Celia's father hadn't sat down with his friends,
Laila and Tuke Speer; he'd merely strolled into the dining-room
with them and then returned to the lounge. He now reappeared

between the Roe twins, Marjie and Marvin, jovially grasping an arm of each.

"Here, Celia!" he said heartily. "I've told these poor children's grandfather they've done enough handshaking and ought to have food. Sit down, twins, sit down; Celia'll look after you." He shook hands with Miley, who'd jumped up. "Young Miley Stuart, isn't it? Mr. Roe told me he'd put you in Augren's care. Good man, Augren, you'll find. You're about twenty-six, aren't you?"

"Next month, sir."

"Bachelor of Science first; then got your engineer's degree and next did a year or so of research at M.I.T., I believe," Lanning continued, to his hearer's impressed astonishment. "We can use all you've got of that, and I think we're going to be glad to have it. Sit down, sit down. Celia, see that Marvin and Marjie have a grand time."

He pinched Celia's cheek and passed cordially on, moving among the tables talkatively and received everywhere with an eager friendliness in which there was also no little genuine deference, Miley thought. The young man, resuming his seat, realized with disappointment that even as a favored stranger he couldn't hope to monopolize Celia Lanning. Already Marvin Roe was talking to her intimately, though not brilliantly.

"Listen, Cele," Miley heard him saying to her. "Where were you last night? Looked almost like you were trying to duck me."

Miley had to apply himself to the entertainment of Marjie Roe, a discouraging task. Shy almost to the point of hostility, she made her responses not only monosyllabic but unintelligible. The excellent festival meal became a dismal one for the newcomer, and when it was over, and the younger diners repaired to the green-and-white ballroom beyond the lounge, he found himself committed to dance with Marjie. Worse, it was a long commitment; the orchestra played and played and nobody showed a disposition to "cut in". Apparently he was to have the heiress to himself all evening—a calamity creditable to the youth of the city who thus unanimously proved themselves at least no fortune hunters. The energy of the orchestra seemed inexhaustible, the pauses in the dancing no more than momentary; but during a somewhat longer intermission unhoped-for relief arrived.

A laughing brisk young woman swept out of nowhere and came to lightfooted poise in the corner of the room where Miley and Marjie stood abjectly together, he drained of his last dregs of talk and she resentfully inanimate. With a leap of new breath he perceived that the vivacious young woman intended to be his deliverer; and he saw her as an angel of grace.

Grace, indeed, she had, and looks too—brown-eyed, piquant, not tall, and with rippled chestnut hair brown enough to let her escape being sufficiently described as "a blonde". At first glance Miley thought her about twenty-two; then, observing with what authority she brought, dragging after her, a frowning boy of eighteen, he decided that she might be twenty-six, and, in enriching worldly experience, older.

"Marjie!" she exclaimed. "Marjie Roe! Think of your living in the same town with Horace Palmer and not knowing him! This is Horace and he's never met you but's crazy to dance with you—so now he can. Celia's at the other end of the room, just to the left of the orchestra, Mr. Stuart, and says she doesn't know how she lost you."

Instantly upon this the brown-eyed rescuer hurried away; and Miley Stuart, dodging among dancers as the music sounded again, had glimpses of her here and there, for she seemed gayly as busy as a honey-bee. He saw her laughing and waving a small pretty hand as she ducked aside when almost danced into by a tall couple he recognized as his play hero and heroine, Ames Lanning and Mrs. Tuke Speer. Celia was where Miley'd been told she'd be; but an interfering young man was in the act of encircling her waist with his arm. They danced, and, half way down the room, Marvin Roe tapped Celia's partner on the shoulder and took her from him. Miley let Marvin dance with her for perhaps a minute; then ran to them, didn't touch Marvin but said to Celia, "May I cut in?"

She swung to him and they were away together without her having lost the step. He couldn't keep her long, however; others "cut in", Marvin Roe most actively; but Miley Stuart had determination. "You're too much liked to be a good Who's Who," he said, after dislodging Marvin for the third time. "There's somebody else I want to know about, though." He danced Celia toward the slight figure that had angelically saved him. The brown-eyed lady was now hustling another frowning boy to dance with Marjie. "There's a professional philanthropist here, though she seems too young to be one. See yonder: that's she with Marjie Roe and the two boys. I'd like to know who——"

Celia was delighted. "You're right again! Yes, she's a philanthropist —and the catchiest silhouette about the place, at that; you couldn't show better taste. Falling for her, are you, at first sight?"

"Yes. You see she told me where I'd find you."

This brought him a full look. "It's true, is it: once a Southerner always one?" Celia asked, and then they laughed together, better than pleased to get on so well. "I'm afraid, though," she said, "if you've really gone grand pash for philanthropy at first sight you may be a bit late."

"She's married?"

"Very definitely," Celia said, satirizing the hard-used phrase. "Very, very, very definitely! Married ten years, and hasn't she a job of it— part of it with me?"

"With you?" The young man began to be enlightened. "She's— she's actually——"

"My stepmother!" Celia said. "No wonder you stare—to see her look like that after bringing me up and Father, too, at the same time. She's always run us both, still does and always will. Having her own way is what keeps her so pretty."

XXVII

Hurriedly seizing upon passing chances, Celia saw to it that her new friend met more and more people, especially girls easy to dance with, and the middle-aged Augren, reappearing from time to time, assisted in these genial processes; but at intervals the young man found himself upon the sidelines, a looker-on collecting more new impressions. The pleasantest of all were those he had of Celia Lanning and her stepmother—a lovely pair of ladies, he thought, and if he could know them better he'd be glad that fate and his great-aunt had dropped him here. Ames Lanning, an impressive and athletic figure, would have interested him even if Mr. Lanning were not a high chieftain in Roe Metal Products and the father of Celia, the man was so plainly a distinguished person seen anywhere or against any background. He'd not grown portly; one could easily imagine his pulling an oar in a racing shell or playing tennis; and, although his look was that of the prodigiously successful American conscious of his power to command, there was no hint of fatuousness about him. Miley thought he looked gay, high-minded and, even at a dance, just a shade authoritative.

The great Henry L. Roe himself didn't appear in the ballroom, though he looked on for a while from a balcony above the musicians' platform; and he was brought there, Miley observed, by Mrs. Lanning. It was probably she who had straightened the old man's white tie; the sulky granddaughter, Marjie, couldn't be imagined as doing anything like that. Mr. Roe didn't seem to care much about watching the dancers; possibly pious scruples, surviving from his youth, still prejudiced him against such a sight and he'd had to be persuaded to pay for it as an advantageous concession to the grandchildren. Mrs. Lanning might have been the person who did the persuading; she had the air of saying to him: "Look! See how harmless and pretty it is." He seemed to assent grudgingly; but they retired from the balcony, laughing together.

Miley's eye followed the handsome Mrs. Speer as she moved adeptly over the waxed floor with a devoted boy of twenty who was shorter than she. Above his flaxen head her large dark eyes seemed to rove, looking for somebody else, and the young Southerner had the impression that their quest was habitual: dining in a restaurant, she'd always be paying less attention to her own party than to the discovery of who else was there. She was better than handsome, he decided, during this second view of her. At twenty-six it is exceptional when "over thirty" doesn't seem out of the running; but Miley began to classify Mrs. Speer as really rather beautiful in a black-and-goldenly way, the gold being traceable to her tan and the necklaces and bracelets, the black to her hair and eyes and the shifting long dark glistenings of the closely-shaped dress. Her youthful partner didn't have her long. She was taken from him by a beaming grey-haired gentleman whose agility failed to equal his confidence. She seemed to rally him, stopped dancing, and a moment later Miley saw her talking animatedly to a group of lookers-on in one of the wide doorways that opened into the lounge. She wickedly mimicked her elderly partner, who still clung to her, and she pulled up her skirt the better to show with her feet what he'd been doing with his.

Her audience became hilariously applausive; but Miley's attention was called elsewhere. The friendly Augren approached, bringing with him the gaunt person earlier diagnosed as lurking villain in imagined melodrama. "Here, young feller," Augren said. "Here's somebody you ought to meet. He's the man who'll be your immediate boss in Plant Three after I've shown you the ropes a little—Mr. Speer. Tuke, this is Miley Stuart."

Miley shook hands with Mr. Speer, who said absently he was sure they'd get on together. He seemed an unsmiling man, rather cold, and possibly not in good health, Miley thought. His pallor was extreme and his gauntness almost emaciation; a whiskeyish whiff seemed to hint that he was one of those men who sustain themselves as best they can while fighting a disease they doggedly conceal. His red hair was seen at close range to have grey in it prematurely; his voice was languid, yet hinted that it could be sour if need be, and his blue eyes, not mild, seemed to suggest a forcible discontent. He wouldn't be easy to please.

Miley said the appropriate modest things; Mr. Speer responded vaguely, and moved on. "Don't be discouraged by his looks," Augren said. "He's a keen hand in the Works; but he's stuck in the same groove there a good many years now and of course that doesn't jolly up any man's manners. You'll find him all right if he thinks your work's up to scratch. He's hard; but he's quiet. There, I won't detain you. Why aren't you dancing?"

"Thank you. I think I am, sir."

Miley crossed the room and presented himself before Mrs. Lanning, who'd just come through a doorway. She smiled upon him and was glad to dance with him.

"I caught a glimpse of you a moment ago, Mr. Stuart. You were speaking to an old friend of mine."

"Mr. Augren? He's been very kind."

"Yes; but I meant Mr. Speer. My husband tells me you're to work under him." She didn't stress the word "husband"; but it picked itself out to Miley's ear as if he'd never heard it spoken before. Only a woman proudly and happily in love with her husband could have said that word just so, the young man thought, and indeed, as her sunny brown eyes glanced up at him, he was sure that he'd never seen a happier, prouder wife in all his life. "You'll find Mr. Speer immensely competent and always fair," she went on. "You mustn't mind, though, if you don't get much praise from him, even when your work's particularly well done. He's not—well, not the enthusiastic type."

"No, I judged he wasn't," Miley said. "He's not very well, is he, Mrs. Lanning?"

"Why, yes, I think he is. His health's excellent, I believe." She changed the subject a little abruptly. "Mr. Roe's been telling me about your great-aunt and her letter to him. He's anything but heartless; yet he said he was glad your bad shoulder'd got you turned down for the army. When we get caught up into this war——"

"You think we shall, Mrs. Lanning?"

"My husband and I think so. Mr. Roe's uncertain and very nervous about it; but he said he wished more of his young men had bad shoulders like yours, so he could be sure of keeping them. You must come to dine with us very soon, Mr. Stuart. Celia'll call you up to-morrow and ask you when. You mustn't let me keep you any longer now." She stopped dancing. "Thank you!" she said, and was away.

He found himself almost touching shoulders with Celia and Marvin Roe, and promptly "cut in".

. . . Mrs. Lanning, having further pursued her ballroom philanthropies, saw her husband surrender Mrs. Speer to a competitor, and joined him upon the sidelines. "All out of control!" she exclaimed, took his arm and appealed upward from the height of his shoulder. "Boys are barbarians, except that barbarians do their duty by the tribe and these won't. They won't dance with Marjie. With the help of his mother, I've got Freddie Cooke at it now; but they're scowling at each other as they dance. Do you think it'd be helpful if you'd go round among some of 'em, threatening, Ames?"

He looked thoughtful. "This party's supposed to be for both the twins and Marvin isn't having any better time than Marjie is. Look at him, helpless and downhearted yonder."

"He's a pig," Kate Lanning said. "He won't dance with anybody but Celia. He can't expect——"

"They don't give him much chance, Kate. This new young Miley Stuart, for instance. He doesn't let Marvin——"

"No, he doesn't." Kate laughed. "Celia says he's a nice boy, Ames, and you can see he's got one of those cheerful open faces you can't be mistaken about. Poor Marvin! Nobody in the world could ever get a girl like Celia to do more than bear with him, dear."

"You think not?" Ames Lanning said. "Aren't there plenty of less attractive young men than Marvin Roe?"

"I can't think where! Did the dinner go off well? I couldn't get back for it and only hoped that everything'd be all right. Was it?"

"Yes, oh, yes—except——"

"Oh, dear!" she murmured. "You say 'except'? Something wrong with the food?"

"No, not the food. I only thought we might have done better about the decorations. This green-and-white scheme we felt would look so springlike and please Mr. Roe——"

"But it does, Ames. He just told me."

"Yes, of course, Kate; but if we'd tried something a little more unusual we might have pleased him and also the kind of people who —well, those who like a more modern——"

"Who's all that?" Kate looked up at her husband, not with any resentment; but she spoke crisply. "Somebody who's been setting up as a critic? I wonder——"

She had no chance just then to say more: Mrs. Tuke Speer and a jovial baldish fat man, he who'd "cut in" when Lanning was dancing with her, came to a halt close by and were at once joined by Mrs. Speer's husband. Mrs. Speer began to talk volubly of her sufferings as the fat man's partner, and at the same time, as if unconsciously, or of familiar friendly habit, rested a hand upon Ames Lanning's sleeve. The fat man, even more familiar, and without Mrs. Speer's palliative advantages, heartily slapped the manly shoulder just above that hand.

"No hard feelings, what, old skeezix?" he said, laughing huskily. "Not sore because I grabbed away the face that launched a thousand ships, are you? Love your fat old Jonesy like always, don't you, Amesy?"

Ames Lanning's sleeve courteously retained Mrs. Speer's hand; but his shoulder seemed to withdraw itself. He didn't laugh with his fat old Jonesy; instead he looked serious. "You get some coffee in the dining-room, and then get some more. Sit down somewhere after that, where nobody's noticing, and take your evening nap." He spoke brusquely, and turned to Mrs. Speer's husband. "Tuke, as young Stuart's to go into your department to-morrow, I wish you'd have a talk with him. He's dancing with Celia just now; but she won't mind if you take him away a while. Size him up a little. Attend to it, will you, Tuke?"

"I've already met him," Tuke Speer said. "Just now my wife wants a highball and I've got to get to my locker. Come on, Laila."

Laila Speer broke off a momentary chatter with Mrs. Lanning, and then, between her two escorts, one of them now a deeply reddened fat old Jonesy, disappeared through a doorway into a corridor. Ames looked bothered. "I don't enjoy doing that to people," he explained to his wife; "but sometimes Bill Jones really needs it."

"You feel so?" Kate Lanning's expression, which had been a gay one during the moment she'd chattered with Mrs. Speer, became somewhat disapproving. "Bill's that way with everyone, of course, Ames."

"Yes, that's just the trouble. I can't always be everyone, you see."

"But you used not to mind him, Ames. You used to be as jolly with old Bill as he was with you. I'm afraid he mightn't understand."

"Then he'd better begin to. There's such a thing as ordinary human dignity, you know, Kate—especially in semi-public. I like Bill all right; but I can't always be with everybody the way I used to be. I can't. When you're in the fo'c'sle with the crew you can be as democratic as you like; but when you're an officer on the quarterdeck—well, sometimes you've got to show your gold braid a little, I suppose."

"Maybe so," she said, "and yet——"

"And yet what?"

"Oh, nothing much." She pressed his arm more warmly. "I just thought people might think—of course you and I know it wouldn't be true; but there are ways of being on the quarterdeck without—without hurting anybody's feelings and giving them a chance to say —to say——"

"To say what?"

"You know!" Kate became a little impatient. "Do I have to tell you what they'd say?"

"That I've got the big-head?" He drew away his arm. "Kate, I wish sometimes you'd understand I do know what I'm doing. Some of 'em are bound to say it anyhow and I can't help it. I've got a position to maintain and it can't always be done without putting people a little in their places."

"You think so? Poor Bill's face troubles me. He looked so——"

"Oh, come!" Lanning said, smiled upon her and restored her hand to his arm. "Stop bossing me and everybody else! I wasn't occupied solely in defending my poor old suffering dignity from Bill. He and Tuke have both been oiling up. Couldn't you see it? I don't want Mr. Roe noticing it, so I told Bill to drink coffee and Tuke to go sit down somewhere for a while with young Stuart. That isn't being too big-headedly autocratic, is it? Mr. Roe's eyes are about as sharp as eyes get made, and Tuke and Bill could easily hurt themselves with him."

"Yes, I know, but——"

"Now, now!" he said, and smiling, put an arm about her. "Let's dance, not argue. Don't worry about how Tuke and Bill'll feel toward me, Kate. They've both got sense enough to think it over and understand."

. . . This was a mistake. Downstairs in a surreptitious small corridor off the locker-room Tuke Speer and fat old Bill Jones, who was now anything but jolly, leaned against the wall, drank and spoke unfavorably of their superior. Mrs. Speer, between them, looked deeply into her long glass and let them talk.

"Easy to see why he wanted me to spend the evening with this new kid, Stuart," Tuke Speer said. "I'm to keep him away and reduce the competition, give Marvin more chance at Celia. Wants to unite the two great houses of Roe and Lanning, does he?"

"Just a step, just a step toward the goal, Tuke." Bill Jones breathed into his glass, drank bitterly. "When Roe dies, or's willing to Chairman-of-the-Board himself into retirement, who'll be the President of Roe Metal Products? The way he acts, Ames Lanning thinks he's got it already. Good old pal Amesy! Got the front to tell me to drink coffee, meaning I'm high, which I'm not, and if I am whose business is it? Which does he think he is, my master or my nurse?"

"Why didn't you ask him?" Mrs. Speer suggested unsmilingly. "Scared to?"

"Me? Likely!" The fat man's tone changed from this preliminary contemptuousness to one of complaint. "Why, Ames Lanning used to be fun! Remember how we'd all get round him at the piano? Now he wants the earth."

"Oh, he'll pull it off all right!" the gloomy Tuke said. "He'll have the presidency."

"No, he won't, Tuke; not if he gets too many people sore. The Old Man's had other big favorites before Ames Lanning and dropped 'em cold. Just 'magine Amesy gets to 'preciating liquor more'n he does now—nice natural thing to do; but let the Old Man hear about it and bingo, Ames'd be out! Or s'pose he never drinks much but maybe makes just an itsy-bitty slip in his morals or anything——" Bill Jones paused. "What's matter? What you staring at me that way for?"

"I'm not," Tuke said. "Go ahead."

"Ahead where, Tuke? Oh, yes, you mean about Ames. Top man for Henry L. Roe has to walk the tightrope, I tell you. Look at the costs and risks Ames's got the business into right now. Me, I say there ain't going to be no war—no, sir, not for Uncle Sam! Dear old pal Amesy might get a jolt."

"No, he won't." Tuke shook his head. "He's got too much ability. What's the use not admitting it? You can't beat him. Look at Metal Products' Defense expansion, enlargement of Plant Three and tripling Plant Two up at Roeville, for instance. If we get into this war Ames is going to be right. He showed the Old Man that even heavier contracts than we've already got'll be awarded here, back from the seaboard and where factories'll be safest. Well, Ames believes war can't be helped, it's coming, and if it does he's fixed correct and Roe Metal Products'll be ready. No, he's got all his own brains and on top of that a mighty good adviser."

"Adviser? Who?"

"His wife," Tuke said. "It makes a team. Kate Lanning——"

"Dew tell!" The interruption came from Mrs. Speer. She gave her husband a side-glance of sheer distaste; uttered a metallic laugh. "That's one of Tuke's theories, Bill. We'd be rich if we could live on theories."

"Listen," Tuke said, and a sulky heat came into his voice. "What did Ames amount to before he married Kate Fennigate? Oh, I know, I know! He had the stuff to go big places; but was he doing it? Laila thought he wasn't, herself, Bill, or she'd have married him, not me."

"Oh, gosh!" Mrs. Speer's tone made audible a kind of disgusted despair—despair of her husband's taste in conversation. "Nice boy!" she said.

He drank and explained. "She doesn't mind my mentioning that Ames wanted her, Bill. She does plenty of that, herself. She only hates to be reminded that she didn't take him."

Bill Jones tried to be soothing. "Now, now, children; it's all in the family—we're talking cordial. You looked like up-and-coming in those days, Tuke. Sure Laila had the good sense to turn Ames down and take you instead, so——"

" 'Good sense'?" Laila echoed, as if meditatively, and, clinking her bracelets, shook ice against the side of her glass into which she again was staring.

"Quit ribbing your husband," Bill Jones said. "What you trying to prove about Kate Lanning, Tuke?"

Tuke removed a somber gaze from his wife. "Look where the Lanning upward march began. I was a defense witness and sat in at the trial of that suit against Roe Metal Products when he made his hit with the Old Man. Ames knocked me for a gool! His whole style had changed; that's the first time he showed he knew how to get the Court on his side, plumping for him. Somebody must have been working on him, and who was it if it wasn't Kate?"

"Kate," Laila murmured. "The brilliant Kate."

Her husband gave her only a glance. "Yes, Kate, of course. Up to then Ames always had the overbearing trial manner used by the heads of his firm: bullying and pretending to be virtue and pure legality outraged by the opposition. Kate really laughed that out of him, got him to take on the tone of a reasonable man sure of what was the law and the truth and being fair and just to all parties concerned. It did the job for him."

"Wonderful!" Laila murmured. "Ames had nothing to do with it, himself, had he, Tuke?"

He disregarded this. "You remember that mother-in-law of his, Bill? She had him buffaloed; he didn't seem to have any energy. When Kate got him out from under that, he began to move. He likes admiration—who doesn't?—and she fed him praise for every little thing he accomplished."

"See, Bill?" Laila said. "That's a wife's only business, praising her husband. Tuke means he'd be in Ames Lanning's shoes to-day if I'd only praised him enough. For what? Tell us, Tuke."

Tuke continued to disregard her. "I'm saying that while Ames's first wife was alive he hadn't found out how to use himself. When he took the big chance and set up offices for himself, everybody thought Roe'd stick with the old Bortshleff firm; but within six months Ames had the bulk of Metal Products cases and right there the Old Man began to depend on him in the business itself. Ames'd been afraid to step out on his own, said they'd be in the poorhouse; but Kate got him bucked up to it. Laila knows that as well as I do, Bill, because they talked it over with me and I told her. Laila knows——"

"Do I?" Mrs. Speer said coolly. "I might know more than you think I do. Isn't it a pity you didn't marry her yourself, Turk? Think where you'd have been by now!"

The gibe cut; but even in hot resentment Tuke Speer showed a dogged kind of honesty. "Did I ever claim I've got half his ability? Kind, aren't you, Laila?" He moved toward the nearby door that closed the corridor. "Want another helping, Bill? I do."

"More liquor?" his wife inquired. "That'll make your eighth since seven o'clock. I've counted them."

"Have you? Then you missed five, Laila. This'll be the thirteenth."

She stooped and set her empty glass upon the cement floor. "Lucky thirteen; it's where I leave you," she said. "Drink yourself to death, honey." She turned her back upon the two men, walked slowly to the open end of the corridor and was gone.

"That's plain enough, isn't it?" her staring husband said to the disgruntled Jones. "Thinks she missed her calling."

"Missed her calling? What you mean, Tuke?"

"Our old pal," Tuke said. "Our former friend, the great man on the steps of the throne. Come on, let's do as she says, Jonesy."

XXVIII

MARVIN ROE, PEEVISHLY SEEKING THE ONE PERSON WITH whom he cared to dance, went everywhere over the clubhouse except where she'd gone to avoid him. She and Miley Stuart sat at the rear of the balcony above the musicians, and, as a row of chatty elderly spectators occupied the chairs nearest the balcony railing, the two weren't easily seen from the dancing-floor, although they could look down upon it when they wished. Celia saw Marvin peering upward in her direction, for the fourth time, and she stooped. "He's near-sighted," she said; "but do you mind lowering your head a little? I've done the polite all evening; but I was never cut out to be an all-time martyr."

"It's all right," Miley informed her. "You can sit up straight; he's gone into the lounge again. I'm beginning to be a little sorry for him, and for myself, too."

"For yourself, too?"

"Do I need to explain?" Miley asked. "I can't flatter myself, can I, that I'm more than any port in a storm?"

"You call Marvin a storm? I wish he were; there'd be some excite-ment to that. For any girl he's just a kind of drudgery and I can't take more of it to-night, even if there's a scolding when I get home."

"A scolding? I can't imagine Mrs. Lanning——"

"No, no; not Kate." Celia smiled and shook her head. "It'd be Father; but don't think I'm too serious about it. He's nobody at all to be afraid of—though I don't mean that a young metallurgical expert just going into the business won't do well to watch his step."

"Student, not expert, I'm afraid, Miss Lanning."

" 'Miss Lanning'?" Celia said. "It would have been 'Celia' by this time if you weren't a true Southern gentleman, wouldn't it, Miley? I'll tell you a secret: you really don't need to be a bit afraid of my father. He hasn't exactly got delusions of grandeur; but you see he truly has come to be quite a whale, and a whale naturally can't help knowing a little something about his own size, can he? I've always heard they're simple-hearted creatures, though, and would rather swim away than do anybody any harm. Here's another secret: when he scolds me I laugh, and I mean laugh. See him now that he's dancing with Kate. Look down—between those two dowagers' shoulders—and say if anybody needs to be afraid of him?"

Miley looked, saw Mr. and Mrs. Lanning dancing together below, and shook his head. "No. I think you're right—at least so long as Mrs. Lanning's with him. If you don't mind my being a bit ecstatic over her, I'll go on to say that she seems to me the best living testimony I ever saw—testimony to a happy marriage. They both look that, I

think. Are they always so—well, so radiant over just getting together?"

"Yes, pretty much." Celia's tone was fond; she became confidential,
as youth often does at such moments. "I was dreadfully young and
dumb when they were married; but it seemed to me they fell more
in love with each other afterward—and more and more ever since.
It's usually the other way, isn't it?"

"Well, if we're to believe Balzac——" he began; but she stopped him
with an outcry, "Oh, how lovely!" Thereafter, not risking Marvin
again for an hour, they devoted themselves to the literature and art
of the French.

At Mr. Roe's party everybody had to be good "the horse-and-buggy
way", as Celia'd said. The orchestra, wholly sober and never once
"hot", stopped playing at half past one. Twenty minutes later Ames
Lanning and his wife motored homeward over curving suburban
roads and under moonlight that seemed a twinkling spray upon the
earliest spring leafage of willow tree and lilac bush. Kate drove, as
she always did when they were out together in the evening; for, whatever the facts, her theory held that the day's work had tired her
husband.

"You danced with me four times to-night," she said. "Did you know
it, Ames?"

"Know it? What do you mean?"

"Nothing—only thank you!"

"Thank me for treating myself to the best dancer on the floor?"
Ames chuckled, patted the hand near him on the wheel; then was
thoughtful. "Toward the end of the evening did Marvin come to ask
you if you knew where Celia was?"

"Yes. I told him I was lucky because he was just the person I was
looking for because it was his party and there were lots of girls he
hadn't danced with yet. He showed real dexterity in getting away
from me. Let's don't talk about him—at least not under this moon."

"Well——" With some reluctance Ames consented to the postpone-
ment. "By the way, what was all that disturbance at the foot of the
stairs just before we left the club? I was talking to people, so I

couldn't tell. You'd got ahead of me and seemed to be in the midst of an arguing group milling about. What was it?"

"Nothing much, Ames. I was only helping Bill Jones keep Tuke from going back upstairs to say goodnight to Mr. Roe. Laila was furious, of course, wouldn't speak to Tuke and stalked out to their car to wait. Bill asked me to help and we finally persuaded Tuke. Too bad it made a little noise."

Ames shook his head. "That was nice of you. Good thing you stopped him. Tuke's got into the way of hitting it up every party he goes to. Lord knows what he does at home. I hate to see it growing on him, not only for old friendship's sake but on account of the business. I'm afraid there's a long disappointment in it, Kate. Tuke's not gone up where we all used to think he would and where he thought he would, himself, of course; but he's still a very useful man in Plant Three. It'll be just too bad if Mr. Roe ever——"

"Yes," Kate said, "we mustn't let it happen. I wish we could ride in this moonlight all night, Ames. Do you?"

"Yes, in a world that held no place where a moonlight night made fear. It's strange to think that moonlight means we have to step up production in all our Plants, isn't it, Kate? What a queer thing that is."

"Yes," she assented sadly. "Queer and horrible and inevitable, Ames."

"I'm afraid so."

They came into their own street, National Avenue's northward extension bordered by broader and deeper lawns than those that Aunt Daisy Cunningham had angrily seen destroyed. Here, in dignified reserve, sheltered by tall trees and a long hedge, stood the simply symmetrical whitewashed stone house that Ames Lanning had bought five years earlier. It had cost ninety thousand dollars to build; but in 1936 the owner had been glad to sell it to Ames for thirty-five thousand, with its four acres of lawn and garden. Kate drove the car slowly along the driveway to the garage behind the house; then husband and wife, hand in hand, retraced their way, came round the house in the moonlight to the front door, and paused there before going in.

Kate looked up at the moon. "Ames, who'd ever have thought that you and I——" she said.

"Yes, who would?" He hadn't needed her to finish the sentence.

Indoors, when they'd lighted the living-room, Kate began briskly to change the water in vases of flowers that her gardener had brought in the day before from the small hothouse in the rear garden. Ames drew forth a pipe from a table drawer, filled it, sat in an easy-chair and smoked. "On the whole," he said, "I suppose we made as much of a success of the party as Mr. Roe expected. I say 'we'; but of course you really did it all. The young people wouldn't think much of it, probably, closing so soon. I suppose Celia and her crowd'll be all over town for hours and then go somewhere for breakfast. I didn't see 'em leave. Did you notice if they took Marvin with 'em, Kate?"

"I didn't see but I doubt it." She applied a pair of scissors to the stems of some roses held over a tin bucket she'd carried in from a pantry. "They've learned lots of ways of avoiding that."

"Have they?" He looked into the smoking bowl of his pipe, seemed not to approve of it. "I suppose at that age nobody's very considerate. I don't see why——" He interrupted himself, turning his head to stare through the open double doorway into the hall. "Hello! Here's something unprecedented. Not staying out for breakfast!"

Celia, who'd just come into the house, appeared in the doorway unfastening her wrap. "Breakfast, no," she said cheerily. "I've been doing a little work for good old Roe Metal Products. Mr. Augren was yawning, so I sent him home. Miley Stuart has to be up early and I'm terribly maternal. We didn't go on with the crowd; I just delivered him at his hotel. Noble girl, what?"

"No doubt, no doubt," her father assented. "If you're as maternal as all that, though, you might have been a little motherly with somebody that maybe really needs it more than our new young friend, Stuart."

"Marvin Roe?" the daughter inquired. "You hospitably saddled him on me for dinner; but no go, my lad, no go! Haven't you done enough for one day, Kate? Bet you're dead on your feet! Let 'em wither, say I! Ain't it ever bedtime for old folks?" She waved a hand, said "Goodnight, all!" disappeared from the doorway and sang herself up the stairs beyond.

Kate Lanning restored cut roses, dripping, to their vase, trotted off to the pantry with her bucket, returned, sank upon a sofa opposite her husband and observed that his look was reminiscently one of chagrin. "Don't be downcast, Ames." She gave him a tired smile. "You're grand in your own field, dear; but when you try to manipulate my sex you're about as subtle as a sixteen-inch gun. Shows you're a man, and I love you for it; but you'll never get Marvin anywhere with her."

"Not if you and she both misinterpret me," he said. "I'm not trying to marry Marvin Roe to Celia. Don't you suppose I know he's not up to her? Yet, though Marvin isn't a genius, there isn't a better boy anywhere and I don't see why she couldn't be a little nice to him, especially when the party was given for him and Marjie."

"Nice to him, Ames? Of course I know you want her to stand seeing more of him on Mr. Roe's account; but she can't, she just can't!"

"Why not?"

"Two reasons," Kate said. "One, he bores her; that's simple. The other reason is simple, too; but not simple to you, because you're the kind of man you are."

"I see." Ames didn't smile. "I'd need to have some woman tell me, would I? Get on with it, then."

"Yes, Ames. Marvin has a high opinion of himself so he thinks toleration means encouragement. Celia knows that if she's more than half nice to him she'll pretty soon have to undo its effect on him. If she allows Marvin to think she particularly likes him it's only piling up trouble for him in the end. He's Mr. Roe's grandson, and on that very account of course I don't want to see him let in for a hard disappointment. Besides, it's preposterous. Marvin's younger than Celia and he's such a drearily immature boy that if she sees much of him, goes about with him, everybody'll think——"

"What nonsense! Just because I'd have liked her to be a little more agreeable to him at his own party——"

"Ames! Why dwell on it so?" Kate looked at him fondly but nevertheless satirically and her tone was a little more superior than she knew. "Celia did dance with Marvin—perhaps too much. That's why she finally hid from him. Ames, you might as well save yourself from worrying over your innocent little schemes; they're as transparent as the day and they never come off, you know. Just you do your grand big work among men and leave the petty little female scheming to us picayune-minded gals."

If she hadn't been tired she'd have been more careful; for she'd realized of late that Ames sometimes found certain advisory things she said disturbing. He set his pipe abruptly on the table beside him.

"I see," he said. "You mean that even in the slightest of my own family affairs I'm not competent."

"How absurd!" she exclaimed. "I didn't mean——"

"Yes, you did, Kate." He rose, looked at her penetratingly for a moment; then began to walk up and down the room, speaking not angrily but in the tone of one to whom a revelation makes itself clearer and clearer. "I'm beginning to be afraid that you often believe me just a mechanism—one that you really run. I'm even afraid it could be the truth and that I've come to be actually only such a machine, with you at the levers. Don't think I'm so petty as to complain of just this one instance. No, you may not realize it, but you've made it a habit; and I see how it came about. I think it began in those old hard times—I mean before we were married. In a manner of speaking, you went to work on me from the very first."

"I didn't!" She laughed. "How?"

"To change me," he said. "For my benefit, of course, and I admit it gratefully. You've proved to be right as rain about any number of important things—most of all about my trial manner and setting up for myself. Don't think I under-rate what your influence has done for me; but that doesn't mean you're right about everything on earth, Kate. Nobody is. Yet from the very start you've pushed me——"

"Pushed you?" She laughed at him. "Ames, does a sparrow push the Great Pyramid? Pushed you!"

"A sparrow can push a straw! It began with a push here and there; now it's every day and everywhere. How many decisions do we make that aren't yours? Why, just in the matter of those decorations to-night, for instance, did I really have anything to say about 'em?"

"No, you didn't even think about 'em," she said. "I took that off your hands because you oughtn't to be bothered to think about such trifles."

"Trifles? My daughter's conduct, for another instance, isn't a trifle, is it? Yet I'm not to have a word to say about it. No, nor about my own conduct with men under me in the business. To-night I couldn't even handle two of 'em who'd been drinking without your jumping on me and telling me how I ought to——"

"Yes, and you ought!" The weary Kate, nettled, now spoke up sharply. "You made them both furious when there wasn't any need for it. In questions of tactfulness perhaps you'd better do as I say a little oftener than you do!"

"You think so?" He'd stopped his pacing and stood near the doorway. "I ought to do as you say oftener? That'd mean the whole time, wouldn't it? Why, damn it, Kate, sometimes I feel as if you were trying to make me into one of those automatic chess players somebody operates from behind with wires! If I try to make a move for myself you jack me up and say it's wrong before you even know what it is."

"That's just silly," Kate began. "When did I ever——"

"Right now," he said. "About poor Marvin Roe. I can't even try to give my best friend's grandson a good time at his own party without your getting it into your head—and maybe into Celia's head, too— that I'm actually trying to marry him to her."

"Ames! Ames! I've never thought anything of the kind; but other people might and I don't want them to. It doesn't amount to any-thing; but when you try to put over such funny little maneuvers as you did to-night—practically instructing Tuke Speer to keep young Stuart out of Marvin's way——"

"Wait!" he said. "Nobody needs to tell me you're the dearest, best woman in the world or what I owe you; but occasionally I'd like to do one single little damn thing without being told either not to, or how to, or that I'm a clumsy ass! If you want to know the truth, Kate, I think you're a sweet thing; but I'm getting good and damned tired of criticism fresh every hour and being instructed at exactly what angle I'm allowed to wear my hat!"

Both his voice and his words had grown more protestive than he intended, and, afraid that if he said more he'd sound actually quarrelsome, he turned through the doorway and went quickly upstairs to his own room.

He was astounded, didn't know just what had happened or how it had come about. Hurt, indignant with both Kate and himself, he had the perplexing impression that he'd made a fool of himself and had been right to do so. Every word he'd uttered had been true and yet to his wife had sounded silly, so that he'd seemed to stand before her like a browbeaten schoolboy at last growling at the teacher. That was a fine dignified position for a man to be in—a man who carried the weight in the world that he did! Ames didn't magnify that weight or his own importance, and he knew that wives and daughters don't see an important man as other people do. He didn't expect at home the prestige he carried when he walked abroad; but surely a man who'd worked as hard and gone as high as he had was entitled to some say in his own household and to protest against being forever held on a domestic checkrein—yes, and had a right to free himself from it!

Long he'd not known he wore that checkrein; but more and more, as he'd moved upward to success on success, its pressure chafed him until this outburst against it came from him to-night—over nothing! No, he insisted to himself, it wasn't over nothing; it wasn't over Marvin Roe, it was over the question whether or not Ames Lanning was ever to be his own man, with his head up because he himself had won the right to hold it high, not because his wife had strapped it there. He admired her, he felt the warmest gratitude toward her and he loved her tenderly—he hadn't been in love with her, so to speak, when he married her; but he'd begun to be and later he was—delightedly and wholly. When their one child, their darling little boy, had died of meningitis, three years after their marriage, husband and wife had been so spiritually united by their grief, both felt, that nothing in this world or another could ever infinitesimally intrude upon such a union. Yet to-night they had quarreled. Ames had rushed upstairs to prevent himself from believing that there actually was a quarrel; but he'd gone too late—the thing had taken place and a difference henceforth was inevitable.

All right, he thought. So be it. Full time that he spoke out to let her know he'd be a checkreined husband no longer! Kate often told him she was proud of him; but in reality she must be only proud of what she felt she'd made of him and therefore proud of herself, since he was only her handiwork! When he did any slightest thing she didn't like, she made it clear she looked upon him as a blundering failure.

In times when every business man needs to be a lawyer as well, and every lawyer must be a business man, she'd done a good wife's part in helping to make him eminently both. Sorely smarting, he acknowledged that; yet asked the walls of his room why Kate couldn't have been the comprehending, easy kind of wife that lots of pleasant women were? Laila Speer, for instance, didn't even interfere with poor old Tuke's drinking, because she so thoroughly understood that a man had to have his liberty even if it hurt him. Why couldn't Kate understand that a man in the midst of making a fine and conspicuous career might like to carry some prestige for it in even his own family —might passionately like to possess some freedom of action? "She won't!" Ames bitterly thought. "She'll join the crowd that think I've got a swelled head. Well, from now on she'll have to think it!"

A suffering husband is unlike a suffering wife. Ames Lanning, filled with grievance, couldn't have suspected that downstairs, stretched flat with her face in a sofa cushion, Kate knew almost everything that he was feeling. Protest against her must have been long pent within him—and was it ironical that he'd submitted so long to Aunt Daisy, yet now rebelled against a wife who gladly spent herself for his advancement? No, the irony was but a seeming one: his slow-grown rage against the rule of women must have been a downtrod seed under the strong feet of Aunt Daisy; but a seed nevertheless. As it grew, had a wife's power withered?

Kate remembered that she was of Aunt Daisy's blood, and so, after all, was she only one of those bossy little women whom husbands finally treat as encumbrances? The critical hour had come and she recognized it; but didn't know what to do. In such a despair a wife can only resolve to do nothing.

XXIX

Mrs. TUKE SPEER, SEATING HERSELF FOR A MONDAY MORN-
ing meal, observed that her husband, across the table, was completing
with orange juice a breakfast that had consisted principally of ice
water. "Got your new spring habit going strong, haven't you, Tuke?"
she said. "Up to about a month ago you'd get high only on Saturday
nights and sobered up on Sunday to be right for business on Monday.
Started your new system after the night of the party for the Roe
grandchildren, I seem to've noticed. Oiled yourself up a few week-day
evenings, too, since then. Curious!"

"Is it?" he asked. "If you want to know the reason——"

"Oh, I don't, I don't!" she protested. "Far be it from me to cast
a gloom on your little pleasures—or even inquire about 'em."

"No, not even inquire? I'll tell you anyhow, Laila. That was the
night that things got really plain to me, and the drunker I got the
plainer they were."

"Is that so?" She looked at him as wholly disillusioned wives do
look at husbands on such mornings. Tremulous in voice and body,
moistly pallid, the red-haired Tuke was hollow-eyed as well as hollow-
cheeked. His best friend wouldn't have found him appetizing to look
upon; and his wife, being by no means his best friend, averted her
eyes. "Just so you don't make them clear to me, Tuke, I really don't
care. Hadn't you better be off to your job—since so far you still somehow manage to hang on to it?"

"No, I'm going to tell you," he said. "Up to then I'd fooled myself.
I'd played tricks on myself a hundred times a day, trying to kid myself
that you cared sometimes, anyhow just a little, whether I was alive
or dead. I'd say to myself, 'No, she doesn't really hate me; she laughed

at that story I told last night.' Or I'd say, 'Look, she brushed the ashes off my sleeve.' Things like that. I'd tell myself you were discontented with me because you saw I never was going to get much higher up in the business or make more money—I know you've had a long disappointment from finding out I'm not built that way—but I kept pretending you didn't hate me. That night I knew you did. It didn't take last night, Laila, to prove. I'd been right."

"Last night?" She looked at him again, and frowned. "What's your objection to last night?"

Tuke glanced at his orange juice, shuddered, rose, went to the sideboard, opened a compartment of it and drew forth an almost empty brandy bottle. He poured the remnant of liquor into a glass, drank, shuddered again and returned to the table but didn't resume his chair. "This is a funny thing," he said. "Here we are, two people each knowing what's in the other's mind—oh, yes, I do know what's in yours, plain as day, Laila—and yet you think you can get away with a question like that, and you'll put on an act of being affronted when I answer it."

"Sorry you find that bottle disappointing." Laila ate slowly and looked toward a sunlit window. "Perhaps you oughtn't to've hit it so hard after we got home."

Tuke glanced over his shoulder and spoke to the empty bottle on the sideboard. "Good-bye. I'm through with you." He looked down at his wife again. "It was my last drink that I just took, Laila; I mean last."

"Yes; likely!" She laughed. "Fat chance! Sunday night supper at the Augrens' doesn't seem to've agreed with you."

"No," he said. "Not when you and Ames Lanning find it necessary to withdraw from the company and sit out in a sunroom for two hours."

" 'Out in a sunroom'!" As he'd prophesied, she looked affronted. "Terrific, wasn't it?"

"I thought so," he said. "Oh, yes, Kate went on chattering and laughing with everybody as if she didn't care, and maybe she didn't —because she doesn't know what's in your mind as I do, Laila."

"What's in my mind? That's pretty simple: if Mr. Roe hears you're falling off in your work because you prefer being a dipsomaniac——"

"It wouldn't take Mr. Roe, Laila. Do you think I don't know where I stand? Ames Lanning can throw me out with two words any time he decides to. I'd be on the town. Ames could do it as easily as that; but it'll be better for you if you don't hope that he will."

"Fooey!" The wife's handsome dark eyes showed a contemptuous anger. "Twaddle and babble! Hadn't you better wait till your brain's unfuddled before you say any more?"

"No, I'm going on telling you, Laila," Tuke said. "I'm in a hell of a fix because I'm a one man dog. I couldn't make a tougher confession; but you've always been the only woman for me and you always will be. I can't help it, even though I know you clear through, Laila. You're the kind of woman that thinks a husband ought to be something that provides her with the envy-builders—minks, new model cars, fifty-dollar slippers. You're that kind, Laila, and maybe you can't help it any more than I can help being your one man dog."

Laila still looked out of the window; but now she smiled and uttered a contemptuous slight exclamation. "Oh, puh!"

"Yes, I hear," he said. "What I want to impress on you is that I may be a horribly disappointing husband; but don't try anything. He could throw me out of the Works; but it wouldn't do you any good. You can't get rid of me. It'd be bad if you tried, Laila." Tuke walked uncertainly to the door, and turned, shaking visibly. "By bad I mean bad, Laila. Don't go too far."

. . . "Can't ever say anything new," Laila Speer murmured to herself, as she heard her husband leave the house; and she continued her breakfast. She did him an injustice. Tuke had never said quite these same things before; but to her it seemed that he had and she was more scornful than disturbed. An old anger with herself was roused, too, and it grew sharper a little later as she dressed to go out.

From her window upstairs she saw between the spring green foliages of tree tops a distant rear gable of a big house that fronted upon a thoroughfare more impressive than the side street where she lived. Laila wished that her window didn't afford a view of that gable; she couldn't look out without seeing it, and seeing it brought always a reminder that she hadn't sense enough to take Ames Lanning when he was a young widower and she had the chance. The gable was part of the house that was a symbol of his triumphant prosperity; but Laila wasn't thinking of either the house or the prosperity as his—she thought of both as Kate's.

Laila, as her own husband had divined, thought of husbands as adjuncts and of married life as a sort of race between wives. She was getting left, and even old Carrie Augren was ahead of her; Sam Augren's wife made quite a show in the town. As for Kate Lanning, she had everything—and didn't know what to do with it, didn't make any show at all except living in that house and tagging round after Ames like a kind of nurse or maybe secretary. Tuke said that Kate had helped her husband up. Laila didn't believe that, and didn't think it a woman's affair, anyhow, to be helping a husband in his business.

"Tuke!" Laila thought she'd stood about as much of him as she could. Talking to her of mink coats and new cars—and in all these years what had he ever given her? Not even a sapphire ring; she hadn't anything except dipped gold things and a few tourmalines and amethysts. She'd sold the only really good "stone" she'd ever owned —the one poor old pushover Barnesy had given her—sold it to buy bride's clothes all worn out years and years ago. Yet here she was, a man's woman, the most desirable in all the town as she very well knew, herself, because she still saw it in every man's eye!

The adjective she liked best for herself was "gorgeous". Only last night Ames Lanning laughed but spoke out in hearty admiration and meant it: "Laila, you're really a gorgeous woman!" Through every process of her dressing, now, she had the confirmation of her mirror but exultantly didn't need it much: she was a gorgeous woman. A gorgeous woman—and tied to Tuke Speer! She who oughtn't even to've been born in this town! By rights she should have grown up in New York where she'd have found the sort of man that would have given her a real chance among real people. Laila was at the age when even a gorgeous woman has to say to herself that she isn't going to get any younger; she knew that if she was to do anything for herself the time had come to do it.

She'd been doing more than a little already, in fact; and she did a bit more that morning. She'd left her gloves, the night before, at "old

Carrie Augren's", and, calling to get them, showed Mrs. Augren a face saddened by anxiety, and shapely tweed shoulders drooping with care. "You don't look well, dear," Mrs. Augren said. "Is anything the matter?"

"Oh, only the same old thing!" Laila seemed to try to be brave. "I suppose I can stick it out. I hope I can."

"But Tuke didn't drink much last night, Laila. I was careful to see that the tray of highballs went back to the pantry pretty soon."

"No, it was after he got home," Laila said. "That's where most of it goes on, you know. It isn't only the drinking, of course. When he stays out at night till—oh, till all hours—how do I know where he's been, or with whom?"

"Oh, dear! That's bad!" Mrs. Augren looked distressed. "I never heard that about him before, Laila. You mean you think he——"

She paused, and Laila, looking away, murmured, "How do I know?" It was not deliberately but almost by instinct that she thus implanted what could become a rumor of Tuke's immorality, and, having done it, she emphasized her manner—betrayed wife's bravery—for a moment; then added, "Let's not speak of it. Do you know anything new?"

"Well, there's a big plum coming for somebody a few months from now, Laila. In the fall the head of Metal Products' whole Eastern Division is going to be called to a dollar-a-year in Washington and the place'll be vacant. Ames Lanning told my Sam last night, and Sam told me after you'd all gone. I'm mad at Sam. He said he wouldn't lift a finger, wouldn't take it if they'd give it to him, because he loves this town too much and whoever gets it'll have to make New York his headquarters and live there. Sam's nothing but an old fuddyduddy! There'll be a block of stock go with it, and oh my, the salary—*whew!*"

"I wonder——" Laila showed interest. "I wonder Ames himself doesn't take it."

Mrs. Augren looked surprised. "Ames? No, he couldn't of course because Mr. Roe wants him here at the center of things and Ames is too much the whole works already, right where he is. Ames'd never think of it."

"No, I suppose not," Laila murmured; and her downcast eyes didn't show that her interest had sharpened.

She walked homeward slowly, engaged in formative thought. She wasn't making plans, however; her mind was seldom able to concentrate itself upon a neatly outlined course of future action. No, her imagination made pictures for her, and vagrant words formed sentences that she seemed to hear spoken in her own voice. The pictures that rambled before her now were of a New York apartment, large, metallic and glittery, incessant cocktail parties, knowing "night spots", pages of reproduced photographs in periodicals—photographs of herself among goblets and carafes with Ames Lanning, with other men, over such a caption, perhaps, as "The Best Dressed Woman in New York". One of the sentences that mingled into the pictures and that she seemed to hear herself speaking was, "Thank God I haven't got any children for Tuke to try to make a mess about!"

XXX

Young miley stuart, after a summer of new experiences, liked his work, liked the city and liked its people. Unassuming, himself cordial, he thus was met with cordiality and was better and better liked, himself. There was an exception, however. The two people who seemed to like him best and whom he certainly liked best, Celia Lanning and her young stepmother, brought him into association with a person who was anything but cordial to him. Marvin Roe, persistently at the Lannings' house, could easily have been defined as outrageous except for his being too dumb (Miley's interpretation) to know better. Consistently and almost genuinely, Marvin wasn't conscious that Miley was a human being, seemed to think him an interfering piece of furniture.

Celia and Miley early completed the first period of youthful friend-ship-making during which the talk consists mainly of autobiographi-cal bits vivaciously narrated. Each of the parties sparklingly describes the "perfectly terrible" mistakes and misbehaviors of his now ancient childhood, and relates the most exciting or embarrassing episodes in his own life and in the lives of his close friends and relatives. For hours, perhaps, the talk springs from "I'll never forget the time I——" or "Oh, *I* was worse than *that* when I was fourteen——" or "The most ghastly thing my Uncle George *ever* did——"

Having thus made themselves humorously known to each other, the two passed to the profundities. They discussed their inmost selves and those of the people about them; they talked of life and death, of war, politics, art, and argued about Flaubert and Spinoza. All this displeased Marvin Roe, who was talented as an interrupter and con-versation-killer.

"Look, Cele," he often broke in urgently. "Listen. Say, let's quit sitting around here. Let's go somewhere."

Heat of late July, all August and early September dried the town to emptiness for Plant Three's ablest young technician. With her step-mother, Celia went to a northern lake cottage of the Lannings', and Marvin Roe followed to a camp he had on that same shore. "He would! Of course he'd have one there!" Miley groaned to himself. Marvin's well-placed camp was hard to bear; but not until an evening a week after the Lanning ladies' return (and Marvin's) did Miley openly prove that he found his dismal competitor maddening.

Marvin seemed finally to become conscious of a third person's pres-ence. "Look, Cele," the heir to Roe Metal Products said, while Miley was describing the military tactics of the Mongols under Genghis Khan. "Listen, let's give all this corny bull the brush-off. The Brooks crowd's out at the Pieplant to-night and I told 'em I'd get you and bring you out there. I've got my car outside. Come on, Cele; listen, let's for heaven's sakes go!"

As this was probably the sixth time the excursion to the Pieplant had been urged upon Celia within the hour, Miley found it—and "corny bull"—intolerable. Habitually good-natured, he nevertheless had a Southern temper, and, becoming now afraid of it, he rose, mur·

mured and departed. Celia's response to his "Goodnight" was indiffer-
ent; she was angry with him and remained so, though she concealed
her feeling, for a while, the next time she saw him.

"When did you turn Presbyterian?" she asked, as he joined her on
the church steps after the Sunday morning service.

"I think it was last Wednesday," he said. "Wasn't that the day you
told me you usually walk home to think over the sermon?"

"Well, I seem to be doing half of it." She smiled agreeably, turning
northward with him. "It's over two miles, you know; but if you need
sustenance at the end of it Kate'll probably ask you to lunch. About
the sermon, you might take some of it to heart, particularly what was
said about the folly of violence."

"You think I'm a violent man, Celia?"

"Boy," she substituted, laughing. "You were a violent boy the other
night, weren't you, when you let me in for an evening at the Pieplant
with the Brooks outfit? Oh, yes, I had to go! It was the best thing
to be done with poor Marvin. I used to be able to depend on Kate
quite a good deal; but I can't any more."

"Your mind skips about too fast for me," Miley said. "What's Mrs.
Lanning got to do with it?"

"She used to help me with Marvin. She'd come and sit by him and
talk to him on interesting subjects, and of course that'd always make
him get up and go home. She hasn't done it for a long while now;
I don't know what's got into her. Something's going on; I don't know
what."

"She's a brown-eyed angel," Miley said. "She seems to know mysterious things of a kind permanently beyond my comprehension; yet
she doesn't show off or let me regret my ignorance. I mean she's like
a professor I had in an art course I took once. I wasn't a month into
it before I saw I'd never really learn anything about art, no matter
how I tried. The professor's mind was a store of goods he couldn't
pass on to me because I couldn't take 'em. He was a specialist, of
course, and so's your stepmother, I suspect."

"You think so? A specialist in what?"

"I couldn't say—not exactly. In life maybe—experience of people
and study of how their works work—I don't know. Anyhow, though,

that old professor of mine let me by in spite of the ignorance he knew I had, and so does Mrs. Lanning. I wish I could hope that some day your father'd be as jolly and friendly with me as she is. I'm afraid he doesn't——"

"Doesn't like you? Don't worry; he does. It's just that he's been growing more absentminded and it makes him seem aloof. It's too bad. He and Kate used to be so gay together. He's good as gold; but what with all the business he has on his mind—all this expansion for Defense and so many people hanging on his every word——" Celia interrupted herself with a meditative laugh. "Funny how hard it is for such a man's family to keep remembering how important he is."

"Is it, Celia?"

"Yes; maybe because I'm a daughter, not a son. To Kate and me he's just our man, you see. Worse: you may be surprised to hear that to the women who try to take care of an impressive man he can seem to be just their infant. Well, at home and in certain ways that's what Father really is, you know. Then again he isn't. He's a business genius—and simple as apples! That mixes things up. I remember telling you the first time I met you that Kate has a job of it. Being married to an important man—yes, of all the kinds there are, that's the hardest wife to be."

"Celia! And you like things easy? That's certainly encouragement for me."

"Southerner!" she cried. "No, I'm in earnest. I mean being that kind of wife intelligently. Father's a big-hearted man; he really hasn't got the big-head at all, and yet he does get so supremely flattered sometimes that I've seen him do a bit of falling for it. The all-out grab Laila Speer makes, for instance, every time she gets near him—why, a dead horse'd laugh; but Kate has to keep a straight face. By the way, Laila's husband's your immediate boss at Plant Three now, isn't he? How do you get on with him?"

"First rate," Miley said; "though he's a bit grim. Looks to me as if he had something the matter with him inside; gets gaunter and gaunter. But he certainly knows the business from A to Z. I've often wondered why he isn't at the top of Plant Three. He looks ready to

drop; but he's always there with the goods. Maybe he isn't appreci-
ated because he's so quiet; maybe it's because that hollow, pale way
of his depresses people."

"There might be other reasons." Celia, thoughtful, looked disapproving. "I'm afraid there's been a lot of talk about him going on—
rather bad. I hope it's not true, because I've always liked him—I even
used to call him 'Uncle Tuke'; he was that sort of man in those days.
People do change, don't they?" Then Celia abruptly looked merry,
but wasn't, as she unexpectedly completed this thought. "You, for
instance!"

"I? What in the world——"

"No, I suppose I'm wrong," she said, beaming upon him. "I just
don't seem to know you very well and thought you'd changed when
it was really only a new facet of your character turning up."

In spite of her kind smile, Miley knew that he was under attack.
"What have I done? What facet? When?"

"When you treated me as you did the other night. Good heavens,
don't you suppose I had enough of Marvin this summer at the lake?
No, you preferred to get angry and not care what happened to anybody else." Celia's laughter was just perceptibly taunting. "Funny!
I'd always heard that Southern gentlemen thought of the ladies first."

"But, Celia, I—I just couldn't take that idiot."

"Oh, I don't know," Celia said coolly. "He's not quite that."

"You think not?" Miley was staggered. She seemed to defend
Marvin, even to be resentful on his account. Then why had she so
minded being left alone with him that she'd preferred going out to
the Pieplant and the Brooks crowd, both detestable to her as she'd
sometimes mentioned? Although he was a Southerner, the young
man failed to comprehend that inconsistencies are the very substance
of such a punishment as Celia felt the necessity of inflicting. "I beg
your pardon," he said. "Of course Mr. Roe's a much older friend of
yours than I am and I'm not entitled to speak of him to you as you've
often spoken of him to me."

"Have I?" Celia hummed a bar or two from a hymn. "Well, at
least I can count on him. He'd never get up and walk out of a room
just to pamper a silly emotion of his own."

"I beg your pardon," the helpless Miley said again. "I'm sorry. I seem to have offended you."

"No, indeed! Not at all. It's not worth speaking of."

Smiling no more, she appeared to imply that nothing else was worth speaking of, either, the baffled Miley thought, naturally somewhat resentful, himself. Looking straight ahead of him, they maintained a long silence as they walked block after block in alternate hot September sunshine and the slightly relieving coolness under big shade trees. Celia quickened the pace at which they'd started and she made it faster and faster, though she didn't do any more religious humming. They were moving briskly indeed when they reached the long shrubbery border of the lawn before her father's house; and at the gate she stopped with an abruptness resembling a jerk. "If you care to come in," she said, "I've no doubt my stepmother——"

"Mrs. Lanning's always very kind." Miley was red and formal, as he lifted his straw hat. "Thank you; but I think I'd best not take too much advantage of her goodness to me."

"Oh, very well!" Celia turned and walked up the flagstone path to the front door, striding. Kate met her just inside the house.

"Celia, what's the matter?"

"Matter? Nothing. We had a very good sermon."

"Did you?" Kate said. "You can tell me about it at lunch. Your father won't be home, because they're having an eating conference at Mr. Roe's about the great New York appointment. It's been offered to Sam Augren; but he doesn't care to be a whale, loves this town too much and is trying to wriggle out of it. What did the sermon have to do with the way you and Miley Stuart just said good-bye to each other at the gate?"

"So you were peeking out of the window, were you, Katie? Well—I've got to blame somebody. It was your fault, you know." She put her arm about Kate's waist, and, looking down at her reproachfully —Celia was a head the taller—walked with her into the living-room, explaining as they went. "Oh, yes, you did it! You stopped helping me chase Marvin off decently months ago and it's led to my not letting Miley call him an idiot. That made Miley furious." Celia withdrew her arm, sank upon a sofa bonelessly; then suddenly sat up, rigid, and said, "Oh, Golly!"

"What now, Celia?"

"I'm a sap!" Celia exclaimed. "Of course he knows I'm furious, too, and how can he help understanding what I got that way about? Men are such conceited swine he'll think it's because I like him so much I couldn't stand his stalking out on me. Now I AM in a rage with him! He has no business to think such things!"

"He doesn't," Kate said. "He's the kind of boy it'd be the last thing he'd think. I don't doubt he's angry, though, because you wouldn't let him call Marvin an idiot. That always hurts their feelings and makes them decline to come in to lunch. You asked him to, didn't you?"

"Practically, but so that the fool thought I didn't mean it." Celia's interest swerved to her stepmother; she looked at her with anxiety. "See here, how do you always seem to know so much about men? You're only nine years older than——"

"Nine and a half," Kate interrupted quickly. "More than that; almost ten."

"Nine years older than I am," Celia insisted. "Where do you get all this? Just from studying Father? That reminds me: What's been going on here, anyhow? I didn't notice it at first; but now I think of it you've been sort of different since quite a good while back. You're altered."

Kate Lanning laughed. "Oh, terribly! Just how?"

"I don't know." Celia was serious. "You are, though. Oh, yes, you're as cheery a sprite as ever, bustling about and hopping from one twig to another; but there's something—— Yes, there is! Wait! I think of three things: one's the dirt you've done me, quitting on Marvin and always wriggling away when I accuse you of it; another's you've stopped singing to yourself when you're moving about the house, and I miss it because you have a pretty voice; and the third's you only talk about one-fourth as much as you used to."

"Murder! Used I to be that noisy?" Kate laughed and moved a Chelsea figurine half an inch to the left for more accurate decorative balance with its mate at the other end of the Adam marble mantelpiece. "Southern imaginations must be contagious, Celia; your fancifulnesses are funnier since our friend came to town. Was that all you talked about on the way from church—just Marvin?"

"No; we got along all right for the first block or so. He was telling me about Tuke Speer, how Tuke's really a very good man for Roe Metal Products, though nobody seems to appreciate it."

"He is," Kate said, and her face was suddenly grave. "He is a good man. What else did Miley say about him?"

"That was about all. I said I was sorry stories were going the rounds that didn't give him a very good reputation and——"

"So they are," Kate interrupted. "They're not exactly stories, though —mainly just smeary implications, the kind that do the most harm and can't be run down and refuted. Of course Tuke's been known to drink hard sometimes and that gives a foundation."

"So does something else, Kate. I mean Laila. Doesn't it ever strike you that she's got the habit of putting on an act about him every now and then? Stops chattering and looks wan when he's mentioned: secret sorrow, suffering wife and so on. You've seen her do it, haven't you?"

"Yes, naturally, Celia. That goes with the rest of it. From all I hear, the 'talk' about Tuke rather died down during the summer. She was away—he'd managed to give her some weeks at Atlantic City—but, since she came back, there seems to be more of it, noticeably more. When a man's getting a bad reputation people ought to observe its timing, oughtn't they?"

"Oh, oh, oh!" Celia cried. "Really I don't think I can stand that woman!"

"Be careful!" Kate said quickly. "She and Tuke are coming this evening, and the Augrens and all of 'em. It's our turn to give the Sunday supper, you know, and it's the first one of the season, so nobody'll miss. You mustn't let her see what you think of her."

"Not even when she's molassesing Father?"

"No. Least of all when she's doing that."

Celia looked her stepmother over with some irritation. "See here, Kate! What sort of woman are you, after all? Don't you ever get tired of being just a bit too damn long-sufferingly noble?"

"I strike you as that, Celia?"

"You do. It may be a pose you keep up—posing at yourself—or maybe it's genuine. How does anybody know? One thing, though: it's time you let out and gave Laila Speer a sock on the ear. Don't you ever *want* to? You hate her, don't you?"

"Something like it," Kate admitted. "The truth seems to be that I'm too sinfully conceited to hate people; I just despise 'em instead! My 'nobility', Celia, is my own form of conceit."

"Oh, well, call it pride," Celia said. "Whatever it is, it oughtn't to keep you from soaking that woman where it'll do the most good. Yes, and Father, too, for letting her make him look so silly! Why don't you ever up and hit out at her?"

"To avenge myself on her? I wouldn't get into a fight with her any more than I would with a tumble-bug, I'm *that* conceited. Besides, *she* does all my avenging for me, Celia; I don't need to lift a finger."

"How's that?"

"This way," Kate said. "Laila Speer lives in a state of envious hatred of me. Every thought of me she has hurts her worse than any intentional blow I could deal her. Benefits from me, not reprisals, are what would put her into a baffled fury. That seems to be the punishment of the envious. If I'd ever smash out at her she'd be gratified; she'd take it for a yelp of pain."

"Got it all worked out, haven't you!" Celia was satiric; then was curious again. "What do you keep on with that old crowd for, anyhow, Kate? There isn't one of 'em you're really congenial with. You really like Cousin Martha and her sort a lot better, don't you?"

"Yes. I see them, too, of course."

"Oh, I know!" Celia said. "The Sunday suppers are only once a fortnight and you think Father needs the relaxation. But there isn't what you'd call an intellect in the bunch, is there?"

"Yes, Tuke Speer. At least he used to——"

" 'Used to'!" Celia echoed. "Must have been a good while ago, and he has to bring his wife with him, doesn't he? Doesn't she ever sour the scalloped oysters for you, Kate?"

"Why, of course!" Kate laughed, but only to show that she didn't take her own feeling about Laila seriously. "She's fun for your father, though; so you mustn't let him get the idea that either of us thinks she's a mental and moral runt, Celia. He was in love with her once, you remember, don't you?—and so were you."

"Was I? Golly!"

XXXI

CELIA DIDN'T NEED TO BE CAREFUL AT THE SUNDAY EVEning supper party. Not present, she was glad she wasn't; she'd scooted away with an impromptu troop of contemporaries that didn't include either Miley Stuart or Marvin Roe. The Lannings' guests began to arrive as she departed, and they were all there within the next quarter of an hour, a noisily informal company. There were a dozen and a half of them, married couples except one widow and one bachelor; and the fortnightly Sunday suppers, carried on through the years except during the summers, still preserved intimacies that otherwise might easily have perished. Thus some of the party liked one another and some secretly didn't; there was goodwill among them and there was hidden animosity ready to poison. Most of the women knew who carried the poison; most of the men didn't know it existed.

Among the latter was the bachelor, fat William Jones, a volatile and forgiving soul. Before the repast he left a group at the piano where he'd been helping to bellow, "The Last Time I Saw Paris", joined Tuke Speer on a remote couch, put his arm about him and became jovially confidential.

"Don't tell, but I got mine at the Valley Club, Tuke; I put plenty enough under this dear old satin vest not to die on me. Bet you fixed yourself good, too, what?"

"No," Tuke said. "I'm not drinking."

"What!"

"I'm not drinking."

Bill Jones nodded and laughed. "I get you, Tuke. You mean you're not drinking the kind of punch Kate Lanning serves, because what's the use? Tastes like there's a magnifico spike in it. You think it's going to kick you right up to the ceiling; but it's only a flavor, nothing doing. Great food she hands us, though. Listen, you heard what they did about the New York job at the Old Man's conference this noon, Tuke?"

"No, and I don't care."

"Me neither." In and out of his cups Bill Jones was frank. "Wouldn't be much more chance their handing it to me than they would even to you, Tukie. Just before I left the club, though, George Cooke sneaked in for a couple on his way here on account of Kate's phony punch and he says Sam's turned down the big job flatfooted; too sot in his ways to leave the home town. George says the Old Man and Ames got the plum on their hands; don't know who to give it to. What you think of that, Tukie?"

"Nothing."

"Well, anyhow it's conversation," Bill Jones explained defensively, continuing to embrace his gloomy friend. "Let's talk about everything. Ames is mighty nice in his own house, same's ever. Never could help liking that fellow. Remember the night at the Old Man's grandchild party last spring when we both got so sore at Ames?"

"Yes," Tuke said. "I remember."

"You had it up your nose a lot worse'n I did," the fat man continued. "All that's the matter with Ames it's at a great big Roe Metal Products party like that he thinks he has to act the semi-official high dog. Look at him now, singing louder'n anybody and got his arm round old hollering Carrie Augren. He's all right, Ames Lanning. Good-looking, too, Ames is. Remember how mad Laila got at both of us that night, Tukie?"

"Yes," Tuke said again. "I remember."

The fat man chuckled gurglingly. "You were a scream, Tuke—jealous 'n' everything—and *was* Laila mad! Whoo! She looks beautiful this evening, old bird, perfectly beautiful! Year after year, wherever she goes, you can always hear her voice, too; get everything she's saying, no matter how many's squawkin' all round. That's a talent. Keeps her looks; hasn't shed a one of 'em. If I had a wife with those eyes and figger and arms and everything in a long black dress like that I'd give up liquor and never go out the house. How long have I been telling you you're a lucky man, Tuke? Broke my heart; but you're a lucky man, Tuke! Listen, Tuke, is our conversation hurting your liver? Don't I exhilarate you any? Can't you ever cheer up any more like you used to?"

"Oh, I do, I do," Tuke said, and rose. "Kate wants us to go out to supper now. Come on."

In the dining-room Laila continued to be the central figure Bill Jones's tribute had described. As he'd said, she had a talent, a long lasting one; but it wasn't only her cuttingly distinct voice that made her predominant, nor was it the bodily symmetry and grace that seemed to justify the claims of that insistent voice. She was Laila Capper unchanged, as able as ever to put forth the cry for attention, the old demand: "Me! Me! Me! Here, where *I* am, shall be the focus. I'm the unusual one; these others are flat. Watch me and listen to me; nothing else will reward either your eyes or your ears."

This she seemed to put upon Ames Lanning, as they sat together at the largest and most flowered of the four tables. Her laughter was a clarinet obbligato to all that Ames said; she made great play with her fine hands, which were continually in swanlike motion and not bloodied upon the fingernails but pinkly silvered, so that argent little highlights seemed constantly to be twinkling and glistening before her face and upon Ames's coat sleeve. He was in high spirits and she kept him so; the adulation of a "gorgeous woman", however humorously revealed, was ever heady delight for a successful man.

Ames liked being with Laila; he thought it was because they always had a good time together. Shrewdest analyst of law and of business, he'd never sought to know just why he always had a good time with Laila nowadays. His enjoyment of it, however, wasn't all; he admired the beauty of this former love of his and he thought she was being a magnificent sport about Tuke, not only about poor Tuke's failure to rise but about his drinking and the worse things that were being murmured. In character as well as looks Laila was still the grand girl she'd always been. He'd had a hurt of her once long ago, yes; but that hadn't been her fault and was an old story anyhow, an episode that time had virtually rubbed out of anybody's memory.

When Ames was with Laila he felt so jolly he forgot business and almost that he wasn't so happy with his wife as once he'd been. His thought of Kate still included a persistent sense of being irked; he didn't realize that never once, since the night when he'd made his vexation known to her, had Kate Lanning advised him or made any suggestion to him whatever upon any matter of any kind. He didn't know this because most men have to be told such things and Kate hadn't told him. He did comprehend of course that ever since he'd expressed his just rebelliousness his wife had withdrawn behind some sort of spiritual stockade. She'd never sulked and she didn't look at him either hurtly or resentfully. She was cheerful and laughed affectionately at his jokes when he made them, made some herself; but as a wholly intimate friend and as a lover she appeared to regard herself as upon the retired list. This left a blank, a queer vacuum in his life; but, "Oh, very well!" he thought. "If she chooses to have it that way, all because I've got to be my own man, so be it! If she prefers our old terms of cousinly courtesy merely because I insist upon freedom enough to hoe my own row, I'll do my best to enjoy that freedom. I don't feel apologetic about it—not in the least! I stand on my rights and I'll do no moping to please her."

He'd seldom been more delighted with Laila than to-night. Broad-shouldered, handsome and hearty, he sat relaxed, all laughter and shining approval, as she chattered, leaning close, dazzling with cajoleries. Bill Jones, nearby at a table with Kate and Tuke Speer and Mrs. Augren, was inspired to ill-advised waggery. These impulses of bibulous jolly men can reach beneath pleasant-seeming surfaces and bring up trouble.

"Look at those two!" the fat man chuckled, affecting slyness. "Honeying all over each other! My, ain't she pretty and him doting! Kate, I sh'd think you and Tuke wouldn't stand for it. If I was either of you I'd put my case in my lawyer's hands first thing to-morrow morning. Look at 'em!"

"Yes, it's terrific," Kate said. "So long as they carry on that way only in public, though——"

"It's all the worse," Bill Jones declared. "Shows they don't care—come right out in the open with it! Look, she keeps manhandling him! Can't say anything to him at all without grabbin' his arm or bumpin' that divine shoulder of hers into him. How do you stand it, Tuke?"

"I don't know," Tuke said, and his voice was so quiet that anybody except Bill Jones might have been made uncomfortable. Mrs. Augren was not a perceptive woman; but she looked at Tuke seriously as he added huskily, "I don't know just how I do stand it; but I do."

"'Cause you got to!" the fat man exclaimed triumphantly. "He's your boss. You'd lose your job if you didn't, and besides, you got to expect to be put through the hoops by a gal like that. Serves you right for taking her away from the rest of us and marrying somebody with that face and hair and those arms and all. Look! Listen to her! Now she's tryin' to coax him to take her on a trip to New York with him or something. Listen!"

"But why not?" Laila's laughing persuasive voice was clear. "New York would belong to you before you'd been there two months, Ames! It would; you'd have it all! Why not be Roe Metal Products there, yourself? We'd all come on and visit you—Tuke could stay home and take care of the house. After all, New York's the only decent place in the country and you'd revel in it, Ames. Opportunity's knocking, old dear! It only comes once; don't turn it down."

Bill Jones became uproarious. "Didn't I tell you? Look! Her fork's absolutely clean; can't eat because she has to grab his arm so often! Oh, yes, Kate, you can laugh; but I bet you're mad as hell! Tuke isn't laughing. Are you, Tuke? Look at him, Carrie! Look at him, Kate!" The fat man pointed a spoon at Tuke Speer's strained gaunt face, and became almost sobered for the moment. "What's the matter, Tuke? Not gettin' jealous, like at the Old Man's party, are you?" Suddenly Bill Jones decided that his suspicions were correct and that everything was funny again. He spluttered, beating the table with his spoon. "He is! The old red-head's got it again. Murder-love-a-day, he *is* jealous! Frisk him, Carrie, if you don't want to see Kate a widow right in her own dining-room!"

"You mean that's a poor place to be one?" Kate said—for the sake of saying anything quickly. "I'd rather be a widow anywhere, though, than a miserable old bachelor getting himself high in order to go out and shine. Don't think I didn't diagnose you the minute you came in. Why else do you think I put you at my table? I have to make sacrifices in my own house, haven't I? Don't talk any more. Just eat as much as you can; that'll help."

She went on making prattle. Bill Jones protested and, as Mrs. Augren joined in the attack upon him, their table was as clamorous as any in the room; but Tuke Speer's voice had no part in this effort. His gaze, whenever he looked up, was upon his wife.

Bill Jones took the offensive, in every sense and shoutingly. "Two on one, no fair! Carrie, I'm as sober as your old Sam and that's not saying much! Kate, stop bossing me; everybody in town knows you're the bossiest little body there is. Look what you did to your own husband! Used to be a good lawyer. It was a treat to go to court and hear him hollering and abusing, until you told him it was ruining his blood pressure because the louder and madder he hollered he'd hear himself doing it and get to believing it, and that'd get him madder and louder and funnier. Used to be a show till you spoiled it. No wonder now he wants to go to New York with Laila Speer!"

The fat man was so noisy that the other tables heard him over their own merrymakings. Laila put a lovely hand on her host's arm. "Do you, Ames?" she asked. "Would you really like to go to New York with Laila Speer?" Turning her head, she called gayly, "We're thinking it over, Bill. Tuke, you could stay at home and look after the house. You'd like that all right, wouldn't you, Tuke?"

"Of course he would!" Kate Lanning's reply for Tuke was instantaneous and loud. "Tuke and I'd both like it and only our consciences would make us go along."

"Spoilsports!" Mr. Jones shouted, and the various tables resumed their own interrupted conversations.

Kate watched Tuke Speer and was conscious that a crisis had been scantily avoided. Some women, like highly sensitive receiving sets, pick up everything that's in the air. Thus she knew that the lively evening was composed of layers of feeling, and that the nether ones held peril. Laila was by no means merely putting on an act of half-mock coquetry, molassesing the great man as Celia'd said. Laila was dreadfully working at Tuke—working at him unremittently.

She hadn't cold-bloodedly plotted to make Tuke disgrace himself to-night; and yet, living from moment to moment, and in every moment's opportunity, that was what she was now trying to prod Tuke to do. She knew that he was watching her and listening to her, and, with every one of her touches upon Ames Lanning's arm and with every provocative word she uttered, she stretched her husband's goaded nerves and tore at his self-control. She meant to tear it all away.

Kate wanted to whisper to him imploringly, "Don't let her get you! Don't let her!" All she said, however, was, "Help me feed Bill sober, Tuke; then he'll go to sleep on a sofa somewhere as usual after supper and we can quiet down again."

XXXII

IN THE LIVING-ROOM, WHEN THE PARTY HAD RETURNED there, Laila finished her arranging and completed her evening's work upon her husband. Kate and Tuke Speer and Mr. and Mrs. George Cooke were at one of the two bridge tables at an end of the large room. At the other end, near the piano, a small but noisy backgammon contest was in progress and it was from among the kibitzers that Laila, pleading with him merrily, drew Ames Lanning.

"You've *got* to, Handsome!" those at the bridge table heard her exclaiming. "Do your stuff, Ames. You haven't done it for years and everybody's dying for it again. What do we care how we disturb all

these old gamblers? They'd love it!" She began to draw Ames down
the length of the room, tugging at his arm. "Kate, come and make
him! Tell him he's got to, Kate! Tell him you want him to!"

Kate looked up from her cards. "Want him to what?"

The two reached the bridge table, Ames laughingly reluctant, Laila
brightly eager. "Tell him you want him to do that old stunt of his—
to sit at the piano and play and sing 'I Adore But Thee', looking
moon-eyed up at me, burlesquing how old Professor Taddi used to
sing it. Don't you remember? I'd loll over the side of the piano,
yearning and languishing at Ames, and he'd make his voice all trilling
and sobby at me, like old Taddi's Caruso-ing—just terribly ga-ga!
He says he won't because it'll disturb all you gamblers; but I say
he's simply got to. You make him, Kate!"

"No!" Ames affected to break from her; but she caught his arm
again and held him. "Unhand me! You're breaking up a bridge game.
I've forgotten that old Taddi stunt. I can't——"

Laila pretended to struggle with him. "Tuke!" she cried over her
shoulder. "Tuke, *you* help me!" Then she turned and addressed her
husband in a charming voice of entreaty, "Tuke dear, *you* ask Ames
to do it. I'm sure he will if *you* ask him to."

She put her hand caressingly on Tuke's head; he looked up at her
with the eyes of a corpse, and Kate Lanning's breath stopped. Play
at both bridge tables had paused, for Laila had forced the attention
of everybody in the room. The picture she made was of herself
teasing Ames Lanning to do what she wished, and, with a wifely
gesture—pretty sporting of her, in view of what Tuke was said to be
up to of late—gayly asking her husband to help her. This was the final
goad to Tuke; Kate knew that Laila'd got him.

"Please, won't you, Tuke dearie?" Laila said winningly. "Laila
wants you to. Tell Ames we'll go straight home if he won't. Tell
him, Tukie!"

Tuke's hand shook as he flapped down his cards on the table. He
rose silently, yet produced throughout the room the hush and arrested
motion of people startled by a sudden crash. Then, closely face to
face with his wife, Tuke Speer spoke three insulting words in a loud
and harsh voice.

"Are you drunk?"

Laila seemed first to struggle to maintain her bright smile, then to succumb to brutality. She drooped; her knees bent pathetically within her close skirt and she put forth groping tremulous hands. "Please—Ames, please take me—out of here." She made her breaking voice little yet audible everywhere, and Ames Lanning, red with indignation, as were almost all of his guests, quickly supported the lovely faltering figure. Dependent upon this manly old friend and kind host, she turned with him and let but a single choked gasp, or sob, be heard as he took her out of the room.

"Poor Laila! Poor Laila!" he said. They moved down the hall toward the open door of his library, and neither was aware that Tuke, striding, was in the hall behind them. He gave them not a look, turned the other way, took his hat from a table and went out into the drizzly autumn night. "Poor Laila!" Ames repeated, much moved. "You poor dear child!" They passed into the library, a long room with an alcove at the far end where there was a leather couch upon which, when he worked at home, he sometimes lay tiredly dictating to a stenographer. He took a step in that direction with Laila. "You'd better lie down, poor child, till I can bring a drink for you. You——"

"No! Don't!" she said, and sank into a deep chair near his desk. "Don't leave me. Just stay with me a minute. I can't——" She began to sob almost soundlessly but with a tragic eloquence, for, although she'd intentionally made Tuke do what he'd done to her, her emotion was as genuine as if the insult had been gratuitous.

She bent and swayed; convulsive, she covered her face with her hands, and Ames's heart was wrung. "Laila, Laila! No wonder, though! It was an unspeakable thing to do to you! Of course it was liquor in him; but, even so, how could he——"

"That's just it," she sobbed. "I've tried so hard to keep it to myself; but now everybody'll know. He's made it public! Now they'll all know what my life is at home. It's gone on and on and on—but—now I can't—— Oh, how long can I—I don't—— Ames, Ames, I can't——"

Sobbing made her incoherent; he was in sharpest distress. "Laila, let me get you brandy or ammonia. Let me——"

"No, no!" She found a handkerchief and wept into it. "Ames, I can't let you see me so. Please turn off that upper light." He did as she wished, leaving in the long brown room only the shaded illumination of a single bulb in the desk-lamp. Laila caught his hand and pressed it to her cheek. "You've always been so good to me. I don't know why; I've never known why. I treated you so badly! Oh, I did treat you so horribly once, Ames!"

"No, you didn't." He was quick with comfort. "That was always all right with me, Laila, after I got over the first disappointment. It was all entirely all right. Entirely."

"Not with me!" she said. "I did a terrible thing to us both, Ames. You never understood the reason. You thought I didn't——" She stopped herself short and, releasing his hand, made a despairing gesture. "No, I mustn't go into what I felt. What could be the use now? Of course I believed then you only had a sort of dreamy fancy for me, or thought you did. So look what I let happen to me—*Tuke!*"

"It can't go on, Laila. If this is the way he treats you—and out of a clear sky with no excuse or reason on earth——"

"Oh, of course!" she said. "It's my daily fare. But to have it happen in public—the humiliation!"

"Oh, *poor* Laila!" Ames's pity for her was almost too much for him and with it he not strangely felt a confusion of mind that was pleasurable, he didn't inquire of himself why. Grief-stricken beautiful women can easily make the compassion of forthrightly masculine men enjoyable. Ames wasn't only rackingly sorry for Laila; he was excited. "Laila, I don't understand Tuke. He isn't what he used to be. I don't know what's come over him of late years. How could any sane man treat you so? How can Tuke——"

"I don't know. He just does! I've never done anything to him—only tried to be cheerful and cover up and not let people see——"

"Laila, you've got to have help to bear this. I'd do anything on earth to help you. I'd——"

"I know you would!" He was bending over her; but with a last half-sob she rose swiftly and was in his arms. "You always would, Ames dearest. Darling! Darling! You always would! I know it. Always!" she murmured, and kissed him warmly and long upon the lips. "Ah—you do love me, don't you?" she whispered.

Ames, increasingly excited, astonished by the pleasure he felt and overwhelmed by tenderness for this injured gorgeous woman, was also embarrassed. He wished to tell her that indeed he did love her deeply a whole lot in a truly friendly way he was sure nobody'd mind; but words to express this succinctly, and yet suitably, evaded him.

"You do love me, Ames?"

"Why, indeed I do, Laila." His arms relaxed a little about her. "Of course I——"

"I know you do," she said in good faith, for her confidence in her gorgeousness, confirmed by experiences, couldn't let her imagine a man who'd once been in love with her not being so again if she'd let him. "Ah, I know you do, Ames!" she said, and kissed him a second time.

Even as he received this favor a part of Ames Lanning was wondering how to be more explicit about his affection's being of the sort nobody'd mind. Everything was happening too suddenly, and Laila's face still touched his when these confused fast moments became yet more involving. Someone, a woman, walking rapidly upon the thick rug in the hall, passed the open door of the library.

Ames saw the figure out of the side of his eye, indistinctly. It was a slight one, seeming taller than his wife's, and he'd have thought it Celia's except that Celia, out with her crowd, never came home this early. Whoever it was, had she looked in and seen him and Laila in the dim library? He didn't know and neither did Laila, for she too had caught a glimpse of the figure. She stepped back from Ames.

"Who was that?"

"I don't——" he began, when they were interrupted grotesquely by the hoarse voice of an aroused sleeper. Intruding as if in an odious French farce, Bill Jones bestirred himself upon the couch in the dark alcove where Kate had put him.

"What *is* all this?" he said. "What you two up to out there? Rehearsing for Romeo and Juliet or a charade or what?" Disheveled, he appeared vaguely in the entrance to the alcove. "That's you, Laila, isn't it?"

She caught Ames's hand. "Quick! Get back to the other room!"

XXXIII

A DOZEN SUBDUED VOICES, MUTTERING MOSTLY ABOUT umbrellas, were heard from the forward end of the hall as Ames somewhat plungingly left the library. The startling domestic scene Tuke Speer had misplaced, presenting it to a jolly party, had broken up the evening. The shocked guests, concluding a suitable period of low-voiced discussion in groups, were departing. After what Tuke had done nobody could concentrate on bridge or backgammon.

Near the front door Kate was busily uttering protestive goodnights when her husband approached from down the hall, loudly declaring that he wouldn't hear of anybody's going, it was only ten o'clock and everything was all right again, entirely all right. Flustered and red, he didn't quite look it. His head was almost full of Laila and a newly reminiscent kind of scented deliciousness; but a modicum of anxiety attended upon the intoxication. Laila, it appeared, was quite a good deal in love with him, astonishingly seemed to have been so even when she'd taken Tuke instead, and naturally nobody is displeased by such a discovery. But—but—— Ames hadn't time to finish the thought that began with "but—but——"

"Home, nonsense!" he was saying, almost shouting, as he came forward. "Break up one of our Sunday suppers at ten o'clock? Don't tell *me* goodnight; I won't listen! We're all going back in yonder and get together round the piano and——"

A soft contour pressing against his right shoulder interrupted him, bringing him a breathlessness. The pressure came from the left shoulder of Laila Speer, who seemed to pause unconsciously in passing. She'd come from the library, looking into the mirror of a vanity-box as she walked, seeming wholly preoccupied in powdering away what might have been the remaining traces of tears; and she was attended by an apparent chaperon, Bill Jones, who looked rumpled and dazed. He advanced, blinking but vociferous, bumping among the leave-takers: "Murder-love-a-day, is it that late? I've overslept; must ate too much. What time is it, anyhow? Where's my hat?"

Under this cover, as Laila's shoulder touched Ames Lanning's, he heard the warning honeyed whisper from the side of her mouth: "Don't look at me, dearest. It's only the least bit but wipe your lips." Then, as he obeyed, affecting to cough into his handkerchief, she held her vanity-box closer before her face and whispered again, rapidly, "I don't know whether Bill saw or not. I'm almost sure the woman that passed turned her head and looked at us. Find out who she was. Don't call me up or try to see me—not till I let you know."

Instantly she moved away from him, and Kate Lanning stepped toward her. "Laila, Tuke's gone home. He left just after that—that mistake. George and Mary Cooke waited to take you home. Here they are. They'll——"

Ames spoke up impulsively. "Why, no; if everybody's bound to be going, I'll look after Laila of course. I'll get out a car and——"

"No, no, you mustn't go out in the rain, Ames." Laila gave him an advising glance and joined in the bustle of departure. "I didn't come in a car; we walked. It's only a step and really all I need's an umbrella; but since George and Mary are so kind—— Goodnight, Kate; you've been lovely. And thank you again, Ames. Goodnight! Goodnight!"

The disastrous Bill Jones was the last of the guests to leave, but finally discovered his hat on the floor beneath a hall table. "What's everybody going home so early for?" he asked, as he groaningly stooped for it. "My watch is right after all. Peculiar, everybody going home just when——" He paused, put his hat on his head, took it off and looked perplexedly back at the library door; then finished his sentence in a manner disturbing to his host. "Just when everything was beginning to get so interesting." He shook hands languidly with Kate at the front door. "I think I'm still dreaming. Kate, keep your eye on Ames. He's one those men nobody ever notices they're good-looking till they begin to get rich. Goodnight, honey!"

. . . Kate turned from the closing door, went into the living-room, to the piano, and, with the soft pedal pressed down, began to improvise Chopinesque recollections. Ames walked quickly back to the open library door, stood and looked in. The place was dim and he couldn't be sure how clearly he and Laila might have been seen from the hall. He entered the room, went to the alcove, extended himself upon the couch, lifted his head and looked toward the desk and its lamp at the other end of the room.

Again he could only be uncertain; Bill Jones might have seen—and heard—or he mightn't. He'd certainly sounded odd when he said goodnight and it'd be just like Bill Jones, half awake, to see something he oughtn't to—and draw wrong conclusions. Ames felt there hadn't been any harm in his kissing of Laila or her kissing of him, whichever it was. She was a dear old friend in great distress—and indeed he could almost wish there *had* been some harm in it! She'd seemed to reveal that she'd always been more or less in love with him, and it was pretty stirringly pleasant to think so. Probably she hadn't meant it too seriously, though.

After all, he hadn't kissed Laila in secret, because wasn't Bill Jones practically right there in the same room and looking on, and the hall door open and somebody else, too, looking, and—Celia! Ames was suddenly almost sure that the figure in the hall had been Celia's. That was an embarrassing thought for a father—and would Celia, maybe like Bill Jones, just possibly draw wrong conclusions? Ames decided that the only thing for him to do was to tell Kate all about it, himself. He'd go straight in and tell her the whole thing laughingly—or, no, maybe not laughingly. First, though, he'd better make certain whether or not it really was Celia who'd passed the open door.

He went lightly upstairs, found Celia's room dark, went down a back stairway, looked into the butler's pantry, the kitchen and the "cold room"; Celia was not in the house. Then the woman who'd passed the library door couldn't have been Celia, and for a moment this conclusion brought him relief; then it didn't. Who was the spy and how talkative was she? Had he been mistaken about her height? Could he be sure that she hadn't been Kate herself? No, not positively. All the more reason, then, for immediate action: the open and frank account of what had happened must be presented to Kate at once. Probably the very act of telling her would make him feel all right about it.

She was still in the living-room, at the piano, touching forth a wistful music, as he came briskly in. "Unseasonably warm," he said. "Drizzling pretty hard, though; might turn cooler." He went to the white marble mantelpiece, stood with his back to its dark aperture and uttered sounds that expressed both meditative regret and a readiness for slumber. "Ah-hum!" She didn't stop playing or look toward him; so he did it again, "Ah-hum!" and added, "Well, well!" Then, as her music continued, he apprehensively stole a long side-glance at her. It reassured him. Her profile, dainty and harmonious, was serene; and he was aware almost surprisedly, as if he'd never seen it before, that Kate had a look of pure goodness. She seemed rather overwhelmingly good, in fact; and he feared he wasn't that good, himself. All the more he felt he'd best get forward with what he had in hand. "Well, Kate, it was too bad—really too bad, wasn't it?"

"Yes." Kate played on. "It was."

"I believe it was one of the worst things I ever saw," he said. "I mean one of the most shocking. In what's supposed to be civilized company I don't recall ever seeing a man treat his wife in so un-called-for a manner before—not in all my life! Laila—poor Laila was —well, I could hardly tell you—— She just couldn't be comforted!"

"She couldn't?" Kate was still playing, though almost inaudibly.

"Well, I did everything I could." He amended this. "I mean I said everything I could. She was broken-hearted, Kate."

"Was she?"

"I never felt so sorry for anybody in my life," he declared. "Laila was—well, it's hard to describe. It got so I couldn't think of anything more to say."

"What did you do then?"

"What? Why, I——" He seemed to have the opening he'd hoped to lead up to; but Kate's music and her preoccupation with it disturbed him. "I'm trying to tell you about it; but if you keep on playing——"

"Oh, I beg your pardon!" Her hands dropped from the keys to her lap, and she swung about on the piano-bench to face him. Her expression was amiable. "Bill Jones was there to help you with her, wasn't he, Ames?"

"Yes; oh, certainly! That is, he may have been partly asleep; I don't know."

"Didn't you see him?"

"Yes—oh, yes, certainly! That is, he spoke to us and——" Ames paused; then added, "There were—there were other people, too—at least, walking through the hall. I thought maybe one of 'em was you."

"No," Kate said, "not I. I was in here until they all began to go."

"Were you?" Again Ames was temporarily relieved. "Well, of course, as you say, Bill Jones was there, too, Kate; but he isn't the kind of man a woman turns to at a time like that—not a woman like Laila, a woman who'd been treated as she had by her own husband and——"

Kate interrupted him. "How'd she been treated by her own husband, Ames?"

"What?" He stared, perplexed. "Why, you saw it."

"Yes, so I did. Did you?"

He was completely at a loss. "Why, everybody did. What do you mean? I was right there beside them, wasn't I?"

"Yes, at the last of it you were. The last of it was all you saw or that 'everybody' saw." Kate spoke rapidly. "I'll explain what I mean. You hadn't been at Tuke Speer's house before they came here. You hadn't been with that husband and wife all day, Ames. You didn't see what had been going on between them earlier, and you weren't conscious of undercurrents between them after they got here. Who knows those things about a husband and wife enough to judge? You don't know what a strain they'd been on together or what Tuke's nerves had been put through before that miserable outburst came from him."

"What!" Ames was astounded. "Why, see here, Kate, there hadn't been anything at all going on between them. I have eyes, haven't I? —and ears?"

"Yes, but they're at a disadvantage, Ames—especially nowadays."

"My eyes and ears are at a disadvantage—'especially nowadays'? Why?"

"For one reason because you've become an important and powerful man, Ames. People don't show themselves as they really are to such men; they put on their best for you—their best and their most ingratiating. When you were on your way up and still struggling you had a lot better chance to see and hear the truth about people. Oh, I know you're called an extraordinary judge of men, and you are when you judge of the work they do or can do for Roe Metal Products; but when you're away from business and——"

"I see!" He looked at her with some satire. "You're telling me that away from business people put on a show for me, their best behavior? Tuke to-night, for instance?"

Kate's color heightened. "No, Tuke wouldn't; he's too honest. I wasn't thinking of Tuke, Ames."

"I see you weren't," he said severely. "Of all the injustice! Why, when Tuke broke out in that unpardonable way, it was right out of a clear sky. She was—why, she'd been charming to everybody all evening, and when he did it she was being charming to Tuke himself! She was being affectionate. Yes, being affectionate! She actually had her hand on his hair and was stroking it. I don't know what you're talking about. Are you trying to tell me——"

"Yes, Ames. Nobody knows quite all she'd been doing to Tuke to get him into such a state or how long she'd been at it. She may have begun it in the afternoon; she may have been at it all day."

"What! Why, when they got here she came in laughing! Kate, you're talking like a wild woman! I never heard——"

The snapping of the lock of the front door, as a latch-key turned in it, interrupted him, and Kate called toward the hallway: "Celia? Hello there! How do you happen to be home so soon? Come in, won't you?"

Celia came in, but only a few steps, remaining near the doorway. She was wet and pallid; she didn't look up and didn't smile, stood downcast. Kate went to her, exclaiming, laid hands upon her.

"What in the world! Why, your hair's sodden and so's your wrap and everything else! You must be wet to the bone. How on earth did you ever——"

"I didn't take my own car, Kate. I got Ellie and Thad Boscowen to drive me home because it was all a sour bore to-night, and I wouldn't let them turn into our driveway but just hopped out and ran in. It's raining, you know."

"That hard?" Kate cried. "It doesn't sound like it. Why, you're dripping! Go get out of these clothes and into bed. Hurry!"

"Yes—I think I'd better," Celia said, and went out of the room without having looked up.

Last doubts were removed from the mind of her father. The woman who'd passed the library door couldn't possibly have been either his wife or his daughter—but who was it? He felt he'd better get on with telling Kate what had happened.

XXXIV

"As i was saying," he began, "no matter what peculiar theories you have about it, Laila was—well, she was all broken up, and, as I was saying, I never felt sorrier for anybody in my life." Kate didn't seem to be paying any attention to him but stood gazing concentratedly at the doorway through which Celia had just passed. "You aren't listening?"

"What do you suppose is the matter with her?" Kate murmured; but the question was addressed to herself and she still gazed at the doorway.

"As I was saying when she came in——" Ames spoke more loudly. "As I was saying——"

"Yes?" Kate turned to him, and smiled. "You were saying I talked like a wild woman."

"I meant about—about Laila," he explained, half-apologetically. "I don't mean in general, Kate, of course, and I didn't mean to be rude. I suppose I was a little surprised because you don't feel more sympa‹ thetic with her, especially when she was going through such an experience." He paused, awaiting comment; but as none came he fell back upon the ancient method of reasoning by dialogue. "She's one of our oldest and closest and dearest friends, isn't she? Why, certainly she is! Well, she needed—she needed help, didn't she? She certainly did, Kate. Somebody had to give it to her, didn't they? Somebody had to help. Isn't that so? Why, naturally it's so!" Then, as Kate still made no response, he continued rather superiorly, "Come to think of it, I wonder you or some of the other women didn't try to do anything for her at the moment it happened—I mean when Tuke was so outrageous to her. You'd think that at such a time all of her women friends would have gathered about her; but not one of you——"

"No, we didn't," Kate admitted. "She didn't seem to need us, Ames."

Upon the pronoun "us" he detected her slight emphasis. "Kate, I can't help thinking that's unfair—really unfair!" he said, and plunged deeper into his hapless maze. The best of lawyers has never yet gained anything by defending to his wife the case of a woman recognized by her own sex as predatory. "It's a queer thing," he went on unhappily. "It's a queer thing that when a wife is publicly insulted by her husband, treated the way Laila Speer was treated in our house to-night, her women friends leave it to the men in the party to try and buck her up. Yes, and then afterward you, Kate, seem inclined to whitewash Tuke for what he did and take his side." Ames's voice had begun to sound indignant; he heard it himself and it made him more so. "My God, don't women *ever* stand up for one another? Why have they always got to pounce on one of their own sex the instant she's in trouble?"

"Because we're just a wolf pack, Ames?" Kate asked, not helping him to be calmer in spirit.

"Indeed it seems so sometimes!" Indignation is a never-failing stimulant to him who feels it. By virtue of it Ames recovered virtue and became sincerely the injured party. Moreover, that sense of being irked by his wife increased upon him. She seemed to feel herself subtly his better, to think she knew things that he didn't and couldn't know—and to be trying to set him against Laila Speer, to control his opinion of that lovely abused woman whom he'd had to comfort. Was it still Kate's intention that he should never, never be allowed to think or act for himself in any matter whatever? "I'm not supposed to have any brains at *all?*" he asked.

"Don't be ten years old, Ames!"

Upon this, two memory pictures flickered within the eyes of Ames Lanning's mind: one was of an Attorney General of the United States receiving the news of a verdict Ames had won against him; and the other was of Plant Three's new expansion, more his creation than even Mr. Roe's, unending walls as busy within, now, by night as by day, where eight thousand men already worked in shifts for the coming defense of the country. Ames Lanning wasn't so vain as Julius Caesar; but could be as sore at home.

"Thank you, Kate!" he said.

She muttered, "Oh, well——" returned to the piano-bench, sat, lifted her hands to the keys, thought better of it and turned to face him again. "See here, I'm not trying to influence you in any way at all. I don't want to. I talk too much. Just forget it."

Nobody so easily forgets one of those instructions not to be ten years old. Ames, applying self-control, spoke quietly. "You say you're not trying to influence me. On the contrary, you're doing your best to make me think that Laila Speer was responsible for what Tuke did to her to-night."

"Think what you like," Kate said. "She was!"

"This is unbelievable!" he cried. "As if I hadn't the evidence of my eyes and ears! I declare I don't understand it. I'm damned if I do! Here you see a woman all gay and good and kind and affectionate go up to her husband and stroke his head——"

"Yes," Kate said, and once more talked too much. "If you care to know it, Ames, that was precisely the most devilish thing of all she did to him."

"Good God!" Ames thrust clenched fists into the pockets of his dinner-jacket. "I'm damned if I ever heard such female poppycock! Why, I thought Laila Speer was a friend of yours! I thought you—— Why'd you wait all this time to show how you hate her?"

"I do not hate her." Kate spoke clearly.

"You don't? Why, of course you do; there's plain evidence. Women! Ordinarily you're big-hearted and generous and your hand is out to anybody; you wear your feet and fingers off working for charities, and yet just let an unhappy wife that we've both always considered one of our most cherished friends—let her get slapped in the face before us all by her drinking husband, and you jump on her as if she were your bitterest enemy! On top of that you try to make me think about her and hate her as you do. Well, I don't fall for it; understand that, Kate—I don't! I'm damned if I——" He brought his hands from his pockets, slapped them together, and said, "Oh, here! This won't do. If we can't talk about it without quarreling we'd better not talk about it."

"I agree," Kate said sharply.

"Very well!" Ames was sad. "I'll never try to discuss it with you again. I'd better get out of here. Goodnight."

Kate began to play again as she heard him stalking down the hall toward his library. He didn't go in there, however; the sight of the desk-lamp and the chair where Laila'd sat and wept seemed to reproach him for listening to slander of her. He'd turned away, had gone upstairs and was in his own bedroom before he remembered, with a considerable shock, something that his pain and anger had temporarily banished from his mind. "Oh hell!" he said; and, with one arm out of his coat, he stood staring at an etching of the small factory building in which Henry L. Roe had begun the subsequently vast projection of the Roe Metal Products Corporation. "Oh hell!" He hadn't told Kate about kissing Laila.

He slid his arm back into the sleeve of his coat, stood for a moment in doubt; then removed the garment because he felt that to go downstairs and again try to tell her wouldn't look well. Besides, it'd probably only prompt her (in spite of their having dropped the subject forever) to talk some more in that inexplicably slurring way about

Laila—Laila, a mistreated, delicious, pitiable, beautiful woman who'd already been insulted in his house enough for one night.

Indignant again, he went to bed; and the comedy began to be serious.

At her piano, Kate Lanning was presently aware that Celia, in wrapper and slippers, had come so softly into the room as to be unheard, and, seated upon a sofa, was applying a towel to her moist hair. Kate stopped playing, looked at the pale girl, and asked, "Did you change everything?"

"Yes, of course. I was pretty wet. I'd have let them drive me in if I'd noticed how hard it was raining."

"You didn't notice that?" Kate shook her head. "I'm afraid you *had* found the party pretty sour!"

"I see what you mean," Celia said. "Miley's not being there. That pig! Oh, yes, he is! They told me they'd actually asked him to come and he said he had some work to do he couldn't let go. Sunday evening! Trying to make me think he wouldn't come because his presence would of course be distasteful to me after our row this morning. Hypocrite! But no, Kate, that wasn't the reason I didn't notice the rain; I was just too tired."

"Yes; you look it. What's really the matter?"

"Why, nothing! Can't a person get tired sometimes without being cross-examined? What went on here to-night, Kate?"

"What makes you think anything special did, Celia?"

"Why—oh, I don't know. They went home rather early, didn't they? Then when I came in I thought it looked as though you and Father had been talking about something uncomfortable maybe. Were you?"

Kate made an impatient gesture. "I'm provoked with myself; I've just been treating him like the devil! What's worse, I've probably made him think I was trying to boss him again. Not I! I've come to agree with the lady from Ohio who said that the only thing we can do about men is to let them do whatever they want to and then nurse 'em when it makes 'em sick."

Bending over, Celia rubbed her head and spoke through the towel.

"But what brought it on? Did something go wrong at the supper—or happen afterward?"

"It happened all evening, Celia, and finished in something sensationally disagreeable. Then your father began a post-mortem on it and I was mean to him and upset his temper. That's all."

"All?" Celia said. "Was it—was it anything about Laila Speer?"

"Of course."

"She's wicked!" Celia leaned back, let the towel drop upon the arm of the chair. "If you want to know what I think, she's a darn dangerous woman."

"She's not wicked." Kate shook her head. "Give her what she wants and Laila'll be as good and happy as a pleased child at Christmas."

"Yes, Kate; probably so would Hitler if you gave him the earth."

"Don't get to hating Laila," Kate said. "When you hate people you forget they're human beings and so you go wrong about 'em. She's a wonderful lacemaker and sells yards of it for the Refugee Aid Society; she's one of the best workers it's got. She wouldn't hurt anybody or anything except to get what she wants, and then she doesn't do it in cold blood or because she gets any pleasure out of hurting people. I've known her to do all sorts of kind things, Celia. She's just a person who follows her natural promptings."

"Yes—like an animal!" Celia cried. "I hate her and I tell you she's dangerous. What was it she did to-night?"

"Goaded Tuke till he couldn't stand it and broke out before everybody."

"But how?" Celia pressed her. "How'd she goad him? Was it anything she did about—about Father?"

Kate spoke negligently. "Yes, naturally it was. You know. You've been calling it molasses, haven't you?"

"Did Tuke threaten Father, Kate?"

"Gracious, no, nothing like that, child!" Kate laughed, for Celia's eyes, fixed upon her, were large and frightened. "Don't be so disturbed. Tuke just spoke out roughly to her and she got pathetically hurt, of course, and had to be helped out of the room.

"By Father?" Celia said. "Yes, of course; that's a safe bet. What happened then, Kate?"

"Why, nothing. Ames took her into the library, where they were chaperoned by Bill Jones, and——"

"Bill?" Celia spoke impulsively. "Bill? I didn't——"

"You didn't what?"

"I didn't imagine she'd want Bill there," Celia said.

"Maybe she didn't; but I don't suppose he was a great deterrent. I'd put him on a couch in the alcove where it was dark; but he must have been awake because your father said he spoke to them. I'm sure even Bill didn't stop Laila from weeping prettily and making poor Ames into a satisfactorily tender champion. It doesn't need much imagination to know just about what she'd do under the circumstances, does it?"

"No!" Celia said with vehemence and sat straight, staring at her stepmother. "No, it doesn't. It may need a little more, though, to know what Tuke'll do about it. What did he——"

"Tuke? He went home, Celia. After he'd spoken as he did to her he didn't look at anybody, not a glance; he just strode out, got his hat and coat and went home."

"What makes you think he went home?"

"What? Why, where else would he go? It was raining. Look at you when you came in. You don't mean he was hanging about the house, waiting outside, do you? You didn't see him when you came in, did you?"

"No, no. When I came in I was all wet and hurrying and didn't see anything."

"Then what's the matter?" Kate leaned forward. "Don't look so worried."

"But I am. Things like—like this make me nervous, Kate."

"What nonsense, child!"

"It isn't," Celia insisted. "Tuke Speer's been pretty queer lately. All these stories about him, they're not like him—not like the way he used to be—and when you see him he doesn't look as he used to look, either. He looks hunted. Yes, he does! He's always been wild about that woman, Kate. You know it. She could drive him crazy; I mean crazy!"

"Celia, no. She hurts him, of course, but——"

Celia was more and more insistent. "Kate, it won't do for you to keep up this passive attitude toward Father. I see what's been the matter with you now, all this time, and I tell you it won't do! With that woman really after him—— Why, she's seductive, I tell you!"

"Celia!" Kate laughed outright.

"She is! She's a lightweight mentally, certainly, and Father's a heavyweight—the very kind that fall for the lightweights without knowing it. He did once, didn't he? I tell you, Kate, we don't know what might happen. There might be scandal—there might be worse."

"Worse than scandal? What?"

"I don't know. Oh, yes, up to now I've laughed over it the same as you; but I begin to see things that are under the surface. I tell you Tuke Speer's face scares me."

"Tuke's face, Celia? When?"

"I mean lately," the girl said hurriedly. "I mean whenever I've seen him lately. Yes, and so's *she* begun to scare me." Celia jumped up, speaking urgently. "Kate, you've got to realize that Father's a marvel in law and in business; but outside of that——" She interrupted herself. "See here! Before you were married Father thought he was a whole lot in love with Laila. I didn't take it all in then; but I did afterward. You don't deny it, do you?"

"Goodness, no!"

"Stop laughing at me, Kate! How long was it after that before he began to see what a darling you are?"

"Not long. Call it a few days, Celia."

"Yes, you had to take him on the rebound, didn't you?"

"Absolutely! It made me cross; but I was delighted."

Celia kissed her. "You sweet thing! How old was he when he married Mother? Only about twenty-two, wasn't he?"

"Twenty, Celia. They were both twenty."

"There you have it!" Celia exclaimed. "Twenty, and they'd been engaged I don't know how long! Why, look at him, Kate! Engaged from the time he was practically a baby; then married and working his head off as he always has. Then heartbroken after my mother died, till Laila stirred him up, then threw him off and you, thank heaven, caught him! About women—don't you see?—he's still not over seventeen. He's still that simple and he's still that good. He oughtn't to be left alone, Kate. From now on, one of us ought to be with him all the time."

Kate rose, picked up Celia's towel, and said smilingly, "You get to bed. I never saw you in such a state; you mustn't have another fight on the way from church! Your father isn't going to run away with anybody else's wife; he isn't going to run away at all. He takes his responsibilities pretty seriously—and you've just mentioned that he's a good man, you know. You get to bed."

"Oh, I will; but——" Celia said, and, leaving this "but" ominously upon the air, obeyed. She didn't remain fixedly in bed, however. Kate had gone to the rear of the house, had dropped Celia's towel down a laundry chute to the basement, and, having returned to the living-room, was putting out the lights when Celia reappeared. "Kate, I keep thinking of Tuke Speer's face. We've got to watch Father. We've got to take care of him. Something might happen that could—— Why, Kate, it could wreck everything!"

Again Kate advised her to go to bed, and again Celia did; but the young stepmother didn't immediately follow. She stood for a time, tapping upon a table with the tips of her fingers and wondering when and where Celia had suddenly developed her fear of Tuke Speer's face.

That poor worn face of Tuke's, how it had changed indeed! Laila's face hadn't, not much, and that was most of the reason why Tuke's had. Well, so had Ames's face changed—broadening and filling, grown masterly. "About women he's still not over seventeen," Celia had said. Possibly, but Kate wasn't afraid that Laila could ever again put a boy's goose look upon him. No apparition of a beautiful Laila once more intruding and disturbing rose before this wife in her meditation.

She looked upon Laila Speer as the other wives of the coterie did, negligently tolerating an old accustomed semi-nuisance—a disappointed woman who monopolized the show at parties and bemused husbands a little but couldn't ensnare them. Long ago, before Tuke and Laila were married, he'd sometimes been able to decline to be jealous; but as a husband he'd lost that control of himself—she could always get a rise out of him. Wasn't a great part of what sickened him, though, the sight of his wife's counting upon blandishments that any grown woman would have thought a high-school girl ridiculous for using?

As for Ames's naïvely manlike outburst on behalf of an unjustly treated woman, it had irritated Kate a little, no worse, and she was sorry she'd let him see that it had. Well, too bad but not important. What had come between her and her husband was incomparably more dangerous than ever could be the worn cajoleries of an envious Laila Speer.

XXXV

AMES LANNING'S OFFICES, A LEATHER AND MAHOGANY clean-smelling air-conditioned suite on the top floor of Mr. Roe's nineteen-story Equitable Trust Building, downtown, gave the occupants a panoramic view of the western and southern sides of the city, the industrial area;—that is, there was such a view when the wind blew hard enough to drive the smoke away. Ames, at his George Washington desk on the Wednesday afternoon of that week, paused in dictation because his thoughts wandered from the letter he was composing, a dull affair, and, through a wide plate-glass window, his gaze had come to rest absently upon the far horizon where rose, ghostlike in haze, the long chimneys of Plant Three.

His pause was only a vague one, lasting but a few seconds; yet a number of thoughts and feelings unconnected with business wandered vagrantly within him throughout its duration. Somewhere under yonder dim immense roofs from which the chimneys protruded was Tuke Speer, and to think of Tuke was to think of Laila—and since Sunday evening, when Ames had last seen her, the thought of Laila was a mixed-up one. It was warmingly pleasant, and something like a delicately stirring perfume seemed to accompany it; and at the same time there was a painfulness. Most of the pain was sympathy—sympathy for a brave woman maltreated by her inexplicable husband and cruelly misinterpreted by other women who were ordinarily good and kind but governed by the strange habits of their strange sex. The rest of the painfulness was a hurt resentment felt by Ames for both himself and Laila. They seemed to be coupled not only as dear friends but as the recipients of unfair treatment. How long would it be before he'd see her again? This thought surprised him—shocked him a little, too. What business had he to be wondering when he'd see Laila again?

He resumed his dictation; then was interrupted. Henry L. Roe himself opened the door of the room and came in—the only person entitled to do that unannounced—and as usual he looked hurried and preoccupied. "Sit down, sit down," he said quickly. "You don't have to get up for me all the time, Ames; I'm not that old, doggone it! I'll go back downstairs if you're on something important, or I'll just sit here and wait."

"No, no, it's nothing." Ames glanced at the stenographer, who departed instantly and softly. "I'm afraid this New York thing is bothering you a good deal, Mr. Roe."

"Well, it is." The small old man sat down and thrust a ruffling hand over the forward edges of his short white hair; he'd already mussed his black bow tie. "It's only three or four times in my life that I've been caught like this—in doubt about the right man for a place, no matter how big the place. As you say, Jennings won't do and Jacob Hensen won't do. That pesky Augren won't take it—idiot! He'd be five times the man he is here and have twice the money, though doggoned if I don't kind of like him for the way he sticks to his city. I've thought and thought, Ames. It's worrying me too much. If we're going to get into the war that job ought to've been filled before now. You still think we're about certain to be dragged in, do you?"

"Aren't you?" Ames Lanning said. "Suppose two men are shooting at each other—call 'em Mr. Churchill and Adolph. I have the information from Adolph himself that he expects to do what he likes to me later, and I don't like what he likes, so I keep handing Mr. Churchill fresh cartridges to shoot at Adolph. Adolph's got a partner engaged in killing a Chinaman, and expecting to be engaged in killing me later, so I'm handing a gun to the Chinaman. Adolph and the Japanese won't include me out much longer, will they, sir?"

"That's how you and Kate feel about it, is it, Ames?"

"Well, I——" Ames knew it wasn't fair to experience a slight irri-tation. "Yes. I don't think the country's going to have any option. The world's more primitive than we thought it was; we're back in the days of the ancients when no law at all prevailed between nations. Where there's no law there's no way to save your life and your goods except by fighting. There's bitter talk and arguing against it; but the country really knows what's coming or it wouldn't be arming."

"I'm afraid you might be right, Ames." Mr. Roe sighed and looked gloomily reminiscent. "Yes, ever since Kate spent all that time in Germany with her father she's been convinced those people were going to fight again some day. Only a question of time, she told me long ago, depending on how soon they got their wind back and felt strong enough again. Talked that way to you, too, didn't she?"

"Yes, sir; and so did others."

"I used to think it pretty far-fetched, Ames. Maybe that was because I hated so to believe it. In the first place I hate fighting, and in the second place I couldn't bear the idea, because how can this country ever get enough united again to fight anybody? Why, just look at us! We've got ourselves all split up into classes, what they call 'blocs' or 'pressure groups'. Labor, agriculture, school teachers, ex-soldiers of the World War, Chambers of Commerce, the silver people, the colored people, the aged people, the youth people, and I don't know what all—every one of 'em with a bunch of politicians in the govern-ment acting as agents for 'em, and all the other politicians promising if elected they'll get all the government money they can lay hands on for 'em. All of 'em trying to get their feet in the trough, all of 'em trying to make the rest of us work for their particular benefit, and all of 'em out to get anybody that's built up a profitable business or's done well by himself and his neighbors and the people he employs. How can a country divided up into squabbling squads of egomaniacs ever pull together enough to fight a war against solidified dictator-ships? I'd like to hear what Kate's got to say about that!"

Again Ames knew his irritation to be petty and unjustified; but it was there just the same. "I don't know, sir. We haven't discussed it lately; but I take it for granted that she'd agree with me. My opinion is that war creates a common fear, and, if the war that's coming is dangerous enough to this country, our fear will be great enough to unite us in an anger unhealthy for the enemy. Well, we're getting that right now; the feeling increases every day. It's under the surface, although most of us are going about our businesses and our pleasures as accustomedly as we can. As I see it, there's an agitation in men's spirits everywhere in the country, and it's of the kind that always precedes a war. Don't you feel it, yourself, Mr. Roe?"

"Oh, my, my!" The old man sighed again. "I'm afraid I do. We'll go on doing what we can. We shouldn't put off our selection of the right man for New York another day, Ames. I suppose you haven't any new ideas on the subject or you'd have let me know."

"Of course. No, I'm sorry to own I'm still stumped, Mr. Roe."

"My, my! When you're stumped it's bad, Ames. This thing's a nuisance; it's got to be settled. God alone knows what's to happen to the world! By the time winter's on us——" He left the sentence un-finished and made a gloomy gesture that meant his helpless abstention from prophecy.

"By winter," Ames said sturdily, "we'll have five Plants larger and busier than Number Three is now. If we can get time enough before Armageddon——"

"Yes, yes, I know." Mr. Roe wearily looked his age. "Ames, I've been wanting to get away a while. I'd like to rest up a bit from all the war talk and the hustle, hustle of the war work we're doing; I'd like to see a mountain lake again somewhere for a few weeks if I could. I want to take Marjie and Marvin with me, Ames. Looks like they're still too young for society around here; they don't seem to enjoy them-selves—act kind of disappointed, both of 'em." Grandfatherly melan-choly evoked another sigh from him. "Marvin, for instance—well, I've had to come to the conclusion he's not exactly a shining light. No, he certainly isn't."

"I'm sorry you feel that way, Mr. Roe. I'm sure Celia and all the others like him and——"

"No, she doesn't," Mr. Roe said. "I can't blame her. I've done everything I could for that boy; but, doggone it, he just isn't there! No wonder, poor fellow, though I've given him the best raising I could. Well, no matter; but at my age a man has to realize these things. If anything happened to me it wouldn't do, Ames, it wouldn't do; it's got to be a trusteeship for both the children and that's all there is to it. They're all I've got, though. Some people might criticize me for taking a trip right in the midst of all our Defense work; but I'm a good deal frazzled up and you're practically handling all of it, anyhow —and tip-top too! The Executive vice-presidency'll give you all the authority you'll need."

Ames flushed with pride and pleasure. "That's pretty gratifying, Mr. Roe; but I don't like to hear you implying that you aren't needed."

"I know what's what," the old man said. "Before I leave, though, I've got to see this New York position settled. There's hardly anybody left I can think of for it. Ransom won't do, Colby won't do, and of course we've got to keep George Cooke where he is. Men like Bill Jones and Tuke Speer are naturally out of the question. Oh, by the way——"

"Yes, Mr. Roe?"

"Speaking of Speer, Ames, I've had it in mind to talk to you about him. Marjie goes around some, you know—not much but some—and she hears the girls talking about what's said in what they call 'the married set'. She's picked up rumors about Speer. For some time back it seems he's been getting the reputation of being too much of a drinking man. You can't contradict that, can you, Ames?"

"Perhaps not, sir; but——"

"I don't like it a bit," Mr. Roe went on. "In business, drinking men can't be trusted. I don't interfere in my people's private lives; but I won't have a hard drinker in the organization, Ames, or anybody there's any scandal about, I don't care who it is. I won't have it, not a sliver of it!"

"No, sir, of course not. Everybody understands that, Mr. Roe."

"I hope so, Ames. This is the home town of Roe Metal Products, and its representatives have got to be examples of high citizenship, above reproach. Maybe Speer used to be all right; but what do you know about him lately?"

Ames didn't answer promptly. It was his custom to speak the truth as best he knew it to Mr. Roe; but he realized that his present feeling about Tuke was a personal one, and he paused to face and examine the fact. Naturally that feeling consisted of indignation and disapproval. Moreover, this former friend of his had of late shown him something like hostility half concealed, never met him but with averted eyes, swallowed and answered necessary questions sulkily. A merely noncommittal word to Mr. Roe now and Tuke would be out; therefore it should not be spoken. At first sight of Ames Lanning the young stranger, Miley Stuart, had divined that he was a square-shooter.

"I haven't heard of Speer's work falling off in the slightest," Ames said. "I don't believe he's been five minutes late at his office in Plant Three in ten years, Mr. Roe. As for gossip I don't listen to it, myself; and you and I have experience enough to know that it gets started over nothing sometimes—and then most likely dies out—about anybody in the world."

Mr. Roe was pleased. "Yes, that's true. I'm glad you speak up for Speer; that settles it. Ames, you're always sound; it's reassuring to me to know you're here, like a rock. You've always understood the fundamentals—the struggle between the agitators and the politicians to get their hands, too, upon the fruits of labor and for their own benefit soft-soap the working-man into destroying the manufacturer. Yes, I used to be called a manufacturer, an honest word; but the jugglers have been at work and of course I had to be called an industrialist—'one of the most powerful industrialists' and so forth. Nowadays the word-jugglers have gone a step further toward public ownership, meaning politicians' ownership; so the latest thing's to call me 'management'. Yes, sir, all I am now, I'm just 'management'. Not so nice! Well, Ames, some day you'll have to bear that odium yourself; but you're strong and——"

The telephone on Ames's desk buzzed, and Ames, annoyed, said,

"Go on, sir; they ought to know better than to put any call through to me when you're here."

"No, no, I was just gassing." Mr. Roe waved his hand toward the desk. "Take it. It might be something. Go ahead."

Ames put the instrument to his ear and said brusquely, "Who is it?"

A voice warmed by the special intonations of a newly tender intimacy replied, "I'd know that's you, Ames, anywhere in the world. Don't you recognize *me?*"

Ames did. "Oh, yes, I—yes, of course," he said, and hoped that he sounded businesslike. Mr. Roe, having turned in his chair, was looking out of the window.

"I've got such a lot to say in a hurry, dearest," the voice said, and Ames pressed the instrument closer against his ear. "It's been such ages since Sunday night! Has it seemed that way to you too, sweet? I've been through—— But first I must have you tell me just one thing. You did tell me Sunday night—oh, so darlingly!—but I must hear it again before anything else. Say it, Ames; say it!"

"Ah——" Ames coughed. "I—I think perhaps you'd better——"

"Nobody'd be listening in on this line, would they?" Laila asked quickly.

"No, but——"

"I understand," she said. "There's somebody besides you in your office. I see. I'll have to take it for granted that you're saying what I want to hear, won't I?" She laughed fondly. "Don't worry; I know it anyhow. I know you do. I'll have to do all the talking, won't I?"

"Yes, I—I believe so; but——"

"I see," Laila repeated, and went on rapidly, "I'm in a public station 'way uptown. I wouldn't have dared at home because I've a very strong suspicion he's bribed both our old fat cook and the colored housemaid to watch me. I wouldn't be surprised if he has somebody following me right now. These days are simple hell, Ames; I couldn't live through them except for thinking of you. He hasn't spoken a word to me since Sunday night nor I to him; but his eyes—oh, it's horrible, darling! If it weren't for the precious thrilling beautiful thought of you——"

"Just a second," Ames contrived to say, as she paused for a gasping breath. "Could you—could you call me again in about——"

"No, I can't," Laila said. "I'm afraid to try it again. I'll have to pour it all out now. Dearest, I just had to warn you——"

"To what?"

"To warn you, darling. We've got to be oh, so careful, Ames, so careful! Dear heart, I'd come straight to you if it weren't for that. You're so open and frank and unsuspicious you'd never think of these things; but a woman has to. You see, if he thinks he's got anything on us—well, you know what he could do. It mustn't be that way, Ames. You and I can't let it be that way. We've got to be right and have everybody feeling that we're in the clear and that if anybody's wrong it's not us but they. The danger is he may have something, Ames. He may! Have you found out who that woman was?"

"No, I—no, I haven't."

"We must, we must!" Laila said. "We don't know what use he might make of it. Then there was Bill, too; it *could* be awful! Darling, you'll keep on trying to find out who the woman was, won't you?"

"Just a second," Ames said. "I'm afraid I——"

"No, wait," Laila broke in. "I mayn't have another chance. We've got to have a little patience. You mustn't try to see me and don't call me on the telephone, whatever you do. I've been afraid you'd get so impatient you might. You see, with the servants listening we don't know what might happen. We must just wait till a really safe chance. We've got to go on pretending, a while longer anyhow, as if Sunday night hadn't happened. Now just tell me the one thing I want to hear again. If somebody's listening they won't understand just one little word. Darling, darling, you meant it, didn't you?"

Something within Ames urged him powerfully to say nothing; but he didn't see how to heed it. "Of course I——" he began, with an impractical intention of going on in a business tone to explain what couldn't very well be explained at the moment—if at all.

"Ah, darling!" Laila said. "If I could tell you what it means to hear you say it in that big manly voice of yours! That's what I really needed, and now I'd better run home again. Thank you, thank you! Sweetheart, good-bye!"

Ames returned the instrument to its prongs and hoped that his

attention didn't seem to wander wildly when Mr. Roe resumed the
subject of the New York appointment. The old man talked of it
botheredly a while; then rose and said, "Well, I'll be on my way. We
don't seem to get anywhere with it and I can see you've got a lot
of other things on your mind. Don't work too hard, my boy. Follow
my example and put your difficulties on other people's shoulders.
Give my love to Kate and Celia, won't you? Remarkable woman,
Kate, remarkable! Don't forget to give her my best."

Ames said that indeed he'd remember; and, left alone, wiped his
forehead, looked at the telephonic instrument fixedly, then wiped
his forehead again. "Don't ever do that any more!" may have been the
essence of the thought he addressed to the telephone, when he'd recovered a sufficient equilibrium.

Laila seemed to feel that the episode of Sunday evening had somehow been much more decisive than he'd thought it; he must have
appeared more ardent—much more—than he'd realized. Anyhow,
there couldn't be any doubt now that she was in love with him—
quite a great deal in love with him, in fact—and took it for granted
that he reciprocated. That wouldn't do. He'd have to explain things
to her, of course. As soon as they'd happen to be alone together again,
with time enough, he'd have to put everything between them on a
proper footing. Tuke was already jealous of him, she'd said, and this
particularly wouldn't do. Somehow Tuke would have to be shown—
truthfully shown—that he had no real cause whatever for such a feeling. Ames could use eloquence when it was necessary, he knew, and,
as soon as there arrived a good chance to talk to Laila, couldn't he
make her see that both their lives might be enriched by a new and fine
relationship, one that Tuke wouldn't mind?

It could consist of mutual devotion, sympathy and the shared sense
of inner companionship. There'd be a secret kind of bond between
them, better not mentioned often even by themselves; and yet, were
it known and fully comprehended, it would merit no just reproach
from anybody. A twilight talk with Laila now and then, when they
could be quietly together, might be both relaxing and inspiring. She
was easy to be with, could be a man's friend without putting pressures
upon him or being forever quoted by Mr. Roe as if her opinions

were the best available and usually necessary for the settlement of important questions. A carefully rare half hour with Laila, when a hard day's work was done, would be rewarding for a man who admitted to himself, as Ames straightforwardly did, that what he really needed from a woman sometimes wasn't advice and control but a little unqualified admiration. Call it flattery if you insist; but no man was wholly without vanity and Laila didn't stick pins into his. Yes, a quiet twilight with her at cautious intervals, so that of course nobody could possibly misinterpret or start talk——

If Ames's daughter and his wife had been invisibly present as he pursued this inviting thought, Celia could easily have proved by his expression that his seventeen-year-old boyishness had by no means departed out of him. One look, and Kate would have yielded the point. He was certain he'd found the best and pleasantest solution of his embarrassing but not disagreeable problem. That is, he was certain for some moments—until his gaze wandered from the telephone to the chair where Henry L. Roe had sat, and from the chair to the window that revealed the long chimneys of Plant Three, distant in the haze. Closer, in the haze of Ames Lanning's mind, faces pressed: Tuke Speer's and Henry L. Roe's—yes, and Kate's. They didn't appear to give his proposed understanding with Laila their blessing or even to believe that he believed in it.

Ames's gaze, returning to the telephone, seemed to regard the instrument as unreassuring.

XXXVI

AMES'S DAUGHTER, AT THE SAME MOMENT BUT AT HOME, was also personifying an identically shaped small black mechanism. In the wide hall upstairs she sat before the table upon which it rested, stared at it angrily, extended her left hand to lift it and her right forefinger as if to operate the dial. Then she let both hands drop in her lap and applied to the telephone her favorite insult. "Pig!"

Kate, coming upstairs after seeing the last members of a Red Cross committee out of the house, overheard the stepdaughter's exclamation, and remonstrated. "Think that's fair to him, Celia? Just because he was cross over poor Marvin and didn't come in to lunch last Sunday?"

"You're on the wrong horse," Celia said. "You don't suppose I'd be goof enough to call that bird up, do you?"

"Pig-bird?" Kate said. "Calling up the poor creature might be a friendly thing to do, though, mightn't it? You haven't seen him since Sunday noon, I believe—three days, the longest absence since we came back to town, isn't it? He might be sick, so naturally you'd want to know——"

"Don't be a brat!" Celia looked up resentfully. "He can be as sick as he likes, I wouldn't send the doctor! Besides, except for a permanently lame shoulder he got from another mule he had trouble with Down South, he's so husky I don't believe he could manage to be sick. My calling him a pig just now didn't have anything to do with him."

"It didn't, Celia? Odd!"

"No, it isn't. I told you I wasn't going to call him up, didn't I? I was thinking of calling Mr. Augren; then, just as I was about to do it, I had a thought and didn't. The reason I didn't was because that pig would be sure to think the wrong thing if I did and so I called him what he is."

"I see," Kate said. "Clear as day. You were going to ask Mr. Augren to tell Miley you didn't mean it, so he could come here again, all's forgiven."

Celia declined to smile. "I was going to call Mr. Augren to ask him for a Defense job in Roe Metal Products. The reason I didn't was because suppose he put me in Plant Three, why, that's where Miley is and no matter what you say about his modesty, of course he'd think I did it because he was staying away and I couldn't bear it. What's riding you?"

This inquiry was caused by the seriousness with which Kate had

begun to regard her. "Celia, you haven't been yourself since Sunday
and you haven't looked like yourself, either. Why have you suddenly
decided you want a job?"

"What could be more reasonable?" Celia cried. "I'm tired of rolling
bandages and tending benefit sales counters and just sitting knitting.
Look at Roe Metal Products' Defense contracts; I'd like to be a
dollar-a-year girl or anything they want."

"No," Kate said. "That isn't it—anyhow, not all of it. What's the
rest of it?"

"There isn't any rest of it!" Celia was petulant. "Why all the fuss
because a girl wants to go to work? You had a job yourself, didn't
you?—yes, and in Roe Metal Products, at that. You were working
there when you and Father got engaged, weren't you?"

"Yes." Kate turned from her and looked thoughtfully at the long
blue rug that covered most of the corridor floor. She sighed and
then spoke abruptly with what seemed a melancholy impulse. "It
might be just as well if I hadn't."

Celia jumped up from her seat before the telephone table. She put
her hand on Kate's arm. "Why would it have been just as well if you
hadn't? You mean something about the trouble between you and
Father. Why not tell me?"

"Oh, well——" Kate said. "When I was there I was most of the
time in Mr. Roe's own office and I suppose I did quite a little absorbing. We might be happier now if I hadn't."

"Why, Kate?"

"Made me think I know too much," Kate answered. "Besides that,
my father was a lawyer, you know, and I'd learned from him a little
of what's useful in setting out cases before a judge and jury. I'm
afraid I went to work on Ames with my father's ways in mind. I
suppose even before we were married I did some hinting and——"

"What!" Celia cried. "You don't mean you imagine Father blames
you for that, do you?"

"No, not blames, Celia. It's a little hard to make you see; but there's
a long list of my advisings and managings." Kate patted the hand
that rested sympathetically upon her arm. "Let's get back to you. Why
do you want to get into Roe Metal Products, Celia?"

"No, you listen to me!" Celia said. "You've been sore at Father for months, so you won't do anything. If harm comes of it, it'll be your fault!"

"Yes," Kate said gently. "That's natural. You're his daughter, so you'd say that."

"Don't waste my time!" Celia was vehement. "I love you both, and you know it; but you're mad at Father just because he's a simple human he-husband."

"No, Celia. I'm trying to do what he wants."

"Yes, not what he needs!" Celia cried. "You've implied he's nourished rancor because of your 'advisings and managings'. Well, why wouldn't he? How'd it look to him? He's always had sense enough to do what you said and it helped him; but it looked as if you wanted to change him and didn't admire him the way he *was*. That wounded him as a lover, Kate. Lovers, both sexes, have got to be *wholly* admired or they're hurt, aren't they? Advice may help; but it hurts, too, because telling a person to change himself is really criticism, and the last person on earth a man can stand to be criticized by is the woman he's in love with. Maybe you've never understood that."

Kate was grave. "Maybe I haven't."

"No," Celia said. "I don't think you have; and yet you're hurt with Father because he was hurt. Hurt means rancor, and you've let the two rancors come between you—and that's all there is to it, except that you've got to do something."

"Have I? What?"

"You know what!" Celia cried. "Don't tell me you don't, because you're the shrewdest woman I know—and yet you choose to be a sorehead, letting your marriage go to pot rather than save it." The girl threw her arms about her stepmother and kissed her. "All right, darling, fold your hands, mope and nurse your wrath, and then, if anything happens to Father, just sit and cry. Don't ask me to follow your example, though. I'll do what little I can. Good-bye!" Celia ran to the head of the stairway, turned there to shout, "You'll be sorry!" and descended rapidly out of Kate's sight.

The stepmother, startled, stood wondering acutely; then she went

to the triple window at the end of the corridor and looked down upon
the lawn and driveway. Celia's car crunched brown gravel determinedly, passed between the stone gateposts and turned southward.

"She *did* see something!" Kate said. "She won't tell me because
she's a good sport—and I'm his wife."

This, half-whispered, formed a connection with another thought, a
suspicion of the reason why Tuke Speer's face brought panic into
her stepdaughter's imaginings. Kate went downstairs, walked slowly
along the broad hallway and paused before the open door of her
husband's library. As she looked in, she couldn't see the alcove at
the other end of the long room; but, in her mental picturing, the
foreground near the desk was occupied by two figures, a man's and
a woman's standing close together—very likely in a consolatory embrace. Across the room, slightly out of line with her and the two
shadow figures, was a window, open and with the shade up for air.
Beyond the window she could see the lawn and shrubberies beside
the house, wanly bright in the autumnal sunshine and only a little
dimmed by the intersecting wires of the fly-screen. In her mind's
eye Kate darkened that scene, put a drizzly night outside and no
strong illumination within the room—for, yes, Laila would have
asked him at once to turn out the upper lights. That would have left
the desk-lamp only, and by its feebler rays could a face outside the
window have been seen through the wire screen? Could such a face
have been seen and recognized from where she stood?

She tried passing and re-passing the open doorway, glancing within
as she walked. "Yes," she thought, "it might. Just barely it might."
Then, being as Henry L. Roe defined her a remarkable woman, she
began to behave in a remarkable way.

She went into the room, sat in the easy-chair by the desk, looked
upward as if to a manly bending figure. After a moment she rose
with extended arms enfolding, and whispered, "Ames, darling,
darling, you're such a comfort to me!" Then she glanced at the open
doorway and looked frightened, her eyes swept to the distant alcove
and she uttered a sound, part gasp, part sob and part laugh. "Yes,
Bill was there, too!" she said, on this note of rueful mirth. Why had
so experienced a hand as Laila taken such chances? Of course because

she didn't care; she thought that Ames would be committed to her
the more if someone saw and heard. Had Laila thought of the ominous window, though? Had she seen the face that Celia must have
seen there? No. If Laila had seen that face she'd not have been so
suave as she was when she joined the departing guests.

The window, now, to Kate's gaze, seemed to frame the climax of
a long tragedy grown at last too keen for bearing. "Poor soul! Poor
Tuke!" she said finally, and drooped down into the chair again to
sit thinking of the truth that lay within the most easily prattled of all
the quotations from William Shakespeare: "What fools these mortals
be!" She included herself passionately.

Celia, meanwhile, drove down through the town, set grimly upon
a course of inconsistency. She reached a parking-space beside the
shorter wing of Plant Three at ten minutes before five, maneuvered
her car until it was directly behind another, a rather shabby one
familiar to her, and then sat gazing toward the nearest entrance to
the huge building some two hundred feet distant. At five the exodus
from the offices began—girls, youths, neat "white-collar workers" of
all ages. Some hurried, some dawdled, chatting, and many went toward a line of waiting 'buses on the boulevard beyond the lot; but
most dispersed themselves among the stagnant automobiles, set them
in motion, backed and buzzed, jerked forward and away, until finally
the open spaces were broad and only a few cars remained. The last
of all was the one just before Celia's, the "used car" Miley Stuart had
thought himself entitled to buy after his first two months in the
great factory.

It was twenty minutes after five when he appeared, walking slowly
and absently but engaged in a cogitation more cheerful than otherwise, Celia fiercely thought. He was beside his car before he saw her
and then he was startled enough to make the rounding of his eyes
a tribute to anybody who caused it. He didn't leap forward, but was
as swiftly beside the door she opened for him.

"Celia! You're waiting for somebody? I don't think your father's
been here to-day. He's probably at his offices in town and——."

"Get in!" she said, adding as he obeyed, "I can talk to you here as well as anywhere. I didn't see Mr. Speer come out. Is he still in there?"

"No; he and Mr. Augren and the other executives have their own parking-space on the other side. Celia, to think I'm seeing you again! I'd been afraid you were too angry with me ever to——"

"I was!" she said. "You treated me with unpardonable selfishness and then blew up because I didn't like it. On top of that you've caused me to give up a plan I had for getting a job here."

"What? How could I when I haven't even seen you?"

"Never mind. I may be all loopy, but I haven't come here to talk about either you or me or any other foolishnesses." Then immediately Celia topped her inconsistencies with a cupola of the same material. "The reason I decided not to ask for a job here's because a lot of people would have said it was darned funny I'd never thought of it before you worked here."

"What? What nonsense! Why, Celia, nobody——"

"Oh, yes, they would! Let's don't waste time on that. Here, I've got to go all out. I've got to make use of you if I can, because I'm in a spot, Miley, and maybe you're in a position to help me a little. It's serious and I'm scared all through."

"What is it, Celia?"

"I've *got* to talk to somebody! First I want to know something: Has Tuke Speer been at the Plant all the time these three days since Sunday?"

XXXVII

MILEY LOOKED AT HER PERPLEXEDLY. "WHY, YES, MR. Speer's been here all the time—during working hours, that is. As a matter of fact I was talking with him just before I came out. He stopped me because he wanted to tell me something."

"To tell you what?"

"Well, it was——" Miley hesitated. "I'm afraid it was a little too good to be true. Of course I had a pretty elaborate technical education, you know, and kept at it rather long, so—well, I suppose it has given me advantages. Mr. Speer's had me at work for several weeks making a mathematical sort of report on the whole of our airplane parts production, here and also at Plant Two up at Roeville, and I handed it to him Monday morning. He's been going over it in detail since then and—well, I suppose he must have been pleased with it, judging from what he said."

"Is that all?"

"Well——" Miley flushed. "He told me there was going to be a vacancy pretty soon, a position higher up in the Plant—somebody was going to resign—and he didn't see why I shouldn't have it. He was going to mention it to Mr. Augren."

"Somebody going to resign?" A leap of intuition made Celia paler. "He meant himself!"

"I don't think so. I can't imagine his thinking they'd consider me for that much promotion, Celia."

She disregarded this. "Resign! That scares me worse. Miley, you've been working mostly with him, haven't you? Has he seemed different since Sunday?"

"I don't know that he has." The puzzled young man thought hard. "Maybe a little. He's always been pretty grim since I've known him and's seemed to be getting rather more and more so all the time."

"Yes!" Celia clasped her hands, appearing to hold them so by main force lest they fly apart in desperate gestures. "There's something I'm going to ask you to do—— Oh, it's really impossible!"

"No, no; tell me, Celia."

"It'll sound idiotic," she said. "I can't do what ought to be done, myself, and I can't go hiring private detectives. I couldn't tell them why and I wouldn't trust them. Miley, I'm asking you to watch him."

"Watch Mr. Speer? Why, what——"

"Yes, I said it'd sound foolish, didn't I? Well, here it is: Sunday morning you and I were talking of the set his wife always makes at Father. Well, it's made Tuke jealous—nobody but me knows how jealous—and he's the kind of man that gets jealous the way Othello did. Don't laugh at me."

"I won't," Miley said. "You say nobody knows but you. How's that?"

She spoke breathlessly. "I saw something. I saw him—looking at them."

"Is that all?"

"I'm not a fool!" Celia wasn't angry; she was too frightened by the picture her memory evoked. "You wouldn't say 'Is that all?' if you'd seen his face as I did. I didn't even see it distinctly, Miley; but I tell you I learned then and there that passion can be so sharp and violent and so hot and so deadly cold, too, that if you're looking on you feel it as if it were something striking straight through you. Miley, it frightened me so that I've been shaking ever since."

He was as impressed as she wished, and he took her too seriously to attempt to be manfully reassuring. "Explain it to me a little more, Celia."

"I'll have to. You'll see why I can't go to Kate fully about it; they're not getting along too well as it is and I won't give him away to her because—well, because he was being—oh, well, just a man, Miley! When as attractive a woman as Laila Speer wants to sob out her troubles on any man's shoulder he'll let her do it, of course. That's what she was doing and naturally Father was falling for it. Well, I'm darned if I'll tell his wife that he was!"

"No; you wouldn't," Miley said. "That's right. You saw Speer looking at them?"

"Yes; but I'd seen him before!" Celia's shoulders jerked in a quick shiver. "It was Sunday night during that rain and I was rushing for indoors when I thought I saw a man lurking round the side of the house; I wasn't sure. I thought I'd better tell somebody; but, after I let myself in, there was a party going on and I thought I'd go see if our house-man was still up and get him to go out with me to look for the man. I didn't because when I passed the library door I saw a face at the window and I knew—I knew it was Tuke."

"That was when you saw the look, Celia?"

"Oh, I did, I did!" she said. "He was looking at them—at my father and Laila. I was scared—so scared of what Tuke might do that I went to watch him. I went out a side door and crept round among bushes till I could see him. Then he must have heard the noise of people beginning to leave by the front door and he moved off through the bushes and stood till they'd all gone—Laila too, because I could hear her voice as she went and so could he of course. What frightened me worse was that he kept staying after that, just standing and standing there and looking at the house. I could barely see him and couldn't make out his face at all; but I knew he was looking at the house—as if he were looking at my father! You won't tell me I'm just imagining, will you?"

"No, I won't. It was raining, you say? You must have been getting pretty wet, Celia."

"So was he," she said. "Yet he kept standing and standing there in the rain—looking at the house——"

"He was probably thinking about his wife, Celia."

"Oh, yes, about both of them of course! I know. But you understand why my nerves have been rather on end, don't you?"

"Yes, Celia."

"Thank you. Have you noticed if Tuke's been drinking harder than usual since Sunday night?"

"Why, no." Miley considered her question. "Of course I don't know anything about what he does after he leaves; but when he's here on his job I'd say he's been entirely sober all the time I've known him. When I first came I noticed sometimes that he'd probably had a drink or two, enough to scent his breath; but since then I haven't noticed any of that. For all I know he may have stopped drinking altogether."

"You think so? Miley, couldn't that be significant? I mean when a man all eaten up by jealousy drinks pretty hard and then suddenly stops——"

Miley assented. "Yes, possibly. I suppose it could mean that whatever he does he intends to have his head about him."

"Yes, it *could!*" Celia exclaimed. "Miley, I *know* it's Tuke that's going to resign! It's as if he were putting his affairs in order before—before he does something he has on his mind to do. Something like —like suicide or—or——"

"No, no," Miley said. "Hold your imagination down."

"I can't. I'm scared—and I'm helpless, too. It'd be silly to ask you to hang about Tuke's house or to follow him, and of course you couldn't do such things; but maybe when he's at the factory you could watch him and study him a little and—and maybe talk to him whenever you have a chance and see what impression you get. I—I——" She broke off with a little cry of distress. "Oh, I don't know! I don't suppose it'd be any good at all or'd help anything. You do think I'm just an idiot, don't you?"

"No," he said. "Speer's got an odd look, no question. Go on, Celia."

"It's no good!" she cried. "I don't know how I got it in my mind that it could be. No, I might as well face it and confess I just had to *talk* to somebody and you're the only one I could think of that wouldn't be certain to call me an imagining fool. Thank you for letting me get it off my chest."

"I don't think it is off," he said. "At least you don't look as if it were. I'll try to be of some use." With that, abruptly it seemed to Celia, he opened the door and stepped down from the car. He lifted his hat. "Good-bye; I'll let you know," he said, went to his own car and immediately drove away.

Celia, blank, said "But——" and then sat thinking, first that Miley Stuart was a queer young man, and second that in his heart he probably agreed with her that she'd been making a fool of herself. She drove home puzzling and inclined to be angry with him again. That was rather a cool thing to do to a girl, wasn't it?—just to say "I'll try to be of some use" and then hop out and be on his way!

Celia's blankness continued all that evening as she sat knitting at home. Her father hadn't been at the dinner-table; he had a meeting downtown with men from Washington, which wasn't unusual, and the two ladies of his family made a silent bleak meal of it. At midnight the telephone bell rang and Celia went from her bedroom to the extension in the upper hall.

When she'd reached it and said "Hello," Kate appeared beside her, speaking hurriedly: "It's your father, isn't it? Tell him he mustn't let them keep him all night. Tell him he must——"

Celia made forbidding gestures with her left hand, and Kate stood silent.

"No!" Celia exclaimed into the telephone, and Kate saw her lips part widely. "No! You didn't . . . You did? You . . . I never dreamed of your doing such a thing! . . . You say . . . Where'd you have dinner? . . . What? Oh, I never meant . . . No, of course not! No, go home and go to bed . . . I said go home and go to bed. Get something to eat first . . . No, get something to eat and go . . . No, no, no; not any later . . . I'll see you to-morrow . . . Yes, to-morrow at noon . . . I didn't dream you'd . . . Goodnight!" Celia's color was high; her eyes were bright. "Well, of all!" she said.

"Of all what?" Kate asked.

"Of all the strange men!" Celia shook her head, marveling. "Miley Stuart! I'll never get over this, Kate. He just said, 'I'll try to be of some use' and jumped out of the car and darted away—and where do you think he was going?"

"What's the answer, Celia?"

"After Tuke Speer!" Celia cried. "He caught up with Tuke's car downtown and followed him!"

"What! You'd better tell me all of it, hadn't you?"

"Well, you wouldn't do anything!" The stepdaughter became defensive. "I had to do something, didn't I?"

"I see," Kate said. "So you went to Miley and told him how you'd seen Tuke's face at the window when Laila was clinging to your father, and you were so afraid of what Tuke might do that you wanted him watched."

Celia shouted at her. "Kate Lanning! Where'd you get it? How do you know?"

"You told me," Kate said, and almost might have laughed. "I don't know how you could have made it much plainer. Your loyalty to your father's been highly honorable and a credit to you—but it isn't needed, Celia; I'm his wife but not his enemy. Naturally, at your age, you believe that when another woman enters the picture, or tries to, a wife necessarily becomes so hostile she can't be trusted; but you see

I know Laila. She was kissing him when you passed the door, wasn't she?—and in his arms—and you saw Tuke's face at the window."

"Truly I'm crazy!" Celia cried out. "Have I given that away, too?"

"Yes; don't worry. What did you get Miley to do?"

"That poor boy! Well, you're right, I did go to him and poured it all out. I just thought maybe he could watch Tuke while they're working together and see if he was getting more desperate and—and things like that—and Miley took me pretty literally about watching him, and followed him home—and, Kate, he's been there ever since, sitting in his car a little way up the street and watching the Speers' house! He said after Tuke went in nobody came out all evening, and about two hours ago he saw the lights go on upstairs for a while but after that they were all turned off pretty soon, so he kept on waiting till twelve, and then, as nothing seemed likely to happen, he wondered if I thought it'd be useful for him to stay there the rest of the night. He'd be glad to do it, he told me, if I wanted him to! He——"

Celia interrupted herself to fling her arms about her stepmother, half weep, half laugh, and cry out, "Kate, Kate, are we all crazy? Have I got Miley crazy, too?"

"No, we're not crazy," Kate said. "That is, I'm afraid we're not. Has something more than seeing Tuke at the window frightened you?"

"Yes. He's cut out drinking and he's going to resign from Roe Metal Products. I'm practically sure of both these things. Don't they scare you, too?"

"They might, a little," Kate said. "That is, they might if you're right and they turn out to be true."

"Then you'd be scared a 'little'?" Celia echoed the word fiercely. "Tuke broke out at her pretty violently at your party, didn't he? If he'd do that he'd do more, and if you think violence never occurs among people like us and the Speers you'd better begin reading the newspapers!"

"Steady, Celia. There are other things about as bad as what you've been imagining, though, and I doubt their being prevented by your having Miley sit all night outside that house."

"I'll give him thunder for it to-morrow! He's certainly proved he's a Southerner." Seeming startled by a thought, Celia expressed it abruptly. "Kate, I'd be afraid ever to get married."

"Yes, it's a wonder fear doesn't stop more of us."

"Do men and women always stay queer to each other?" Celia asked, in a child's voice, she being but recently out of childhood. "Do husbands and wives never get to know each other—as women know other women, I mean, Kate?"

"I can't tell you, Celia."

The girl's startling thought persisted. "Kate, you just said you were Father's wife but not his enemy. It sounds as if the natural condition of husbands and wives—in a sort of way—is being enemies. It seems to me I'm beginning to understand what I read long ago in Virginibus Puerisque that marriage is not a bed of roses but a field of battle. Oh, I'm afraid it might be true! There's you and Father and——"

Kate's interruption was sharp. "I'm not fighting him, Celia!"

"You are—at least you have been!" Celia cried. "And think of that grim house Miley was watching to-night! What awfulnesses do you suppose go on inside it between that husband and that wife? Why, Kate, almost every married crowd you know anywhere has a woman like Laila in it, playing hell with it, ruining her husband and keeping other wives heartbroken or furious. The world's at war and you and Father have both said for months we're going to be in it. Is marriage and even life itself and everything just war? We can't stay out of life, we haven't any option; but if marriage is war, too, isn't any woman a fool that goes into it?"

"Any woman?" Kate repeated, and her face was shaped to contours of sorrow so unfamiliar to the stepdaughter that again she was startled. "Any woman? Any man, too, Celia! Isn't that what I've made my husband feel?"

XXXVIII

THE "GRIM HOUSE" MILEY STUART HAD BEEN WATCHING till midnight had long been dark; but even at that hour it was not wholly silent within. Laila'd gone up to bed early and had lain listening before she went to sleep. She heard Tuke ascend the stairs and click off the light in the narrow corridor outside her locked door; but he didn't go into the bedchamber opposite, the "guest room", where he slept in their small house. Instead, in the dark, he began to pace up and down the hallway. Its narrow floor was carpeted; but his footsteps were audible to her, from one end to the other, regular and unceasing.

"Thinks that's the way he talks to me," Laila said to herself, alluding to the fact that no vocal word had been exchanged between her and her husband since Tuke had said, "Are you drunk?"

Seven steps forward, seven steps back she counted, seven, seven, seven—Tuke walking in the dark outside her door and thus talking to her.

Afterwhile she slept, and afterwhile woke: seven steps forward, seven back, seven, seven, seven. "To hell with you!" Laila whispered. "How long do you think I'll let you do this to me? I'll finish it pretty soon, my fine fellow!"

In the morning she had breakfast in bed; then watched from one of her windows until she saw Tuke go into the small garage for his car. Upon this, she came downstairs to find the morning paper, but had a surprise: Tuke had re-entered the house and he confronted her at the foot of the stairway.

"I told you it'd be bad if you ever tried," he said. "Just now I decided to speak to you again because I want to make a suggestion, one for you and him to remember: the next time you clasp and kiss and tell how long you've loved each other, don't do it before three witnesses."

"Get out of my way!" Laila said.

"No. You listen!"

"I won't!" Laila tried to thrust by him, and he put his hand on her shoulder to detain her. Instantly she screamed, then she shouted: "Don't you dare strike me!" The fat white cook and the colored housemaid appeared in the dining-room doorway, staring. Laila screamed at them, "He struck me!" and stood rubbing her shoulder.

Tuke stepped back. "I never knew what a rotten sport you are!" he said, and left the house.

"He struck me!" Laila called to the two goggling faces. They retired, perhaps not wholly convinced, and Laila returned upstairs to her room, to dress.

"Anyhow, he was *going* to strike me," she said pathetically, facing her trembling gorgeousness in a long mirror. "He the *same* as did, really."

It was the left shoulder that Tuke had grasped. Baring it, now, and still watching the sympathetic mirror, as she tossed her wrapper to a chair, she felt over the insulted area tenderly with her right hand, convincing herself that she was bruised—or, at least, almost bruised. Such convincings are a necessity for such wives when they find a new love; they must first make themselves see the husband as a domestic ruffian or they cannot hate him sincerely enough to make others see him so.

Laila easily believed herself now, at last, virtually struck by her ruffian; therefore she acquired what she wished—an almost genuine bitter belief in her rightness. Thus she felt well justified in taking a new love, for, in a measure and in her way, somewhat as a child is in love with a Christmas tree, she was in love with Ames Lanning. His image burned brightly in her heart; she saw Ames not only as a manly human being, handsome and stalwart, but as the wielder of all the power of Roe Metal Products and the controller of its wealth. To her his success had transfigured him. Generous and hung with gifts, he seemed beautiful; he was distinguished, too, and his wife a great personage—not trotty little old Kate of course; but when he'd have a wife fit for splendor.

The ugly old word from the turn of the century, "gold-digger", doesn't cover Laila Speer, if indeed it ever covered anybody. Laila liked comforts and bedizenments but her passion was to dazzle surpassingly—surpassing other women. She wouldn't have thrown Tuke out for Bill Jones if Bill sought her and had money enough. Part of her love for Ames sprang from thoughts of a calling-card: "Mrs. Ames Lanning." What that could mean—if it meant a woman who knew how to be Mrs. Ames Lanning!

That Ames was really hers Laila hadn't a doubt. Rejected, he'd turned from her to Kate in the sore mood of a man who consciously takes second choice because he's lonely. Laila couldn't think of all the other men who'd made love to her—no, nor look in the mirror— and doubt that she was still Ames's first choice. That was what had been the trouble with Tuke for a long time back, his fear that some day she'd drop him for Ames who of course wanted her, as Tuke, too, never questioned. Who indeed could question a thing so obvious, seeing Ames's radiant face whenever he was with her? For months, this year, he'd been more and more openly proving that he'd always been in love with her and always would be, and on Sunday night, and again over the telephone, he'd said it. New York, pictures in the New York magazines, doormen helping her out of soft-rolling cars, people in restaurants or at the races murmuring "Look! Mrs. Ames Lanning!"—foreign young diplomats whispering to her—it was all moving to be ready for her, with Ames himself a happily adorning figure in the fore part of the background.

Laila brushed aside thoughts of the woman who was to be dispossessed of a husband. In such exchanges as Mrs. Tuke Speer now contemplated the other wife must be looked upon as disposable. Naturally, a pair of thoroughbreds can't be expected to starve because of a dog in the manger. Laila'd seen the shadow on Ames's brow sometimes when he looked at Kate; and other people, too, had noticed, had commented. Laila decided to go and talk with one of them this morning, because Tuke had been ominous.

He'd said that there were three witnesses to the Sunday night embrace. So either Bill Jones or the woman in Ames's hallway, or both, had talked, and Tuke had heard but hadn't got it straight. He'd said there were three witnesses, whereas there were but two, the woman and Bill Jones. Where had Tuke picked up that stuff about three?

Of course Laila'd dramatized everything in her telephone talk with Ames. She was living in drama these days and it was good for Ames to feel how much she was enduring on his account. She didn't thoroughly believe, for instance, that Tuke had bribed her servants; she only thought it possible. However, she didn't intend to take any chances: she meant to emerge spotless and with the smears all on Tuke, upon whom a strong hand would be needed. He wasn't going to stand still and be smeared like a gentleman.

"Three witnesses. Three," she said to herself, as she walked toward Mrs. George Cooke's, round the next corner. So far as Ames was concerned, the more witnesses the better—to show him how completely he'd compromised her. On the other hand, three witnesses against her and Ames and for Tuke in a courtroom—no, that wouldn't be useful. Nevertheless, "three's a crowd"; so couldn't her lawyer simply laugh at Tuke if Tuke tried to produce three? Anybody knew that embraces before a crowd, virtually in public, couldn't be made to imply secret relations between the parties. Laila didn't believe there'd been three witnesses; but suppose there were. She laughed. "Just let Tuke try to put that on us! What a boomerang for him!"

At Mrs. Cooke's, after they'd talked a little about Red Cross work, Bundles for Britain and Refugee Aid, Laila asked, "Know anything new, Mary?"

"No, I don't think of anything."

"You sure?" Laila smiled ironically. "Not even any gossip about me? That'd be something new, wouldn't it?—if there weren't any going the rounds about me. You surprise me. I was practically certain that Ames's kindly trying to buck me up a little the other night after Tuke broke out at me might have started something."

"About you and Ames?" Mrs. Cooke shook her head. "No, I haven't heard anything like that, Laila. Not a word."

"I'm absolutely crestfallen!" Laila burlesqued disappointment. "It'd be so exciting to have people thinking that Ames and I were renewing our romance after all these years. Seriously, I'm rather surprised, though, that no one's taken up that idea—especially in view of the way we hear things seem to be going lately between Ames and Kate."

Mrs. Cooke was interested. "You think there's something in it—that they're not getting along together?"

"Me? I don't know!" Laila waved a disclaiming hand. "I only know what some of the crowd are saying—and of course how he and she *are* when one sees them together. Of course Kate always puts on an act—everything all sweetie pie—so how can you tell? I used to try to do that, myself, until Tuke made it impossible. You've heard the rumors about Kate and Ames, though, haven't you, Mary?"

"Well—Carrie says she thinks something's sort of going on there, nobody knows just what, and of course we've all noticed they aren't the same together." There was a moment's silence; then Mrs. Cooke added, "I hope you've accepted Tuke's apology for what he did, Laila."

"Do you?" Laila asked. "What apology?"

"You mean to say he hasn't?"

Laila spoke in a low voice. "I'd show you my shoulder except it might make you rather sick."

"Laila Speer! What on earth do you mean?"

"Until this morning he hasn't spoken to me," Laila said. "Of course, though, he makes noises all night in the house with the idea of keeping me awake till morning. Oh, yes, on purpose, all night every night —war of nerves! That's nothing, though, Mary, you see, because this morning, when I thought he'd gone and went down to get the paper, he sneaked back indoors and explained he'd decided to insult me some more, and when, instead of listening, I made an effort to get away and not listen to what he was calling me, he—— I don't know whether he tried to strike me in the face or not. I must have moved instinctively, because it was my shoulder that got it."

"Laila! Why, this is horrible! What did he do it for? How could a man strike a woman in cold blood like that?"

Laila made her brief laugh sharp. "You heard him insult me in cold blood the other night, didn't you?"

"Yes, I did; but to *strike* you—it seems too terrible! What for? Why? Didn't he even say why he did it?"

"He scarcely needed to, do you think, Mary? When a man with Tuke's habits finds he prefers—prefers other companions—and wants to get rid of his wife, he's likely to go to rather extreme lengths. So I've always heard and now I seem to be finding out."

"But, Laila—a blow! You ought to leave him! If you go on living with him after this, you haven't any self-respect. You ought to pack up everything that's yours in that house and go straight to a hotel—straight!"

"You think so?" Laila said. "Maybe I might do something like that."

" 'Maybe!' " Mrs. Cooke cried. "Why, it's an open and shut case of cruelty and the law gives divorces for that! Laila, you ought to leave him this very day!"

Laila said perhaps she would, she was thinking of it and didn't know how much more she could bear. She was, in truth, thinking of it, and, when she'd returned home, toward noon, continued to think of it acutely; for, accompanying her thoughts, was a rising alarm. She was accustomed to use numerical figures loosely herself, not distinguishing carefully between two and three or even, indeed, between hundreds and thousands; but she remembered that Tuke wasn't like that: when he said two he meant two and when he said three he meant three.

All morning his words, "before three witnesses", had returned again and again to her with a growing emphasis. After all, had there been three witnesses of that embrace—three people who'd seen it and who'd heard her and Ames declaring that they loved each other? After all, mightn't testimony upon such a scene bear a sinister interpretation in court? If there were three witnesses, who was the third? Maybe neither Bill Jones nor the woman in the hall had talked—yet —and Tuke knew because there really had been a third witness. Where? What about windows? Thereupon Laila began to understand what Kate Lanning had understood—Tuke outside, there in the rain and the dark, and his face at a window!

"I told you it'd be bad if you ever tried," he'd said a few hours ago at the foot of the stairway; and, as she recalled the expression of his face as he spoke, there now seemed to have been a disastrous certainty in it. Laila's hands trembled as she sat alone at lunch and she didn't eat much nor did she finish the meal; instead, she went upstairs to the desk in her bedroom and wrote a note.

"Darling something's happened and I've got to take the risk. I've got to see you immediately. This can't go on any longer and I must talk to you first. I'm sending this by a messenger and he'll be under instructions not to deliver it to anyone but you yourself and then he's to go and phone me instantly that you have it. If you're not there he's to bring it back to me. The moment he phones me you're there I'll start downtown to your office in a taxi.

"Please arrange that there'll be nobody in your own private office but you yourself—but be sure there are stenographers or secretaries in the next room and leave the door open after I come in so people can see us and there won't be any possible chance he can prove we were out of their sight—though of course we'll have to keep our voices so low they can't hear us.

"This is all frightfully important dearest. Trust me to know what I'm doing. Darling darling I've thought it all out and we'll take council together. I'm trembling with happiness—that so soon I'll be looking at you! I'm frightened too—but don't you doubt any more than I do that we're going to make the future pay us for all we've been through. This goes now and I follow."

XXXIX

NEARLY ALWAYS IMPULSIVE AND INTUITIVE, LAILA RAN the danger of becoming impractical when she tried to be a deliberate schemer. Acutely self-centered people whose lives are only an expression of their own desires are too credulous about themselves and about the effects they produce; and their encasement within self easily keeps them ignorant of general human affairs. Laila derived from the sending of her note something not unlike the pleasure felt by a stage director who has inspiredly "created just the right atmosphere for a great scene." Her fate and Ames's, and also the destinies of several other people, were now to be decided. The crises of their lives had been reached; though for Laila there was present only the crisis in one supreme life, of course. She felt herself the master of that crisis; she was as confident as she was gloriously excited.

Ames was going to be startled, of course; he'd have to face a radical change in his life and he'd need to be overwhelmingly swept into it before he could think much about it. Good enough! She was an expert overwhelmer, with exultant proficiency in such rapid outpourings of words as had often made even a roomful of competitors of her own sex into helpless listeners. Ames wasn't to think much; then she'd best not let him talk much. She'd do all the talking.

When she entered his quiet office her color was high and her eyes were brilliant; she'd never looked more adventurously beautiful. Ames came forward, took her hand for a moment; and, after a quick deep glance into his disturbed eyes, she advanced and sat in the chair before his desk, with her back toward the door she'd left half open behind her. Ames glanced at the doorway, saw that view was possible for the half-dozen people variously busy in the next room; then he went to his own chair across the desk from Laila.

"What it means to see you again!" she half-whispered, as he sat down, and her dark eyes examined him eloquently. "No wonder you look a little anxious, poor darling: I'm afraid I've frightened you about what's been happening to me. In this big office they can't hear me from in yonder, can they?"

"No," he said. "Especially not with those typewriters going. We can talk. I—I'm afraid we'll both have to do quite a little talking."

"Yes, of course we shall," she murmured. "Darling, I do love to see a man wear grey tweeds to business! When I was a young girl and first knew you, I used to think you wore funny clothes. You never seemed to care how you looked. I adored you for it; but now I adore you more because you always dress so nicely! Inconsistent of me—all except the adoration that's never changed. Yes, you see I've found out I must always have been in love with you, Ames. Darling, when I'm away from you, even a few days, I forget a little that look of power and resourcefulness you have, because I keep thinking all the time of your tenderness. Your tenderness to me, I mean, because that's all you've ever showed me, so I forget the strength you show your enemies."

"Enemies?" he repeated, necessarily in a lowered voice but as if the word bothered him. "I don't like to think I have enemies, Laila. I suppose I've made some; but I've never meant to be any man's enemy, myself."

"No, Ames, you dear thing; of course not! Maybe I ought to've said our enemies, because we've got some, Ames, and we're going to have more. We can't help that, you see, dear love. Tuke, for instance, hates us both like vitriol."

"He does?"

"Does he!" Laila's bitter laugh rose a little. "Why the surprise? Haven't you seen him look at you, Ames? Haven't you any idea how long he's been jealous of you? God, how he hates you! But there, let's take things in order, dearest. As I drove downtown I've been trying to straighten them out in my mind into firstly, secondly, thirdly and so forth, and firstly I want you to send me to the best divorce lawyer you know in town, Ames."

The gravity of Ames's manner, already profound, became still deeper. "You think it's come to that, do you? You're sure that you——"

"Ames! Of course it had to come before long anyhow, didn't it? This morning, though, he settled that it'd be right now, himself, and gave me my grounds. Mary Cooke knows about it and she says it's more than ample to charge him with, and this state grants divorces for cruelty. She can testify I told her about it right after he did it, and besides I have two more witnesses that practically saw it, my cook and housemaid—and even if he *has* bribed them they'll have to tell the truth when they're on the stand. We could almost thank him for doing what he did, though it wasn't very pleasant to take. I must have jerked my head away, so my face wasn't bruised, but——"

"Laila!" Ames was all horror and compassion. "I can't believe it of him! He actually struck you?"

She smiled pathetically. "With the door open I'm afraid I can't show you my bare shoulder, dear."

"Laila! Poor Laila!"

Her smile became a rewarding lover's. "It was worth it—to hear you speak my name so sweetly! So we'll go ahead with the whole thing now, won't we?"

"I——" He hesitated. "If I'm to advise you——"

"Oh, I know!" Laila quickly assured him. Ames, a careful chooser of words and hard put to it to find the right ones, could only wait for such pauses as she chose to make. "Don't think I'm lightheaded enough to imagine you could take my case yourself, Ames dearest. Naturally we know what they'd make of that before we got through with them. You're not that kind of lawyer, of course, anyway. I never thought of such a thing. All I want is for you to give me the name of the best firm. When I get home I'm going to begin writing out all I've got against Tuke, and the names of witnesses, everything. Then I'll take it to whichever lawyers you say."

"I'm afraid no one has a right to dissuade you, Laila. A blow—that's pretty bad; it's sufficient. Then there was that brutality of his on Sunday night. You have plenty of witnesses to that."

"Ah, haven't I, though!" she exclaimed. "About seventeen, I think! But I'll not let you be one of 'em, Ames; it'll look better if you aren't. Now just tell me who to see."

Frowning, he sighed. "I suppose you'd better go to Gus Meyers. Meyers, Bayliss and Born. Gus is away; but he'll be back the first of next week; you'd better see him, himself. Here." He wrote the address upon a memorandum slip, and Laila, extending an ungloved hand, touched his fingers, pressed them with sly fondness as she took the paper from him. She placed it in the gilt-trimmed black bag she carried and smiled triumphantly across the desk at him.

"There, honey," she said. "The thing's as good as done—only we've got to take all our steps pretty carefully and just in the right order. It's your turn next."

"My turn, Laila? Very well. The truth is I've been hoping for a

chance and perhaps this is as good a one as we'll have for some time.
I've thought pretty hard, Laila, about how we could put ourselves
upon a—upon a basis—that would be right and good, so now, since
you say it's my turn, I——"

"No, I didn't mean it was your turn to talk, Ames; I meant it was
your turn to do something."

"What? I don't see——"

"You will, dear. That's really the main thing I came to show you.
You'll have to fire Tuke just as soon as you can, Ames. I mean right
away. To-day if it's possible."

"What?" he began. "Why, I——"

"Listen!" She leaned forward. "He saw us, darling; I'd swear to it.
God, if we weren't a pair of innocent fools! He saw us, and heard us,
too."

Ames's face was quickly red. "Saw us and heard us when?" he
asked, though he greatly feared he knew.

"When?" This echo would have been an outcry except for Laila's
remembering the people in the next room. "Good Lord, when you
took me in your arms and we were kissing each other and you were
telling me how long you'd loved me, and I telling you! Sunday night
in your library! Tuke was at that open window, and he as good as
told me so this morning. He was there, Ames—Tuke, don't you understand, *Tuke!* He was spying on us. He saw us with his two eyes, and
he heard it all! How often do you suppose he thought we'd done the
same thing before, and don't you see what of course he believes that
means about us? He's been putting me to torture for it, and what do
you suppose he'll go on to do now when he's got two other witnesses
—that woman and Bill? We're not going to just sit still and let him
ruin us, are we, darling?"

She'd spoken of Ames's resourceful look; his crimsoned face didn't
wear it now. "Why, see here, Laila, I—Laila, I——"

"Don't worry." Laila was more and more eager. "We'll beat him,
dear heart! I know what's in that vindictive mean little mind of his.
Don't think I don't! He's been trying to frighten me and he'll try to
frighten us both if we don't act before he does. We'll both be served
with papers, Ames; that's exactly what he'll do. If we give him time

he'll go to a lawyer first and bring suit against me and name you. Or else he'll have his lawyer threaten us with that and try to make us back down. Or if I bring suit first, as I'm going to, he'll oppose it and bring a counter-suit and take the stand and testify to what he saw, and try to get Bill and that woman as witnesses, too. And maybe he can—if you don't act quickly, Ames. It's got to be quick."

"Wait a minute." With effort Ames kept his voice steady; but he wiped his forehead. "Let's go a little more slowly, Laila. You say——"

"I told you what to do," she said. "You've got to throw Tuke out of his job practically this instant!"

"Laila, you——"

"You can do it!" she urged hurryingly. "Mr. Roe'll let you do anything; he thinks you're God. Tuke hasn't got a cent; he's in debt, and the minute he's out of Roe Metal Products the people he owes'll be down on him like wolves. That'll be just right for us, darling, because he won't be able to hire even a shyster lawyer. I mean literally he won't have anything to do it with, and think of the tremendous influence you've got in this town, with the weight of Roe Metal Products behind you! Except for a whole lot of money nobody'd dare take a case against you, and Tuke won't have any money at all. So he can hate us all he wants but can't do a thing to harm us. He'd kill us if he could; but when you throw him out he's licked. You see it's got to be done quickly, don't you, honey?"

"Laila——" The red had left Ames Lanning's face, departing as he stared unbelievingly at her who thus exhorted him. "I'm afraid I haven't quite taken all this in. I don't see——"

"Don't look so shocked; it's all going to be all right, sweetheart!" Smiling, Laila talked fast but was almost motherly. "Here's another thing. I've got it all in my head. I've often urged you jokingly to take that New York job; but underneath I really meant it. You'll have to do it now, Ames—and a grand thing, too! As soon as I've got my divorce I'll go there and wait. Then when you come—oh, darling, darling, I'll make up to you for ruining both our lives the way I did years ago when I didn't think you loved me enough and crazily let my soreness over that betray me into taking Tuke. You've never understood what a jam I was in. I couldn't tell you. What I did to us both!

Me—with Tuke—and oh, poor, poor Ames, anybody can see what your life's been with Kate Fennigate! Nobody'll blame you and there won't be any scandal for Mr. Roe to get to muttering about. That'll all be on Tuke, you see, and you can make Kate let you go quietly— for one of those causes everybody knows means nothing, like desertion or something. Everybody'll see you just couldn't stand her boring and bossing you any longer, darling."

"Laila——" Ames had stopped looking at her; he stared at the shining brown surface of his clean desk. "You'll really have to give me a chance to speak."

She didn't—not yet; she didn't intend him to speak until she had it all settled. "Oh, I know it's a jolt to you, beloved! Don't think I can't realize all the uprooting and change in routine it's going to be —leaving your work here and taking the new position; but, darling, we'll simply have to do it. We wouldn't want to hang around here, running into Tuke and Kate. They'd be popping up everywhere and of course they'd have a few champions; it's got to be expected. After all, though, aren't you pretty sick and tired of our old every-other-Sunday-night supper crowd? Of course you are and so am I! Darling, darling, we'll leave all that stodgy provincial dumbness behind us, and you and I—ah, just you and I together, dearest—in New York! You and——"

"Wait!" Ames continued to look at his desk; but he made an imperative gesture. "I'll have to stop you, Laila. I'm sorry; but I've got to make you listen to me. I'm afraid you've been seeing things not—not as they are—and I'm afraid it's my fault. We've got to straighten it out."

"But it is," Laila said. "It is straightened out. Haven't I just shown you?"

"No, not—not exactly, Laila. I'll have to have a talk with Tuke."

"With Tuke? Why, you can't, Ames! He wouldn't listen, and anyhow, what's the use?"

"I'll have to have a talk with Tuke," Ames repeated, not looking up. "I'll have to explain to him."

"Explain?" Laila leaned back, apparently to stare at him the better. "Explain? Explain what?"

"What he saw through the window." Ames spoke slowly and painfully. "I mean if—if he did see it as you think, or if somebody's told him. There wasn't anything really for him to complain of if it's honestly and frankly explained to him."

"Ames, what's the matter with you?" Laila stared harder. "I just told you that if you throw Tuke out he won't be able to——"

"I can't throw Tuke out, Laila."

"You can't? You can! Everybody knows that Mr. Roe'd never interfere with anything you——"

Ames looked up. "I mean I wouldn't, Laila. I mean I won't throw Tuke out. As a husband he may be detestable, and now that he's struck you as well as openly insulted you at my house the other night you'll have everybody's sympathy if you get your divorce. If it makes enough talk when it happens, very likely Mr. Roe'll ask for Tuke's resignation; but I won't do it, Laila. Tuke's been with Roe Metal Products for many years and always done a good job. You know of course that my sympathy's all with you; but so long as Tuke serves the business as well as he does I won't be a party to his dismissal."

Laila stared and stared. "It seems to me you're talking gibberish. You're queer. What's the matter with you, Ames? Something's wrong with you!"

"Indeed there is," he said, and the trouble in his suppressed voice made it husky. "I'm sorry I couldn't make you listen sooner. I didn't know anybody thought there was any difficulty between Kate and me, Laila. I didn't dream anybody thought such a thing. There isn't."

"What?"

"Why, no," he said. "Not a thing."

Laila rose. "What about me?"

"What about you?" he said, like a boy who still tries to postpone a dreadful moment that he knows has arrived. "What about you, Laila? I don't understand—exactly."

"You don't? You don't understand that when a man's in love with another woman it's usually supposed to mean at least a little trouble between him and his wife?"

"Yes; but I——"

"You what?"

"I'm not." Ames's honest face was red again. All he could do was clump to the end of the blind alley into which the most chivalrous and kind-hearted of men are sometimes forced by attractive and attracted members of the opposite sex. "I'm not in love with any other woman, Laila."

She dropped back into her chair, and for a moment her face was as red as his; then color left it. "What did you say?"

XL

AMES'S DISTRESS WAS MANIFEST. HE WIPED HIS BROW, swallowed hard, blinked rapidly and looked anywhere except at the eyes of Laila Speer. "I—I've been wanting to tell you, Laila. I—I haven't had a chance to. This is the hardest thing I've ever had to say in all my life and I don't know how to do it. I've always thought you and I had a—a friendship, one that wouldn't hurt anybody or need be objected to. I thought we could go on having it. I——"

She interrupted him. "You just said you weren't in love with any woman except your wife. I thought I heard you say that, Ames. Did you?"

"Well—yes, I did, Laila. I'm not."

She spoke in a clear quick whisper. "Then why did you say you were? Why have you been making love to me all this time? Why did you tell me you loved me?"

His gaze was again upon the desk. "It was fondness I meant, Laila. I meant an old long-standing affection. I didn't have a chance to go into it much with you. I felt a genuine and sincere affection and——"

"Affection! Fondness!" Laila's whispering was like fire upon him. "My God, only last Sunday night you told me you were in love with me! You said you'd always been! Wednesday you said it again over the 'phone! Wednesday was yesterday! Just yesterday you said you loved me!"

"I know you thought so, Laila, but——"

"Thought so? You said it!"

"If I did——"

"If you did?" She spoke out. *"If?"*

"If I did," he repeated doggedly, "I didn't mean it the way you thought or—or in any way that would do anybody any harm."

"I see," she said, with inordinate slowness. "You only meant to express fondness—fondness and affection. Is that what you're trying to tell me?"

"It's the truth, Laila; I'm sorry."

"Sorry? That's very kind, Ames." Laila wasn't whispering now; but she still maintained some suppression upon a shaking and breaking voice. "Yes, it's very sweet of you to be sorry for me; but that doesn't accomplish much, do you think? You just say 'sorry' and that makes everything all right?"

"Laila, I don't know what to say. I'd do anything I could."

"Yes; you'll have to!" He looked at her then, saw that her face was contorted; tears were disordering her eyelashes. "I'm afraid you'll have to, Ames! A woman can be struck in other ways than Tuke uses, you know. Do you think I'm just to be battered to death between the two of you? Do you think you can kiss and kiss me and tell me in one breath that you love me and in the next that you've never cared for anybody except your saintly little Kate Fennigate? I'm to get a divorce, am I, and then just traipse off alone and try to pick up a living somewhere to keep me half alive in a boarding-house? Is that your idea of what you can do to a woman? Do you think you can——"

"Laila, what a miserable way for us to have to thresh this out and what a hell of a place to do it in! With that door open I'm afraid in the next room they'll——"

"Yes, yes, I know." She set her hands to her wet face slappingly, speaking between them. "I'm not to make a noise; your Kate might hear of it!"

"Laila, please!" The unhappy man sent an anxious searching glance

through the open doorway; but the typewriters were thudding steadily and no one seemed aware. "Laila, I wouldn't have had this thing
happen for——"

"It has, though. It has happened, Ames! You know that, don't you?
What do you think's the rest of it?"

"The rest of it? I don't——"

"You don't see?" Laila said, weeping in bitter soundlessness. "No,
of course not! And you don't care because 'the rest of it' means only
what happens to *me!* You think you can do this, do you, and just go
home to Kate? Well, you can't, Ames; I'm sorry but you can't! Men
think they can have their cake and eat it too; but they can't. I'm
afraid you'll find I'm on your hands. You hadn't thought of that, had
you?"

"I don't know what I've thought," he admitted, being now only a
strong and unusually clear-headed man helpless before an agonizedly
accusing woman. "I don't even know what I'm thinking, Laila."

"Then I'll tell you what you'd *better* think!" In her passion she
believed with a carrying conviction every flimsy untruth she uttered.
"You'd better think of the woman who's given up everything in life
for you because she trusted in your honor when you said you loved
her! You'd better think of the woman who's been tortured and made
to suffer a hundred hells because of you! You'd better think of the
woman whose reputation is going to be ruined on your account!
Maybe you'd better think a little of what Tuke's going to do to you
as well as to me, Ames Lanning! You don't think he can?"

"I don't know, Laila."

"You *will* know!" she said. "Tuke can—and oh, won't he, though!
You think you'll not be pulled down from your high horse? You want
to stay on it; that's why you've gone back on your word to me. You
didn't think it'd go this far; you didn't know you were playing with
fire—but you were, Ames, you were! What'll happen when I tell this
town the truth in court? I'll be ruined because of you, and I guess
then you'll find me on your hands pretty thoroughly, won't you?"

"Please!" He made a movement as if to rise and close the door; but,
though she wept on, she lowered her voice.

"Oh, I see what's hit you," she said. "You've been scared out of it.

Either your darling Kate was the woman who saw us or else the woman told her and Kate's pinned it on you and made you afraid of Mr. Roe. That's a nice way of keeping a man—my God but isn't that a fine way to hold 'em! So Kate——"

"You're wrong," Ames said. "It isn't true."

"Of course it's true! It won't do any good, though; I can tell your darling Kate that much! She and you and that damned Tuke aren't going to bandy me about among you; I don't stand for it and to hell with all of you!" Laila's fierceness was augmented; she spoke with the wilder intensity because of a need she still mechanically felt, in spite of everything, to keep her voice decently inaudible in the next room. "You'll find you took on quite a responsibility, Ames Lanning, when you made love to me and took my life into your hands!"

"I didn't intend——" he began. "I don't like to say it again; but——"

"You don't like to say what again?"

"That you've been taking too much for granted—both lately and all along, Laila."

"That's the last damned lying insult I'll stand from you!" Laila rose. "I think you'll get a chance to try it for an alibi in court; but if I were you I wouldn't—it won't sound pretty." Her breath had begun to come almost noisily from her fast-heaving bosom. "After— after my divorce this town may feel that you—that you've got to do something about it, Ames. Even your good little Kate mightn't want you then; but I'll tell you this: if you spend the rest of your life on your knees doing penance to me it won't pay me for what you've done to me this afternoon. I think you'll have to try, though, damn you; I think you'll have to try!"

The fact that even still she strangely felt a compulsion to keep her voice repressed made both her anguish and the threat in it the more poignant. Ames, master of many fates but plainly not now of his own, sat speechless as through indicting tears her eyes predicted the fate she held in store for him.

"Just you wait!" she said, and, turning suddenly, walked to a window out of view from the room beyond. There, with her back toward him, she used her handkerchief; then took a gold "compact" from her bag and employed it for hurried but attentive renovations. When the little mirror assured her she'd finished these, she clicked the small box shut, restored it to the bag, and, still with her back to Ames, spoke briefly. "You'll see!"

The prophecy was but too convincing. Having uttered it, she swung about, and, without looking even toward him, walked quickly to the open door, passed through, crossed to a door beyond and was lost to his sight.

He sat looking at nothing, afraid that without self-conscious and exposing timidity he couldn't glance into the room where the typewriters thudded; but presently he rose, did cast an eye about that room, saw nothing untoward and nobody furtively observant of him. He closed the door, returned to his desk, tried to smoke a cigar and couldn't. Showing a barely perceptible rim of ash, it went dead in an agate tray.

Ames was a "man of affairs" but not of such affairs as this. People spoke of him sometimes, he knew, as "on top of the world"; he wasn't there now. The scene Laila'd made might have badly shaken even an old philanderer but it was wholly new and tasted like death to this able and diligent man whose previous experience had never explained how many kinds of women there are, or that one he thought he knew could be atrociously surprising. In these moments Ames Lanning wasn't aware of himself as an up-and-coming great captain of industry; he was only a mortal creature like any other who discovers the world not to be his oyster but a jungle path whereon may fall the shadow of the leaping panther.

The revulsion within him had come when Laila'd said, "You'll have to fire Tuke." Her jolly but semi-caressing coquetries had long been among the pleasantest rewards of Ames's success; but, after years of admiration of her, when she said "Fire Tuke" he began to know her. Then, quickly, he knew more of her. Overlooking even his daughter completely, babbling infantile folly about New York, brushing Henry L. Roe's convictions aside as of no consequence, self-persuaded that a man was life-and-death in love with her because he'd stumbled into comforting her too pleasantly for a few minutes—why, the woman had weeds for brains!

Of all creatures the weed-brained can be the most fatally dan-

gerous; and the manner of Laila's departure brought him sure fore-
taste of calamity. She was going to splash mud sky high—all over
herself and all over Roe Metal Products; but Ames would be blackest
with it.

By a strange order of nature it is the innocent of this world who
suffer the most from their consciences; and it is they whose imaginations are busiest with thoughts of supposedly deserved impending
punishments to be endured. Would a monstrous public opinion believe that he was honor bound to spend the rest of his life "making
amends" to Laila Speer? "Honor"? What a word! For years he'd been
a greatly honored, honorable man. When such a one is dishonored,
what's left of him?

XLI

ON THE CITY'S HORIZON, VACANTLY HALF-SEEN THROUGH
the window at which he stared, dark movements against the sky
finally reminded him that a convicted man has to go on living until
the drop falls. So was routine compulsory. The dark movements were
the far away upward pulsations of smoke from the stacks of Plant
Three where a great stoking went on: Roe Metal Products was hurrying. "All right," Ames said faintly, as if in resigned answer, and
with a flaccid hand pushed buttons on the rim of his desk. He resumed his work, interrupting it for a moment late in the afternoon
to give instructions that his house should be called and his wife
informed that he couldn't come home for dinner and might be out
late.

He worked till after seven; then went down to the street, where
the varicolored lights were begging into the evening dimness for
customers, and groups in the sidewalk crowds began to weave toward
the movies. A speeding young couple, linked, bounced into him.

Ames apologized mutteringly, annoying the boy and girl but the more and making him wonder why it was he who asked pardon. Was his threatening future already so humbling him that he must beg every heedless idiot to forgive him for still remaining a corporeal presence?

Yes, he'd just proved it, thus showing himself to be not much like himself—not like the assertively rising Ames Lanning of yesterday. It was in this mood that he entered the quiet downtown restaurant where he sometimes lunched with other Roe Metal Products men; he had the waiter give him the small table that was farthest from the glass front door. The place was almost silent; only a few tables were occupied and these by diners too serious over food to talk much. Ames ordered a thin dinner and had about stopped trying to finish it when he heard the street door open, and, glancing up absently, saw Tuke Speer coming in.

Tuke went to the table nearest the door, the length of the room from Ames, of whom he didn't appear to be aware, and, when the waiter came, gave his order in a low voice, not looking away from the "Carte du jour". The tables between Ames and Tuke were all vacant and the two men sat facing each other across these intermittent shapes of white cloth and twinkling cutlery. Ames looked steadily at Tuke for some moments but had no return of his gaze from Laila Speer's husband. Tuke kept his eyes upon the restaurant list until he was compelled to look up by the greeting of an acquaintance. This was young Miley Stuart, who came in briskly and appeared to be much surprised, and cheered, too, by the sight of a friend unexpected in that place.

"This is luck!" the young man said brightly. "I've got seven or eight things on my mind I've wanted to ask you about those new blueprints ever since you closed work for the afternoon, Mr. Speer. Do you mind if I sit at your table and eat while I ask 'em, sir? They're really rather important, and if you don't mind I'd like——" Miley interrupted himself, seeming equally surprised to see Ames Lanning, who had paid his waiter and was rising to leave. "Well, Golly me!" Miley exclaimed. "Just a minute, Mr. Speer, and I'll be back." He hurried down the room toward Ames. "Mr. Lanning, is your car parked somewhere? Wouldn't you like me to go with you to see if it's all right? I thought I noticed the other day you seemed to be having a little trouble with the starter. I'd be only too glad to——"

"No. No, thank you. It's in a garage nearby, where I always leave it," Ames said. "They keep it in condition and I don't think there's anything wrong with the starter."

"But I'd be delighted if you'd let me." Miley walked up the aisle between the tables, keeping beside Ames and making a flutter of polite offers. "Do let me go along, Mr. Lanning. It would only take me a minute to see if that starter's as right as you think. I'm not in the least hungry. You may have had a pretty tiring day; but I haven't and I'd only be too glad. I'm pretty sure I'm right about the starter, and the garage people may have neglected it. I could straighten it out very easily for you if you'd let me and I'd be only too glad to——"

"No, no, it's not needed," Ames said; and, as Miley renewed his flutter, the two passed Tuke's table with the over-courteous young man on the side toward Tuke, who did not look up.

Outdoors, on the pavement, Miley abruptly became less insistent. "Well, sir, if you're sure there's no trouble with your starter——"

"None at all," Ames said. "Goodnight, Miley."

"Goodnight, sir."

Ames walked away, thinking not of Miley Stuart's eagerness to be useful to the father of a pretty girl but of the hollow-eyed concentration Tuke Speer had bent upon the menu. Never before had Ames been confronted by a former friend who'd come to hate him so openly, for surely hatred must be both open and hot when the hater is willing for you to see that he cannot bear even to look at you. Ames asked the neon-lighted night what he'd done to incite that passion. If he'd really done anything Kate would have told him, wouldn't she? "Wait, though," he admonished himself with misgiving. She hadn't been telling him anything much for quite a time, had she?—not until last Sunday night when she'd gibed at him for his solicitude about Laila. Remembering that "solicitude", he felt a chill rising from the pit of his stomach.

Sunday night and Tuke at the open window of the library! Irretrievable, but it had all been a kind of accident. So, then, accidents could happen to anybody—even to the strong, to the proud and the confident. Accidents don't care whom they destroy. Ames was like a dreamer who strolls balmily in a grove of shady trees—and the dream turns into nightmare with all the myriads of leaves become scorpions and centipedes and the very path beneath his feet reptilian.

He went to the garage, got his car and drove northward, but not through the long street that passed his house. Beyond the city he reached a three-ply highway into which he shot at a great speed immediately afterward increased. Thus he covered fifty-six miles and reached Roeville in three-quarters of an hour, coming to a stop before an unending dimness of brick wall and the floodlighted sign seventy yards long, "Roe Metal Products Corporation of America". From within Plant Two's vastness came a muffled chugging, a deep noise that meant America growing and growling in the dark, preparing its defense of the world; and Ames Lanning, hearing such stout sounds, might rightfully have taken some credit to himself for them, since it was he who was responsible for their disturbance of what other-wise would have been the silent night. Not giving himself credit for anything whatever, though, he went into the vibrant building and treated its night staff to a surprise inspection that lasted two hours.

He drove homeward more slowly than he'd come, hoping that everyone at his house would be wrapped in slumber when he arrived; but both Kate and Celia came to greet him as he opened the front door. Celia told him that he looked tired and both asked if they couldn't get him something to eat.

"No, no," he said. "I had dinner at Frederic's, plenty. I'm afraid you're right about my being tired, though. I had to go out to Roeville and I'll have to be out there again early to-morrow morning. Probably be there all day. I'd better go straight up to bed now if you don't mind. Goodnight. Goodnight."

They watched him go up the stairway; then looked at each other as anxious women do. "White as a sheet," Celia said, when they'd heard his door close. "Did you see his expression and notice his voice? Just stricken! I think something's happened."

"Yes, all the time, Celia, these days. A great many men are wearing themselves out as he does."

Celia shook her head. "No, he's an ox for work; he's always been so and I'm sure it isn't that. Do you want to know what I think? I'll bet you——" She interrupted herself, as four notes of the chromatic scale were whistled outside. "It's Miley!" she said, ran to the door, opened it, and echoed the whistle.

"Saw you were still lighted up," the young man explained, appearing in the doorway. "I had something to mention and thought maybe you'd come out and—oh, good evening, Mrs. Lanning!"

"Come in!" Celia bade him, and glanced toward upstairs. They took him into the living-room, closed the double doors, and Celia said, "You haven't been doing that again, have you?"

Miley looked embarrassed. "Mrs. Lanning, I—— Celia——"

"Speak up," Celia said. "She knows now what I'm worried about and maybe it'll be no harm if she gets a little that way, herself. I've told her a dozen times Tuke Speer hates Father for no reason on earth. We all understand. You can speak out, Miley."

"It's all right, of course," he began. "Mr. Speer went home about nine o'clock and the lights went out along toward eleven and——"

"Didn't I tell you not to do that again?"

"I had nothing else to do," he said. "I thought I might as well sit there in my car; but nobody came out and I'm pretty sure they must be asleep by now. Celia, I thought maybe you'd want to hear about what happened earlier."

"There!" Celia's brow darkened at Kate. "Didn't I tell you something had? Go on, Miley!"

His embarrassment returned. "It seems to have begun in the afternoon really." He paused, glancing dubiously at Kate; but Celia gave him an imperative nod, which he obeyed. "I might be mistaken but it rather seemed to me to have something to do with—with Mrs. Speer."

"All right, go ahead," Celia said. "I just told you that Kate and all of us know perfectly well that Tuke's crazily jealous of every man his wife so much as speaks to, and that includes Father. Go ahead!"

"All right, if you say, Celia. It might be nothing of course; but toward closing time Mr. Speer and I were working together at his long table, and Mr. Lanning sent down some blueprints he'd checked over. It was that talky young clerk, Eckling, who brought them. Eckling handed 'em to Mr. Speer, and, because he always has to have something to say, said he'd made it from your father's office, Celia, to the Plant in twelve minutes in spite of the traffic. Mr. Speer wrote a receipt for the blueprints and then Eckling wanted to give himself a nice gabby exit, so he said, 'Well, gents, I'll skim back to headquarters!'" Miley, sometimes a mimic, imitated the high voice of the too-chatty messenger. "'Oh, by the way,' the fool said. 'We had a beautiful visitor there this afternoon, Mr. Speer, as I suppose you know. We're all hoping she was seeing Mr. Lanning about joining us in our war work. Yes, your good wife paid us quite a call, quite a call!'"

"That was helpful!" Celia exclaimed. "Laila'd been to——"

"To Mr. Lanning's office," Miley said. "Yes, so it seems; and this idiot, Eckling, just to make more conversation as he left, put in, 'A marvelous-looking lady, Mr. Speer; we all envy you!' and then got himself out in a state of affability and pleasure, though Mr. Speer only looked at him. Mr. Speer didn't speak to me either; he just pushed the blueprints over to me and went to his desk and sat down and didn't do anything."

"This world's full of Ecklings!" Celia cried. "They ruin people! Don't stop, Miley."

"Yes, Celia. I couldn't help but be sorry for Mr. Speer, he looked so tense and so forlorn and so strange. Of course he's been a pretty strange-looking man ever since I've known him. I don't suppose he was always like that, though."

"No, he wasn't," Kate said. "I don't mean to interrupt you, Miley. You followed him when he left, did you?"

"Yes, Mrs. Lanning; but he didn't go till very late. He just sat there. I'd worked through the blueprints and finished up the other job we were on long before he left. He didn't speak to me—just suddenly got up and went out. I let him get a start, then trailed after him. He drove all the way home but didn't get out—only sat in his car and looked at the house—and then he turned round and went downtown again, to Frederic's restaurant."

"Frederic's!" This was an outcry from Celia. "But to-night Father went to Frederic's!"

"Yes, he was there," Miley said, and made the picture for them.

Before he'd finished, Celia was shaking. "Haven't I been right?" she asked her stepmother. "If Miley hadn't been there and kept between them—and think of how Father looked when he came in the door just now! That woman in his office this afternoon—what for?—and Tuke knows that she went there! You still think I've been hysterical, do you?"

Kate didn't answer. Standing, she seemed to be intently studying the floor; but, coming out of this contemplation, she said, "You're a dear thing, Miley Stuart!" and left the room.

She went upstairs, and, seeing light beneath her husband's door, rapped gently. He opened the door, stood before her in a bathrobe and spoke rather roughly. "What is it?"

"Nothing, Ames, except that in the morning before you leave there'll a basket packed for you and enough in it for three or four others if you want to ask them to eat with you at Plant Two tomorrow and keep on talking instead of bolting food in the cafeteria."

"Thank you; that's very thoughtful."

"Is there anything wrong at Plant Two, Ames?"

"No, not so far. There could be some labor trouble out there if we're not careful."

"Don't let it worry you," Kate said. "If I were you, I wouldn't let anything worry you, Ames—not anything at all." With that, she stood on tiptoe, put her arms about his neck and kissed him quickly.

He looked tragic. "Kate!"

"But that's nothing," she said, and gave him the sad hint of half a smile over her shoulder, as she opened her own door. "A kiss doesn't mean anything, Ames; but don't forget what I told you: don't worry about Plant Two or about anything else—and of course please don't think I'm trying to be advising you. Goodnight."

XLII

IN THE MORNING KATE WAITED UNTIL ALMOST ELEVEN; then she walked half way round the block and rang the bell of a small white house that stood in a narrow neat lawn. A languid young colored woman, responding, said, "No'm, Miz Speer ain't home at all this morning. No'm." Kate was as conscious of tensed ears at the top of the stairway as if they buzzed; and, departing, she felt herself watched hotly.

A polite generation preceding this stylizedly mannerless present one held that no gentleman ever raises his glance to the upper windows of a house as he approaches it or as he leaves it afterward; but Kate Lanning, though aware of the old rule, felt that it didn't apply to a lady in emergency. Apparently absorbed in thought, she reached the pavement before the small lawn, then looked up unexpectedly and caught a glimpse of the withdrawal of a face from between closing folds of chintz at a bedroom window. This disappearing face, pallidly haggard beneath wisps of unkempt black hair and not beautiful to-day, seemed to send a deadly message whirring on the air as if fast to a steel-pointed arrow: "I'll get YOU if I die for it!"

At home Kate waited again, then tried to call Laila on the telephone; the housemaid's voice was still uninterested. "No'm, Miz Speer ain't home, so she say she ain't go' answer no 'phone-calls . . . No'm, I couldn't say when . . . No'm, I on'y come in by the day up to four-thirty, so I couldn't say when . . . No'm, I pos'tively couldn't say."

Kate called Plant Three and asked to speak to Mr. Speer. "This is Kate Lanning," she said, when he answered. "I've been trying to see Laila; but I'm afraid she isn't going to let me. I wanted to talk to

her first of course; but if I can't I'll just have to go ahead with you
—if you'll let me. Could you come here any time to-day or this evening—or I'll meet you anywhere you say?"

There was a long pause; then he said, "No; I believe not, Kate."

"I think we'd better have a talk, Tuke."

"No; I believe not."

"Is that all I can get you to say to me?"

"Yes, Kate. Good-bye."

She went to her own room, wrote a letter to Laila, and, having
finished it and read it over twice, made a confetti shower of it for
her wastebasket. "Trying to reach that mind!" she thought. "Am I
hysterical—struggling to be square and put truth into such a mind
when it's frantic with disappointment, cursing amid the wreckage
of its delusions? I see it can't be done; but trying has at least satisfied
my womanly honor." Toward sunset she was carefully writing another letter, not this time to Laila, when she was interrupted by Celia,
excitedly gloomy.

"Kate, here's a little more simple hell for Father; they'll break his
back. I've just taken a call from him and he says he won't be home
to-night or to-morrow or to-morrow night, either—not till Sunday
morning. He's had a cot put in his office at Roeville and he wants a
bag packed and sent to him. I've got Miley coming as soon as he's
off and he and I'll drive up to Roeville with it."

"Yes, Celia. Is it trouble with the union, did he say?"

"Between two unions, he said, Kate. Told me Mr. Roe and Sam
Augren have been up there all day, too, but are on their way home,
because Mr. Roe's practically frantic and knew, himself, he wasn't
doing any good. Father thinks he'll be able to talk the squad of labor
leaders up there to death if he can keep 'em awake long enough."

Kate smiled feebly. "He was able to joke about it?"

"With his words only," Celia explained. "His voice didn't sound
particularly jestful. How about that bag?"

Kate packed it, and, having watched its hustled departure, returned to her letter. This one she didn't destroy and it was handed
to Tuke Speer the next day, Saturday, at noon, by an apologetic Miley
Stuart. "I hope you'll excuse me for bothering you, sir," the young

Southerner said, "but Mrs. Lanning asked me to let her know if yo
thought there'd be an answer. If you don't mind I'll just sit around
till you've read it."

"All right, sit around." Tuke read the letter, put it in his pocket,
said, "Tell her yes"; and, at a little after five in the afternoon, walked
into the Lannings' living-room where Kate awaited him.

"It's no good," he said. "All the talk in the world isn't going to
change anything; but when you put it on the ground of old friendship and that your life's as much involved as anybody's, I couldn't
keep on saying I wouldn't even listen to you. You've got a right to
talk to me if you want to, I guess; but your own intelligence ought
to've informed you by this time that you can't accomplish anything
by it. Go ahead, though."

They hadn't shaken hands but stood looking at each other. "You
won't sit down, Tuke, to listen?"

"Oh, certainly, certainly!"

They sat, facing each other, and, after a moment of scrutiny, she
said compassionately, "You ought to take some vitamins, Tuke."

He didn't laugh—apparently he hadn't been amused for a long time
and never would laugh again—but he made a rusty sound that was
like a dried bone of laughter. "You don't need any, yourself, I see.
You're as pretty as ever and as healthy-looking. The more luck for you
—that you're not a real worrier. The people that don't worry about
things are those that don't care. You're supposed to do the talking,
though, not I. Get going, why don't you?" Then, as she only sat,
thoughtful, he added, "By the way, since you think I need vitamins,
you haven't advised me to stop drinking. Why don't you?"

"Because I think you already have, Tuke."

"What? You don't think I was drunk the night I asked my wife
if she was?"

"No, I knew you weren't."

"You did? Curious; but you're right. I cut it all out for good months
ago, longer than anybody's noticed. I got the idea I'd like to die sober.
Get ahead with it now. I'm listening."

"No, you aren't," Kate said. "You aren't, because you're in a state
of terrific emotion and a person in that state can't listen, because

listening has to be done with the mind. How am I going to reach that part of you?"

"I don't know, Kate; that's your headache."

"Yes, I know," she said. "Poor old fellow, you've been suffering so long and so hard that sometimes you wonder if you have any mind left. Your work at Plant Three ought to be the answer to that, though; nobody there doubts that your mind's still operating, Tuke Speer. Your work hasn't suffered."

"Automatic, Kate, automatic—and a hell of a lot anybody in that set-up cares or even notices whether my work suffers or not." Tuke flushed, as an old soreness burned within him. "After I'd been there a year and a half I'd caught up with Sam Augren and we were running even. Look where Sam is now and where I'm not! I know more about Roe Metal Products in a minute than he does in an hour. How I do run on! Reminds me of the way I used to brag to you in Mrs. Cunningham's library about how high I was going to go in the business. Well, here I am bragging again about how really good I am, all appearances much to the contrary! Frustration, what? Think it's just my vanity talking?"

"No, Tuke."

"They've passed me over," Tuke said, still flushed, "how many times in these last years? I used to think maybe it was most likely because on top of being red-headed I got to be skinny-looking a good while ago and quit being talky. Besides that, I'm nobody's back-slapper. No, don't give me that wise look of yours, Kate. I know well enough it's been partly because they thought I took too many drinks now and then; but I wouldn't 'a' been taking those drinks if they'd ever given me a chance—and of course if my damned home life had been different. Want to hear me beef some more?"

"You don't need to, not to me, Tuke; I'd do it for you. I knew something about the business when I was in Mr. Roe's office, you might remember."

"What's the use?" Tuke said. "It's all over. I've been fixing things to get out and I've handed in my resignation. Put it in a note of less than twenty words Thursday night, mailed it to old man Roe yesterday; he certainly has it by to-day. Surprise you?"

"No, not any, Tuke. What are you going to do?"

"How the hell do I know?" His straight gaze at her seemed to glitter for an instant. "I'm not living much in the future these days; I don't know that there'll be any. A reason for my resignation right now's pretty plain to you, though, isn't it? I just thought I'd beat your husband to it and that I wouldn't give my wife and him the pleasure of throwing me out. See?"

Kate looked at him calmly. "My husband wouldn't do that."

"Oh, he wouldn't?" Tuke's dry bone of laughter was heard again. "She spent a good part of the afternoon day before yesterday in his private office. That jolt you any?"

"No, Tuke; I know she did."

"You do? Not from him I'll swear."

"No, he didn't tell me."

"I thought not," Tuke said. "What do you suppose they talked about?"

Kate smiled. "About almost anything that people can talk about in public, Tuke. You've been in that office, haven't you? It's about as private as an excursion train to Niagara Falls."

"You don't know Laila," Tuke said. "I'm surprised; I rather thought you did—at least that much. She can make any place private, if there's a man there she's taken a fancy to." At this, Kate's gaze drooped; he saw the wince and continued: "Yes, I see you get it. That same morning she'd faked my striking her, put on a screeching act before our two servants. Gives her away, doesn't it?—she'll sue for divorce pretty soon. She went to him for further planning. What'd be the step they'd take first? Me summarily discharged, therefore discredited. Broke, too. That'd be their idea, wouldn't it?"

Kate, looking up again, shook her head slowly. "I know your wife better than you know my husband. She's furious with you, and Ames is an old friend. She probably relies more on his judgment than on anybody else's; naturally she'd ask him for advice—yes, sympathetic advice—but if she was so raging with you that she'd ask him to put you out of the business—Tuke, she'd merely horrify him. Nothing on earth could make him do a thing like that."

"Nothing but Laila, I'm willing to admit," Tuke said. "Women like you think they understand men; but there are some things about 'em they can't. You're worth ten thousand of Laila; you're that much more intelligent than she and in your way you're even about as good-looking as she is; but Laila was born, I swear, knowing one thing completely out of your field of understanding—and that's how to get men insane about her and keep 'em that way. There isn't a man in the world you could hold, Kate Lanning, if she decided she wanted him."

Kate spoke gently. "Poor Tuke!"

"Meaning I'm witch-ridden?" Tuke said. "Maybe; but she'd take any man from you like rolling off a log. For one thing, you wouldn't do what she would; you couldn't. You're proud and if you saw him sliding away you wouldn't lift a finger to keep him."

"No." Kate inclined her head. "Not just to keep him."

"You think she hasn't got him?" Tuke said. "She took him away from you once, you know."

"No, she didn't. I didn't have him then, Tuke."

"What! Why, you worked for him night and day. You kept house for him. You took care of his child. You did nothing else but plan and work for him. You made him completely dependent upon you, whether he knew it or not; and yet Laila only gave him a look or two and a pat on the sleeve and she had him! Well, maybe he's still dependent on you, whether he knows it or not; but do you think she couldn't do it again? Couldn't? She has."

"No. She couldn't and she hasn't!"

"No?" Tuke said. "I'll settle that for you. I'll tell you what I saw. A while ago we spoke of my asking her, before the crowd here, if she was drunk. Hardly more than ten minutes after that I saw——"

Kate interrupted him. "Oh, yes!" she said serenely. "I know all about it, Tuke. I know what you saw."

"You do? Celia told you?"

"Practically; but anybody'd have known what was bound to happen," Kate said, and smiled again. "Anybody'd know almost exactly what Laila'd do—yes, and what Ames would of course do—under the circumstances."

Tuke didn't understand. "God, but you take it coolly! Yes, I suppose you're right, saying anybody'd know what they'd do. After all the cooing at each other and arm-grabbing and shoulder-pushing every time we saw 'em together for months, even I ought to've known what I'd see as soon as they thought they were alone! I *didn't* know, though—up to then I only suspected—and since then I've been walking round with red inside my skull as well as on top of it. You wouldn't know!"

"I wouldn't know how you hate my husband?"

"Hate him?" Tuke didn't make a gesture; he sat motionless and his voice was quiet. "I remember the day I loved that man. Thursday night I went into Frederic's restaurant, and he was there. I knew that if I looked at him I'd do something crazy; I was afraid I would anyhow. If young Stuart hadn't happened to barge in, chattering and skipping about between us, I think I would have. Hate him? Yes."

Kate now didn't look so healthy as he'd said she did. "You aren't exactly an assassin, Tuke. Ames could have looked after himself pretty well. All you'd have done was make a brawl."

"Maybe," Tuke said. "Even that'd have been enough, wouldn't it? —if it got into the papers or old Roe heard of it and what it was about? It might happen yet—any time. I couldn't answer for myself under certain circumstances."

"Couldn't you? I could."

"Think you know me better than I know myself? Old stuff, Kate Fennigate!"

The two were looking at each other steadily. "What are you and I doing, Tuke?" Kate asked. "Are we having a sort of duel? It mustn't be like this." She rose, went to a table, took up a silver box, opened it and offered it to him. "These cigarettes are Celia's. Won't you light one?"

"No, thank you."

"Not even Celia's?"

"No."

XLIII

KATE RETURNED TO SIT IN THE CHAIR THAT FACED HIS. "So far we've got nowhere, have we?" she asked.

"Yes, and nowhere's where we'll stay, Kate."

"That'd be a pity," she said, "because you've dug up a good part of your misery out of yourself, Tuke—out of a jealous man's imaginings."

"I didn't imagine what I saw, did I? I didn't imagine their kissings and murmurings of 'dearest' and 'darling' and 'love' with their arms about each other, did I? When two people do that as soon as they think they're alone together, it doesn't need much imagination to understand what it means, does it?"

The determined woman facing him didn't look sickened; she smiled. "Thanks. Thanks for that!" she cried, and leaned toward him. "Thanks because it makes your condition so clear. No, you didn't imagine what you saw. Yes, you did imagine what it meant—because it didn't mean anything, Tuke."

"What? Have you actually slicked yourself into believing——"

"Wait!" she exclaimed. "You said they thought they were alone together. They couldn't have thought anything of the kind. You saw the open door just beyond them, didn't you?—yes, and the very window you looked through, with the shade up and the light upon them! You saw Bill Jones, didn't you? Why, he talked to them! You saw Celia, didn't you? Anybody could have passed that door or come in at any moment, and can you imagine their not realizing that? What's more, they weren't doing anything that any other two people in the same position wouldn't have done. Nothing, I tell you!"

"You're his wife and you call it nothing?"

"Certainly! Laila had deviled you all evening; but there were only

three people who knew that—you and she and I. Then, you poor
thing, you let her get you, and, even though she'd asked for it, it
threw her into a state of emotion, and any man will comfort and pet
a woman when she's like that. Think of this: Haven't you ever had
a weeping woman throw herself into your arms before the funeral
when you've had a friend die? Women do that, I tell you. Nobody
was dead; but Laila wanted some man to say he loved her enough
to stand by her. When she went to his office it was probably about
how she persuades herself you've been treating her. Ames has always
been fond of her and——"

" 'Fond'!"

Kate drew a deep breath; she saw she hadn't shaken him. "You've
been letting it eat into you a long, long time, haven't you?" she asked.

"Yes, a long, long time—ever since my wife began to go out for
him."

"Naturally she did!" Kate spoke urgently. "That wasn't to her
discredit, was it?"

Tuke frowned; this puzzled him. "I didn't know you were so
liberal. I was under the impression you believed in marriage's being
respected."

"Yes, Tuke; but many an attractive wife has been thought rather
clever and not undutiful for making up to her husband's boss. It's
been thought to have advantages. Don't you realize it's supposed to
be an entirely innocent way of helping on the husband's preferment?"

Tuke's expression seemed to show a bony kind of pity. "Has it
helped my 'preferment'? No wonder you haven't got any lines in your
face; you can kid yourself into believing anything. So it's all been
on my account, has it?—just to get him to give her beloved husband
a better salary that hasn't happened?"

"No, Tuke; I didn't say all on your account—not all—but if a husband gets jealous when his wife's making up to the Boss she'll
naturally think herself insulted and behave like the devil, especially
if she wants to get her husband a bigger salary on her own account
as well as his."

" 'As well as his'!" Tuke echoed. "I wonder that didn't choke you,
Kate!"

"No!" Kate wasn't baffled. "You know what Laila wants, the things she has a passion for. Why haven't you given her these things, Tuke?"

He'd slumped a little in his chair; but at this he sat straight. "What the hell do you mean? What with?"

"I'm only trying to show you," Kate said. "If you had given her the things she wants she'd have been kinder to you, wouldn't she?"

"Kinder? She'd have sweetied all over me. My God, you don't suppose I know her too little to understand that if I were in your husband's place and he in mine, I'd be the one? What Laila wants, her life blood—clothes, clothes, clothes, jewels and jewels, shiny cars, head waiters and the damn society column, other fool women yearning and rubbering and their husbands cackling, 'Hi, Beautiful!' Spill those over her, she'll be in heaven and love you to death. You and I both know that, and what the hell's it got to do with anything?"

The gaze of Kate's brown eyes became even more piercing than compassionate. "But if you could spill those things over her, you still would, anyhow, would you, Tuke?"

"I would, God help me, I would!" Tuke's voice for the first time had violence. "I would; I couldn't help it and I wouldn't even *want* to help it. Call me any kind of crazy fool you like; but don't try to understand it. People like you couldn't possibly. Laila's over there at the house now, locked in her room and brooding on how to get rid of me, dig me so deep into the gutter that I can never reach high enough to harm her or the new husband she's planning for; but if I had a diamond mine I'd use it to buy her and keep her bought!" With this, the passion that shook him seemed to pass; he spoke quietly again. "You've let yourself in for this, Kate. If you don't like the exhibition——"

"Wait," she said. "How long has Laila kept herself locked in her room?"

"This time? Since night before last, after she'd been—'for advice'! —to your husband."

"Does she know you've resigned?"

"Yes, she had that information from me last night—through the locked door. I wanted her to know that I was beating her and Ames to it. Well, anything more? I suppose what you really got me here for's to find out what I'm going to do, isn't it?"

"Yes, partly."

"Well, I've already told you I can't tell you," he said. "I'm not living by plan. She means to get rid of me; but I'll block her. It can't be done to me while I'm alive. What you want is for me to leave your husband out of it. You don't want me to ruin him—not even ruin him a little. That's it, isn't it?"

"What are you telling me?" Kate asked, and her voice was still steady. "That you'd wreck us all?"

"Yes. You too. I'm sorry; but you too. I'm gone already, myself, you see—my resignation has settled that—and I really don't give a damn about anything except Laila."

"You like me, though, I think, Tuke."

"Not enough to spare you," he said. "Like you? Yes, I like you better than I do anybody else in the world. I don't like Laila; I think she's despicable. What's liking you got to do with it?"

Kate's voice now was tremulous. "We've liked each other pretty thoroughly—and a long time, haven't we, Tuke?"

"Yes. What of it?"

Kate rose, advanced the few steps that separated her chair from his, looked down at him with an illimitable sad comprehension. She put her hand on his shoulder. "Liking is really a good small form of love itself, isn't it? In that sense you really love me, don't you?"

"Why, yes." Looking up at her wonderingly, his widened eyes showed that she moved him, at least a little. "In that way I suppose you could say so—that I love you, Kate."

She stepped back from him, pointing to the open double doorway. *"There,* Tuke! Imagine Celia's standing in the hall yonder, and Bill Jones down at the other end of the room, you just outside looking in at the window—and what's the difference?"

Tuke jumped up. "What a trick!"

"No!" she said eagerly. "Not a trick at all, because it's the truth, Tuke. We've always had a good and true affection between us, and just now, if I'd been hurt and crying, you'd have put your arms about me, wouldn't you? Why isn't it the same?"

"Why isn't it?" The violence returned to his voice, unhappy passion to his whole being. "Because you're not Laila. You're a busy good little woman, Kate Fennigate, full of schemes to make men do what's best for themselves. That's what you live for, to put your way of being good and happy upon us, and you've spent your life making your husband walk the chalk for his own benefit—*his* success, *his* health, *his* happiness. All wasted, Kate! Do you think you could ever for an instant make him feel what Laila's made him feel?"

"Oh, dear!"

Tuke heeded this inadequate little exclamation, saw the startled look in her eyes; and, for a moment, it was his turn to be compassionate. "Yes, I'm sorry. I told you talk wouldn't change anything; but perhaps it has—at least to make you unhappier, Kate."

Again, as upon his arrival, he didn't take her hand. He only said "Good-bye," then left the room and left the house.

XLIV

AFTER A HARD EXPERIENCE PEOPLE SOMETIMES SAY THEY feel as if a steam-roller'd been over them. Kate's talk with Tuke hadn't so flattened her; but she seemed to have been picked at, tweaked and pricked with sharp instruments. She felt shredded, and, although she had accomplished a part of what she'd hoped to do—that is, had learned some things she wished to know—Tuke was right when he said her struggle with him made her unhappier. For a time she stood as he'd left her, a lone small figure in a big handsome room; then she sat down suddenly, not knowing that she did so, and said "Oh, dear!" again, but more faintly than before.

Tuke had said there were things about men that some kinds of women couldn't know and that Kate was one of those women. This

rang true. Out of the strange talk of that afternoon there seemed to
have emerged two portraits, scratchily painted and unfinished but all
too visibly contrasted—the one of a dry little dun-colored, put-on-
your-rubbers sort of woman and the other of a glorious-bodied, en-
rapturing Aphrodite, pin-headed and self-adoring but with wily
knowledge of hidden fire in men's hearts. After all and after all, had
Laila Capper struck again? Was that old ruinous intrusion repeating
itself once more—and mortally?

There were no echoes in the darkened living-room; faintly, faintly
"Oh, dear!" was whispered, small sounds not even reaching the walls.

. . . Celia arrived, bringing Miley home with her; they came into
the unlighted room and exclaimed when the abrupt glow of a lamp
revealed the inhabitant. "What in the world!" Celia exclaimed. "You
with your hands folded! Sitting in the dark for fear somebody'd catch
you not doing a lot of things at once? Miley's willing to lay off secret
service with Father out of town. Of course *you* still think we've both
been silly about that, do you?"

"No—no, I don't."

"Of all the inconsistent women!" Celia cried. "Wouldn't do anything when I was urging you; but now when everything's safe for
a while because Father's away, you sit here worrying about it. Can't
you worry just as much with the lights on? What's the idea of the
blackout?"

"No idea at all, Celia."

"Golly, what a voice!" Celia said. "You got a headache? I almost
have, myself. Had a note from guess who? Just nobody but Marvin
Roe—after I was sure I'd brushed him off for all time. Said he's going
to take a trip with his sister and grandfather pretty soon and very
definitely wants to see me oftener before leaving. Yes, oftener very
definitely! He would! Got a bad case of 'very definitely', Marvin has.
Miley and I'll hop to the movies quick after dinner so it'll be true what
I wrote Marvin in answer—that I was going to. My note wasn't as
mean as I'm telling it; but how do you get out of being dirty sometimes? You can't do everything everybody wants you to, though you
seem to, Kate. How do you manage it?"

"I don't."

"Golly!" the stepdaughter again exclaimed. "Have you heard from Father? Something's gone wrong at Roeville?"

"Not that I know of. I haven't heard."

"Then why so downcast, now that we've got a breathing space? What sort of dinner you giving us?" Celia talked on inconsequently, and, helped by Miley, kept up a prattle throughout the meal. Both were conscious of the stepmother's unusual solemnity and more disturbed than cheered by the too evident efforts she made to disperse it. They returned to the living-room for coffee, and on the way Celia caught Kate's arm tightly, whispering, "What new thing's wrong? You've got to tell me!"

"Nothing. It's all right."

"It isn't! See here, I'm going to call up Father and——"

"Yes, do. He'll be glad to hear you and you'll find that he's all right."

"I'll see!"

Celia turned back to a telephone under the stairway, and Kate went on into the living-room with Miley. There she made small talk until after the coffee'd been set before her and she had given him his; then she startled him. She said: "I'm afraid Celia'll have trouble getting through to the Plant at Roeville; their lines have been busy all day. What kind of woman would you be most likely to fall in love with, Miley?"

"Good heavens!" he exclaimed, and, recovering, added seriously, "I think you know, Mrs. Lanning."

She shook her head. "No, I mean if you fell in love—violently."

"So do I," he said.

This was eloquent enough; but she didn't seem to be satisfied. "Don't you think most men, especially if they're natural and good and manly and—and absorbed in their work—don't you think they're likely to be most deeply stirred by—by flashingly beautiful women, the bewitching, dazzling——" She came to a wistful stop.

"Yes," he said. "Indeed I do!"

"You do?"

"Yes, of course, Mrs. Lanning." Miley, reddening somewhat, spoke apologetically. "I'm afraid you'll be accusing me again of being just a Southerner if I take it that you're referring to dazzling women like —like you and Celia, Mrs. Lanning."

He was rewarded by a sudden and charming change in her. She blushed; her eyes sparkled. "You *are* a help!" she cried, as Celia came in.

After the two had gone to their movie Kate sat at her knitting. The picture most often in her mind's eye was one of Tuke at home walking the floor but perhaps, perhaps with a rag of hope in his eye— hope that a door might be unlocked? On the other side of that door was the same old Laila Capper but desperate now; the door would never be unlocked to a husband out of a job. Tuke knew this, of course, and so—— No, there'd be no flicker in those sunken eyes of his to-night. None of the attempted reasonings of that afternoon had made either him or Laila less dangerous.

In the morning, late, near noon, Ames arrived looking thin and so preoccupied that he may have been unaware how meager he made his salutation.

"You all right, Kate?" he said. "I telephoned Miss Stillweight to be here. Has she come?"

"Yes; she's in the library." Kate, as well as he, seemed never to have heard that wives and husbands after absence from each other usually make demonstrations of affection. "Have you got to begin dictating right away—on Sunday, Ames?"

"Yes. I think I'll lie down while I'm at it—talked almost the whole of last night. You might send lunch in there for Miss Stillweight and me, when it's ready—sandwiches and coffee'll be enough." He began to move toward the library; but she spoke to him.

"Ames——"

"Yes?"

"Is that all you——" She changed her tone quickly. "Have you got the labor trouble at Roeville settled?"

"No, but I will," he said, and there was anger in his voice. "Nobody need have any doubt of that; I'll settle it! I'll have to go back there to-night and I'll be there most of the week probably; but it'll be done. Please don't let anybody disturb me now while I'm working, Kate."

"No, nobody shall, Ames."

Tuke Speer's gaunt voice seemed to be repeating: "All wasted, Kate!" Ames had kept his eyes averted from her—as if the sight of her had grown distasteful to him, or was a reproach, or both. Wasn't his manner precisely that of a man whose wife has become his martyrdom because she is what separates him from a supreme happiness he believes he'd possess if she didn't exist? Three nights ago he'd come home tired and much troubled. Some of this he might have got at Roeville, but not most of it. Laila'd been to his office that afternoon, and Kate had built her own interpretation of the scene between them: Laila saying "But you love me, don't you?" and Ames saying "No."

That would have meant a scenic fury of disappointment, enough to crush any man cozened to think himself responsible for it; but another interpretation was as well confirmed by that bitter shot from Laila's eyes between closing chintz curtains: "I'll get YOU!" How if Laila'd said, "But you love me, don't you?" and Ames had answered, "Yes, but there's Kate—Kate and my daughter and Roe Metal Products!"

How was the truth to be had? One way to it might be open by nightfall.

Yesterday morning she'd met Mr. Roe in the lobby of the bank she used; he'd stopped her and said, "Ames'll be home to-morrow, I understand. I'll drive round to your house some time in the afternoon and he and I may have a tough session. A hundred things have turned up while he's been away, and, besides that, he and I've got to get a particular matter settled, one that's been hanging fire too long. I don't intend to crack my head over it any longer. 'Bye-bye, child."

The quiet Sunday hours moved slowly into that irretrievable fixity, the past; but for Kate they were empty of all save waiting. The old man arrived late in the afternoon and she met him smilingly, making a little fuss over him as she brought him into Ames's library. There, after asking about Marjie and Marvin and telling him how hearty he looked, himself, in spite of all his burdens, "Ames'll be down in a minute or two," she explained. "I sent to have him wakened as soon as I saw your car drive in. He was pretty tired when he got home this morning and he dictated till after three; but then he went up to his room to try to get an hour's sleep before you came. You're anxious to be off on your trip and rest up a little, yourself, aren't you, Mr. Roe?"

"Yes, I've got to, Kate. The world's grown too pressing, and do you know how old I am?"

"You'll be younger when you get back, Mr. Roe."

"I don't know," he said. "I'll be seventy-seven next month. I've got to put even more responsibility on Ames." He sighed. "These unions fighting——"

"That's going to be all right." Kate's voice was as cheerful as her face. She beamed upon him. "Ames'll have that straightened out within the next few days." She laughed. "I know he will because he sounded savage when he told me he would."

"Think so?" Her bright assurance seemed to cheer Mr. Roe a little. "Yes, I guess if Ames says so and sounds mad it'll happen. He's got a load on him, though, a mighty big load. I'm glad he has you to fall back on; you always were a great one to be full of confidence and brisken things up."

"Why not?" she asked gayly. "For instance, look at the record Roe Metal Products is making. When you think of all the intelligence and energy and strength of the men in that organization—the devotion and ability they're all showing—doesn't it make you feel proud, Mr. Roe? It ought to!"

"Yes, maybe." He frowned. "And yet when I look 'em over to find one to fill a special big place—well, I'm stumped. That's the main thing I'm here about to-day."

"Yes, I thought so, Mr. Roe. Of course the trouble is you've got so many good ones it's hard to select from 'em."

"No, it ain't," he said querulously. "That's where you're wrong. Practically ever since spring I've been looking for a crackerjack top man for our Eastern Division. You know that as well as Ames and I do, don't you?"

"Yes, Mr. Roe."

"Certainly you do," the old man said. "Got to be an A-1 general manager and a production genius—and where is he? If we took somebody from outside the organization he'd practically have to learn Roe Metal Products from A B C up; but Ames and I have both been over our whole personnel a hundred times and there's nobody that fits the hole—nobody! What you laughing at?"

"At you and Ames, Mr. Roe."

"It's no laughing matter!" he said testily. "I tell you we've looked 'em all over——"

"Oh, yes!" she interrupted. "Looked 'em all over and overlooked the right one!"

"What?" He spoke crossly. "Who've we overlooked? Who you talking about?"

"Oh, just somebody right under your noses. That's probably why you've overlooked him."

"Who?" Mr. Roe said angrily. "Who?"

She hadn't time to tell him, because Ames came in just then, shook hands with the guest, and, without turning toward Kate, asked her to see that if Celia buzzed into the house with a crowd they'd not make too much noise. Kate said, "Yes, of course," glanced at Mr. Roe and moved rather slowly toward the door. Mr. Roe made a petulant gesture.

"No!" he said. "Sit down, sit down. Sit down both of you! I want Kate here too, Ames. You and I've been racking our brains for months and she's got a few, herself. She's just been acting like she has some superior secret insight that we don't possess, and I want to hear what she has to say. Most likely amount to nothing; but in my long life I've noticed there are times when a woman'll hop right into the middle of a passel of men with an idea they've been looking and looking for. Sit down, Kate."

"If you say so," she responded, obeying and slightly but gravely emphasizing the pronoun. She'd become serious. "Mr. Roe, I believe you asked me——"

"Wait just a minute," he said. "There's a matter I want to get out of the way with Ames first, smaller and not important but bothersome. We've got to make another replacement, Ames. Here,

the other day, I was talking about letting Tuke Speer go on account
of his drinking and getting gossiped about; but you said no, so we
let him stay. Yesterday I found his resignation in the personal mail
addressed to me at my house. What's the matter with him, do you
know?"

Ames didn't answer promptly. "No, I—I can't say I do."

"Well, anyhow he's resigned," Roe said. "I got hold of Sam Augren
and he's worried about it; says Speer was always to be depended on,
kept things running smooth and never put any bothers up to Sam.
Sam says Speer himself suggested young Stuart for the place. That'd
be pretty radical, wouldn't it? Everybody says Stuart's already showed
he's a great technical man; but he only came in last spring. What
you think about it?"

"About young Stuart?" Ames asked. "About young Stuart?"

"That's what I said!" Mr. Roe spoke crisply. "You still asleep? I
asked you what you thought about young Stuart for Speer's place?"

"I—I don't know. We might try him."

"All right, then, we'll try him. That settles that. Now we'll get
down to business." Mr. Roe turned in his chair. "Who in thunder were
you talking about, Kate?"

"Tuke Speer," she said.

XLV

The old man didn't understand. "No, no," he said
peevishly. "We're through with that. I mean who were you talking
about when you said we'd overlooked a man right under our noses?"

She seemed to be amused. "I've just told you. Tuke Speer."

"Oh, me!" Mr. Roe looked distressed. "You're mixed up, Kate.
Before Ames came in we were talking about all our mushing around

for months trying to find a man for the head of our Eastern Division. You told me——"

"I know," Kate said. "That's what I'm talking about. Just now you asked Ames why Tuke Speer's resigned and Ames said he didn't know. You did say you didn't know, didn't you, Ames?"

Ames's profile, reddening, seemed to be conscious that Kate was looking at it. "Yes. I suppose he has his own reasons for resigning; but nobody's stated them to me."

"They don't need to be stated," Kate said. "Isn't it perfectly plain what they are?"

"Plain? I don't——"

"You don't see?" Then Kate turned quickly to Mr. Roe. "For my part, I wonder Tuke Speer didn't resign long ago. If I'd been in his place I'd have been out of Roe Metal Products long before this; I wouldn't have stood the treatment he's had there. I wouldn't——"

"Oh, see here!" Mr. Roe interrupted fussily. He'd begun to pull at his neck-gear and already had it well disarranged. "Maybe it was a mistake asking you to sit in with us, Kate. What you keep harping on Speer for? He's out and we'll try young Stuart in his place, so that's settled. What you mean talking about the treatment Speer's had? Nobody's been interfering with him. You mix me all up, I tell you. The way you sound to me it's exactly as if you're telling us you think Tuke Speer's the man we've been looking for to be head of our whole eastern set-up and we ought to appoint him to it because he's resigned his job at Plant Three! Is that what you——"

"No! I'm telling you that you ought to've appointed him months ago! You ought to've done it long before he resigned because he was disgusted with your neglect of him. Your failure to recognize his ability after all the proofs he's given you, year in year out, that he knows the business——"

"Well, I'll be doggoned!" Mr. Roe used his expletive with acute feeling. "This looks like one of the craziest things I ever had happen to me! To sit here and be told that Ames Lanning and I haven't been using our brains, don't know how to pick our men, pass by what's right under our noses and——"

"Why, look at you!" Kate cried. "The pair of you! You began by offering this great position to Sam Augren. Good old Sam, yes; but compared to Tuke Speer he's only a good old pack-horse. I challenge you to compare his grasp of the organization with Tuke's! You've talked to them both about the same problem sometimes. Which was the one that understood it right away and which the one that didn't? I knew which, I can tell you, as long ago as when I was in your office. Tuke Speer's always known more about Roe Metal Products in a minute than Sam does in a year. You accuse me of saying you haven't used your brains. Well—have you? Here's exactly the man you need and you haven't even considered him."

"No, we haven't considered him." Mr. Roe, resentful, became stern. "We never more than mentioned his name as one of the impossibles, and a very good reason for it, too! Your husband wouldn't even have suggested Speer to me, because he knows my principles. There are rules I never break, and Speer's ineligible. I've put up with him where he is because it's true, as you say, he's always done good work there and his private transgressions with liquor, though known, were not notorious. For any higher position than that, though, I wouldn't consider a drinking man. Never! Not for a minute!"

"He's not a drinking man, Mr. Roe."

"What?"

"No," she said. "We've usually seen quite a good deal of the Speers. Ask Ames when was the last time he saw Tuke take a drink. Not since a good many months ago, was it, Ames?"

"No," Ames answered uneasily. "I believe not. Not for some time."

"No, and I'll tell you both why," Kate said. "Tuke Speer's stopped altogether. Yes, for good, Mr. Roe—because he saw it was doing him harm—and when a man sees that and stops, he's through. He didn't advertise it; but he stopped. Mightn't it strike you that knowing this position was open, he respected your principles and tried to make himself eligible—from *your* point of view—and with what result? That you didn't even consider him!"

"You wait a minute!" Mr. Roe made his point truculently. "Neither did you. You knew what we were looking for all these months and so far as my knowledge goes you've never said a word about this fellow, not a single word. Has she, Ames?"

"No—not in this connection, sir."

"I thought not! If you were sure he was so good all this time, Kate, why didn't you ever speak out for him? It wouldn't have been any use because he's not the right man; but you make me curious. I'd like to know why you waited until right now to——"

Kate interrupted him. "Two reasons. I hoped that maybe either you or Ames—at least one of you—might take note that he'd stopped drinking and begin to think about him for yourselves. That was correct of me, wasn't it?"

"What's the other reason?"

"It's rather a private one," Kate said, and, though she didn't glance at her husband, her voice shook a little. "I've had occasion to think that sometimes I've been rather too forward with my—my advice. I've tried to turn over a new leaf, Mr. Roe; I've been trying not to push my ideas on—on anybody. I haven't wanted to——"

The old man stared at her, astounded. "Yes! This looks like it!" He laughed satirically. "Don't want to push your ideas on anybody, and sit there squealing at your husband and me and giving us fits because we won't consider handing over one of the biggest jobs in the whole business to a grouchy, red-headed ex-souse that's already resigned himself out of it!"

"That's how you think of him, is it?" Kate asked. "No wonder he resigned! Why wouldn't he? Well, are you going to keep on not considering him?"

Mr. Roe was frowning at her. "One sufficient reason'd be his resigning. In Roe Metal Products I don't like a man to resign. He's supposed to stay on——"

"On the job!" Kate cried, and she sprang to her feet. "Yes, to stay and eat his heart out—and keep his wife contented—on the same old pay—the pay a boy'll get now, a boy that was taken into the business only last spring! Tuke Speer was on that same job when I was in your office, Mr. Roe. He was there when Ames and I were married and Ames wasn't with you at all. Now, at last, you've had the chance to show Tuke you know what he's done all these years and appreciate it—yes, the chance to have the good sense to make the best use of him—and what do you do? You don't even consider him! Why *wouldn't* he resign, I say! I tell you that if any man so treated had the spirit of a mouse he'd get out and shake the dust of your old Plant Three from his feet and tell you two to go to the devil!"

Ames had turned his head, and both men were looking at her now, as she stood before them vehement, high-colored, high-spirited and seeming almost tall. Mr. Roe was greatly disturbed; his fingers fumbled at his collar and his voice was thin with complaint. "Now, now, now!" he said. "Outside of everything else, this fellow Speer's been getting to be the kind of looking man most people wouldn't likely consider for anything of A-1 importance. He's red-headed to start with, and besides that, why, nowadays he's white-complexioned, kind of burned-up-inside hungry-looking, and so far off weight he looks more like a skeleton than a——"

"Then feed him!"

"What?"

"Feed him, I say!" Kate cried, and she struck her small hands together resoundingly. "Feed him this job and see him begin to look like a man again and not a skeleton! You'll see what he gives you for it in return! You *know* he's the man you want; in your hearts, you both already know it now, and all you can say is that you've starved him so thin that his looks are peculiar! That's a brilliant reason for not 'considering' the best man you've got, isn't it? Subterfuge!"

The old builder of fortunes and of men turned uncertainly to his younger colleague. "She's a pretty smart woman," he said feebly. "What you got to say, Ames?"

Kate advanced a step toward her husband. "Yes, what have you to say, Ames?"

If he heard the ring of the personal challenge that was in her voice, he either didn't comprehend it or refused to meet it promptly; apparently he was somewhat dazed. "I'm not sure," he said slowly. "Simply it's—it's an idea that hadn't occurred to me."

"Why not?" His wife's question was quick.

"Well, perhaps because——" He paused. "I can't say just why not."

"You see?" Kate spoke to Mr. Roe. "It hadn't occurred to him for the reason that he hasn't been thinking of Tuke Speer in that way,

Tuke Speer's such an old friend of his that he's always thought of him personally, so to speak, and not in his business capacity. That's one reason why it's our most intimate friends that often get overlooked, isn't it? Mr. Roe, are you going on overlooking Tuke Speer because he's grown thin working for you and's always been an intimate friend of Ames's?"

"Don't be so snappish!" the old man said, snappish himself. "You've had your say, haven't you?"

Kate looked from one of them to the other, and her scrutiny of her husband, though brief, was of a penetrative intensity, yet yielded her nothing that she needed to know: his face was a handsome sculpture expressing profound cogitation only. "Oh!" she said. "I see. You want to be left alone to consider whether you'll consider Tuke Speer or not, do you? Well, before I go I'll say just one thing."

"I bet you don't!" old Roe gibed at her. "I bet you say a dozen!"

She looked him in the eye, turned away and swiftly crossed the room.

In the open doorway she sank in a mocking curtsey. "Good-bye— you myopic astigmatics!" she said, and, skipping instantly out of the curtsey and into the hallway, closed the door behind her.

For a moment or two they heard her sing, loudly at first, then with decreasing distinctness:

"There was a man in our town, and he was wondrous wise,
He jumped into a bramble bush and scratched out both his eyes——"

This sauciness of hers was deliberate; part of her performance, it was the finale to the scene of provocation she'd created. Her face had no impudence but only anxiety as she let her pertly singing voice fade out on her way back to her eternal knitting. She knitted fast, not looking at her hands; but time was long while she waited for the two men to come from the library. More than an hour passed; then she was called to the telephone to speak to Mrs. George Cooke.

"It's about next Sunday night," Mrs. Cooke explained. "You and Ames remember it'll be my turn to have the every-other-Sunday supper for the crowd, don't you? I just wondered if you have any

ideas about food, how maybe George and I could give 'em something
a little different. Any suggestions?"

Upon this subject, after Kate had spoken, Mrs. Cooke was verbose,
held to it for ten minutes; then said, "Well, that ought to do, especially with the iced tomato ring to top the salad. We might be fewer
than usual: 'Neely Wayne's got a really terrible cold, Jessica says, and
mayn't be well enough, and to tell the truth I'm hardly expecting
Laila and Tuke." Mrs. Cooke giggled. "I'd be pretty surprised if *they*
turned up, wouldn't you?"

"Why?" Kate asked. "They've always been among the regulars.
Why do you think——"

"My good gracious heavens!" Mrs. Cooke was loudly exclamatory.
"Look at what happened at your house last time, and where have you
been all this week? They're having a most shocking to-do. Laila told
me herself he actually hit her!"

Kate laughed. "So Laila says?"

"You don't believe her?" Mrs. Cooke asked, and added, "Well, of
course with Laila it *is* always hard to tell. Anyhow, though, this time
everybody's certain she's going to leave him. Me, I'm looking for
the announcement of a divorce suit any minute."

"Are you?" Kate laughed with exaggerated skepticism and made a
risky quick decision. "If I were you, I wouldn't take them that
seriously."

"You wouldn't? But, Kate, you don't know! Why, they're *at* each
other; it's just a cat and dog——"

"The cat might be sorry," Kate said. "Suppose, for instance, something rather magnificent were coming Tuke's way pretty soon and
Laila's dog turned out to be Prince Fortunatus instead. She might
regret any too hasty action, mightn't she?"

"Kate Lanning!" Mrs. Cooke's voice was as excited as Kate intended it to be. "You know something! What are you hinting at?
You don't mean the New York appointment? Has Ames been
telling you——"

"No, no; he doesn't talk business secrets to me."

"He does, too; everybody knows he does! Listen! Has Tuke been
told? Does he know it yet?"

"No, no, no, and neither do I. It isn't certain. It hasn't happened."

"Listen!" Mrs. Cooke's excitement was mounting. "You can't shut down on me like that! You say it hasn't happened; but you know it's going to. You mean the powers that be are talking of it, that they're considering Tuke for it. You've got to tell me that much!"

"No, I can't; I can't tell you anything," Kate said hastily, for a moment earlier she'd heard the library door open and close. "Good-bye! There's something I have to attend to; I've got to run!"

This was true, and, after running, she was able to confront her husband and Mr. Roe near the open front doorway, through which the colored house-man was just disappearing with Ames's traveling-bag.

"Well?" she said demandingly.

Mr. Roe took the explanation upon himself. "I'm carrying Ames along with me to supper at my house; the children won't be there and we can keep on talking till he has to leave. Then I'm going to take him to Roeville in my car and come back. You send his to him to-morrow morning for him to use while he's up there. What's the matter? Mad because he didn't trot all over the house, hunting for you to say good-bye?"

"No," Kate said. "He knew I'd be here for that. Good-bye isn't what I came for, though. You both know what that is. I'm waiting. Well?"

"Don't 'well' me!" The old man's irascibility suddenly had the better of him. "You expect to pop up with a thing like that and put it over and have the answer, yes or no, all in two minutes and a half? Think we haven't any other questions to decide, either? Boss of the whole shebang, are you, and just about ready to stamp your foot at me?" He grasped Ames's arm, urging him through the doorway. "Come on, Ames. I bet you lead a life! If I had a fireball little sergeant of a wife like that, why, doggone me, sometimes I wonder you don't leave her!"

XLVI

HENRY L. ROE'S ACERBITY, MOST NATURAL AFTER HE'D
been verbally handled as he hadn't been during forty prodigious years
of success, was a childlike but effective revenge. His departure into
the twilight with her husband, who hadn't said a word to her, first
staggered Kate, then floored her. Accustomed to command her own
intelligence, she found shockingly that she knew neither what she'd
done nor what she could further do. Nightfall was here; but the truth
she'd expected to look upon was not.

The New York appointment was in Ames's hands, and if he did
what she believed merely right—right by Tuke and right by Roe
Metal Products too—his career was saved from an hourly rising peril.
It was in Ames's manner, when he perceived the choice she'd given
him, that she had thought to find her answer. She'd hoped that he'd
feel and show the relief of a man unexpectedly freed of a great fear.
He hadn't. He'd looked—well, to put it in a word, hangdog! What did
that imply? Taking it simply, usually the best way to take anything,
did it mean that he was ashamed of how miserable he knew he was
going to feel if he let Tuke carry Laila off resplendently?

On the other hand, maybe Ames couldn't make himself believe that
Tuke was up to the great position; conscientiously felt he couldn't
give it to him. Would that make Ames look hangdog? It might, or it
mightn't. Kate had long been convinced that she knew her husband.
Well, she didn't. He who'd seemed an open book was an enigma.
Women laugh knowingly when men complain that women are unreadable; they laugh because they know that men are the more
mysterious of the two.

Flattened at last, Kate couldn't eat, gave herself a sick headache and

an indigestion. She took to her bed, not so much because of a preoccupation with physical anguish as for the sake of a pillow upon
which to weep at intervals. Bafflement so complete can be prostrating.

She had a lifting message on the third evening of this nervous
illness. Celia came in after a telephone call from Roeville. "I obeyed
you and slicked it over, Kate. Mr. Augren was up there to-day for
a while and happened to mention that his wife had been here and
was told at the door you weren't well. So of course Father was worried and——"

"Not about me," Kate interrupted. "It's about a possible strike."

"No, it was about you, Kate. I lied like a good girl—told him you
weren't really sick abed, just lying down a good deal. He kept
insisting I must send for Dr. Prudens; but I told him you absolutely
wouldn't let me and were sure to be all right by to-morrow morning."

"I shall be," Kate said in a strengthened voice, and bodily she kept
her word. Mrs. Augren called again and found her downstairs, briskly
knitting.

"Kate! I've been crazy to see you! Thank goodness you're up!
Everybody's absolutely crab-eyed about the Speers. Sensation? Oh,
my! Tessie Seybolt and Joanna Tyne are practically sitting on my
gate-posts right now waiting for me to get home and tell 'em what
you say about how it happened."

"About how what happened?"

"Good Lord! About how it happened that Tuke Speer, of all people
on earth, got the plum!"

Kate stopped knitting. "He has got it?"

Mrs. Augren was skeptical. "You mean to tell me you don't know
it? Of course you do! You want us to think your husband is as close-
mouthed with you as all that, do you? You can't put it over. I take my
oath you've known it for days!"

"No, I haven't. I don't know it now. Where did you hear it?"

"Why, from everybody. It's all over the place, and was it a surprise!
Joanna says her Harold claims he's always thought Tuke'd have a
chance if he'd cut out hitting it up, and Tuke did. Murder, when I
think of how that woman would put it over the rest of us if they
were going on living here I'm glad it's New York that'll have to

stand it! Won't she make the money zing, though? Come down to cases, Kate: How long's it been on the cards?"

"I don't know that it's on them yet," Kate said. "No; I mean it! What makes you so sure it's true? Has Sam told you?"

"No, he says Mr. Roe and Ames haven't taken him into their confidence about it; but he heard it downtown and he thinks it must be so. I heard it, myself, Sunday evening and it had gone round practically everywhere by yesterday. At first, when I told Sam he didn't take much stock in it; but he does now, and he says while he probably wouldn't have thought of Tuke, himself, for such a position, he won't be surprised if the poor old thing'll hold it down all right. My! Think of how he and she have been fighting—right up to the very edge of divorce! She'll have to make up with him and keep the peace, or Mr. Roe wouldn't dream of it. Don't you love it!"

"You think she will?"

"Think so?" Mrs. Augren laughed aloud. "Why, we all know Laila, don't we? Mary got her on the telephone day before yesterday, Monday, and began talking about New York, and at first Laila didn't know what she meant, hadn't heard a word. So Mary screeched and said, 'Tuke hasn't *told* you?' She says Laila almost choked to death over the telephone; then, soon as she could get her breath back, she asked Mary if George knew if Tuke was still out at Plant Three or where was he? Mary says she talked so fast and so much she could hardly understand her. Make up with Tuke? *Will* she! You've known her all her life; I should think you'd——"

"Yes, I suppose you're right."

"You know it!" Mrs. Augren, though they were alone, lowered her voice to the confidential wheedle women use at such moments. "Listen, Kate: Seriously, don't you think her honeying up to Ames all this time's been a good deal so's she could coax this out of him— on her own account of course, not Tuke's? Just girl to girl now, you're clever as they make 'em and don't you think there's something in the idea?"

"Laila's stupid," Kate said, with apparent carelessness. "She ought to know Ames better than that, though, don't you think?"

"Well, maybe." The caller was not convinced, but shifted ground.

"Even Mary Cooke says it's going to be nice to have her out of town, and while they're getting ready to move I guess we won't have to listen to any more of her complaints of Tuke, what a godsend! I wouldn't be surprised if it even brightens up that funny old face of Tuke himself! Queer sight, wouldn't it be? Look, dearie, those girls are waiting for me, they really are, and I've got to go. Aren't you going to warm up enough now to let's hear how it happened? Come on out with it!"

"I can't," Kate said. "I don't know, I tell you. I don't know that it has happened."

Mrs. Augren made denunciatory outcries; Kate was the most stubbornly tight-mouthed woman in the world, she declared, repeating this till she was fairly outside the front door. Kate was left asking herself what she had done. She'd started the rumor deliberately, taking the chance that it was on the way to become the truth—but if it didn't?

"Merely a damaging fool?" she'd asked herself, when she was told that Mr. Roe wanted her on the telephone.

"You made me mad the other day," he began crossly, and added at once, "I still am."

"I'm sorry, Mr. Roe. I didn't——"

"Yes, you did," he said. "You thought you'd get more action that way. Fresh as paint! I'd hate to be your husband and I keep telling him so. I been up there since early this morning; only got back an hour ago. He says you been sick but Celia 'phoned him you're up again. That's too bad; women with as flip a tongue as you got ought to stay sick. People'd like 'em better."

"Yes," she said gently. "I'm afraid so."

"Here!" He sounded crosser. "Don't all of a sudden go so Christian on me; it ain't like you! All I called you up about, it's to insult you some first."

"First?" Kate was breathless, as he paused. "First before what, Mr. Roe?"

"Oh, have it your own way!" he said. "Have it your own way!"

"About—about Tuke Speer?"

"What else are we talking about?" he shouted into the telephone.

"You weren't nagging us to give it to Hitler, were you? I never saw such a tantrum—squealing at me, stomping your foot at me——"

"I wasn't, I wasn't! I didn't stamp my——"

"You wanted to," he said. "That's why I hate like poison to do what you say."

"Mr. Roe! You mean you're going to?"

"No, I don't. I said 'Have it your own way,' didn't I? Ames and I finally got it talked out and I've just sent your friend Speer out of my office with a bug in his ear. I told him if he didn't make a better record in New York than he has here I'd——"

"Mr. Roe! Mr. Roe!"

"Quit hollering at me!" the old man shouted. "Think hollering's going to help you run me and your husband and that red-headed friend of yours, too, and the whole Roe Metal Products Corporation? I only hope you stay out of Washington; they already got too many bosses down there."

"Mr. Roe! Mr. Roe!"

"Hush up!" he said. "You got your way, so quit hollering at me, can't you? G'bye!"

Providence doesn't always take care of drunkards and of women who act upon risky impulses, but sometimes does; the rumor sent forth to stop Laila had become truth. Laila could even "save face" a little, and so could Tuke by letting her pretend that her cajoleries of another man had been but wifely art practised for her husband's advancement. Tuke would always know the truth about what Laila'd tried for, of course; but maybe now he could stop hammering his head with it. What he wanted was Laila, and he'd have her.

This didn't save Kate Lanning's marriage. Months ago it had begun to perish because she was too bossy and too snappish in her bossings. Now she'd just shown that she was snappier and bossier than ever. She had virtually taken a great matter out of her husband's hands by forcing it into them. She waited for him as a stranger awaits a stranger.

XLVII

"Yes, that hole's plugged," Ames told Celia, who met him and kissed him enthusiastically in the sunshine at the opening front door. "Told you I'd talk 'em to death, didn't I? They saw the light at last: the country's in too much danger to stand for many more jurisdictional strikes. Neither will Congress, and things are moving too fast but have got to move faster. Anyhow, the wheels were turning all the time we talked. Powwows, powwows, powwows! The last one till three this morning! Almost forgotten which day's which. This is Sunday again, isn't it? I don't want anything to eat. Stopped at Mr. Roe's and had an early lunch with him, and he'll be off on his trip next week. Here! What are you doing?" The question was indulgent; Celia had again thrown her arms about him and kissed him. "Why all the daughterly exuberance? You're not usu-ally——"

"Yes, I am!" Celia cried. "You're such a good man, Father, and you look all worn out but still so pretty! I'm having a little congratulation dinner here to-night—just a dozen or so of my crowd—but you won't mind, because you and Kate'll be out of course, so you'll——"

" 'Congratulation dinner'? What kind of a dinner's that?"

"Why, for Miley Stuart because he's been promoted, you angel!"

"Oh, I see!" Ames looked at her thoughtfully. "You've felt that it's you who are called upon to give such a dinner, Celia?"

"Yes." She took his hand gravely and a little timidly. "Yes, I'm sure I'm the one. He's here waiting to thank you, Father. Will you——"

"Just a minute." His expression, briefly emotional, was questioning, as if he wished to ask her how much she had just told him. "Are you saying——" he began; then interrupted himself, postponing the question that already had an answer. "Just let me get my bearings. Ah— you said that Kate and I'll be out this evening. Where?"

"Why, at your every-other-Sunday-night supper. It's at the Cookes' and terribly exciting—at least, I hear they're all excited about it because it'll be the last appearance of the Speers before they step out into the higher spheres. You're expected, because of course you're the one that really gave the great appointment that makes the Speers happy for life. Kate told Mrs. Cooke you're both coming."

"She did?" Ames's voice was sluggish. "Well—I don't know—I hadn't thought of going out to-night. I'd probably better be catching up on sleep if I can get the chance. I don't think I'll——"

"You can sleep the whole afternoon, Father. Anyhow, settle it with Kate. Miley's been waiting quite a while, about three hours. Aren't you going to come in and give him a chance to——"

"Yes, yes, of course."

Still retaining her father's hand, she led him into the living-room where Miley stood, somewhat embarrassed. Someone else was there, too, a silent figure at the other end of the room; and Ames, in a quickly removed glance that way, seemed to have seen nothing but a pair of intolerably searching brown eyes. "You're—you're sure you're as well as ever again, Kate?" he asked. He took an uncertain step in her direction; but she helped his evident inclination not to come nearer.

"Yes. Entirely all right. Miley has a little speech he wants to make, Ames. We mustn't postpone it any longer or he might forget it. Begin, Miley; we're waiting."

Miley obeyed, spoke gratefully, with modesty, and was surprised to perceive that the recipient of thanks for the promotion was more embarrassed than he was, himself. The two shook hands, however, not without heartiness; Ames expressed confidence that with increasing experience Miley'd make an excellent record in Roe Metal Products, and, turning again toward the other end of the room, said "Well, Kate——" before he discovered that she was no longer present.

"I think she was afraid she'd cry," Celia explained seriously. "She's so fond of Miley and so proud of him, you see, Father. Besides that, she's so careful never to let anyone see her cry that nobody really knows whether she ever does or not."

"Yes—yes, I suppose that's so," he said absently, and made no effort to learn whether Kate was weeping now or not.

He didn't see her again, in fact, until just before seven o'clock in the evening when she called his name outside his bedroom door.

"Yes, what is it?"

"Don't you want to come down and see what a pretty table Celia's going to have for her dinner—white chrysanthemums and the Bristol candelabra and everything? Wouldn't you like to take a look at it before we start?"

He opened the door. "Before we what?"

"Oh, dear!" she exclaimed. "You haven't changed! I'm afraid you'll have to hurry into your——"

"What for? You mean the Sunday supper?"

"Yes, of course. We needn't drive; we can just walk round there. It's only a step. It's at the George Cookes', Celia says she told you, Ames."

"Yes, I believe she did." He hadn't looked up; he didn't now. "Do you really want to go, Kate?"

"Why, of course! I told Mary we'd be there." Kate's tone was decisive. There was even something like gayety in it, not genuine. Thus far since he'd entered the house he'd glanced at her just once, and now, standing before her, he was abject, still wore the hangdog look that might mean anything. "You'll have to hurry, Ames."

"I don't feel——" he began. "I'm really still pretty tired, you see, Kate. You could go all right without me, couldn't you? I don't believe I'll——"

"I'm afraid they'd be disappointed, Ames. The supper to-night's something of a celebration—for the Speers—just as Celia's dinner is for Miley Stuart. Wouldn't you be afraid that if we didn't go some of them might think we aren't enthusiastic enough about—I mean don't you feel we really ought to join in the send-off for two such old friends?"

"Ah——" He was most reluctant. "I don't feel—I doubt if I really feel up to it."

"Yes, you *do!*" Kate said. "You've slept almost five hours. I'll be waiting for you downstairs. You'll have to hurry!"

She turned briskly from his slowly closing door, and, after a dozen steps along the corridor, was confronted by Celia who'd just run up the stairs. "I've been thinking," the stepdaughter said. "I've changed my mind. I'm afraid it'll be altogether too tough for him to face those people after what's happened."

"To face what people, Celia?"

"Tuke and Laila Speer of course—particularly Laila. Oh, you pulled it off beautifully, Kate! I'm giving you full credit for a great maneuver but——"

"I don't know what you're——"

"Don't know what I'm talking about?" Celia said. "Oh, no, you don't! Stop stalling! I say you're a miracle—getting the Speers out of town for good, feeding the fat to Laila and feeding Laila to Tuke— but after all this if you make Father walk in on 'em at a party, why, you know what he is; the situation'll be too much for him. I've been thinking about it, I tell you, and after all I don't believe you ought to make him go. Only think how he can't help but be dreading it! Do you feel sure you're right to put him through it?"

"No," Kate said. "I'm going to, though."

"You are? I shan't blame him if he hates you for it."

"Nor shall I, Celia."

"Stubborn, aren't you?" Celia said, and, after a moment of frowning, added: "You think he's got to show 'em he can stand up to 'em. You've gone bossy again. Maybe it's just as well; but thank heaven I'm going to be at my own party and not at that one. I'd hate to be looking on!"

Ames didn't hurry with his dressing. His daughter's friends were filling the house with loud girlish chirpings and boyish outbursts of inexperienced laughter, all in sudden crescendos and unexpected stoppages, before he draggingly joined his wife at the front door.

"We'll be at least half an hour late," she said, as they set forth. "That won't matter, though, because Mary's making it a buffet tonight so there's no trouble about places at tables. We'll come home as early as you like." She spoke apologetically. "I felt we ought to go—because——" She let "because" seem to finish the sentence for her.

"Oh, of course, of course!"

Kate said that it was a fine mild evening for the season, now they were getting well into the autumn, and he agreed, adding that a year ago, at the same time, the weather had been more blustery. They spoke of Hitler in Russia; his troops would soon be running into trouble there where the winter came early, both thought; and thus, like a pair of polite acquaintances, they got themselves as far as Mary Cooke's house and into it. The party was already vociferously in being when they arrived; and a fat-choked voice was heard over other shoutings from the dining-room at the end of the hall.

"I'd forgotten him," Ames muttered, when he'd removed his hat and overcoat. "If I'd remembered Bill Jones was certain to be here——"

"You wouldn't have come? Yes, you would!" Kate all at once transformed herself, put on a gloss of bright-eyed gayety, and, smiling, took his arm cozily. "Don't look like that; it's a party! Come on!"

As they stepped into the noisy and rather small dining-room it was Bill Jones, of course, who first saw and greeted them. With emptied plate in one hand, re-filled glass in the other, he pushed his fat way through to them. "Look who's here! Arm-in-arm—loving couple, what? Can't shake hands; I'm eating and drinking, laughing and joking. Made up with the old boy, have you, Kate? Let bygones be bygones, says you; forget all about the party at your house only two weeks ago when he and Laila were telling us all how they were going to take a trip to New York together. Forgiven him now, have you, for the sweet and simple reason he's sending her husband to live there with her? Mag'nimity, what? I mean Ames's."

Mary Cooke tried to push him away. "Go sit down, Bill! Kate, you and Ames'll find plates yonder at——"

"Don't interrupt!" Bill Jones wouldn't go. "We've been trying to get Tuke to go out and march in so we could all sing, 'See the Con-quering Hero Comes'! Tuke and Julius Caesar are both red-headed. Did you ever notice the resemblance?"

"Yes, often," Kate answered. "Tuke's head's very like that one of Caesar in the Louvre."

"Is it?" The fat man looked concerned. "Still there, you think? I heard Goering's using it for a paperweight. Not Tuke's, I mean; but anyhow it oughtn't to be permitted. Here's a coincidence: Laila says Tuke and Julius Caesar have been getting lots alike ever since Tuke had the big joy-shock. She made Tuke laugh. Yes, sir, you won't believe it; but he's been laughing—once, anyway, and four of us heard him. We'll all four swear to it! Why wouldn't he, him with the New York job and a wife like that? Look what she's got on! Already working Tuke's new credit at the dressmakers', hair-doers', jewellers', what? She's got what it takes; I call it *la volupté.* Told her so. Venetian red-and-silver slippers, what? Magnificent Venetian feet, what? But look at her all over!"

He wasted his breath, a powerful one; both Ames and Kate had been doing nothing but look at Laila. Nobody, indeed, was doing much else. Transfiguration had been accomplished; the tragic disheveled head Kate Lanning had seen withdrawing viciously from a bedroom window, a few mornings ago, seemed to have been hallucination. This radiant woman in red and silver, with a platinum basket of diamond flowers below the complete bareness of her left shoulder—shoulder as fluent as the incessantly laughing and chattering voice—was a new Laila. Heretofore, accompanying all of her turned-on fascination, there'd ever been an undercurrent as of complaint, push for greater importance. This had gone; she stressed herself, thrust herself upon everyone as of yore, but did so now commandingly; and cooks, chauffeurs, waiters and love-making gentlemen would henceforth need to be on the hop for Laila or they'd have a rough time of it.

She stood swaying, widely gesticulative, killing other voices, and all aglow with starring for her audience, an adulatory semicircle. She appeared not yet to have observed the belated entrance of two of her oldest friends.

"Yes, sir, *la volupté!*" Bill Jones repeated. "Gorgeouser'n ever, what, Ames? She's what I call a *femme fatale.* I'm having a French evening. *Femme fatale! Ravissement!* She's got the world by the tail and going to swing it round her head. Brains too, believe you me! You admit she's used 'em on you, Ames, don't you? What you think, Kate?"

"I think you aren't going to last long to-night."

"Spiteful!" The fat man became sly uproariously. "Laila's been kind of giving it away that she worked her cuteness on your old man to get what she was after for her and Tukie. Guess she did, at that. 'Member that night at Sam's and Carrie's she had you in the sunroom the whole evening, Amesy? Yes, and this other time lately I woke up on your sofa and she was crying or something all over you? Trying to get New York out of you right then, wasn't she? Well, she got it, didn't she? Brains? By the barrel!" Through his alcoholic mist he perceived that he wasn't being enlivening. "Ames, why the monkish visage? Why Saint Jerome dying in the desert?"

Ames tried to look genial. "Aren't you used to that when you're being funny?"

"Naughty!" Jones said. "Old, too. Your feelings are hurt. I see why. She always used to rush for you the minute you came. Not doing that now. Looks like ingratitude. Listen, I'll *make* her notice you! Laila! Look who's come, Laila! Here's your Mr. Big all cast down 'cause he thinks you're going to quit grabbing his sleeve from now on."

"There might be something in that, Bill!" Laila, laughing extravagantly, looked at them between heads of the group about her. She put only the hint of a genuinely acid derision into her laughing voice; but the effect was that of a triumphant gibing. "A gal doesn't have to go on grabbing sleeves all her life—not after she's shaken out the trump cards that were up inside 'em, does she? Many might be the true words spoken in jest, Bill Jones!"

At this, everybody except Ames laughed with her, though for the most part a little startledly.

"Why, Laila!" Jones's tone was reproachful. "Don't be so open! Aren't you even going to say howdy, good evening?"

Laila waved a hand in intentionally negligent, amused greeting. "Hello, Kate. 'Lo, Ames."

"Is that all?" the terrible Jones asked. "Just ' 'Lo, Ames'? Oh, I see! No sentimentality in public. Scene of the thanking already done in private. You and Tuke rushed right over to Ames's house and poured forth appreciation the minute Tuke got his notification. Did, didn't you, Lovely?"

"Well, no, I believe not—not exactly," Laila said coolly. "After all, there does exist a certain Mr. Henry L. Roe, you know, Bill. Unless I'm mistaken, it's Mr. Roe we all work for, so I seem to have heard— you and the Lannings and all of us. Just to satisfy you, though, Bill, my Tuke wrote Mr. Roe one of the best letters of acceptance I ever read."

She stretched a long arm to where her husband stood, a little aside in the group, and drew him to her. Kate and Ames had come farther into the room, and this movement of Laila's, dissolving her semicircle, made a new grouping; so that she and Tuke seemed just then to be confronting the Lannings, confronting them victoriously—such was the scene Laila somehow created. Her hand, caressingly upon Tuke's arm, expressed a loving proprietorship. Kate looked cordial, Ames guiltily downcast.

Abruptly Laila laughed aloud, and, with open effrontery, asked, "What's the matter, Ames?"

The allusion to his crestfallen look was direct, and nothing could more clearly have said, "See this laughable poor fool speechless because he's lost me and sick with chagrin because he never won me while I gulled him, got what I wanted and yet was a true wife all the time!"

She spoke again, rallyingly. "What *is* the matter, Ames—really? Do tell us! Why so downhearted?"

"But isn't it natural?" he said, and began to appear less confused. "Aren't we all sorry to be losing you both, Laila?" He glanced briefly at the solemn Tuke. "Of course it was proper for Tuke to write to Mr. Roe; but I think perhaps you'd both like to know that it was Kate who got him to go over Tuke's record and study his qualifications. It was merit that brought Tuke the place, of course; but sometimes merit needs an advocate, so perhaps——"

"He means we ought to thank Kate!" In Laila's merry voice there rang an incredulity that was frank ridicule. "Thanks, Kate!"

XLVIII

Laila turned away. "Here! somebody get me some more anchovy paste. Not you, Bill; you'll drop it! You get it for me, Frank. George, where'd you put my Old-Fashioned—or is it you that's holding it for me, Harold?" She went to the buffet, pulling a trail of other women's husbands after her, and from there she could be heard offering fantastic suggestions for the cheering up of Ames Lanning. He mustn't be allowed to remain the skull at this feast, she insisted, and made everybody hear her frequent inquiries, followed by her own knowing laughter: What in the world could be the matter with the poor old thing? Just being Kate's husband couldn't account for it, could it? No, must be something he hadn't got used to. Some sort of disappointment, maybe?

Jones, ecstasized, went to lean abdominally upon Sam Augren, who'd begun to talk seriously with Ames, standing in a doorway. "New thing for you, Amesy, what, all this ribbing?" the fat man chuckled. "Trying to get in your hair, isn't she? Good for you; helps tie your head in so you can keep on wearing the same hat a while longer, what, Mr. Big? Superb woman! Takes a really glorious gal to bite the hand that fed; got to be glorious to get away with it. Everybody round her's laughing at you. Look, Ames! Upset you some?"

The tall Ames smiled down upon him good-naturedly. "You're upsetting Sam's plate with your head, Bill. When's your nap?"

Bill Jones stared up waterily. "What! You don't mind? Looking agreeable again? *Mille tonnerre!* Bravo, old boy!"

He wasn't the only one pleased to see Ames smile. A dozen feet away Kate sat beside Tuke who was talking to her as they ate; but her eyes were upon her husband, and a new knowledge she had grew more certain: Laila was truly jubilant, reveling genuinely, but malice grumbled in her voice of victory—hate that in the crude belittling of Ames Lanning took what poor vengeance it could. Vengeance—what for? Surely, surely because Ames must have said "No." Laila wouldn't have been like this if he'd said, "Laila, I love you; but there's Kate." Laila, inveterately dull-minded, made it plain that he'd said "No."

"I suppose I was a little crazier than ordinary when I had that talk with you, Kate," Tuke was saying. "You've pushed me for the place and Roe's given it to me; but it was Ames who really had the say. It's very strange to me; but you were right, he didn't want her. She's proving that now, pounding at him with her adolescent jokes. There's vinegar for her in our new pie because she can't help wanting every man to want her. Trying to punish Ames to-night for not. She's a wonder! Thinks she's broiling you, too—trying to make it seem you get to keep him only because she dropped him as soon as she'd used him. You're right to look as if that doesn't set you back any, Kate."

"It doesn't," she said.

"No, of course not. You wouldn't even try to flatten her out with the truth if you were alone with her. That's right, too: showing up people like Laila to themselves never does anything but get 'em hostile. They only think you're insulting 'em. Does Ames see that, too, maybe?"

"I don't know," Kate said.

"I take it back about him, Kate. You could have talked to me till Kingdom Come but you couldn't have proved anything by talk. A single action outweighs a dictionary of words. His deed proved your case. Hope it pleases you?"

"Yes, Tuke."

"Hope you're pleased by something else, too," he said. "Ames didn't know it but he gave her something to swallow when he told her it was you we really had to thank for the big job. She tries not to believe it; but she's afraid it's true. The most enraging thing you can do to some people is to return good for evil. Poison and fury, what? Doesn't hers gratify you—a little, anyhow?"

"I don't know. Perhaps it does—'a little, anyhow'."

"So I've got her again!" He looked sheepishly cheerful. "Think of our old talks in your aunt's library and on the front steps as the lights came out on National Avenue! You ought to know by this time that a fool's paradise is the kind of hell I like to live in. Can't help it. People can't change themselves much. All of 'em here telling me I'm a new man now I've got this job, and so I am—but no, it's only the old me with a pressure lifted. Same with Laila. Think you could ever change yourself much, Kate?"

"No. I've been trying to; but I can't."

"Lucky," Tuke Speer said. "I mean lucky you're still Kate Fennigate."

Laila's mockeries, playing always about the same theme, were incessant, continuing as the groupings of the party shifted and long after her most consistent applauder had been left behind, a plastically irregular rotundity snoozing in a dining-room chair, and the other guests had moved into the next room for bridge, gin-rummy and backgammon. She wrung her derided subject dry; dried up, too, the politest mirth of her hearers as well as all unction in her own laughter; and yet, with briefest intermissions, she gibed at Ames to the very end of her glorified evening. Her jokes omitted nothing: there were witty-sounding implications of pomposities in him, vanity and false success, that Tuke had won his way by hard work, Ames his by cozening, by looking rich, by toilsome preservation of his waist-line and even by the possible dyeing of his hair for the continued capti-vation of Henry L. Roe.

These quips, sometimes loud and sometimes pretendedly half-suppressed but always successful in reaching the ears of their objec-tive, had not the desired effect upon Ames—nor upon Ames's wife. Laila's first shot at him, upon his arrival, had begun to make him breathe easier; he'd been able presently to smile, and, with every repetition of her fire, he became more comfortable, not only within himself but outwardly. The experience seemed to expand him; some-times he was the only one—except Kate—who still laughed with Laila and, when goodnights came to be spoken, he shook her hand heartily.

"The best luck in the world to you both!" he said in a full and honest voice. "Laila, I can't tell you how glad we all feel over this new——"

"Yes, you do!" Laila withdrew her hand in a manner implying that he was hopelessly trying to retain it. "Take care of the precious health and do try to be a comfort to Katie again pretty soon. Good-bye, little Mr. Big!"

Outdoors and turned toward home with his wife, the man who'd been badgered all evening uttered a sound that was not a word but an eloquent exhalation: "Whoo!"

"You're that glad to get out to the air, Ames?"

"Yes, I——" Embarrassment returned; he was confused and downcast again. "Kate, I—I've wanted to explain about my overlooking Tuke, as you said. When you championed him to Mr. Roe, one reason I didn't speak right up for Tuke was my habit of overlooking him because of his drinking. I hadn't realized he'd cut it out. In order to consider him for the post I had to readjust my view of him. I had to do that in several ways. It took a little time."

" 'In several ways'?" Her tone was unemotional, rather brusque. "I see. You had to readjust yourself to begin thinking of him as a non-alcoholic and also as not a mean-spirited husband whose wife would be justified in leaving him. I——"

Ames interrupted her. "No. I already——"

"You'd already decided he wasn't a wife-beater?" Kate said. "Or that if he beat her, he was right? I'd like you to answer one question. Tuke and I both knew she went to your office that day and——"

"What?"

"Yes, certainly," Kate said. "This is the question: She *did* ask you if you were in love with her, didn't she?"

"Why, I—I——"

"Just answer my question!"

He was distressed. "Well—no, she didn't ask me, not exactly. She —she rather assumed that I was."

" 'Rather'!" Kate echoed. "Yes, I can imagine Laila's way of 'rather' assuming that! Poor man, what a jam that put you in!"

"No, I—— At least I——" Ames was stammering. "Well—it was complicated."

"Not so very," Kate said. "You're a one-track man: Roe Metal Products. Even if you'd have liked to be in love with her—a little and only on the side, say—you saw you couldn't, because of Roe Metal Products. You are built into Roe Metal Products so solidly that of course you couldn't entertain any idea that might cause a disruption."

"Kate, please listen——"

She didn't heed him. "Here's another reason why you couldn't speak up for Tuke promptly when I urged him upon you and Mr. Roe. You're so incarnately and conscientiously Metal Products that you were afraid to trust your own judgment. You recognized that both Laila and Tuke were threats to your position, and for your own sake you wanted nothing better on earth than to get them out of town and where they wouldn't be a danger to you. For that very reason you wouldn't appoint Tuke hastily—you had to take time to be sure that Roe Metal Products wouldn't suffer because you did a thing that was for your personal self-interest."

"Maybe so. I don't know." Ames humbly admitted his confusion. "I suppose that was part of it. I've had so many things on my mind lately I'm not very sure of anything." He paused; then uttered a whistle of self-pity and went on: "Laila made me look a fool all evening, especially to you, I'm afraid."

"Not at all. Not to anybody, Ames. Maybe she might have if you hadn't braced up and laughed. The more she sniped at you, the cheerfuler it made you feel. So, as you took it that way, all that her jeering at you did was to give her away."

"Give her away? I don't——"

"Why, yes, certainly," Kate said. "If she'd cut it milder, and if you'd kept on looking guilty, it mightn't have been so clear; but everybody saw how pleased you were when you found that she was only vindictive."

This took him aback. "I don't seem to see——"

"Don't you? She's got what she wants; she's in ecstasies over new riches, new importance that she couldn't have had except for you—and yet she showed everybody that she hates you. Laila always overdoes, and overdoing as she did to-night made her real rage with you much too plain. On top of that you, yourself, cleared up the cause of it."

"I?" He was astonished. "How?"

"By happening to be a gentleman," Kate said. "When a gentleman is compelled to tell a woman that he's not in love with her he's distressed, and when he meets her afterward he's apologetically unhappy because he thinks she's suffering about him. Then if she begins to bark and bite at him he brightens all up because he's pleased to find her only furious and not downed by unrequited love. Well, to-night you brightened all up. Nothing could have made the whole thing plainer."

Ames said, "Uh——" and stopped short upon the pavement. Kate walked steadily on ahead, as if she hadn't noticed his halt. He said, "Uh——" again; then strode on and overtook her. "Kate, I——" He coughed, rubbed the lower part of his face with one hand, then with the other. "There's something I should have—should have mentioned. First, there was a matter I intended to mention some time ago. There —there've been several things since then, too, that I'd have liked to go over with you; but this threatened strike and—and other matters— seem to have prevented. I——"

"You don't need to bother," she said in a light voice, casually. "Anybody really interested in you enough to understand you a little couldn't have more than a passing doubt that the play the poor goose made for you could never amount to anything or get anywhere. Of course it could worry you——"

"Worry me!" he burst out. "Do you think I haven't been worse than worried? Kate, I've been scared—scared and——"

"That's too bad," she said, as lightly as before. "Scared what of?"

"Of—of you mostly. Now it's come up, I think I'd better go ahead and tell you the whole——"

"Not at all; there's nothing to tell, Ames. Naturally Laila threatened you and conjured up hobgoblins to gibber at you; but the only chance that any real mess could have come of it was through poor Tuke's being outside the window and seeing her shed tears all over you so that you had to make love to her. He understands her and you, too, now, and so does Celia. Celia did all the time."

"Celia! You say Celia—— Then it *was* Celia! But, Kate——"

"It's all right," Kate said. "You don't think Celia's so stupid she didn't know it was only Laila putting on another act at you, do you? No, there's nothing for you to tell me, Ames. Anybody in the world'd know Laila was going to follow that up—follow *you* up—to your office or anywhere—until you'd have to tell her as decently as you could that you weren't going to break up the Roe Metal Products Corporation to oblige her."

Ames came to a stop again; but now they were upon their own ground, before the many bright windows of the house, and Kate stopped with him. "Kate, that wasn't what I told her. I told her I wasn't in love with anybody except my wife."

"Of course you did. What man wouldn't?" Kate said. "You had to. It was the only way to convince her that you genuinely did not care for her. You were wise to make use of it."

His gesture of protest went unseen; she'd begun to move toward the house, her back to him. "I was 'wise', was I, Kate? My wisdom is what's been conducting me through this damned nightmare? My wisdom's what's extricated me, is it? Well, God save the mark!"

Kate didn't speak; he followed her ploddingly till she once more stopped, this time near the front steps. From within the house the piano could be heard hammering out jocose rhythms delightful to the ears of the young. Figures unrestrainedly capering passed across the illumined oblong of the nearest window. Its shade was not drawn down, and beyond, at the piano, Celia could be seen, seated and patiently beating the keys in spite of Marvin Roe who hung over her doggedly. Miley Stuart, looking sacrificed, passed the window dancing with Marjie. Kate murmured, "Oh, dear!"

"Would you be willing——" Ames began. "Would you be willing to—to give me a hearing? I think there's a good deal that each of us would like to say and so if you can bring yourself to listen I'd like to——"

"Oh, dear!" Kate murmured again, and seemed not to have heard him. "They don't have to do that. They could use the phonograph and it'd be a lot better. I'll have to get this straightened out."

She tried the front door, found it unlocked, passed quickly within
and was out of Ames's sight when he entered after her.

He walked down the hall as far as the door of his library but didn't
go in. A young Gilpin girl, seated upon his desk, was trying to smoke
one of his cigars for the entertainment of a boy who was betting her
a dollar that she couldn't. Ames turned to the stairway, ascended
to his own room, left the door open and sat waiting for Kate to come
upstairs. There were things that had to be said before he could sleep,
he thought; and, though he was anything but sure he knew how to
say them, he wanted to try. Before long he heard the distant big
phonograph playing dance music. "Now she's done that she'll surely
come." She didn't. "What's she doing now?" he asked himself. "She
knows they don't want grown-up people mixing about with them.
Yes, and she knows I'm up here waiting to talk to her. Why doesn't
she come?"

Again Kate didn't; and after a while he began to understand where
she was and what delayed her. His mind's eye offered him a picture
of her—busy in the kitchen, getting things out of the refrigerator,
piling dishes upon the dining-room table, arranging for the youngsters
to resume their perpetual eating. There were servants to attend to
this if need be; but she was doing it herself and taking her own time
to it, too, though she knew he was waiting in great perturbation of
mind to talk to her. Men never did this sort of thing—pottering, busy-
ing themselves with nothings in times of crisis—but women did.

How many more trifling delays would occupy her before she'd come
up and give him a chance to explain himself? He wanted to do this
humbly, almost entreatingly; but she kept him waiting so long that
when finally her steps were heard upon the stairway his confessional
mood had changed to the reproachful. He went to the doorway and
she stopped before him in the corridor.

"Kate, how many more footling things do you think you have to
do before you give me a chance to talk to you? You knew I was waiting to."

"Did I?" She looked at him absently. "Celia never knows where to
find anything and they're always hungry. I wonder if I oughtn't
to——"

"Wonder if you oughtn't to go downstairs and keep me waiting some more?"

"No. I remember I did put out the chafing-dish, if they want to use it. What is it you want to say, Ames? I'm a little tired to-night. Couldn't it be postponed?"

"Oh, certainly!" he said, stepped backward and closed his door. Yes, women specialized in such bafflements, and there was a reason. Only lately he'd begun to suspect that women had reasons for doing these things—and for the other unreasonable things they did.

XLIX

THE HUSBAND AND WIFE DIDN'T SEE EACH OTHER AGAIN until late the next afternoon. It was a raw wet day with winds now and then whirling rain against windows so intrusively that people glanced up from work to frown at the watery panes. Neon lights began to redden the wetness downtown as Ames drove homeward, and the house was dark when he came into it. Then, before him in the dim broad hall, he saw the vague effulgence of something that was like a small tree with spreading white foliage. Its odor came to him, slight but tangy, and he recognized it as a great cluster of white chrysanthemums mushrooming out above a long glass vase that moved toward him, borne by a slim grey figure.

"Just a minute," Kate said. "I'll turn on the lights as soon as I've put these in the living-room. The fire's going in your library if you're cold, Ames."

"Thank you. Will you come there with me, please?"

"Just a minute," she said again, carried her vase into the living-room and returned, empty-handed. They walked together as far as the library door, and, as he entered, she said "Just a minute", absently, for the third time, and went on toward the rear of the house.

He looked after her, sighed, and crossed the room to warm his hands at the wood-fire she had lighted for him. Some minutes later she reappeared with another white tree in a vase, placed it upon his desk, smiled vaguely at him, and turned to depart. He spoke gravely. "Aren't you going to say 'Just a minute' again, Kate?"

"I—I was only going to bring my knitting if you don't mind."

"I do," he said. "I've been trying to remember if there was ever a time in our lives together when I made an effort to talk to you and you weren't doing something or other with flowers, dusting dust that wasn't there with your handkerchief, or fixing your attention upon a table, a sofa, or a chair that you were planning to alter the position of. I suppose you've never listened to me, Kate, because you were always sure that you already knew everything I could possibly be going to say. Could you bring yourself to make an exception—this one time?"

For answer, she sat down in one of the two armchairs that flanked the hearth, and, although her husband was preoccupied by what he had in mind to say, the firelight upon her was so rosily becoming that he didn't speak at once but stood looking at her. Reflected flame danced upon her eyes; but there was no dancing within them, for they became wistful and melancholy as gusty rain clattered lightly across the windows.

"Do you remember that day?" she asked. "I mean the day so like this, the day Aunt Daisy went out on the roof. High wind and a cold rain always bring it back to me—and the wondering I did about her."

"Wondering?" Ames stood leaning against the mantelshelf, the upper part of him in shadow. "Wondering if she meant to do it?"

"No," Kate said. "I always knew she did. What I wondered about was her encasement within herself. She was so set into the small iron cell she'd made of her life that really she had no communication with anybody. For Aunt Daisy there really didn't exist any other people or a universe. She was a hermit and her eyes couldn't see an inch beyond her hermitage."

Ames considered the word "hermitage". He asked, "You mean the old house?"

"No. She'd made the house a part of herself. It didn't even look to her as it looked to the rest of us: she saw something different because she couldn't see actualities from inside her encasement. I've always thought about her a great deal, Ames, and, looking back upon her now, I wonder and wonder if the encasement was her own fault. Her shell closed in on her and she wanted it to; she liked it that way. Well, did she have to wish to let it close her in? Did she have a choice?"

"Ay, there's the rub!" Ames sat down in the big chair on the other side of the fireplace. "I haven't been much of a theologian, or a philosopher either, since I left college. I was pretty well encased, myself, when you first knew me, wasn't I? I don't believe I had much real communication, as you call it, with even Mary. Or else—or else, maybe, Mary's mother closed her own encasement in on both of us. It isn't a happy thought that so long as they lived I'd never have got out of it. That sounds pretty brutal. 'Realistic' I believe we call it nowadays."

Again, as he too well perceived, Kate hadn't listened to him; she was continuing to think of Aunt Daisy. "Nature seems to make her points by setting up exaggerated examples, Ames. I mean Aunt Daisy was one of those extreme cases we find anything but rare if we're interested in what people are made of. I say she was 'extreme'; but that only means she was more encased than many of the rest of us are—so the rest of us must be encased, too, some of us more, some of us less. I'm not speaking of just our mere egoism, you know—or do you know, Ames? You wanted to talk and I'm doing all of it. Perhaps you'd better begin."

"I did," he said. "I began when I asked you if you were going to say, 'Just a minute' again. You put me off last night when you knew what a stew I was in, and it's your instinct to keep on putting me off right now and for the same old reason: you're always sure you know beforehand everything I'll say. Well, you don't. You talk of 'encased' people who haven't any communication with others. What about you and me? How much communication has there ever been between us two?"

"What?" She looked surprised, almost startled.

"Yes, how much?" he insisted. "We've cared about each other, certainly, and at times we've felt closely united, as we did when—when our little boy died. We were very dear to each other then. At times we've been more than dear to each other; but as we sit here now, Kate, it seems true to me that we don't really know each other enough to talk together with a whole understanding."

She was grave. "Is there such a thing? It's a hardworn old truth that we know even ourselves very little, so how could——"

"Wait," he said. "You've always thought that you knew me pretty thoroughly, and, so far as character goes, I suppose you did; but I doubt if you do just now. On the other hand, I think I've scarcely known you at all, Kate. It's about due, isn't it?"

She'd been looking into the firelight, but now her gaze was upon his face with sharpest scrutiny. "I'm not sure what you mean."

"I'm not sure I can tell you," he said. "I'll try. I had a talk with Tuke to-day."

"You did? You wanted to?"

"Yes. There was a Directors' lunch and we had Tuke there. Afterward I asked him to come up to my office with me. He seemed more like himself than he's been for a long time. I don't mean like his old self in looks, though there was a little of that, too. Of course no man who'd had ten years of Laila Capper could ever be expected to look as he did before that experience began. Speaking of encasements, *there's* a sample!"

"Tuke?"

"No," Ames said. "Laila. If ever anybody's spent her life in a self-made little iron cell, she has. Not even a candle in it. Dances round and round in the dark of that tiny space all by herself; it's horrible to think of! Oh, yes, I know what you mean by 'encased' people! The tighter their shells are about them, the more miserable they make the human beings who've got to live with them. Even when I was up at Roeville arguing and exhorting I couldn't help thinking of such things in the back of my mind. I've been through quite an experience; I doubt if you realize what it's done to me. The scare she gave me opened up a brain area I'd never put to much use."

"Your fright did that?" Kate spoke gently; but her incredulity was made audible and he heard it.

"You still think I couldn't?" he asked sadly.

"Couldn't what, Ames?"

"Couldn't say anything that would interest you. Couldn't have been
thinking anything unexpected of me. I'll have to see. For one thing,
I thought seriously about the nature of women. I discovered I'd neglected doing that before, heaven forgive me! It was a shock, and I
had another to-day as I listened to Tuke and looked at him and
thought about what ten years of Laila have made of him and what
ten years of you have made of me. Good God, Kate, are men *only*
what their wives make of them? If Laila'd married me when I asked
her, would I be now what Tuke is?"

"Never!" Kate was sharp with this. "You'd have drooped a while;
then you'd have seen some of the truth of her and you couldn't have
stood it. You'd have left her—or she'd have left you. Tuke's always
been really in love with her, you see; so he's stayed."

"Stayed damned by it, hasn't he?—till you got this job for him,"
Ames said. "Suppose you'd married him, wouldn't he have had all
that I've had?"

Kate shook her head. "No. With a quieter married life he'd have
done well enough; but he never had your special abilities. He'll carry
on excellently for the business now and he's got a hold over her that
he hasn't had before; but no, he never could have arrived where you
have."

"No? Who developed those 'special abilities' that I have? You or
I?"

"You, Ames."

"So I thought, once," Ames said. "Well, I had them; but they ran
to seed till you took hold of them. As a reward for you I finally asked
you to keep your hands off! Laila scored a sharper hit than she knew
when she called me 'little Mr. Big'! Why, when I told you to lay off
and let me strut alone I didn't even know that my rudimentary
ignorance of women was dangerous and could get me kicked into
the gutter in a minute—*any* minute! Pleasant to think that if you'd
kept your hands off, as I asked you to, that's where I'd be to-night!"

"I did keep my hands off, Ames. Quite a while."

"Yes, I know," he said. "At Roeville I was able to review these last
months and observe that you'd stopped even suggesting. Your anger

wasn't hard enough to see me thrown to the lions, though. When it came to the test you preferred me to it."

She leaned forward, looking at him inscrutably. "I preferred you to my anger? How do you know I didn't prefer my own position, Celia's, Roe Metal Products, and all of that?"

"I don't," he said. "That's what I'm coming to." He paused, rueful, and added, "I think you wouldn't let me talk to you last night because you thought I'd only be apologetic in a usual mannish way. Do I interest you now at all? Did you know beforehand that this was what I was going to say?"

"Well, maybe—a good deal of it," she answered. "Perhaps all except what you've just said—that you don't know whether I gave up my anger because I preferred you yourself or because I preferred to have things go on as they'd been going for all of us."

Ames didn't speak for some moments. Then, "Poor old Tuke!" he said. "To-day I saw he wanted to get back on the old footing with me. He talked a lot. There's a part of him that just looks on at things. He could see himself burned at the stake, or burning somebody else there, and that part of him would still be just looking on. As he left he said something pretty cutting, though he smiled when he said it. He said, 'Good-bye, Ames. Have a thought to Kate sometimes.'"

"Did that——" She hesitated; then began over and finished as if in casual inquiry, "Did it leave you feeling rather angry with him?"

"No. I didn't need any such jolt; but, except lately, it was justified. That's partly your fault, Kate, because all along you've made me the absorbing one in our two lives. It's you who've made everything center upon me—not that I didn't fall for it only too easily! I find the result not satisfactory now because I see I've never had a good perception of you. I feel as if I were beginning to talk to you for the first time in our lives."

"Then we'd better go on, hadn't we? I mean you'd better go on, Ames."

"There's one thing that'll have to be settled between us first of all," he said. "You made a systematic man of me long ago, so I believe in putting down a foundation before anything else is done. We've had a disruption—at least I have—and now I want to know where I stand with you. I mean we've both got to know where we stand toward each other."

"Do we? Why?"

The question astonished him. "Good Lord! Because we've never had anything basic between us and if ever we needed solid ground under our feet we need it now. The world's turning into a hundred hells before our eyes. 'It's later than we think'; every seeing man in the country's telling us that. War's coming at us hour by hour and nobody knows what it'll do to us all when it comes. I've been a soldier once, Kate, and even for Roe Metal Products I don't believe I'd like a desk job either here or in Washington. Mr. Roe might have to take hold again."

"Yes, I've understood you might feel like that. What else, Ames?"

"I'm trying for the foundation," he said. "We had an affection for each other when we were married, and then pretty soon it seemed to me that I was in love with you; but I see now that my way of being in love with you didn't amount to much." He paused; then spoke up manfully, though his voice had a tremble in it. "I mean that now at last when I've discovered I don't really know you, I'm so in love with you, Kate, that what I felt then seems to have been a feeble delusion. You'll—you'll accept that as a fact, won't you?"

Her unreadable look didn't alter. "It sounds as if you were proposing to me—at last—Ames."

"Yes, I know what you mean—and I am. I'm frightened, too, because I don't know the answer. I don't know whether you pulled me out of this hole for my own sake or because you preferred things to go on as they were. Kate, I don't know if you began building me up in the first place, and went on with it afterward, for my own sake or because you're just made that way."

"There are other things you don't know about what happened 'in the first place'," she said. "For instance, that Laila'd have married you if I hadn't stopped her."

"You?" He thought his wife's memory at fault. "Why, no. She decided——"

"I decided her," Kate said. "She thought she could park Celia out and I convinced her she couldn't. She thought you had more money

than you had and I showed her she was mistaken. At first I didn't
know how much I'd shaken her. I didn't know until you told me she'd
jilted you. That's how you married me instead, Ames. You may think
it's a bit late to hear of it; but so long as you thought her a charming
woman it didn't seem useful to tell you. Now that at last I've informed
you, perhaps you feel you begin to know me a little better?"

If he was at all astonished, as she seemed to expect, his expression
gave no sign of it. He looked only the more rueful. "No. You only
prove what I already knew—that you were always the Guardian
Angel. It's your nature to prevent calamity and to take hold of things
and straighten them out and develop them, so I don't know whether
what you've done with me and for me's been done because it was
your nature or for a reason I'd like better."

"What?" She spoke the word vaguely.

"Kate, does this interest you?"

"Yes."

"Then I'm telling you, upon my soul, I don't know whether you've
ever loved *me* or not and if you do now. Do you?"

Upon this, she leaned back slowly and gazed into the fire. "I'm
not sure what that means, Ames. When I was a girl I went through
the experience people call falling in love. It was with you, and in time
the state of being in love with you made me try to make all that I
thought and did useful to you. Trying to be useful to you became the
habit of my life. There's my own question: When love turns into just
a habit of life is it still love? Is a habit the kind of love you mean?"

"No." His voice was slightly unsteady again. "You seem to be telling me that you don't know whether you love me or not."

With her gaze still upon the fire, she assented. "That's how it seems
to me."

He rose abruptly, strode down the long room and back again.
"Once I'd have assumed that you were the last woman in all this world
to say such a thing. I mean the last woman to tell her husband after
ten years that she doesn't know whether or not she loves him. I'd
think it's because you've finally seen what kind of fool I could make
of myself, except you must have known that much about me all
along."

Kate's deep look into the fire changed; her expression became absentminded as she glanced toward his desk. She left her chair, went to the vase of chrysanthemums and began to rearrange them thoughtfully, seeming engrossed with them. He stared at her; then strode to the door before he spoke.

"At least I've been able to talk with you a little, for the first time; I can hope that it may happen again. For me that would be a great hope. I can have it, can't I?"

Her back was toward him as she busied herself with moving the chrysanthemums about in their vase; and, finding that she didn't answer his question, he turned through the doorway. Kate heard the departing step and her lifted hands became still. Again the wet gale splashed the windows. She looked into the long past, looked into times before that other rainy day of which this one reminded her. "I like to hear the rain splattering on the window-panes," Mrs. Fennigate had said upon her deathbed; but Kate was remembering a larger tragedy than her mother's. More clearly than her memory had seen it for years, there rose upon her inner sight the wasted face of Malcolm Fennigate, and the melancholy eyes searched her through and through with a question: "You'll keep to your own encasement forever?"

Over his shoulder Ames saw how motionless she was, standing unaware with uplifted hands poised above the flowering vase. The attitude was that of one who brings a votive offering to the altar, and so was a true symbol of her and of her sort: compassionate good women, creation's loveliest work; they give and give and always give. Ames Lanning, desiring no gift, sorrowfully turned once more toward the stairway in the hall.

Then there was the faintest sound, as if she meant to speak; but the one appealing word that came from her was not so much as clearly whispered. His heart heard it well enough.

"Wait."

bw.T1745k